Beautiful...

Just The Way You

Are

Written by

Alan Gaines

This is a work of fiction. Names, characters, businesses, places, events, locales, and incidents are either the products of the author's imagination or used in a fictitious manner. Any resemblance to actual persons, living or dead, or actual events is purely coincidental.

Copyright © 2020 by Alan Gaines

For more information:
rejectingthenarrative@gmail.com

Order this book at:
www.flippingthescripts.com

Cover designs (front & back) by: Charity Neal

ISBN 978-1-5136-5536-9

Dedication

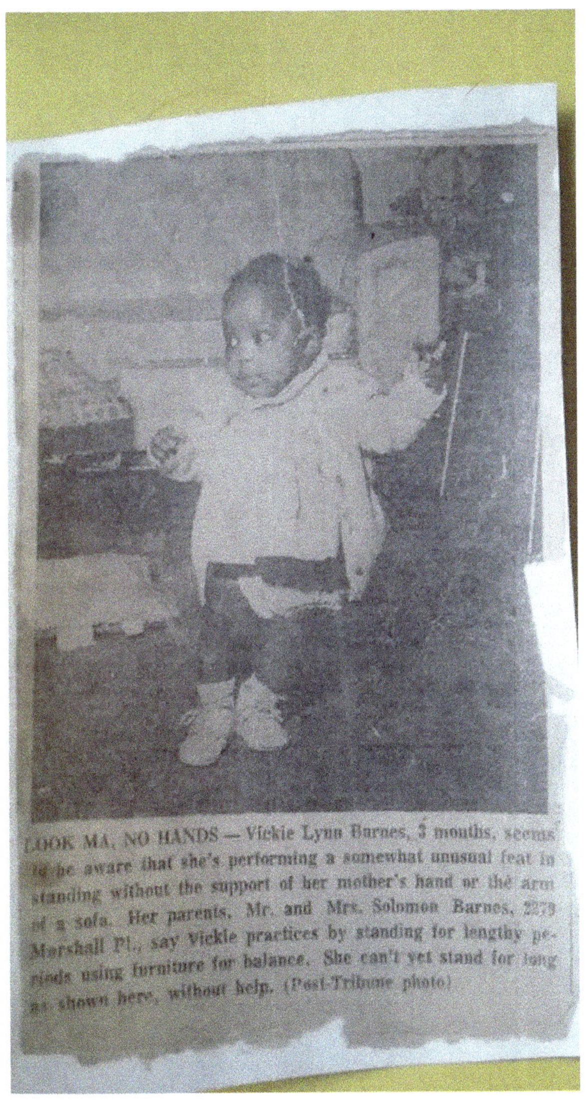

LOOK MA, NO HANDS — Vickie Lynn Barnes, 3 months, seems to be aware that she's performing a somewhat unusual feat in standing without the support of her mother's hand or the arm of a sofa. Her parents, Mr. and Mrs. Solomon Barnes, 2379 Marshall Pl., say Vickie practices by standing for lengthy periods using furniture for balance. She can't yet stand for long as shown here, without help. (Post-Tribune photo)

To my mother who let me know each and everyday that I could do anything, that no one was better than me, encouraged me to let my light shine and made me feel that I was the greatest in the world. Thank you Ma! I love you and I want you to know that no other honor will ever mean more to me than being one of Vickie's Kids!
(This image is a newspaper clip of my mother standing unassisted at 3 months old. #Blackgirlmagic)
Vickie Lynn Barnes - Stansil

Dedication

To my 3 Daughters:
Assata,
Nehanda
and
Anayah

You all will never understand the joy I have had in raising you
but that joy is no comparison to the pride I take in seeing you all
blossom into the young woman who will change the world...

I am forever grateful for the man
you all have helped me to become!

Daddy Worships You...

Dedication

To My Wife
Carla

No one person has had a greater impact on my life than you...

Your support, brutal honesty when something I wrote wasn't good, your encouragement and overall belief in me has made this particular book possible...

This book, just like me would be nothing without you.
I dedicate this book to you simply because you dedicate so much of yourself to me & for that I could never say thank you enough...

I Worship You...

Beautiful... Just The Way You Are

Order of the Essence

Roses

The Contributors & Their Work

Charity Neal
Contributions: Art
Illustrated Front & Back Covers
Pages 76, 84, 179 & 181 - 204

Karma Griggs
Contributions: Painting
Pages: 16, 89, 215, 227 and 233

Daisjah Ball
Contributions: Art
Pages: 11 & 241

Lacist Wortham
Contributions: Art
Page 118

D Marie
Contributions: Art
Page 112

Janiyah Browning
Contributions: Art & Poetry
Page 151

I would personally like to send an extra special thank you to each
and every one of the people who lended their talent and time to this
project. I truly feel that this book would not be what it is without
you gracing your abilities to this book.

Thank You
From the Bottom of My Heart

Introduction

This book for me personally was a journey that shattered narratives that I had accepted in regards to women. Writing this book forced me to explore issues and emotions that I had previously only dealt with on a surface level. Beautiful... Just The Way You Are, exposed to me my hypocrisy of thought on so many levels. No one individual is perfect and in writting this I have been criticized for attempting to capture the truth and reality of so many people who are living the issues that are dealt with in this book. The irony of both the criticism and writing this book was that I had to confront these notions within myself 1st in order to be able to honestly, depict the truth and pain that is being lived by so many people who are going to connect to the words in the following pages.

It is my hope that this book is as therapeutic and liberating for every reader as it was for me as the author. As cliche as this may sound, I honestly laughed, I cried and I cringed throughout the journey of writing this book. Some of the issues that are dealt with in this book are no laughing matter and I tried my very best to respect the pain and trauma that will be discussed to the utmost. I know 1st hand from my own experience as well as 2nd hand from situations and individuals that I have worked with in my career as a mental and behavioral health professional as well as a teacher that the reality a lot of individuals face in their home life is truly heartbreaking. So many individuals I have worked with feel isolated within their pain and experience that they can't see an escape from the things that has happened to them. This book, I hope will be their voice.

Beautiful... Just The Way You Are is an anthology of 8 short stories that deal with; Seeking validation from others, The Criminilization of Black Girls in Schools and Society, Child Molestation and Sexual Abuse, Domestic / Dating Violence, The Rape Crisis in Africa, The Effects of an Absent / Unengaged Father on Young Girls. the 75,000 Missing Black Girls and Women in America and finally the idea of Beauty.

As you can see this book is going to take it "there." However, we can't heal that which we won't reveal. I don't pretend to have all of the answers, only God has that. It is my hope that this book will allow us the space to have the conversations that we tend to avoid as we wear the masks of complicity and silence. Both complicity and silence have created an incalculable amount of pain and trauma which manifest in broken relationships that have been built by damaged people.

Lastly, I want to urge you as a reader to be honest and respectful of the matters covered in the pages to follow. If you or someone you know is experiencing any of the issues that will be discussed... Please Speak Up!

For Everyone
Who Has Been
Told To Love Themselves
And Wondered...

"How?"

Section 1:

Roses

Roses are a global symbol of Beauty and Love.

The Rose is one of the world's strongest flowers. Roses are one of the few flowers on earth that can be grown in extreme weather conditions.

Roses can be found in climates that are brutally cold as well as locations that experience scorching heat.
Roses simply adapt to their environment and then grow relentlessly towards the sun.

In This Section You Will Meet
Two Young "Roses" Who Represent The Undeniable Beauty of Millions of "Roses" Just Like Them...

"The Essence of A Rose"

An Original Drawing By:
Daisjah Ball   Age: 14

This Beautiful drawing was
inspired by the book
Beautiful Just The Way You Are

Chapter 1
Just Because They Can't
See Your
Beauty

At this very moment, there are countless girls all across the world staring into a mirror, clearly looking at what they know to be true. Yet they are unable to see...

The fact that they are Beautiful...

Nothing needs to change. These young ladies are Beautiful... Just The Way They Are

Unfortunately, all too often young ladies feel the need for outside validation to confirm the Beauty they possess inside of themselves...

Typically, girls compete amongst themselves to impress one another and on occasion young ladies look for the validation to come in the form of male attention...

Allow me to introduce to you
Lisa...

Lisa feels Beautiful and thinks she is attractive.
However, she can't understand why she hasn't caught the eye of any male worth talking to.

Well, all that is about to change. Lisa is about to be faced with more than she could have imagined when she meets Trey.

Will Trey's validation of what Lisa feels about herself come at a cost that will be too great for Lisa to return from?

Let's Find Out What Happens When They Can't See Your Beauty...

"Feelings... So deep in my feelings... / No, this ain't like me... /Can't control my anxiety / Feeling like I am touching the ceiling... / When I am with you I ca ----"

"LEEESSSAAA!!! .... Girl hurry yo' self up and get in here! ... I ain't got all day! Girl I gotta go to work in the mornin'! You takin' all doggone day... Shoot! Hurry up!" Yells Vickie, Lisa's mother, from the bottom of the stairs imploring her daughter to stop taking her sweet time.

"Okaaay.... I'm sorry! But that is my song..." Lisa says to her mom, after realizing that she was lost in a daze. Lisa was in the bathroom mirror feeling herself. "Here I come..." Lisa turns back to the mirror and says "Aigh't boo... I'll be back... I gotta go get dolled up for you okay!" Of course, the mirror doesn't respond. While there is no boo yet to speak of, she feels she is ready for one. Not because she is boy crazy... Nope, this is all about her. Lisa knows that she is pretty but is craving the interest of a guy to validate how she feels about herself.

Lisa has an explanation in her mind for exactly why no guys are into her... The culprits are most definitely her parents. Between their over protective parenting and strict no social media rule, Lisa surely places blame for her nonexistent love life on her parents. Lisa feels that her best shots at becoming 'Boo'd Up are being defended by the two most influential people in her life, her Mom and Dad. Truth be told, Lisa may have a point, she is a beautiful, tall and slightly skinny caramel complexioned 17-year-old. Fully equipped with hazel eyes a nice shape and a smile that lights up the room. Lisa knows that she is pretty, so why else wouldn't a guy want to be into her? Too naive to recognize how the game goes and a bit too stubborn to believe what her mother is telling her, Lisa simply has come to terms with the theory that her parents are preventing her from living her best life.

Lisa is a bit optomistic that her fortunes may soon be changing because her parents have finally agreed to let her go out to a skating party with her friends. Super excited for the rare opportunity to go out, Lisa stops in her room and grabs her phone charger before finally making it down the stairs to the kitchen. She sits in the chair before showing her excitement "My bad Ma..." "Girl just sit down here so I can put these passion twist in your head. Let's get this over so I can get in the bed for work tomorrow." Her mom says a bit irritated by having to wait for Lisa. "Ma, thanks again for letting me go to Taty's and to the party," Lisa's mom has started on her hair when she responds,"Girl you better be thanking your Daddy, he the one who said you can go. And Lisa please clean that bathroom and kitchen good tonight so I don't have to hear his mouth in the morning complaining about every little thing. You know your Daddy think he Inspector Gadget when it comes to cleaning up."

13

Lisa smacks her lips before letting out an "I already know..." "Hey... I'm trying to help you out. Don't get upset with me, this your skating party or whatever y'all calling it... My time done came and went, I've had my fun. I'm just letting you know that you gotta take care of everything before you can go out and enjoy life... Now, who all 'pose to be at this little skating thing anyway?"

Lisa rolls her eyes again knowing that her Mom is behind her, so she can't see the face she is making. Lisa wants to respond, "I've told you like a thousand times! Ain't nobody new been added since the last time you asked me like an hour ago!" However, she responds with the answer that will not result in being killed by her mother, "Taty of course because we leaving from her house. Jazlyn, Takeia and Ashanti. Trinity was supposed to come but her mother said she got something to do with her little brother or something I don't know... Ma, thank you for letting me go." "Hey you gone be in college before we know it, so it's about time to start allowing you to do more things and go more places." Lisa's mom says and as the words are leaving her lips, she begins to reflect as well as come to grips with the fact that her baby isn't that much of a baby anymore. Lisa likes what her mother said so she shoots her shot, "Aww Ma... Does that mean I can get an Instagram and Snapchat account?" Lisa's response snaps her Mother out of the self-reflecting moment she was having, "Say what?! Girl Bye! Yeah right... You tried it!"

In true motherly fashion, Vickie asks, "So what lil' nappy head boys supposed to be meeting y'all up there? I know Kevin is gone be up there with Takeia so don't say nobody... I know Dre gone be up there for Ashanti... So what lil boy you call yourself having meet you up there?" Lisa turns her head and says to her mother, "Oh we got jokes... Really Ma?" Lisa's Mom did know the answer before she asked the question, but she has a bigger motive behind asking, so she slyly plays it off. "What? Hey, as a Mom I gotta keep asking... I mean just because you ain't told me about no Lil boy don't mean you not into one." Lisa is a touch in her feelings when she replies, "Yeah... But no! Ain't nobody been checking for me. Well, nobody I would want to. I mean guys don't like me for whatever reason... (Lisa blinks her eyes rapidly as she thinks of her theory. Yet she wouldn't dare tell her mother so she keeps right on expounding about the vacancy in her room of validation.) And I know what you are going to say, 'Your mind shouldn't be on boys anyway.' (Lisa says it in a mocking voice to indicate she has heard her mother say that 50 million times)

Surprisingly, her Mom changes her tone a bit. "True, but I understand that you are still going to think about boys... I ain't crazy. So there isn't anyone you got a crush on or who has a crush on you?"

Lisa wasn't expecting this would be the conversation when she sat down in the chair, but she doesn't want to ruin it either, so she keeps the conversation flowing. "Its some boys that are cute or whatever but you know... Most of them I have heard too much stuff about so I know that they ain't really my type." Her mother nods to herself with pride as if she is happy Lisa has been paying attention before saying, "Okay, so what is your type?" "My type is... Tall, he gotta be tall... Attractive, he needs to have some nice size arms and a nice size chest. I don't want somebody all small and skinny. Ain't nothing wrong with that but I just would want someone with an athletic body... Oh, and he has to have a nice smile. Like if a guy has a really good smile then that makes him sooo attractive to me. That is it for the physical stuff... I really need someone who is smart and makes me feel secure. They have to have good conversation and they gotta want to do something with their life."

Lisa's Mom stops putting twists in Lisa's hair to interrupt the laundry list of the perfect guy Lisa is giving. Lisa feels it and slightly turns over her right shoulder and looks at her Mom trying to figure out why she stopped when her Mom responds. "Well it seems like you have put a lot of thought into all this." Lisa is a bit embarrassed but is feeling she can talk freely, so she gives it no thought when she says, "Yeah I have. Ma I know I look better than a lot of these girls, like even some of my friends but dudes don't be checking for me and I don't get it. Like what is wrong with me? Am I ugly or something like what? Low key, I feel some type a way about it sometimes... Ok like most times... I know I get good grades and I got my dreams and all that but still like... I don't know... I mean I am excited to go out and all but I know ain't no dudes bout to try to be all up on me or nothing like that."

Vickie is feeling for her baby as Lisa is having an honest moment. Vickie knows that she is going to have to offer both sympathy and per-spective. "Is that a bad thing that guys ain't going to be all up on you? I get where you are coming from, but as my old teacher, Mr. Denson used to say Boys Before Books, Brings Babies... Stay focused on your goals... The right one will come along in due time... Lisa ain't nothing wrong with you. Anyone who can't see what you have to offer is the one missing out. What I learned about boys along time ago and men, in general, is that they fear rejection. Guys don't want to be shot down and if they don't have the confidence that they are going to get the girl for sure, then to be quite honest they aren't likely to try... I know it doesn't do you any good in terms of your confidence but trust me, it's saving you a lot of wasted time in the long run... I hate to call a young man no good so I will put it this way. A lot of the guys your age have accepted the narrative that they have to get as

"Lisa"

An Original Oil Painting By:
Karma Myles   Age: 14

This Beautiful painting was inspired by the story, Just Because They Can't See Your Beauty

Instagram: @paintitkarma

many girls as they can. Trust me, you don't want to be just uh, what is it you told me that guys are calling it now?

Lisa knows exactly what she is talking about and responds, "Body count!" Disgusted her mother responds, "Ugghh y'all kids today is so trifling. Where do they come up with this stuff? Body count, oh my gosh... Anyways... You deserve and were made for more. I know that you may not like it now but you are going to respect it in the long run... And hey, you never know, someone might approach you at this little skate party." Lisa is feeling a little better because she knows her mom is right so she says with a touch of optimism, "Yeah you right Ma, what do you always say 'why not me?'" Lisa's Mom goes to lighten the mood, "Okurrrrrrrrr!" They both laugh before Lisa pleads with her mother in a laughing tone, "Ma, please stop! Don't ever do that again!" Lisa's Mom is laughing pretty good when she responds, "I'm sorry, I couldn't help it! Even though I hate when people say that!" Lisa rolls her eyes and continues to laugh. Lisa is feeling the genuineness of the moment, so she turns around and tells her mother, "I love you Ma." "I love you too Lisa." A quiet moment passes before they spark up a less serious conversation.

Pre- Party Preparations

Friday rolls around and Lisa is in her room watching Beyonce's Homecoming on Netflix for the thousandth time, but we all know it never gets old. Lisa is waiting on her Dad to get home, so he can take her to Taty's house. Her mother comes into the room and asks, "You all packed up and ready to go?" Lisa is an obvious amateur at going out so she doesn't really know that this question is loaded. Lisa responds unsuspectingly, "Yeah I am. Ma thanks again for letting me go." Ignoring the attempt by Lisa to butter her up, her Mom continues the mission she came into the room to complete. "Un-huh, what you call yourself wearing to this little party tomorrow night?"

Lisa gets out her outfit, which she is feeling confident about because she thinks it's "cute." And it is, she has a gray and black Ivy Park jogging suit with a black Ivy Park haltered top and a pair of Silver Surfer Airmax 720s. Lisa's been wanting to slay in this outfit since she got the news that her father agreed to let her go. Lisa holds it up and says, "I'm wearing this and my grey Airmax's that we got from daddy friends store Maxxed Out." "Ok, ok... I see you! Periodt! Periodt!..." Lisa likes the confirmation but is playfully annoyed by her mother's attempt at the pop culture reference. "I can't with you! Mama!" Lisa says as she puts her clothes back in the suitcase.

With what seemed like no warning, Vickie kicks into 'Mommy Mode' and is giving Lisa a long speech about how to act and behave appropriately at this skating party tomorrow night. Lisa is halfway paying attention to her Mom's warnings but all in all she is thinking that her Mother is just being overprotective because her girls do this all the time and nothing ever happens, so she is thinking to herself "This party is going to be Lit and nothing is going to go wrong Ma, just chill out will you..." However, her response to her Mother is an appeasing "I understand Ma, everything is going to be fine, stop worrying please." Vickie stops herself, takes a sentimental look at Lisa and says, "You're right." Speechless, she leans in and gives her daughter a hug. As they embrace, they hear Lisa's Dad's car pull into the driveway.

Lisa lights up immediately when she hears the sound she had been waiting on. "Oooh Ma! That's Daddy! Let me get my stuff!" Lisa excitedly hops out of the arms of her lovingly protective mother. "Well Dang! Just knock me down why don't you!" Vickie says at the abruptness Lisa is moving with. "My bad Ma, but I gotta go!" "Alright... You sure you don't want to continue our Regina King binge?" Vickie says already knowing the answer yet fishing for a reason to keep her baby close. Lisa let's her mother down easy as she continues gathering her things and heads out the room. "We can keep it going on Sunday when I get back." They both walk out of the room and to the front door of the house. Vickie gets the door and Lisa sets her bags down and gives her mother one last hug. "Thanks again Ma and please stop worrying, I am going to be fine. Love you!" Vickie utters the same words simultaneously and is a bit choked up as she takes the moment to realize that she is watching her daughter grow up into a little lady. Lisa grabs her bags and walks to the car. Through all the layers of protection it never crosses Vickie's mind that 'the Lisa' that is leaving her house may never come home... 'The Lisa' that will return may be totally different because of one chance encounter with a guy she never saw coming...

Ladies Night!

Lisa is the last one to arrive at Taty's house. The squad has been waiting on her to have their "photoshoot" that will most definitely end up on "the gram." So after a few hours of "Girls being Girls," they start talking about the party. Jaz asks Lisa the big question. "Lisa, girl what you wearing tomorrow night? We know this your first time we can't have you out there bad with no granny outfit." Lisa takes the friendly teasing in stride as she gets up and goes towards her suitcase. She holds up her outfit and naively responds, "My Mama said the outfit was nice..." Everyone immediately stops what they are doing and all eyes shift in shock towards

Lisa. She notices the shift in energy innocently asks "What?!"

Much to her surprise, Shanti who rarely speaks up says, "I got this one y'all. Girl, this is not that type of party..." Lisa is confused. Taty jumps in, "Yeah, ain't no dudes gonna be all up on you if you all covered up!" Lisa is lost, she wore something similar to this last year to the homecoming dance and Antoine was trying to get all up on her. Lisa says what she is thinking because she doesn't see what's wrong with her outfit. "When I wore my blue Aeropostale suit like this to the homecoming dance, Antoine was all up on me." Keia bursts out laughing "Girl you know Antoine stay thirsty! Don't forget he was on Buck Tooth Brenda! That boy don't care..." Lisa is taken back a little bit because up until that point, she thought it was how she looked that night that had caught his attention.

Taty is the voice of reason, "Girl look, that outfit would be lit about any and everywhere, ok, but for this party, you gotta show a little something if you want to get them up on you! Your shirt is cute and you can wear that. Now look in my top drawer and get my ripped shorts, you a little bit taller than me so they going to be about mid-thigh on you. You can still wear your shoes with them. With that outfit, you will definitely do better than just thirsty Antoine on tomorrow night." Everyone laughs, even Lisa. This seems to settle the matter. As Lisa goes to the drawer and gets the shorts, she holds them up and says to herself, "My mom would kill me if she saw me in these..." However, Lisa is not brave enough to tell her girls, that she wants to wear what she picked out. Inside, she feels uneasy about it, however this is her first time going out and she doesn't want to make too big of a deal of it. In Lisa's mind, her girls know what they are talking about. Her friends know how to get what male attention, which she wants, so Lisa rolls with their suggestions.

The Skate Party

Let's fast forward to the skate party and the girls are arriving at the skating rink. Taty's mom, Ms. Jeanene is dropping them off and as the girls file out of the car, she calls Lisa to get a last look at her outfit. Lisa doesn't know it, but Lisa's mom texted Ms. Jeanene about what Lisa was supposed to wear to the party. Taty was a bit ahead of the game and already told Lisa not to wear the shorts to the party; she told Lisa to put the shorts in her Michael Kors bookbag purse. She told Lisa to change into the shorts once they got inside. Lisa is naive so she didn't question the strategy too much, excited about the chance to go out for once, Lisa's mind frame is simply go along to get along. So as Lisa walks toward the driver's side window, she looks back at Taty who has a little smirk on her face, because her suspicion was right. Taty had a feeling that Lisa's mom was going to talk to her mom about Lisa's outfit.

Lisa passed the "outfit" test.

After paying the cover charge, the girls make their way into the packed skating rink. Lisa is mesmerized by the beautiful commotion when she hears the DJ say, "Alright fellas, I know some of y'all been trippin' on your ladies this week so if I was you I would grab them tight... Because this next song is for all the single fellas out here taking shots in your ladies' DM's... This one is for the real Heavyweights." The DJ drops the beat and the words "Your girlfriend wants to be my girlfriend / she be calling me telling me about you..." come through the speakers. The place goes crazy! Everyone rushes over to the dance area. The whole squad rushes over as well and begin to dance.

All the dudes are checking them out and Lisa is definitely liking how this attention feels. Lisa momentarily losses herself in the music and is dancing carefree when something tells her to look up. When she does it is as if those words had been spoken by the deep brown eyes of a tall almond complexioned guy that would definitely fit the physical must have list she gave her mother a couple of nights ago. Lisa gives a seductive slight smile as she mouths the words "Ya slipping/ I think it's time I slip in." Lisa looks this guy up and down and gives him that inviting look. He smiles at the obvious flirting that Lisa is doing. He gives a slight bite of his bottom lip while slowly blinking his eye. He begins to flirt back while mouthing the words, "Baby he ain't what you need/ whatever you want, Girl I got it, come to me." Lisa's smile widens as he flirts back. She knows that she has gotten his attention, so now it's time to play hard to get. Lisa turns around and continues dancing with her girls, thinking to herself that if he is about something then he will approach her at some point during the night.

As soon as the song ends, Taty grabs her by the arm and they go to the restroom to change into her outfit. As soon as the door opens, Lisa starts the 21 questions. "Girl who was that dude with Kev in that Black Victory Lap shirt and them LeBron's? Girl he was fiiinnnneee and he was flirting!" Taty is gassed up for her friend, "Girl I saw that! Girl that is Trey! That's Kev cousin. Girl, he works at Footlocker in the MetroMall. Hey, if he push up on you, then you should find out what he talking about! I would. I know he a senior so he probably looking for Ms. Right Now, more than he looking for Ms. Right, but hey girl... Tonight, live it up! No shade, but you don't get out that much. So, if you get one of the finest dudes up in here to try and get at you. Girl go for it!" Lisa continues to change and Taty's words only serve as fuel to the fire that has been lit by the flirtatious exchange she just had. Lisa buttons up the ripped shorts, looks at Taty and says, "You right... Now let's go get turnt up aaayyyeeee!" Lisa put her pants in the bag and they head out of the restroom.

At the same time Taty and Lisa were walking to the restroom, the guy that Lisa was flirting with walked over toward Keia. He goes up to Keia and asks "Yo, who is your girl?! You been holding out on me Keia? He nods in the direction of Taty and Lisa "Why don't you put your boy on?" Keia responds, "That's my home girl Lisa... She single, this her first time coming out with us. Crowds ain't really her thing but she wanted to come tonight. I'll introduce y'all when they come back out here." Trey plays it cool, "Naw, I'm gonna introduce myself. I just wanted to make sure she ain't got a man. Good looking though, for real." Keia is a true friend, so she tells him straight, "Hey if you trying to just play my girl, please don't even waste her time. I ain't gonna hate on you or nothing but if you ain't gonna be about the right then I am telling you, Trey, you can let that this one go... I'm for real don't play with her emotions. She a good girl Trey" Trey's face turns up in surprise as he begins to reassure Keia. "Hey, I feel you looking out for your girl and all, but I ain't even talked to her yet. If I am feeling her, then I promise you, I ain't gonna do her dirty. You got my word aight!" Keia can tell the sincerity in his voice and says, "Aight Trey... That's my girl now... I'm for real..."

Trey is 18, and he is definitely a ladies man. Trey is a Senior, and he has already been accepted into Jackson State on a Computer Science scholarship. Trey is 6'3" and plays basketball, so his arms and chest are banging! His grandmother on his Dad side is Puerto Rican, so he has curly hair. All the girls want him despite his reputation as a playboy.

Tonight, he is shutting all that down because it is something about Lisa that has caught his eye. Trey can't put a finger on it which is a little weird because usually, it's the girls who are all over him. Trey is trying to hold onto his ego as he is dealing with the fact that he is feeling a little awestruck by Lisa. It's as if Trey could sense Lisa's innocence and despite his usual laid back, 'let them come to me' approach when he is out, Trey is just a bit thirsty for Lisa.

Shortly after Lisa and Taty come from the restroom Trey is looking to make his move on Lisa. Trey thinks he has game so there is no hesitation with his approach to Lisa. "Wsup Lil Ma? Where you been hiding at? Keia and her girls always out but I here this your first time... Wsup with that?" Lisa is feeling some emotions that are very unfamiliar to her because although she was looking forward to a guy trying to talk to her, she had no idea that it would be arguably the best looking and one of the most popular guys in the building. She smiles at him and tries to play it cool with her response... "I don't know... but I ain't been hiding nowhere... All this really ain't my thing, to be honest skating and dancing is cool but I ain't really into going out or being in big crowds..."

(Lisa is lying, she loves being out in this environment, but she knows that telling Trey that her parents don't let her out could blow her chances with Trey.) Trey senses she is playing a little hard to get and respects that. Trey is thinking two steps ahead in his mind, so like a seasoned vet with the ladies, he knows coming off too thirsty could blow everything up.

"My bad, that pretty smile of yours got me losing my manners. My name is Trey. It's obvious everyone calls you gorgeous but I would like to know your name..." Lisa is blushing super hard. Lisa reaches out to shake Trey's hand that he extended as she says, "Well thank you... My name is Lisa... Oh and that lil pickup line you using is kinda cute, I'll admit... I just got one question though?" Trey looks her dead in the eyes and says, "Shoot." Lisa leans over to his ear and says, "Is that the line that you always use? If so please use something better because I'm not basic..."

Trey is shocked, but laughs it off. "Okay I see you... I can respect that... No cap, it usually does work! I like that in you. Keeping it one hunid, it was something about you that I couldn't put my hands on at first when you was giving me the eye... Now, I see it's beauty and brains... I like that... Well, I ain't gone hold you from your friends too much but uh... it was nice to meet you." Trey says as he gently grabs her left hand and says "If you don't mind dancing at some point tonight, I would like to have the privilege of dancing with you, I mean, you say this (Trey motions to the large crowd of people as he looks around) isn't your thing but if your song comes on and you feel like dancing, holla at your boy Lil' Mama..." Trey slowly lets her hand go, almost finger by finger as he backs up 3 or 4 steps still looking a blushing Lisa in the eye before he turns and walks away back into the crowd of people in the skating rink.

Lisa tries to play it cool, but she is bursting with emotion. She is smiling from ear to ear. Lisa has played out in her mind a thousand times how it was going to go when a boy finally did approach her and she will be the first to tell you that this is way better than she imagined it! In what feels like the best moment of her life, Lisa bum-rushes Keia. "Girl he asked me where I been hiding at? And why I ain't never been out with y'all before and -" Keia abruptly cuts her off... "LISA!" "Girl calm down with the extras! I was right there the whole time, I heard him..."

Lisa quickly comes to the realization that she is super loud and extra excited. Lisa is a bit embarrassed as she looks around trying to see if anyone else noticed the scene she may have been causing. Lisa takes a few deep breaths trying to calm her excitement while asking Keia, "So what do I do now?" To which Keia replies, "Girl do what you want to do, skate, dance, whatever..."

Lisa replies, "No girl, about Trey and his fine self..." Jaz interjects, "Look Lis – we all know that Trey ain't looking for no girlfriend, he going off to college pretty soon, so I'm pretty sure his mind is only on his body count. I guess it's cool that he trying to holla in all but, you don't need no dude like that. If I was you, I would dance and flirt with all that sexiness but after tonight I wouldn't waste my time." Lisa knows that Jaz always tells it straight. Ironically, Jaz sounds like her mom right now and although she doesn't want to hear it, she knows this is what she needs to hear.

Now is Lisa listening to Jaz? That's up for debate she hears her but what she is feeling for Trey she can't ignore. Taty jumps in with her two cents, while rolling her hips and putting her butt out "Girl go dance with him and see what he is working with" they all chuckle. Taty continues, "Look we know that he gone be on to the next one, but we always hurt because we try to be wifey and these dudes out here doing what they want... Girl you ain't had your little heart broke yet, so before you go down that road, have you some fun like they do! We not marrying any of these dudes in here... except for maybe Shanti, with her lovey dovey self with Dre..." (They all look over at Shanti who is hugged up with Dre against the wall.) Taty keeps speaking "Girl I know your Mama keep you on lockdown, so who knows if you are ever going to be out again so live it up!"

Lisa's head is spinning as she is getting advice from her friends and none of it sounds the same. Lisa is conflicted about what she should do. She came wanting to get attention from a boy to justify how she felt inside about herself and Trey's approach did just that. To have one of the finest, most popular boys trying to get with you should have been more than enough to make Lisa or any girl lacking confidence and self-esteem feel good about herself. Truthfully, it was enough for Lisa, but once you open Pandora's Box of emotions, it is hard to control it. This is why Lisa finds herself in a world she is completely unprepared for now that Trey has approached her.

Like most young ladies who don't realize that looking for confirmation from a guy is a mistake, Lisa finds herself in a situation that she hadn't thought out all the way. Lisa's confusion is growing by the second because she knows inside that getting advice from your peers is not always the best decision. On the one hand, she is happy about what is happening. On the other hand, she doesn't know what she should do next about Trey now that she has his interest. Lisa usually talks to her Mom about everything. With that not being an option at the moment, Lisa decides to fall back and take in everything that is going on.

Well, Lisa's plan to fall back doesn't last too long. Trey is making his way over to an unsuspecting Lisa. Just as Trey gets close to Lisa, the DJ plays "Press" by Cardi B. and the whole party erupts. Just so happens, Lisa loves that song, so as the roar comes over the skating rink, Lisa notices Trey coming her way. Lisa instantly gives Trey a smile while she dances with a look on her face that says "Come Get Me". Trey's face lights up and he slides right over to her and she reaches for his hands. Lisa quickly turns around putting her butt near his midsection while wrapping his arms over her shoulders and then out to her side before she places his hands on her hips as she continues dancing. Lisa looks around and notices all her girls dancing with someone and she feels, euphoric (extremely excited and happy). This carefree feeling is what she wanted from going out with her girls. Lisa is taking it all in as she realizes this will be the first time that she will not have to get all the details on Monday in science class or trying to live through the moments on someone's Instagram the next day at school. Lisa is happily living in the moment, as the music plays Lisa is loving every bit of... This night, this feeling, this guy, This... Is everything she thought it would be and more...

Now, the story could end here with just the girls having a good time. However ladies, in the world of teenage boys this is never the case, they are always going to push it to the limit. So as the song is ending, Lisa turns to face Trey, who grabs her hand and gives it a little kiss and says "Thanks for the dance." Lisa says "Oh, you are most definitely welcome..." The two are gazing into each other's eyes as Lisa slowly backs away in the direction of her girls. Just as she goes to release his hand the DJ announces, "Alright ladies, we about to slow it down. So grab you a man... or someone else's man that you are using for the weekend..." Instantly, the intro beat to SZA's "The Weekend" blares from the speakers and all the girls in the building let out a simultaneous AAAAYYYYYEEEEE...

Lisa gently grabs Trey's other hand while clutching the one she was about to let go. Lisa places both of his arms around her waist as she draws in close to his chest. Lisa reaches up to put her arms around his neck. Trey bends down ever so slightly to help her get her arms comfortably around her shoulders. Lisa is loving every moment of this as she closes her eyes and mouths the words to the song because in this seemingly magical moment in time, Lisa feels what she always knew inside that she is... BEAUTIFUL.

The song is coming to an end and as Lisa opens her eyes she notices that Keia has walked off with Kevin towards the door. Keia has Kev's hand as he is leading her through the crowd and towards the exit. Lisa is a little shocked because she has no idea where they could be going. Lisa hasn't noticed that she has stopped dancing and leans her head back off of Trey's chest and looks him in the eye with a very puzzled look on her face, only to ask, "Where they going?"

Slightly nodding her head in the direction of his cousin and her best friend heading in the direction of the door. "Who? Oh them, girl you know what time it is... Oh, that's right this is your first time out with them... Yeah, they always go out to the car after a while being in here." By this time, Lisa is in complete defensive mode and has taken a step back from Trey and says with her face frowning, "For what?" To which Trey responds, "Chill out Lil Mama, they ain't doing 'That', well I don't think they are..." Trey says with a second-guessing look. "You know Keia mom don't really like him all like that after she saw some of the stuff in Keia phone. So, they just go outside to get a little closer than they can in here... Why you tripping?" Not knowing what to think, Lisa has a confused look on her face, yet she doesn't want to mess up her night and chance at Trey. So she just says with a fake laugh, "Nawl... it's cool, I was just asking."

By this time the song has ended and she slowly taps a few fingers on his chest and gives him a smile looking deep into his eyes and says "Thanks for the dance, don't go far I might want another one..." Trey looks back into her eyes and says "Anything you want, you can get it." Being naïve, Lisa missed the innuendo and slowly walks away as she gives him a smitten smile. Lisa snaps out of it quickly as she turns and is headed straight to Jaz. She knows Jaz is going to tell her the truth about Keia and Kev. What Trey just told her wasn't a good enough answer for Lisa.

Lisa makes her way over to Jaz, grabs her by the wrist and walks off to the corner where they can talk rather privately. "Girl Keia just went outside with Kev, what's that all about?" Jaz rolls her eyes in disgust and replies, "Girl, she always go out to the car with him. I don't know what they be doing. She say they just be talking but I am sure it be a little more than that because they can 'just talk' in here. I don't judge them, but you ain't gone catch me outside with anybody, girl it ain't worth it..." Lisa is still a little lost and says, "Wait, they go outside in the cars and talk, or to get freaky?" Jaz replies, "Girl, to be honest, I tried to talk to them about it a long time ago, but they do what they want, so I just left it alone..." Lisa is still trying to comprehend, "So what is wrong with going out to the car if they are just talking?"

Jaz responds with an annoyed look on her face... "Look you can't never trust any of these dudes, who knows what can happen to you in they car? They liable to try anything when they got you alone. In here, you safe, you want to dance, to talk, you can do it inside, ain't nobody going to do nothing in here... you know? Outside, in they car, they think you must want to do something if you are willing to go out there. Look Lis – it is just not a situation that they should be putting themselves into, but hey, I tried to tell them and if they don't listen... Oh well, I just hope nothing goes wrong while they are out there." Jaz has made her point very clear. Lisa looks at Jaz and notices how much this bothers her and says convinced... "You right Jaz."

After two songs pass, Trey makes his way back over to Lisa and asks "Wsup Lil Mama, you hungry? I'm heading over to the snack bar. Lisa responds, "I don't know what I want" so Trey simply suggests, "Well come see..." and definitely meaning more than food Trey slyly adds, "You can have whatever you like." A gullible Lisa is quick to say "Ok" with a shrug of her shoulders and the two walk off. As they make their way through the crowd, Trey reaches back for Lisa's hand to make sure she gets through safely. Lisa again is living in a fairytale because in her mind, this is too good to be true.

When they make it to the line, Trey turns to Lisa and asks, "So how you liking this? I know you said this isn't your thing and all but I can't tell because I been watching you the whole night and you haven't stopped smiling..." Lisa doesn't try to hide her emotions so she speaks from the heart, "This is so fun. I think I am going to be doing this a lot more. It's lit in here!" Trey continues to play it smooth, "That's wsup Lil Mama, that sounds like I am going to be seeing more of you. Why don't you give me your snap so I can keep seeing that pretty smile until I can see you again in person" Lisa's worst nightmare just came true. She has no social media and doesn't know how to explain that her parents will not let her have one.

Luckily for Lisa, fate intervenes. As Trey was going to his grab his phone he realizes that he doesn't have his wallet. So instead of waiting for Lisa to give him a response, Trey says, "Dang it, I forgot my wallet in the car... Come with me real fast to grab it?"

Although Lisa just dodged a bullet, she now has a bigger problem on her hands. Lisa is thinking about what Jaz just said and immediately thinks going out to the car with Trey is a bad idea. Awkwardly, she doesn't respond because she is literally processing all that Jaz said and even louder she could hear her mother going off if she found out that she was sitting in a boy's car alone. Lisa says to Trey, "How about I just keep our space in line."

By this time Trey has already begun making his way out of line because he assumes Lisa is following and he only turned back because he heard Lisa say something about keeping their space in line. Trey turns back with a half disgusted, half puzzled face at Lisa, because although he did leave his wallet, he is not used to a girl turning down his request to go to the car. In his mind, he is "Trey". Which to him means that he could have anyone he chooses, so for Lisa to be resisting him, is an attack on his ego. He looks back and says, "What?! You ain't coming?" Lisa sees the change in his demeanor and is a bit uneasy because she doesn't want to mess up a "magical" night. Lisa reluctantly gets out of the line.

Lisa knows it is a bad idea and all she keeps thinking about is how her mom would kill her if she finds out. As Lisa is walking towards Trey, she is trying to figure out a way to not get in his car and not mess up her chances with Trey. Lisa makes a quick plan, "Ok when we get close enough to the car, I am going to bend down to tie my shoe, that way he can keep walking to grab his wallet and I don't have to get in the car with him. He won't be mad because I came out with him and I don't have to get in the car... I'm good."

As Trey and Lisa walk out the door, Jaz looks up and sees the two leave, she is shocked, "I know this... Uggghhh" Disgusted Jaz doesn't know what to make of what she is seeing so she sits with her thoughts for a moment. She thinks about telling Shanti and Taty but doesn't know if that's the right move. Jaz can't live with not knowing what Lisa is doing or going to do with Trey. Jaz knows that doing anything could ruin her life and her reputation. Jaz leans over to Taty and tells her, "I'll be right back" and then heads for the door. Jaz hurries through the crowd to make it out the door and into the parking lot to see Lisa walking with Trey.

Lisa's arms are folded because it's a bit chilly outside compared to the heat generated by the bodies inside. Trey notices that she is a bit cold and walks behind her and rubs his hands up and down her upper arms and gently asks, "Does this help?" Lisa responds, "Oh, thanks and yes it does..." Changing the subject she turns to look back at Trey and says "Hey, Keia and Kev been out here talking for a minute, what they talking about?" Trey gives a sarcastic "Ha" Trey is still missing the naivety of her voice... "You know they needed to "talk talk." Trey says attempting to insinuate that maybe more than just talking is going on, but Lisa is playing the dumb role and wants to hear it from Trey.

Lisa stops him and looks into his face while making eyes at him attempting to get him to explain more. Trey looks down at the shorter Lisa noticing she wants more of an explanation, so he expounds, "Alright Lil Mama, my bad, I see you the pushy demanding type, it's cool. I like my women to know what they want... Real talk though, "It's more than one way to have a conversation" Trey says seductively while looking deep into Lisa's eyes. He licks his lips and slowly leans in like he is going for a kiss, so Lisa closes her eyes anticipating the passion, but Trey moves slowly to the right side of her face and in a deep sexy whisper he mutters "Sometimes your hands and body can say all the right things." Trey slowly walks around her and to his car that is parked about 10 feet away and Lisa is standing there shocked trying to figure out what just happen. Lisa is thinking,

27

"Wait, wasn't I supposed to be tying my shoes or something? – Is this why my Mama told me 'Boys gone be there, stay focused on what you want in life?'" Whatever this is that is happening, I like it..."

As Lisa slowly opens her eyes with all these things running through her head because she could have sworn 10 seconds ago she was about to get her 1st kiss, she sees Jaz standing near the entrance looking at her with a face full of disgust. Lisa feels guilty but she doesn't know why because she hasn't done anything. Jaz's face is burning a hole full of guilt into her right now. While Lisa and Jaz are having this unspoken communication, Trey has found his wallet and is thinking "Why not see if I could get her in the car?"

Now truthfully, Trey isn't really trippin' if she comes to the car or not because he is actually feeling Lisa, but his ego is feeding him right now so he has nothing to lose in his mind and says "Hey Lisa!" Lisa slowly breaks eye contact with Jaz and turns around where she is facing Trey. Lisa doesn't say anything she just raises an eyebrow acknowledging that she heard him. Trey slowly bites the bottom of his lip and raises his head simultaneously as he lets his lip go and ask "You Wanna Talk?"

Lisa knows that everything is wrong with going to get in the car with Trey, but she has never felt this way and this feeling is strong. She has always wanted to feel beautiful and be desired. Trey is making her feel both right now... She takes a second to turn around to look at Jaz and she knows that going back toward her friend is the right decision and she wants to do that so bad. Lisa turns back to Trey and says...

28

The Big Picture

Ok, I know that you want me to finish the story right now because it just got really good, but first let's take a look at why Lisa is in this position. Lisa is like many young girls around her age, who for whatever reason lack self-confidence and doesn't have the highest self-esteem. Lisa is trying to gain validation from Trey for something she already knows to be true... That she is beautiful.

If you are like Lisa, you are probably saying to yourself... well if that was the case, then why aren't I getting the attention that other girls are getting? The answer is simple, you are giving off something that the other girls are not giving off, strength. Truth is, most males fear rejection and the girls that they feel may reject them, they don't dare talk to, regardless of how you look.

If we look at the image that I painted of Lisa, we find a girl who has both parents, you would think makes good grades, is opinionated and appears to be on her way to achieving her goals. Lisa isn't always out at every social event, although not by her choice. She looks nice, is well dressed and smart. Lisa is almost ideal, which is usually the problem when it comes to attracting males. Lisa is the type of girl that most guys feel they are not good enough for, especially if they don't want to be in a relationship and just want to see how far they could go with as many girls as possible. Fortunately, Lisa isn't the type of girl who fits that list, so she will continuously get passed over. Consequently, this makes Lisa feel as if something is wrong with her. When in actuality, Lisa being passed over is a reflection of the immature and misguided mind frames of young men. A fact that Lisa is too young to realize for herself.

I named this chapter "Just Because They Can't See Your Beauty"... for the simple reason of making you aware of that your beauty can't be determined by anyone but yourself. It is my hope that this chapter shows a lot of young ladies that seeking validation for things that you feel inside can often lead to trouble. Usually in the form of situations that get out of your control much faster than you can ever realize. Since Lisa lacked the confidence and self-esteem she finds herself thinking about going into a car with a boy that she just met simply because he has confirmed what she has felt her whole lifetime. That she is Beautiful.

Ok, ok, ok, I know you are feeling what I am telling/preaching about but you want to know if Lisa gets in the car, right? Well, I really want to leave that up to your interpretation and ask you what would you do?

And here is why. There are so many different ways this could play out. Lisa could say no to Trey and Trey could say okay; remember he was just trying to see how far he could go any way. Lisa could say yes and Trey could be on some real player stuff and sit in the car and actually just talk to her and get to know more about her because Trey is the rare type of guy who actually is attracted to the strength in a girl. Lisa could tell Trey no and he could get an attitude because he feels like she wasted his time, so when they go back inside Trey is off of Lisa and she could feel like she messed up what could have been a good thing. Lisa could say no and gain Trey's respect because he has been looking for a girl who stood by her morals and the two could begin dating and this was the start of a long five year relationship. Lisa could say no to Trey and Trey could be cool with it upfront but inside he wants the challenge of "getting her." Trey keeps pursuing her and eventually after months she thinks Trey loves her and she allows him to be her first. Out of nowhere, Trey flips and stops talking to her because he got what he wanted, leaving Lisa crushed and emotionally scarred forever. All of which are possibilities and while they make a good story they don't make the point I want to make.

The point I am making is that with boys you don't always know how things are going to play out. So you have to control what you can control. How I would want the story to end is with Lisa saying no to Trey, he is cool with it and they go back inside and having a good time. Trey eventually tells Lisa that he doesn't want anything serious because he is going off to college and doesn't think it is fair to lie to her. Lisa went home that next day and told her mom about everything that happened with Trey and her mom gave her good advice and they celebrated her making a good choice. Lisa gained not only the confirmation that she was beautiful but also the confidence that she could make the right choices when it comes to guys and have her self-respect if nothing else at the end of the day.

So listen carefully, 'Just Because They Can't See Your Beauty...' It doesn't mean it isn't there, nor is it worth you compromising your future trying to find what is in your mirror... Remember you are Beautiful... Just The Way You Are...

A Message From The Author

Beautiful Just The Way You Are is both my personal and proffessional homage to the women in my life and the beautiful young ladies that I have taught and mentored. Besides the obvious, that all of you are beautiful, I wanted all of these girls and women to know that not only did I have love for you, I wanted you all to know that I hear and see you; then, now and forever...

To my readers, the stories that follow are an amalgamation of both my imagination and true stories of women I have encountered, scenarios I have been faced with as a teacher and coach and even storeis that have moved me from national headlines. It is my hope that this book and the stories within it move you to have the passion-ate discussions, heighten your awareness and if possible inspire you to advocacy for at least one, if not all of the issues covered in the book. So as you read the pages of this intimate look at Black Womanhood from A Man's Perspective, I want you to know that this book is a labor of love that not only reminds you but also confirms that God made you Beautiful, Just the Way You Are...

With Love and Compassion
Alan Gaines

32

According to the 2018 Discipline Data for Girls in US Public Schools released by the Department of Education office for Civil Rights Black Girls are:

6x More Likely Than White Girls to be Suspended

4x More Likely to be Arrested in Schools Than White Female Students

3x More Likely to be Reffered to Law Enforcement Than White Females

3x More Likely to Receive 1 or More In-School Suspensions Than White Female Students

3x More Likely to be Restrained Than White Female Students

2x More Likely to Receive Corporal Punishment than White Female Students

Chapter 2
A Rose By Any Other Name…

Black Girls in particular and Girls of Color in general are being consistently adultified by both the perceptions and consequences they receive in schools.

The long held belief that Black Women are "Angry" has manifested into young Black Girls being viewed as "Smart Mouthed," "Loud" and "Grown." None of which justify the disparities presented on the previous page in regards to how Black Girls are punished differently in relation to their racial counterparts for the same violations of school rules.

The Criminalization of Black Girls in schools unfortunately hasn't received the necessary attention that would enable policy makers to address this obvious racial bias.

Due to the lack of awareness around this issue, Black Girls all across America are being systematically victimized in what appears to most people as isolated incidents. Sadly, these incidents are not isolated and speak to a much larger issue that we must view as a crisis.

In recent years we have seen police officers who have been hired as school security guards flip Black girls out of desk, drag them down flights of stairs and even arrest a 6 year old. This has to stop!

Please allow me to introduce to you
Destiny.

Destiny is like every other girl regardless of her color who goes to school to learn. Despite the fact that she is a Black Girl Destiny is A Rose Who By Any Other Name Still Smells Just As Sweet…

33

A Look into Destiny's World Before We Get Started...

As much as I would love to tell you that Destiny is trying her hardest to stay up in class right now, I can't do that with a good conscious. Destiny has just nodded off for the 3rd time this class period, much to the annoyance of her teacher Mr. Paneli. Destiny doesn't like Mr. Paneli nor the school for that matter. But before you go labeling Destiny as just another girl with a bad attitude who doesn't care about school, she actually has an understandable reason as to why she is having trouble staying awake today in class.

Destiny was up until 1o'clock in the morning tending to her little brother who was sick. Her mom is the manager at the local grocery store and usually works the 3 - 11 shift. Unfortunately, that leaves a large part of the household duties to be handled by Destiny. From cooking and cleaning to homework and baths, an awful lot is requied from Destiny.

Destiny who turns 17 in the fall, is the oldest of 3 children. Her mother divorced the father of her 2 younger siblings who are 10 and 8 years old. Destiny's Dad was 17 and her Mom was 18 when they had Destiny. It never worked out for them as teen parents and her Dad went off to college at Jackson State University and runs the IT Department at a medical center in Zachary, Louisiana. Destiny's mother and her two younger siblings (Xavier and Jalayia) Dad got divorced 5 years ago and things have been tight ever since. Both her Dad and ex-stepfather pay the appropriate child support but that doesn't replace the psychological toll that has been placed on the household. So as you can see, Destiny is dealing with a whole lot before she even makes it to school every day.

Let me be clear, this is not a reason to fall asleep in class. I am simply telling you this so you can have a clear picture of Destiny's reality. Destiny like many other children has an non ideal home life. While some educators take the time to get to know their students and become empathetic of the circumstances that each child brings, the reality is that it is not a requirement for teachers to care. In the performance based climate that is school today, empathy has given way to standards and school ratings created from high stakes test. None of which matters to Destiny who is simply tired from a long evening and at a school she hates...

<u>A Rose By Any Other Name Would Still Smell As Sweet</u>

It's 8:37 am on a Tuesday morning and Destiny is in her homeroom class. Destiny's head is down and her eyes are closed. Yet, she still hears every word that is being spewn (to vomit or release under pressure) at her from her "teacher" Mr. Paneli...

"Ms. Brooks! This is the third time I told you to sit up and stop putting your head down! What's wrong with you, did you stay up all night watching episodes of Hip Hop Love or whatever it is your people watch? I don't know why you come to school... You are a waste of space... You'll never pass my class... Just get out!"

His rant obviously lacked compassion and definitely is being said with the intent of embarrassing Destiny. Not to be outdone, Destiny who hates the "good school" her parents are forcing her to go to, picks her head up after she hears Mr. Paneli's last verbal jab. Time to let the show begin, Destiny pushes the paper that she has in front of her onto the floor and the desk she is sitting behind down along with it. Destiny screams, "I HATE THIS STUPID SCHOOL!!! I SWEAR TO GOD!!!" Mr. Paneli is calling the office while Destiny is attempting to safe face with her disrespectful actions. Destiny knows that security is on their way and she kicks over the garbage can on her way to the door. Destiny has her bookbag in her hand because she knows she isn't coming back to class and probably just earned herself a few days of suspension. Despite the disrespectful display of be-havior, Destiny stoicly, takes the all too familiar escort to the Principal's office from the security guard who has made it to the door by the time Destiny is exiting Mr. Paneli's class.

<u>Destiny Revealed</u>

It's been a little more than twenty minutes since the show she put on in Mr. Paneli's class. Destiny sits in the office while the Principal, Mr. Dumbrowski types on his computer. Destiny sits quietly looking out the window, at nothing in particular. Destiny is questioning everything in her life as a million thoughts, very few of which are positive, run through her head. The silence between her and Mr. Dumbrowski is largely rooted in the overall frequency of Destiny being sent to the office. Destiny knows what is coming next. Any minute in now, her Mother will be here and Mr. Dum-browski will go on talking about Destiny as if she is not in the room. Mr. Dumbrowski's lecture will definitely insinuate the environment she grew up in and all the social ills facing African Americans as to reasons why Destiny is consistently being put out of class. None of which are the reasons for her actions, which they would see if they looked at Destiny for what she is, a human.

While some of the behavior Destiny exhibits warrants consequences, Destiny's attitude has landed her in the purgatory of being labeled a trouble maker. With that label attached to her name, every little thing she does typically receives more scrutiny than if someone else did the same thing. Or as she often pleads to her Mom, the teachers are always "picking on" her.

The underlining issue is that Destiny doesn't like the school. She never has. Her parents felt that sending her to a predominately white private high school, after she had spent her whole life in local public schools would give her an advantage they never had. Her parents didn't take into account other factors such as socioeconomics, race and general social adjustment to a new predominately white environment. When those things are coupled with having to get up an extra hour earlier to get to school that is fifteen miles outside of town, Destiny is over it. When Destiny tries to explain her frustration to her mother, it is usually to no avail.

"I Didn't Know What Else To Do"

Destiny's Mom gets to the office and in what has become a routine procedure she sits through Principal Dumbrowski's whole spill about Destiny's behavior. The conversation is playing out pretty much the way Destiny anticipated it moments ago as she was waiting for her Mother's arrival. Destiny is a little taken back by her mothers calmness which is different from her typically agitated demeanor when Destiny is in trouble. Perking her ears up Destiny begins to pay attention to what her Mother is saying to Mr. Dumbrowski, "... again I totally understand your frustrations with Destiny and I am completely aware of school policy. Under no circumstance should my child or any student react this way. I want to apologize and you can be sure that I will talk to Destiny about this situation. Her Father and I are working very hard on getting Destiny to focus on the things she needs to be successful." Mr. Dumbrowski is pleased with her Mothers response and confidently ends the conversation. "Well Ms. Smith I appreciate your support of our mission here at Paramount. I'm sure if we keep plugging away we will find the right solution to help get Destiny on the right path." "Thank you Mr. Dumbrowski, you have a blessed day." Destiny's mom shakes Mr. Dumbrowski's hand and leave the office.

Destiny is still puzzled by her Mothers calm affect. Little does Destiny know, she is in for a big shock when they get in the car. Destiny's Mom casually walks out of the building with Destiny a few steps behind and heads to the car. When Destiny gets in and closes the door, her mother burst into tears. Destiny's Mom begins apologizing to Destiny for all the responsibility that she has put on Destiny:

"I know I put a lot on you and it's not fair, but you gotta work with me Dess. I am trying so hard. I know you hate this school but we put you in this school to give you a better opportunity. We know you wanted to go to Wirt with some of your friends from middle school, but we gotta do what's best for you. It's our responsibility to give you the best opportunities in life. That is why I work so hard. I hate coming up to this school and having these people look at me funny because you have been put out of class or getting suspended. I know that it isn't always your fault but you have to take account-ability in a lot of this Dess. Life ain't fair and everything ain't gone work the way you like it. But you are going to have to do your best and make the best out of your situation. You know how I feel about my job. But the reality is that I put myself in this situation because I didn't take care of business when I was young. Now everyday I got to deal with people and things that I don't like. I want to snap out and go off like you did today but if I do that, we all would be living on the street. So guess what I gotta deal with it and that is all I am asking you to do, is deal with it. Do your work and what is asked of you...

    Look, I didn't know what else to do so... I called your Daddy and told him that something has to be done about your behavior. I know that a big part of what you are going through is that you miss him. You might not like this but you going with your Daddy for the sum-mer. His job has him in Jackson doing something with computers, I don't know what but you going down there with him. I don't know if you are going to get to go to Louisiana while you are down there but I know that you going to be in Jackson with him mainly. Dess I am trying so hard with you. What happened today, I ain't tripping on, but you got three weeks left in school so just ride it out. Do what you are supposed to do and stay out of trouble. Your Daddy is booking your flight for the 15th of June so I need you to just chill out. Can you do that?"

    Destiny has been crying since her Mother began to breakdown. Des-tiny can't remember the last time she saw her Mother cry. Her Mother usually is superwoman and keeps it together through everything. So Des-tiny knows that her Mom is hurting. Destiny wipes her tears and responds to her Mom, "I'm sorry too Ma. As much as I can't stand this school, I promise you I'm not gonna get into anymore trouble... You got my word, no more trouble."

Destiny went the final three weeks of the school year without incident after returning from her 3 day suspension. It's the 1st day of summer break and her flight to Jackson, Mississippi has just landed.

Change of Scenery

Destiny is coming down the escalator from baggage claim when she hears, "Laaaddddyyy Buuuggggg!!!!" Destiny looks up from her phone and screams back "Daaaddddyyyy!!!!" She puts her phone in her pocket and begins to walk fast but cautiously down the escalator before running the few steps into his arms. A father's embrace never gets old, yet it is a bit different when there is an extended period of time between the last time you felt it. Destiny feels the passion in the hug and tears of joy begin to stream down her face. "Ahhh Lady Bug, I missed you so much!" "I missed you too Daddy!"

Destiny wasn't expecting to hear this type of enthusiasm seeing that she practically spent her entire sophomore year in some form of trouble at her school. What Destiny doesn't know was that her parents had a long talk and both agreed that they would focus on creating a positive future for Destiny instead of what has already happened. Her parents both agreed that she was getting more than enough criticism and judgement from the outside world. A strategy of positivity and a temporary change of scenery was what they decided was the move they were going to make to spark a change in Destiny. They hoped that it would revive her once vibrant personality.

Destiny and her Dad are in the car when Destiny's Dad got into his normal joking and playful vibe right away:

Dad: "Dang girl you growing up so fast. You looking good baby girl, I like that outfit, it's On Fleek."
Destiny:"Really Daddy?"
Dad" "What?
Destiny: You so laaaaame!!! Don't nobody say On Fleek any more Daddy.(She says laughingly)
Dad: "My bad... But let me check out those edges tho!" (He says while laughing and leaning in and slightly lifting her hair. They both erupt into laughter. Destiny hasn't laughed and felt this free in Lord knows how long.)
Destiny: "Okay baldy! I know you ain't talking... At least I got hair! With your old milk dud head!"
Dad: "Yea my lining was starting to creep back so I had to be like Frozen."
Destiny: "Daddy please tell me that you are not trying to say 'Let it go.'

Just drive Daddy please...(Destiny says while shaking her head at her Fathers corny joke.)
Daddy: Alright, I'm done... You wanna get something to eat? I know you hungry. Don't worry, I know just the place.
Destiny: That's fine.

Destiny's Dad drives over to Cool Al's which was his favorite restaurant while he was in college. They both got a Super Burger and laughed and caught up as they enjoyed the food. When the meal wrapped up and they were walking to the car Destiny's attention turns to the summer plans:

Destiny: "So what am I going to do this summer? I know you out here for the summer working on some techy thingy or whatever you do? Staying in that hotel room is going to get old real quick Daddy." (Destiny is talking as the two are getting in the car.)

Daddy:"First it's not a techy thingy, I am developing the main frame code for the database that will be used at the medical center. As for what you will be doing, didn't your Mother tell you?"
(He is joking because he knows that she didn't. Destiny gives him that 'C'mon' look as she smacks her lips.)

Daddy: "Ok, Ok" (He says as he starts the car and begins to drive off,) "I signed you up for the Magnolia Bar Associations Summer Youth Debate Series." (Destiny replies with a puzzled look on her face.)

Destiny: "Aaannnddd what is that Daddy?" (Destiny replies with a puzzled look on her face.)

Daddy: "Oh, we gone put that attitude of yours to work Miss Thang!" (Destiny's Dad is mimicking a girlish attitude by snapping his fingers and rolling his head and eyes. Destiny cracks a smile and presses for more.)

Destiny: "Ok, but what is that?"

(Turning on a more serious tone, her Dad begins to explain.)
Daddy: "It's a summer camp for high school students that gives them an introduction to becoming a lawyer. You are going to learn how to do research to properly formulate an argument. You get to travel and debate against other teams. I think you are going to love it. You are going to be on a college campus five days a week. Not just any campus either, you going to be at thee JSU, my Alma Mater."

39

Destiny smirks and rolls her eyes with a here we go again look on her face because she has heard about the "Mighty JSU" from her Dad at least a million times. Destiny's Dad continues

Daddy: "The program this year is focused on Social Justice and issues of race in America. More importantly every day there is a daily financial literacy component that shows the students how to budget and manage money. It's for rising Sophomores and Juniors. There will be different speakers coming in... I can keep going but you are going to love it. And the best part of it is.... I get to take you shopping for some outfits so you can be On Fleek!"

Destiny: "Daddy!!!" (Destiny screams in irritation because she just told him about saying that and they both laugh.) "That sounds cool... Are some cute boys going to be there?" (Destiny says jokingly as she leans away from what she anticipates would be a joking grab or hit from her Dad. As she anticipated, he gives a half reach in her direction and answers.)

Daddy: "Yep... Did I mention that I got my gun?"

40

Again, the two share a laugh. This feels so good to Destiny. Stopping to smell the roses, she looks over and says in a very endearing tone.

Destiny: "I Love You Pops."

Taking his eyes off the road momentarily to reciprocate the sincerity he hears in Destiny's tone, her Dad responds:

Daddy: "I Love You Too Ladybug."

The two share a warm silence as they ride the rest of the way back to the hotel. The rest of the weekend was spent with a lot of laughter and bonding. The two head over to the mall where Destiny's Dad fully intends to splurge on her a brand new summer wardrobe as well as outfits she will need for the debates at the end of the summer.

We catch back up with the Daddy Daughter duo while out shopping. Destiny begins to inquire (ask questions) about what to expect when she gets on campus Monday.

Destiny: "Daddy, I seen a couple of episodes of The Quad, is that what being at an HBCU is going to be like?"

Destiny's Dad nearly drops his phone at the sound of Destiny's unintended insult at the illustrious history and legacy of HBCU's.

Daddy: Are you serious? You're joking right? Ladybug, College Hill and The Quad are so far from what life is like at an HBCU! Please don't ever say that again... I know I love to joke with you but I am dead serious. Please don't throw any covers at HBCU's?

Destiny: Daddy you mean "Throw Shade."

Daddy: Well a shade "covers" the light doesn't it?

Destiny: Daddy... I can't with you... (Destiny says laughing before continuing to look at the shirts on the rack.)

Daddy: I got the perfect thing for you... When we get back to the room, we are going watch A Different World."

Destiny: "I've seeing that on Netflix but I never watched it... Is it good?" (Destiny's Dad is shaking his head in disbelief and jokingly claims.)

Daddy: "I have failed as a parent... If my baby doesn't know that A Different World was more than just good, I have failed as a parent. A Different world exposed the world to the beauty of Black Colleges. It was more than just good, A Different World was On Fleek!"

Destiny: "Daddy!!!" (Destiny says shaking her head.)

Daddy: "Ok it's fiery"
Destiny: "Daddy!!! Oh My Gosh! You are so lame... It's LIT, It's LIT not fiery! It's LIT."

(Laughing at his own intentionally annoying sense of humor.)
Daddy: "Trust me you are gonna love it..."
    They finished shopping went back to the room and started their binge. And of course, Destiny was hooked from the first episode.

It's Monday morning and Destiny's Dad is walking her to class in the Liberal Arts building. Immediately, Destiny is beginning to notice how many people are speaking to them as they pass by. Destiny is getting a really good vibe. As they walk into the lecture hall where the class will be held they are greeted by Mrs. LaTanya Williams who is the site Director at JSU and an Urban Studies Professor on campus.

<u>It's A Different World From Where Destiny Comes From...</u>

"Good morning Mr. Brooks." She shakes Destiny's Dads' hand and looks over to Destiny. "I take it this is your lovely daughter Destiny. I have heard so many nice things about you. It is my pleasure to finally meet you. I am Mrs. Williams, the site Director for the Program."

Unfamiliar with these emotions Destiny can't remember the last time she was embraced by an adult in a school setting, Destiny shyly responds, "It is nice to meet you as well." Destiny looks at her Dad with a surprised look in regards to the unexpected hospitality Mrs. Williams is showing her. "OK Dad we are going to see you later, you know she is in good hands..." Mrs. Williams says eager to get the program off to a good start. "Thank you so much again for giving her this opportunity." "Your welcome."

Destiny's Dad turns to her and says, "I'll be in the same parking lot after it's over, just call me... Love You" Destiny who experiencing those new environment jitters responds, "Love you too."

Destiny finds a seat a few rows from the front and begins getting out her a pen and notebook. A young lady from a row above leans over to Destiny and introduces herself. "Hello, my name is Crystal. I'm from Yazoo City. What's your name?" Destiny is taken back because she didn't know that people still go up and introduce themselves. This is the south and southern hospitality is alive and kicking down here. Destiny responds, "My name is Destiny and I am from Gary, Indiana. It's nice to meet you." The two begin to exchange small talk before promptly at 8 o'clock Mrs. Williams calls the class to attention. Mrs. Williams:

Good morning, this is a day that the Lord has made, so let us rejoice in his glory, Amen. On behalf of Jackson State University and the Urban Studies Department, it is my pleasure to welcome you all to the Civic Engagement and Social Advocacy Summer Youth Program. This program is sponsored by the Magnolia Bar Association. We are extremely grateful for the work and contributions on their behalf to make sure that this program is available to the future world leaders and policy makers.

I greeted each student here upon arrival but again my name is LaTanya Williams. I am a happily married wife and loving mother of two beautiful children Rodney & Shannon. And I'm Ma Dee to six amazing grandchildren.

In addition to the role I have here on campus, I have led a few mayorial campaigns and served as the head of the Youth Service Bureau. I also teach a stocks and financial literacy enrichment course at a local high school. A course that you all will take every morning with me. But that is enough about me for now, I want to bring up a person who was very integral to making this program a reality across the 5 Historically Black Colleges in Mississippi. It is my honor to introduce you all to the Executive Director of the National Organization of Black Elected Legislative Women and Mississippi's own, Ms. Waikinya Clanton.

A beautiful black woman emerges from the front row and comes to the forefront of the room. She begins to speak:

"Thank you so much, Mrs. Williams. Good morning, as you just heard, I am Waikinya Clanton. I am a proud Tougaloo graduate. As a former member of the U.S. House of Representatives, I was able to see first hand the importance of having the representation of people of color in the room when the policy was being both written and voted on. That is why I am overjoyed to see so many young faces before me today. I know that the knowledge you are going to learn this summer will go a long way to help mold not only the leaders you are going to be but also the world you will leave the generations yet to come.

This summer we are going to tackle social and civic issues. You will be placed in groups and your task will be to create a policy that if enacted would serve as a viable solution to the issue you are tasked with addressing. Your team will research the issue, find if or if not a precedent has been set and create a mandated policy with the appropriate checks and balances to ensure that your policy can be implemented feasibly. Your presentations will be judged by a panel of members from the Magnolia Bar Association. The winners from each category will receive a prize. You all will be competing against other high school students who will be representing the four other Historically Black Colleges and Universities in Mississippi; Alcorn State University, Mississippi Valley State University, Rust College and the one and only Eagle Queen, the illustrious Tougaloo College.

As I wrap up my time here with you this morning, I want you to know that you are destined to become an agent of change. In order to fulfill the calling God has put before you, one must embrace their gifts. Your passion must turn into perseverance. Your intellect must become the basis of sound judgement and analysis. Students, never let anyone tell you that being aggressive or loud is a bad thing, you simply need to learn how to use your aggression at the right time and if you are willing to listen we will teach you that. As for being loud, was Dr. King considered a quiet man as he continued to fight for justice until the day that he was taken from us? I know that's a little outdated for some of you all. What about Nipsey Hussle, he used his voice and his brain to proclaim loudly that we need new narratives in our communities. Silence very rarely changes situations, you have to learn to use your voice appropriately through social and political activism. Thank you for your time this morning, again I am looking forward to the phenomenal presentations at the end of the summer."

Destiny is in awe, she pinches herself to make sure she isn't in an episode of *A Different World*. Destiny wasn't dreaming, this was real life, Destiny was seeing Black Excellency in a whole new light.

Ready To Embrace Her Name...

The rest of the day at the program didn't stray too far from your general orientation and greetings. At lunch, Crystal introduced Destiny to some of the people she knew prior to coming to the program. During lunch the students sat around and talked about how they were excited for the opportunity to debate issues such as Colin Kaepernick, NBA Players being told to "Shut Up and Dribble" and The Black Lives Matter Movement. Destiny followed these stories on the news and she had extensive conversations with her mother about them in her home as they were happening. Destiny was always very passionate about these types of topics and wanted to discuss these issues in her classes at school during the school year. Unfortunately, her teachers would hide behind the state-mandated standards as reasons not to discuss these issues when she tried to bring them up in school. Which only added to why Destiny really wasn't feeling her school.

The discussion was amazing, Destiny really hasn't ever been in a situation where the majority of the people she was surrounded by wanted to actually do something with their life. Seeing her peers doing more than simply posting on social media was inspiring to Destiny. She chimed in from time to time in the conversation but mostly took it all in. Destiny was pleasantly surprised at how the first day was unfolding. More importantly, she is beginning to see herself in the light her parents always tell her to expose to the world.

As the day wrapped up and it was time to go, Destiny walks right up to Mrs. Williams and says "Thank you so much, Mrs. Williams, I think I am really going to enjoy the program. I can't wait until tomorrow to see which topic I am going to have..." Mrs. Williams smiles and politely says, "You are welcome, we are glad to have you. Trust me you are going to not only love the topic but you are also going to learn a lot about yourself. Enjoy the rest of your day and I'll see you bright and early tomorrow morning."

After she turned away she saw Crystal waiting for her and they walked out to the parking lot together.

Destiny's Dad is right outside as he promised and when she spots him, she decides to act like the summer program was boring and that she isn't really feeling it. Destiny makes it to the car and as she gets in the car she gives him a dry unenthusiastic greeting.

"Hi Daddy..."
(Her Dad doesn't answer, instead, he leaned in anticipating more conversation. Destiny turns and says)

Destiny: "WHAAAT?"
(She says with a straight face because she knows he wants to hear all about it. Destiny's plan is working perfectly, so she continues keeping him in suspense.)

Daddy: "Sooo that's it??? Nothing about how everything went today?"

Destiny: "It was Okay. I mean people talk funny down here but it seemed cool... How was your day, Dad?" (Destiny is still messing with him.)

Her Dad's face turns in disappointment at the fact that this all she has to say but he keeps his cool and gives her a half-hearted:

"My day was cool. Thanks for asking."
(He says as he looks out the window trying to mask (hide) his emotions.

Daddy: "So did you me--"

Destiny: "IT WAS AMAZING!!! I'm sorry I couldn't hold it any longer! Dad this program is "On Fleek!" (They both begin to laugh uncontrollably at the perfectly timed joke.)

Destiny: "Ahhh Dad, this program... It felt so, so freeing! I felt like I could breathe... Wasn't anyone judging me! It was, ahhh man, man I can't even describe it... This girl, Crystal Lewis, came up to me and introduced herself?! Dad! I was like... "Where they do that at? People don't make friends no mo! I guess they do down here... This ain't Gary, that's for sure... Crystal was cool though. It was nice to have someone do that. It was a little odd, but it was cool... Aww and the class - Man Daddy it was lit... It was lit... This lady she is over the National Organization of something I can't remember right now but her name was Ms. Waikinya Clanton. When she got up and got to speaking about using our voice and she even knew about Nipsey Hussle, it was moving Daddy. She was talking about how it is more important how we view ourselves than how others view us. And how we gotta use our characteristics as tools of empowerment for ourselves and others. I know Mama would always say that to me but the way she said it, sounded different..."

Daddy: "It wasn't different, it was the same. It was just someone different who said it. Your Mother has been telling you your whole life what Ms. Clanton said in about ten or fifteen minutes and now you get it. Ladybug, you only get it because your Mother has already planted the seed in you. Without it, what she was talking about was likely to go over your head."

Destiny: "I know, Mama always says I need to use that mouth to make some money as a lawyer... But this was different Dad..." (Destiny's Dad reemphasizes his face, to which Destiny realizes how what she is saying sounds to her dad.) "Ok, but hearing her talk and the things she was saying, I think that is what I want to be a Civil Rights Attorney."

Daddy: "Ladybug you can do that and more. Don't limit yourself to only being a Civil Rights Attorney. Dream big! Become the first Black Woman to sit on the Supreme Court. Why not you? Somebody has to do it. Continue the legacy of Constance Baker Motley and all that she did for Black People."

Destiny: "Hey, Mrs. Williams talked about her in class today, I put her in my notes, her and Charles Hamilton Houston. Daddy what you know about all this?"

Daddy: "Hey I know a little something, something" (The two share a small laugh. Destiny leans over and kisses her Dad.

Destiny: "Thanks Dad. For everything. I really needed this program and I am excited about everything that is happening for me. I love you."

Daddy: "Love you too Ladybug."

Destiny came in the next morning excited to find out what topic she was going to be assigned. Destiny's group has the assignment Letting Her Magic Show: Designing Policies and Programs to Circumvent the Criminalization of Black Girls in Schools. When Destiny sees the title, she thinks to herself "Ok God, what are you up to now?" The irony of the assignment is that she is usually the one getting into trouble. Destiny is eager to see what information she is going to learn as she completes the project. Mrs. Williams gives each group last instructions before sending them off to the library to get started. Destiny's group is all females and she was lucky enough to get Crystal along with, Monica, Sherita, Tai, Comora, Angela and Stephani. The group is in the library and looking over the materials when Destiny breaks the silence:

Ain't I A Woman?

"Hey y'all, I like this topic.." Crystal jumps right in, "Yeah this is pretty heavy stuff, I mean just looking at some of the things on here, it's crazy. I know we all see that one girl in school, who always in trouble and we think like, that is just her. But looking at this information, I had no idea it was this bad." Comora says, "Wow, looking at this data, it just makes me motivated to do something. We all have seen the images of some messed up stuff involving black girls on social media, but this is laying out how bad what we don't see is. Like, I heard about some girl in Florida getting in trouble for a science project but I had no idea that she was handcuffed, arrested and charged with a felony. How can your life be the same after something like that." Tai is shaking her head in disbelief as she reading when she says, "It's like what Pastor Traci Blackmon said, "It is impossible to be unarmed when my Blackness is what they fear."

    The mood in the room is low, when Destiny gives a more sobering fact, "Hey, it's not just them, we do it to ourselves, look at this... Turn to the eighth page of this packet right here." (Destiny holds it up so everyone can see the one she is reading from. The girls turn to it when Destiny begins reading it.)

47

"Historical analysis information can be used help develop your position. Image perception of young Black females dates back beyond the civil rights movement. Be sure to include how executive decisions based on perception such as the one made by the members of the NAACP & Montgomery Improvement Association who decided that Claudette Colvin was not suitable to be the centerpiece of the Montgomery Bus Boycott. The decision was made when it was found out that she was pregnant, despite being a straight A student and refusing to give up her seat on a bus in Montgomery Alabama nearly 9 months before Rosa Parks. Information such as this can be used to strengthen your position and provide historical credence to your argument."

Angela chimes in, "That is so sad. I read about her before on one of those Black History cards. I feel bad y'all, being that I am a good student, it feels like I am a bit detached. When I see other kids in trouble, I feel like, that's just them. I didn't consider that it is something bigger. This study right here that was published in the Sociology of Education Journal in 2017, suggest that Black girls like us are two times more likely to receive discipline for minor violations such as dress code or being late to class. And three times more likely to be sent to the office or get detention for "disruptive behavior." It's almost as if just being ourselves is the reason we get in trouble. I know that we can be a little extra at times but I never thought about just who we are being the source of trouble at school."

Monica speaks up, "This is really lighting a fire in me right now. It makes so much sense what Ms. Clanton was talking about when she said not to let people tell us something is wrong with being loud and all that stuff. It's like that Sojourner Truth speech, Ain't I A Woman, my Mom had me memorize it a few years ago. Basically, she talking about how Black women go unnoticed, this kinda feels the same to me. All this is happening to Black girls like us and nobody is noticing it. It's always some type of program that mentors black boys. If more people knew about this information maybe they would do more for girls like us. We gotta do something about this y'all for real for real." Sherita stops the onslaught of emotions, "Let's just decide who is going to look at what information and take which roles so we can get started, okay?" The group knows that she has just given the best course of action and get to work.

The Unexamined Life Is Not Worth Living

The day wrapped up and as Destiny's Dad is in the parking lot waiting for her, he notices that her energy is a bit low as she walks to the car. So as the door opens he asks,

Daddy: "Wsup Lady Bug... Are you okay? How was class?"

Destiny: "It was great." (She says with no true emotion to back her claim.)

A bit puzzled, her Dad responds,

Daddy: "Oh that was the most unenthusiastic great day response I ever heard, but ok." (Destiny changes the subject.)

Destiny: "Can we go get something to eat?"

Daddy: "Yep we sure can... Where you wanna go?" He's still wondering what has her down but is respectful of her emotional space so he lets it go.

Destiny: "I don't know, it really doesn't matter to me."

Daddy: "You want to sit down? You wanna get something to go? What you in the mood for Lady Bug?" (He says trying to be accommodating.)

Destiny: "To go, let's grab something to go. I got some work I gotta do."

Daddy: "Lady Bug, I hope that is not what got you in a funk. You knew it was going to be some work involved didn't you?"

Destiny:"Nah, I'm not tripping on the work. I like the stuff I am doing. I'm actually really excited about it. It's just that... I'll tell you later, can we just get something to eat and go back to the room?"

Daddy: "Sure thing Lady Bug. I got just the place! Here take my phone and call E&L Barbeque. I got the number already saved. Tell them we want two steak sandwiches and sauce on the fries."

Destiny: "What about me? What they serve there?"

Daddy:"One of the steak sandwiches is for you. Just get whatever you want to drink, order me a -"

Destiny: "Lemonade with no ice" (Destiny says sarcastically, before continuing) "It's only been a couple of days and I figured that out already."

Daddy: "Well, thank you, my dear... You sure everything is good?" (The question brings back the frustration that Destiny is trying to surpress.)

Destiny: "Yeah, I'm cool..." (Destiny says as she looks back out the window. Her Dad raises his hands as if he is backing off and leaves the conversation alone. Destiny orders the food and the rest of the ride is silent.)
     Destiny is still feeling some type of way about the topic. Destiny's Dad is giving her the necessary space because it's obvious that something is bothering her. A few hours have passed now and Destiny's Dad is sitting on the sofa in the suite reading, Black// White: A Poetic Concept by Carol's Son a book by his former classmate JD Phelps, while Destiny is reading over the information for their assignment. Figuring he would check in Destiny's Dad, looks over at her and smiles proudly to himself before asking, "How's it coming over there, Chief Justice Brooks?"

The question triggered a different reaction than what he anticipated, Destiny begins to cry. Hearing the slight whimpering he gets up out of concern and asks more firmly,

Daddy: "What is wrong Destiny?!"

Destiny: "I know I been telling you nothing all day, but it's this assignment... It's not that it is hard. It's just... It's just that I see myself in the middle of this and I don't see how I am going to ever be able to escape it!!!"

Daddy: "Destiny, what is going on? See yourself in what? What is the topic? I am not understanding, what about it has you so upset?"

Destiny wipes her face as she begins to explain.

Destiny: "We have to design a policy to help stop the criminalization of Black girls in schools. I'm excited about the topic because it hits home with the things that I have been going through at school. It's just that after reading this research, I am realizing that this stuff is bigger than me. I know I can control my own attitude but this stuff is talking about studies that go into the psychology of how people feel about Black girls and how that plays a role in why the suspension rates of Black girls are so high."

Destiny's Dad wasn't anticipating discussing her behavior this soon. He felt it would come up organically at some point later in the summer. Being that he is never one to sugar coat things, he offers his opinion.

Daddy: "Destiny, you know my number one thing is taking accountability. You get in trouble because of your mouth nine times out of ten Lady Bug."

The agitation is still strong inside of Destiny as she quickly responds to her Dad's point.

Destiny: "Daddy, I am not trying to avoid anything, I know my mouth gets me in trouble a lot of the times, but read this. This is from Girlhood Interrupted: The Erasure of Black Girls' Childhood. Read right there Daddy, read it.
Destiny's Dad takes the booklet and begins to read what Destiny pointed out to him.

Across all age ranges, participants viewed Black girls collectively as more adult than white girls. Responses revealed, in particular, that participants perceived Black girls as needing less protections and nurturing than white girls, and that Black girls were perceived to know more about adult topics than… than their white counterparts.

These results suggest that Black girls are viewed as more adult than their white peers at almost all stages of childhood, beginning most significantly at the age of 5, peaking during the ages of 10 to 14, and continuing during the ages of 15 to 19. In essence, adults appear to place distinct views and expectations on Black girls that characterize them as developmentally older than their white peers, especially in mid-childhood and early adolescence - critical periods for healthy identity development.

The significance of this result lies in the potential for adultification to act as a contributing cause of the demonstrated harsher treatment of Black girls when compared to white girls of the same age. Simply put, if authorities in public systems view Black girls as less innocent, less needing of protection, and generally more like adults, it appears likely that they would also view Black girls as more culpable for their actions and, on that basis, punish them more harshly despite their status as children. Thus adultification may serve as a contributing cause of the disproportionality in school discipline outcomes, harsher treatments by law enforcement, and the differentiated exercise of discretion by officials across the spectrum of the juvenile justice system.

Daddy: "Oh wow!"

Destiny: "I know right? This is so sad. This research explains so much. I never put it together that because individuals see Black girls as "Grown" it unjustly validates stricter punishments and harsh treatments. I can't stop thinking about things like… when the girl in South Carolina was flipped out of the desk at school by the officer. Or the girls at the pool party who were slammed down and the cops put knees in their back! Daddy they arrested a 6 year old girl at school… This is crazy… This stuff goes viral and we think it is just a racist cop. This is saying its deeper than that. All this stuff… (Destiny gestures to all the work she has in front of her) Is explaining my life. Going to that "good school" I feel like I am treated unfair and now I understand why. It makes sense now that they are always calling security to the class for me. But when other people get in trouble, they just tell them to go to the office. I'm sorry Daddy, I just don't see how I am going to escape someone else's perception."

Her Dad is shaking his head in a bit of disbelief as he tries to find the right words to sum it up.

Daddy: "Well Ladybug, the only thing that I can really say is, Pain is inevitable, suffering is optional. I read that in Jasmine Guy's book about the life of Afeni Shakur, Evolution of a Revolutionary."

The names sound familiar to Destiny so she ask to be sure,

Destiny: "Isn't that Tupac's Mom?"

Daddy: "Yep. It means tha-" (Destiny interrupts)

Destiny: "Jasmine Guy, why does that name sound familiar?"

Daddy: "Whitley. Jasmine Guy plays Whitley on A Different World."

Destiny: "Okay, I gotta learn our legends, but keep going..."

Daddy: "Anyway, what that means is that no matter what, everyone is going to experience something that causes us pain. How long we allow the pain to have control over us is our choice. Racism, prejudice, and biases have been here long before we got here and by the looks of things, they are going to be here well after we are gone. Now, reading that was eye opening. Not so much the racial portion of it, more so the fact that I am guilty along with other Black people in general of viewing you and girls like yourself as able to 'handle' certain things."

Destiny hears the sincerity in his voice as he tries to help her make sense of it all.

Destiny: "Thanks for that Dad, but what am I going to do about everyone else, my school, the world, like everybody... I mean, this is how they see me, this is what they see when they look at a young black girl, what am I going to do?"

Destiny's Dad looks her in the eye and says,

Daddy: "Your question Ladybug, is your answer, What are you going to do?"

A silence overcomes Destiny as she sits back in her seat speechless.

Now the summer program went on and Destiny and her team learned how to formulate arguments. They spent hours in the law library, practiced for their mock trials and even had a few outings that really allowed the team to bond. Every single day, Mrs. Williams greeted the students with a hug, affirmations and was a continuous source of positive encouragement. Mrs. Williams and Destiny developed a special relationship as everyday she was positive and encouraging to Destiny. Mrs. Williams could be hard on her and demanded that Destiny develop the perseverance to see things through. Destiny did a lot of growing during the summer and discovered a lot about who she is and how to channel and properly express her emotions.

Destiny's Dad has been supportive the entire way, helping her study and even playing the role of the judges and giving her constructive feedback. Each day Destiny grew more and more eager to make a difference. The more she delved into the topic the more it became personal for Destiny. She felt compelled to be more than just a number in the statistics she read about. So with the day of the presentation being tomorrow, Destiny was unusually subdued. Destiny was sitting on the sofa with her airpods in her ear, just zoning out when her Dad brings her some lemonade.

What is Your Why?

Daddy: "Shouldn't you be reviewing your documents or going over what you have to say for tomorrow?" (Her Dad says while handing her the drink.)

Destiny: "Thanks. Nah, I'm good. You always say if you stay ready, you ain't got to get ready right…"
    Proudly surprised by Destiny's response, her Dad nods in agreement with her sentiments.

Daddy: "Ok, ok, I see you been listening. Cool, I am going to let you do you. If you change your mind, I am in the other room aight…"
    Destiny takes the airpods out of both ears before saying,

Destiny: "Dad you can stay, I was just sitting here visualizing how things are going to go tomorrow. You know how you always tell me that you gotta see it first." (Even more impressed with that response, her Dad reaches up and touches her forehead as if to see if she has a fever.) "What, what you doing Daddy?"

Daddy: "I am checking your temperature to see if you are sick?" (Destiny laughs)

Destiny: "Daddy, you so silly…"

53

Her Dad replies with a straight face,
Daddy: "No Cap! I'm trying to see if you are sick! No Cap"
Destiny laughs out loud at her Dad trying to be cool.

Destiny: "Oh my Gosh Daddy, I can't with you! Just go!"
The smile finally comes across his face when he says,

Destiny: "No real talk... Is that how you say it? Ok, I quit... I am super proud of you Lady Bug, I see you are applying the things that your mother and I have been trying to get you to see for the longest. She is going to be so happy with the Destiny that returns to her Sunday."

Destiny shows obvious disgust in the thought of having to go back,
Destiny: "Dad I don't even want to think about going back. I am just trying to focus my energy on this victory tomorrow."

Daddy: "I like the sound of that. Your Great Grandma Barbara Jean always said you claim it and it is yours... Well, let me give you a last piece of advice and I am going to let you get back to visualizing and manifesting your victory. Make sure tomorrow those judges can hear what is your why?"
(Destiny is a little puzzled and squints hoping that her Dad will give her more of an explanation. Seeing the uncertainty on her face he explains.)

Daddy: The difference between those people who do things and those who excel at them, usually is the motivation behind their actions. Those who excel tend to have someone or something that separates and drives them to levels beyond most people who are doing it just to be doing it. Your why will drive you to reach heights you never knew you could reach. Tomorrow what is going to be your why? The reason that is bigger than just winning?"
(Destiny knows exactly what he is talking about.)

Destiny: Dad, you know what is crazy, I already know. I mean I didn't think about it as my 'why' but all I been thinking about is all the girls who I saw on video being mistreated by cops or security guards in schools. Seeing that girl being dragged down the stairs in Chicago, then punched, kicked and tased by those cops, for having her cell phone out in school really messed me up. Only to find out that she was charged with felony aggravated battery because the cops lied. I mean something has gotta be done and now I got the answer to the question I asked you. Dad I am going to do something about it. These voiceless girls in a system that doesn't protect them is my why. I am going to be their voice."

The Presentation

...Thank you and now I will bring up our group member Destiny." Crystal closes her portion of the presentation before taking her seat. Destiny grabs her materials and walks to the podium. She gets to the podium and begins her presentation. "Good morning..." Destiny freezes. She looks out at the judges and then over towards her group. She is contemplating doing something that could likely cause her team to lose the debate. Destiny looks out and sees her father. Her Dad slowly nods which gives Destiny all the reassurance she needs...

"Uh, I'm sorry but I know I am supposed to follow the points on this my paper but, uh I'm sorry, I need to speak from the heart." Destiny takes her paper and flips it over before taking a deep breath. "Okay... I am sorry but I can't get these images out of my head. I mean, I can't stop seeing that cop flip the young lady in North Carolina over in that desk. I can't stop seeing those girls being slammed and arrested at the pool party. I can't stop seeing those cops drag the girl down the steps in Chicago, before they kicked, punched and tased her. Only to lie on her and say that she attacked them, which led to her being arrested and charged with a felony. I can't stop seeing Sandra Bland being slammed and man-handled by that cop. Only to know that less than 48 hours later she would no longer be with us. I can't stop seeing them this morning as I am up here to present because those images remind me that I am them..."

Destiny continues, "What I am about to say may come as a shock to my group. Before coming here this summer, I spent most of the school year in trouble. I was escorted to the office by security so many times that I lost count. Now, some of these situations I made worse by how I reacted to the petty stuff the teachers were doing to me. Like being sent to the office because the teacher could see the 'top of my cell phone' in my pocket. Or when I got sent to in-school suspension for a being late for class when my books fell and I was picking them up in front of the class-room. But I was late because I wasn't in my seat. Those things made me hate my school. I felt the whole time they were just keep picking on me. Even worse was all the 'You should know this, or You should know that.' So many expectations placed on me for whatever reason, made school a place I really begin to hate. Yet and still I am fortunate to not have had to deal with the emotional trauma that these young ladies I mentioned had to deal with being assaulted and arrested by cops in a school or at a party. I am sorry but I had to get that off my chest because, I know that they didn't have a voice and today that changes, I am going to be that voice. Here at this mock legislation competition and with the rest of my life. I wanna thank the Magnolia Bar Association for helping me find my purpose. So lets begin."

55

With confidence exuding from her voice, Destiny flips her papers back over and starts again. "First, we must remove all cops from schools. Our proposal to have cops removed is based on the historically problematic relationship between the police and minorities, specifically Black people. The current social climate and the exposure of our generation to the countless murders of Black people at the hands of cops caught on both body cams and cell phones has generated a negative ideal in regards to police amongst youth. We feel to expose students to the presence of police in their schools is contradictory to school policies that often state that they seek to ensure students are in a safe and stable environment. The presence of police in our schools, we feel creates a hostile environment based on the perception of Black people by police. Seeing countless officers and neighborhood watchmen walk free from assaults and even murders after grand juries rule that officers used necessary force or did not act outside of routine procedures we feel has created an unsafe environment for students in general and leads to the criminalization of Black Girls in schools.

Furthermore, our proposal is backed by the research of Dr. Phillip Goff and Dr. Matthew Jackson. In February of 2014 they published "The Essence of Innocence: The Consequences of Dehumanizing Black Children" in the Journal of Personality and Social Psychology. I'm sorry, just talking about this stuff makes me emotional. I know that this is a presentation, but this is real life. Ok, let me just read some of the findings in the report. Ok, so it reads:

Researchers tested 176 police officers, mostly white males, average age 37, in large urban areas, to determine their levels of two distinct types of bias — prejudice and unconscious dehumanization of black people by comparing them to apes. To test for prejudice, researchers had officers complete a widely used psychological questionnaire with statements such as "It is likely that blacks will bring violence to neighborhoods when they move in." To determine officers' dehumanization of blacks, the researchers gave them a psychological task in which they paired blacks and whites with large cats, such as lions, or with apes. Researchers reviewed police officers' personnel records to determine use of force while on duty and found that those who dehumanized blacks were more likely to have used force against a black child in custody than officers who did not dehumanize blacks. The study described use of force as takedown or wrist lock; kicking or punching; striking with a blunt object; using a police dog, restraints or hobbling; or using tear gas, electric shock or killing. Only dehumanization and not police officers' prejudice against blacks — conscious or not — was linked to violent encounters with black children in custody, according to the study.

The authors noted that police officers' unconscious dehumanization of blacks could have been the result of negative interactions with black children, rather than the cause of using force with black children. "We found evidence that overestimating age and culpability based on racial differences was linked to dehumanizing stereotypes…

I'm sorry, I know I keep apologizing but this is crazy. Like this real life. I am going to do something about this. Not enough people are educated on what is going on at these schools and parents too often are siding with the schools when their children are complaining about things being unfair. We have allowed the perception of us as a people to make it alright for police with these types of views to be the security in the place that we are told is so important to our future. This is crazy. I'm sorry but like for real the cops gotta go from our school."

Destiny gathers her emotions and continues. "Solutions. The solutions that we came up with are threefold. First, staff members in schools should be made aware of the disparities in discipline in regards to minorities. Being made aware of the disparities we feel will allow staff to reassess the discipline being put out and will help them reflect on the behavior being displayed by the student. If the student's behavior is age-appropriate then the punishment or discipline should be treated in accordance with how students from other ethnicities would be disciplined for displaying the same behavior.

Secondly, administrators should be required to identify each student with a staff member with whom they have a positive relationship with. This will enable students to be sent to "Buddy Classrooms" or to be de-escalated by a staff member that the student feels has their best interest in mind. These systematic implementations we feel will reduce the disparities in the discipline of students of color in general and Black girls in particular.

Finally, schools should be mandated to provide opportunities for mentoring for young Black girls. We feel that very little is done by the schools to embrace young black girls as they journey into womanhood. Schools across the country, specifically in urban areas, have a shortage of extracurricular activities in general and the numbers are reduced drastically with activities specifically geared toward girls. Young Black girls in some cases have little to no opportunities to participate in activities at school that are not related to sports. We are proposing that school districts mandate enrichment programs and activities be made available for Black girls in schools. Organizations such as Gyrl Wonder, Black Girls Rock and Pretty Brown Girl, all have initiatives to help empower young Black girls and can be used as viable resources to help change the mindset of Black girls in school. This proactive approach we feel will engage Black girls in schools and allow them to feel connected and involved in the culture of the school.

Thank you... We hope you find our presentation and solutions to be plausible and worthy of winning the top prize. Whatever you all decide we would like to leave you with the sadly still relevant and true words of Malcolm X who said of the Black Woman:

"The most disrespected person in America is the Black woman, the most unprotected person in America is the Black woman, the most neglected person in America is the Black woman."

Destiny goes back and takes her seat. When one of the judges, Trey Baker from Grenada MS, stands up and says, "I am breaking protocol by doing this, however young lady, I want to say that in all my years of working with youth, I have never felt any young person more passionate about something as I feel that you are about this. You still need some work on how best to articulate your thoughts, however in law, there aren't any style points. Hardwork and dedication are what get the job done in this field. I want you to keep that burning desire inside you at all times. Let that passion drive you to be the change you want to see in the world. I think you have found your calling and I will make myself available to help you in any way possible as you go on your quest to change the lives of so many people. Thank you for caring."

58

Destiny's JSU Debate team came in second to Tougaloo College. The group is getting off of the van as they have just arrived back on campus. Destiny is emotional because she knows that Monday morning she has to fly back to Gary. She is dreading all that comes with going back into that environment. She simply is not looking forward to taking care of her siblings and the school she hates. Destiny is feeling some type of way. So as the team enters the lecture hall that has pretty much been their home all summer, Destiny grabs Mrs. Williams.

Epilogue

"Can I speak to you in private." Mrs. Williams says "Sure" and the two go outside into the hallway. An emotional Destiny begins to speak, "Mrs. Williams, I just, I just wanted to say thank you for everything this summer." Destiny is trying to control her emotions and is fidgeting with her purse strap. Mrs. Williams can sense that it is more to what Destiny wants to say, so she just comes right out and asks Destiny, "What is going on sweetheart? C'mon say it now, I know you ain't shy so say what you feel, you been doing a great job f it all summer and you know that you carried us today. It's okay, let it out." A tear begins to roll down Destiny's cheek and she opens up. "It's just that I gotta go back home. I mean it's different there then it is here... I mean it's different, the teachers, the school... It's Different..."

Mrs. Williams grabs both Destiny's hands and looks her in the eye, "Destiny, it is different, but you can choose to be the same Destiny that you showed everyone here... When you get back home. Destiny if there is nothing else that you take from this summer I want you to take what I am about to tell you right now, okay..." Destiny wipes her cheek and gives a silent nod of reassurance to Mrs. Williams. "Destiny, as a Black woman, we must always maintain control of who we are, regardless of what environment we find ourselves in... This is a cold, ugly world that is going to give you some very dark days and take you to some very dark places...

But wherever you find yourself, you must always show the world the light that is who you are... Don't ever dim your light because of what is going on around you and how the people around you are treating you... They can't change your light unless you give them the power to... You must keep control at all times Destiny. This is more than a choice, it is your conviction to remain strong... Destiny let me tell you something before you ever came to this program, we called and talked to the people at your school. We do that for all participants. They told us about your attitude and the trouble that you got into. I made a choice not to listen to those negative things that they said about you. I hadn't met you and I made the decision to allow you to show me the Destiny that you wanted me to see. I did that because that is exactly the one power that everyone has, the power to show the world who they would like the world to see. I never saw that person they described. I saw a beautiful girl who desparately wanted to just be herself.

In fairness to the people I spoke with at your school, they also said something that I want you to always hold on to. They said that you were intelligent. They didn't say that you were smart, they said that you were intelligent. People who are smart, know a lot of facts and information. People who are intelligent know how to appropriately apply facts and information to the situations that they find themselves in."

Mrs. Williams continues, "So when I heard the word intelligent, I knew that I would not have any problems with you. For whatever reason Destiny, you don't care for that school and that was the reason you got in trouble consistently this past school year. When you walked in here with your Dad, I knew that I had to make sure that this was an environment that you knew cared about you and was judgment-free. Now you are nervous about going home and back to school because you think it is going to be the same way it has always been. Let me tell you, it doesn't have to be the same. Here is why. You are not the same Destiny that came here six weeks ago. You have a different set of tools than the ones that you came here with. Now, it is your choice to use them or not. However, I have confidence that you are going to show the world the Destiny that your Mama always tells you to be." Destiny's face looks surprised because she wonders

59

how Mrs. Williams could know what her Mom always tells her. Mrs. Williams continues, "Destiny, your name holds power, it's Destiny... Do you know that Destiny means to have a choice of what you will become? Everyone's Destiny is the result of the choices that they make... There is no escaping that... I know that you came out here to thank me and you are very welcome, but thank me Destiny with your actions... Go home and begin the habit of making choices that will make greatness, your Destiny."

The End

This story is largely based on the research done by the
Georgetown Law Center on Poverty and Inequality
in addition to my own experiences as an educator.

Links to the studies used in this story can be found on the next page.

I would also like to thank Waikinya Clanton for allowing me to use her
likeness in the story. I am truly humbled.

The Big Picture

The fact that Black women and girls have been under attack in America dating back to slavery is not a news flash. However, the lack of awareness and outcry being made by us as parents and community members has allowed our babies to be systematically victimized. This is a serious problem. It is as simple as that. Awareness must be raised around this issue and safeguards need to be implemented immediately to protect all students in schools and Black girls in particular.

The research that I did for this story was particularly heartbreaking and I want to thank the Georgetown Law Center on Poverty and Inequality for the studies they have done around the systematic mistreatment of girls of color. I am leaving a link at the bottom of this page to the phenomenal work they do.

I would be remissed to not mention Monique W. Morris who does an excellent job of championing this issue and wrote the phenomenal book Pushout: The Criminalization of Black Girls in Schools. I sincerely urge you to read it and allow it to fuel you to become passionate about this and other issues surrounding young ladies of color.

Lastly, if you or someone you know are experiencing the unfair treatment that Destiny faced in this story, I urge you to speak up and consistently advocate for yourself. Embrace your story no matter how dark it may be. Just remember that exposing your truth may help others find their light.

Links to the Research for A Rose By Any Other Name:

https://www.law.georgetown.edu/poverty-inequality-center/wp-content/uploads/sites/14/2017/08/girlhood-interrupted.pdf

pushotufilm.com
(A book and film by Monique W. Morris)

Section 2:

Diamonds

Diamonds are a universal symbol of Beauty and Elegance.

Diamonds are created under intense pressure and heat. As a result, diamonds are one of the worlds purest gems.

Diamonds are formed deep in the earths core and must be mined from within Mother Earth.

In This Section You Will Meet
Two Young "Diamonds" Who Have Been Formed By Extreme Circumstances.

Enjoy their journey as they emerge from life's depths to take the shape and form of a Beauty that like Diamonds, will last forever...

Chapter 3
Ebony And The Happy Place

CHILD MOLESTATION IS AN ISSUE IN AMERICA.

This issue transcends race and gender.

By no means would I ever trivialize this issue in any shape form or fashion. My attempt with this chapter is to encourage victims to break their silence.

Movements such as #MeToo are doing a tremendous job of empowering people to speak out about what has happened to them. In my human experience as well as my professional experience, too many family members and friends are being allowed to victimize children and young adults because of a code of silence that protects perpetrators at the expense of the victim.

Ironically, in some instances, victims often become the one thing they do not have, protectors.
Victims will sometimes endure the abuse in order to protect a younger sibling who they fear could potentially be the next victim.

Allow me to introduce Ebony.

Ebony is the victim of Child Molestation. If this chapter is personal or gets to be too much please skip ahead I understand.

Also, please allow me to apologize for the lighter moments in this chapter. I understand that this issue is not a laughing matter, they were implemented in hopes that we could laugh to keep from crying...

"Secrets"

An Original Drawing by:
Charity Neal   Age: 16

This Beautiful drawing was inspired by the story:
Ebony and the Happy Place

Ebony and The Happy Place

Ebony lays in her bed, she is trying her hardest to go to sleep but the fear and anxiety make it hard to simply fall to sleep at night. She knows that any moment the all too familiar sequence of sounds are likely to begin. A few moments pass then it starts. Ebony hears the toilet flush from the bathroom which is right next to her wall. Followed by the water running from the sink. Ebony knows what is coming next, the slow, squeaky, opening of the door to her bedroom. So she closes her eyes tightly and boom, she is there! ..."There" is one of the many fantasy places that she has created which enable Ebony to keep her soul intact while her body is being violated by her mothers boyfriend. The smile that has come over her face is mistaken as pleasure but Ebony has lost all control of her physical presence and is having fun in the "Happy Place". Ebony's older cousin Janae and her journal are the only two things in the world that know about the "Happy Place" and why she goes there.

Ebony's body is stoic during the entire encounter. Unfortunately, Ebony has to take these mental journeys at least four times a week. This has been her reality for what feels like her entire life but in actuality it only been the last 8 of her 17 years on earth. It only takes one such event to change the trajectory of an entire family for generations so it's complete understandable that Ebony's burden feels like a lifetime.

Nearly, 15 minutes go by before, !Boom! Just like that she snaps out of it. No longer in the happy place, Ebony opens her eyes and quickly realizes the furnishings of her grim reality which are a stark contrast to the places she goes in the "Happy PLace". Ebony is a bit surprised because she usually gets to spend more time in the Happy Place. Ebony looks over to the other side of the room and notices that her sister Felicia is tossing and turning in her sleep. The unusual restless sleep from Felicia has to be the reason that her recurring abuse is over tonight just as soon as it started.

Ebony lays there emotionally disconnected for a few more moments until she hears the fourth and final sound that she has sadly grown accustomed to, the door closing. Upon hearing the sound, Ebony reaches under her bed and grabs her journal with the pen in it and begins to write. The Journal is nothing more than a "composition book" that she inscribed the words, "The Happy Place" on the cover. Ebony carefully records the date and time of each entry. Once the night is time stamped, Ebony recounts her adventures in the fantasy worlds she creates to emotionally disconnect from the fact that she is being molested. With pen in hand, Ebony begins to write:

"Bon jour Mademoiselle Ebonee... I see you are alone tonight, will you be dining alone or will you be entertaining the likes of some handsome gentleman this evening?"

"Ah Monsieur Ernest, your pleasant greetings only come second to the amazing entrees served by the chef! Please give my regards to Pierre will you? I'm looking forward to what he cooks up tonight... And to answer your question, I will be dining alone tonight, there is no gentleman to indulge with tonight... But who knows, some fine young gentleman man see something he likes and come give me a very entertaining conversation... Let's see what the night holds..."

"Touche' Mademoiselle... I see optimism is the mood for tonight! Well, I will give you your favorite seat in the house, equipped with breathtaking ocean views and your first round of spirits will be compliments of the chef! Right this way Mademoiselle..."

After being seated by the Garcon, I took my customary gaze at the ocean. The water usually reminds me of the infinite possibilities that life holds, but tonight, the usually calm waves were crashing against the shore. The uncustomary happenings are worth noting. I am a virgo so it is not unlike me to overthink a situation.

Could the crashing of the waves be a sign that something in my life is attempting to get my attention?

Does unsteady water symbolize that what lies ahead will be rocky?

Before I knew it I had gone down the rabbit hole in search of clarity for the symbolism of uneasy shores... My quizzical meditation was pleasantly interrupted by a deep subtle voice...

"Good evening Mademoiselle, may I have this dance..."

This pleasant surprise snapped me out of my soul searching... Excited to partake in the happenings of the dance floor, I didn't truly get a good look at the face of the gentleman prior to accepting his offer. However as I made my way towards the dance floor, something said to look back one last time at the water as something in the darkness and the unusual noise I knew was attempting to get my attention...

Ebony closes the book and puts it along with her pen back under her bed. She grabs the sheets and curls into the fetal position. No easier to fall asleep, she just lays there emotionless. After enough time has passed, biologically Ebony is sleep.

Just an average morning

The next morning comes and she is awakened to yet another sound which she has sadly become emotionally numb to by now. The most unusual of alarm clocks sounds as soon as Tabitha, their mother, enters the room, "Would you hefa's get out the dang bed! Get Up! You whores get on my nerves! Every day I gotta wake y'all tramps up! I get so tired of having to do the same stuff every day! Y'all tramps need to hurry up and get ready for school! Hurry up so y'all can get y'all Lil funky selves out of here!" The violent verbally abusive tornado stripped off covers and snatched sheets as it swept through the room leaving emotional destruction in its path.

Both Ebony and her sister Felicia, who is 19 months younger than her, have grown so accustomed to the toxic environment, that their response is as if they were awakened by the sweet melodies of an angelic harp. Ebony and Felicia are among the countless black children being raised in a toxic environment under the harmful yet widely accepted code of silence known simply as, 'What happens in my house stays in my house.'

So as the door closes and their mother exits the room, Felicia pops up and starts talking to her big sister. "Morning Ebs, how you sleep?" Felicia is unaware that Felicia is being molested by their mothers' boyfriend so the question is genuine. Ebony responds blankly, "Alright." "I had a crazy dream…" Felicia says eagerly to share with her big sister, "I was fighting some girl I didn't even know, it was wild. I don't feel like I got any sleep." Ebony looks down at her headscarf that she took off while Felicia was talking. Yet Felicia's "nightmare" explains why Ebony's trip to the "Happy Place" was so short-lived. Felicia is a hard sleeper and usually is "out" when everything takes place. Felicia is going on with the details from her dream yet Ebony gives it no more thought and starts her day.

After finishing her morning routine Ebony makes her way to the kitchen, where her mother sits at the table in her sports bra, boy shorts, furry slippers and head scarf. Tabitha is chain smoking cigarettes as she scrolls through her phone yet makes it a point to give Ebony a cold stare when she walks in. Ebony takes the senseless nonverbal insult in stride as she heads over and opens the freezer. As soon as she grabs the eggos she hears, "If you don't put back my Eggos! You hefa's always eatin' my stuff! You and your Lil funky sista can grab some pop tarts. And you betta hurry up for y'all miss the dang gone bus!

You tramps gone be walking cause I ain't taking y'all nowhere!"

As her mother is going on her normal tirade, her mothers' boyfriend walks into the kitchen. Her mother immediately changes her tune, "Morning Bae... Do you want some Eggos? I can put you on some bacon and grits to go with it if you are hungry?" Ebony nonchalantly grabs her and Felicia some pop tarts before looking at her mother with disgust. Ebony rolls her eyes and shakes her head at her mothers pitiful contradiction between how she treats her boyfriend opposed to how she treats her own children. Fully aware of what Ebony is thinking but will dare not say, her mother flicks the ashes from her cigarette into the ashtray and sits up in her chair. With an even colder stare than she is getting from Ebony, she looks directly into the eyes of her firstborn and without saying a word clearly articulates to Ebony, "SO". Ebony knows that this battle isn't worth it and simply heads for the front door. (Her mother leans back in her chair with an inflated sense of a meaningless victory.)

"Felicia, come on, I got you a pop tart. Come on before we miss the bus!" Ebony says from the end of the hallway. "Okay, here I come!" Felicia says as she grabs her book bag and comes out of the room. Ebony opens the door to leave out the house when she sees Felicia turn the corner from the hallway. At the sound of the door opening the last attack of the morning comes from the kitchen, "Y'all tramps ain't gone tell me bye this morning? I swear y'all some unappreciative hefas! Y'all keep on treatin' me like this, your little fast tails gone need me before I need you, watch what I tell you!" Unwilling to give their mother any more energy the door closes and the sisters leave out.

<u>Without vision, your dreams will perish</u>

The sisters are walking to the bus stop when Felicia turns to Ebony and says, "Hey Ebbs, you wrote any new stories yet? I see you were writing in your journal that you never let me read. I saw you writing in your other notebook too. C'mon Ebbs, let me see it! I know you got something good!" "Nope FeFe... When I write something new... I will let you know." Felicia gets excited as she starts thinking about the future, "Ebbs, I can't wait! Your stories are going to be made into movies or like TV shows! Man, it's gone be crazy! I'ma be like, yep that's my sista!" Ebony lacks the confidence that Felicia has and dismisses her sister. "FeFe cut it out. My work isn't that good. I just write to take my mind off of stuff that's it! But, I doubt I ever let anyone read my work like that anyway. FeFe I know Mama be talking crazy to us but she probably right about my work. People don't really like reading so who is going to read my work? And what writers do you know who make money? Being a writer ain't gonna make no money... She right..."

Felicia has the will that Ebony needs and pushes back against her sister, "Well if Momma is so right then you tell me how your two favorite authors make it? You always talking about Natalie Baszile and Tiphani Montgomery. They made money and people read their books! So what you gotta say about that?" "Girl you must be crazy if you think I can be like them. Have you read their work?" Ebony retorts to her sisters' optimistic persuasion. Felicia hates that her big sister lacks confidence, yet she gives her the response that Ebony never considered, "Ebony why not you?" The bus pulls up and opens its door as Felicia's question rolls off her tongue. Ebony can't find the excuse and luckily doesn't have to as the sisters get on the bus.

"Look, Felicia, I write to take my mind off stuff. I mean it's my outlet. It's for me. I let you read them because you my sister. I know you think the stuff is good but I don't think it's all what you making it. Mama might be right about this one." Ebony says. "Ok 1st off, Mama not right about this... And 2nd, the Bible talks about the parable of the three servants. The para-" Ebony cuts Felicia off after she mentions the Bible, "Oh boy here we go again with your Bible talk. Ever since Ms. Dilosa been coming to get you for church, all you talk about now is the Bible." Felicia takes offense to Ebony's position. "Ohhhkay, what is wrong with me talking about the Bible? I'm lost?" Ebony states her case, "First off, you too loud, everyone ain't got to hear our business on this bus... But hey I ain't hating on you and God. I just don't see it... If God was all that they say then he wouldn't let all this stuff happen to me..." Felicia becomes concerned, "Let what stuff happen to you?"

Felicia's question makes Ebony aware that she may have said too much. Ebony is quick to keep the cover on the abuse by changing up her words, "I mean, to me, if there was a God then he wouldn't let all this crazy stuff happen in the world. Like, look at that movie we was watching, 'when they see us' stuff like that, those boys were innocent. Where was God? Look at all this mess with R. Kelly, why God allow him to do all that to them girls?" Felicia's faith is strong yet she isn't the most well versed on the Bible so she answers the best she can. "Ebony I don't know, but I know that Ms. Dilosa always tell me that the Bible say that everything works for your good. I heard the preacher say that God's timing isn't our timing so, who knows... I just got faith Ebs and you need to have some too..." Ebony's circumstances are fueling her reluctance to the idea of faith but instead of continuing to indulge in the debate over the existence of God,

69

she hits her sister with a quick, "Mmhmm, whatever FeFe."

Felicia stays persistent, "Anyway, back to my point. The Bible talks about the three servants and basically, God gave them all some money and then went away. When he came back, oh yeah it was a different amount for each of them. Yeah, but basically he gave them all some money and when two of them did something with their money. God gave them more money. The last one just held on to his money and God was mad. So he took the money and like made him work or something, I'm not sure. But when I asked Ms. Dilosa, what she said is that the story is a parable. God didn't really give them money, he gave them talent. Or a gift. Like he gave you the gift of writing. So she was saying like when God give you a gift and you do something with it, he gives you things like money, cars, house it's like God rewards you for using what he gave you. Ms. Dilosa say it's how you get abundance, from using your gift. If you don't do nothing with your gift then God make you like normal or whatever. Like you gotta go to work or something... I can't explain it like she did, I just know we supposed to use our gift and when we do, God gives us more... So, I believe God over Mama Ebs. You got a gift and you keeping all that writing to yourself is gone make God mad." Ebony has no comeback so she simply asks Felicia, "Are you done?" Felicia looks up and smiles, "Don't be mad at me, I am just the messenger." Ebony cracks a smile as she smacks her lips, "Whatever!" The two sisters laugh. Ebony feels there is some truth to Felicias point so she lets the words sink in as she stares out the window.

Your gifts will make room for you

It's later in the same day and Ebony is in her 4th period English class. Her teacher, Dr. Dease is walking around the room while the class is working on an assignment. Dr. Dease stops at Ebony's desk and softly whispers "Ebony, I need to speak to you after class. Ebony nods her head in agreeance.

When the bell rings, Ebony takes her time and allows the majority of the class to get toward the door before she makes her way to Dr. Dease's desk as she requested. "Dr. Dease, you wanted to speak to me?" "Yes, Ebony I did. I won't hold you too long, I know you want to get to lunch but please have a seat." Ebony sits down but the request draws a bit of concern. "Is everything okay Dr. Dease?" Dr. Dease doesn't quite know how best to answer that question so she jumps right into it. "Ebony you are not in any kind of trouble but I am a bit concerned. Ebony, you are an exceptional writer. Your responses are always very articulate and of course, during our poetry unit, your work was magnificent. The reason I asked you to stay is because I submitted your work into a statewide writing competition. The school got the application to me last minute. The district stated that every high school had to have at least one submission and I chose yours. Ebony, you won the competition, however, they ran into a problem."

Ebony wants to feel happy but is a bit accustomed to things not going her way so she asks, "What was the problem?" Dr. Dease begins to get a bit emotional, "Ebony the prize was a $10,000 scholarship but at this point, you couldn't academically qualify for any college. The office sent over your grades and it seems that you are missing 13 credits. I had no idea that this is your 6th high school in 3 years... Looking at your transcript, the only class that you have done well in throughout the different schools has been your English or writing courses. I spoke with some of your other teachers and they all said that you have shown that you can do the work, however you simply choose to write poems or in your journal all class period. Ebony, I don't want you to miss out on this opportunity because you are an extraordinary writer. Honestly, in all my years of teaching, you are amongst the best writers I have ever taught. I'm just perplexed about how we can get you on course to make you eligible for college?" Ebony lets everything register for a bit before responding.

"Dr. Dease, to be honest, college ain't for me, I barely like school now. So I doubt that after high school I will sign up to do four more years. I appreciate what you doing, trying to help me and all but maybe they can give the money to whoever got second place or something. I don't know..." Dr. Dease can't believe what she is hearing, "Ebony, you have a gift. I understand that it may be hard for you to recognize your own talent, most people with exceptional abilities often lack the general awareness of their skills because it comes naturally to them. However, I can't allow you to waste such a promising future simply because you don't have the foresight or confidence in yourself... Ebony, I am going to have to call your mother and -" Ebony explodes immediately as soon as she hears 'mother'.

"NO! NO! DO NOT CALL MY MOTHER! DR. DEASE NO! DON'T CALL HER!" Dr. Dease has never seen Ebony become so animated. "Whoa, Ebony... Alright. I won't call her but is everything okay? I have never seen you like this." Ebony gathers herself but does not relent on the urgency. "Dr. Dease, please do not call my mother. Whatever you do, do not call my mother. I thank you for all this but it's not for me. I would truly appreciate it Dr. Dease if you didn't call my mother and just, I don't know, find someone else or give the money back, whatever, just don't call my mother, okay!" Dr. Dease is trying to process this alarming reaction from Ebony. Wisely she doesn't offer any push back because of Ebony's volatile mood. "Alright, Ebony I won't call your mother, I promise. As for the scholarship, I will talk to the Principal to see what other options are available." "Okay, Dr. Dease can

71

I go now, I'm really hungry," Ebony says looking only to escape. "Sure thing, I'm sorry. This went longer than I anticipated." Dr. Dease says, releasing Ebony to lunch. Ebony gets up hurriedly and walks out. Dr. Dease has been blindsided but knows something must not be right at home based on Ebony's reaction, Dr. Dease knows its time to do a little detective work into Ebony's background.

Ebony goes straight to the cafeteria to the table where her and Felicia sit every day. Ebony is in a rush as she sits down next to Felicia who is eating and a bit puzzled as to where Ebony has been. "Ebs I was just about to come looking for you." "FeFe if anybody asks you anything about us or Mama, remember what Ma always tells us, what happens in her house stays in her house. So if teachers or anybody get to asking, everything is great at home, do you understand me?" Felicia is taken by surprise, "Yeah but... what is going on?" "FeFe just do as I say okay, nothing is going on but I just don't want us to ever get split up. I can't let them take me from you because I need to protect you at home! So just if anybody asks everything is good at home, alright?" Felicia has put her food down by now and is looking at her sister like she has two heads. "Ebony, protect me from what at home? Everything is okay at home, I mean Mama always tripping and stuff but my friends say their mothers be tripping too so what's the big deal?" Ebony is both relieved and saddened by her sisters' naivete, Ebony shakes her head as she tries to calm her emotions. "Nothing FeFe, nothing is the big deal, just if anyone asks you, please tell them everything is fine. Don't go into details FeFe, just tell them everything is cool." Felicia is dismissive because she doesn't know where all this is coming from with Ebony, "See all this you doing. This right here. Is why you need to come to church with me and Ms. Dilosa. Girl, give your burdens to the Lord, he will take care of that..." They both laugh as Ebony gets up to go get in line to get her lunch.

Dealing with the pressure

Ebony returns to the table with a look of distress on her face as she begins to eat her food. Felicia can still see the anxiety in her sister so she asks, "Everything okay Ebs? And what took you so long to come to lunch today?" Ebony is still a bit wired from her conversation with Dr. Dease and decides to get relief. "Nothing, uh, Dr. Dease was talking to me... FeFe watch my stuff, I need to go to the bathroom. I will be right back and whatever you do –" Felicia anticipates what Ebony is about to say, "I know, don't read my journal titled "The Happy Place." I won't, I know you said you gonna let me read it when the time is right. I'm gone be patient. Going to church is teaching me to let go and let God." Ebony grabs her purse and says,

"Girl you crazy... Just watch my stuff..."

Ebony leaves the cafeteria and heads for the restroom. Ebony enters the bathroom and sees two girls in the mirror. She tries to be discreet while checking to see if anyone else is in the stalls. Feeling confident with the amount of privacy, she goes into one and locks the door. Ebony quickly goes into her purse and pulls out a pair of nail scissors. Ebony takes her left arm out of her shirt and raises it up. Ebony grabs the scissors and begins to dig into the area right outside her under armpit. As she moves the scissors slicing her arm she begins to grimace "MMMMMMM... AHHHH... Hmmm hmmm hmmmm." Ebony tries to control her voice as she lets out the hushed groan. Ebony sits back on the toilet and begins to take deep breaths as the self mutilization has ended and she has the pressure release she desired.

The abuse has mushroomed into anxiety, depression and a constant feeling of hopelessness which has turned Ebony into a cutter. Ebony felt she needed the release, this time her usual therapy of writing wasn't available so she turned to the other outlet she uses from time to time, self-harm. Ebony wipes her arm with the piece of tissue, a slight wince comes across her face as she begins to put back on her shirt. Ebony walks out the stall looks aimlessly in the mirror seeing only the pain she is enduring. Based on the circumstances of her life, it's easy to see why Ebony's mirror doesn't yield a reflection.

All things work for the good

A few days have gone by and now it's Friday of that same week. Ebony and Felicia are walking out the school for the bus when Ebony sees Dr. Dease who appears to be looking for her. "Ebony, I missed you in class today?" "Yeah my stomach was hurting so I went to the nurse and she let me lay down. I meant to come by so I could get the work, I'm sorry." Dr. Dease can sense Ebony's lame excuse, "I see. Well, I hope you feel better. Also, I spoke with Principal West and she told me to speak with you again to see if you would reconsider. We can get you into some credit recovery courses to get you caught up. Ebony ten thousand dollars is a lot of scholarship money. Just think about it... I know you have a bus to catch so I won't hold you. Enjoy your weekend ladies." Dr. Dease walks away. Felicia turns and gives Ebony a look that only she can. "Uhhh Ebony, what is she talking about?"

Ebony has been trying to forget about the scholarship since the moment she told her about it earlier in the week. Ebony knows that if she tells Felicia the truth that she would keep nagging her about it, "It's nothing FeFe, she wants me to apply for some scholarship for writers but you have to go out of town to make the presentation and you know Mama not taking me out of town." Felicia trusts Ebony and cosigns the sad reality of their home life. "Yeah, Mama fa sho ain't taking us nowhere," she says as they walk towards their bus. When they get on the bus, Ebony pulls out a notebook and begins to write.

The bus pulls up to their stop and the sisters get off. They are making small talk as they walk the two short blocks home. When they make it to the door, the house is surprisingly quiet. Felicia uses her key and they open the door to a pleasant surprise. Lexi, their 2-year-old cousin runs toward the door when she hears it and says, "Fe." Felicia immediately walks over to her and says, "Awww come her Lexi!" She gives her a hug while picking her up. Ebony is happy because she knows that Lexi must mean that her mother Janae must be there also. Janae is Ebony's favorite cousin but is more like a big sister than a cousin.

Ebony looks over to the couch and locks eyes with Janae. "Aaayyee!" Ebony rushes over to give her a big hug." Janae is equally as happy to see her, "Wsup Ebs girl... Oh, it's so good to see you!" Janae says as they are still hugging. Ebony feels the much-needed security she hasn't had in Lord knows how long. The unfamiliar feeling causes a tear to come out of Ebony's eyes. Janae can feel Ebony's emotion shift from excitement to vulnerability so she squeezes tighter. "It's okay... I know, I hate it for you Ebs but, It's okay Ebs... It's okay..." They share a hug and after a moment Ebony lets go so that she can collect herself. Ebony steps back and wipes her face. "Where is Ma at?" Ebony asks Janae. "Yo Momma went with "him" to the store or out to run some errands. I don't know, they said they would be back in a few hours. That was about twenty minutes ago."

Ebony sits down on the couch and looks around. Janae knows what Ebony is about to say, "The social worker came over to do a scheduled wellness check on Lexi. So she had no choice but to clean up." Ebony nods in agreeance of the rare site of the house being so clean. "I knew it had to be something. I can't remember the last Friday that wasn't one of their little junkie parties. It feels a little weird actually, I'm used to music blaring and drunk old people in the kitchen playing cards who are shootin' up or snortin'..." Janae gets a bit reflective of her time in the house, "I know... I couldn't take it, I had to get up out here between that and well...(Janae pauses and mentally braces for the response to the question she has to ask but already knows the answer to...) How's that going? You still have to go to the 'Happy Place?'" Ebony looks down and gives an embarrassing nod of agreeance. Janae knows Ebony's pain because she went through the same thing while she lived with them. She takes a deep breath knowing that she can't do what she really wants to do, which is to tell that Ebony is being abused.

A helplessly silent moment of pain passes prior to Janae switching the subject. "How's school going?" Ebony rolls her eyes, "School is just like everything else. It is what it is?" Janae dropped out of high school herself so she doesn't push too hard. "Well, how's your writing going? I know you got some bomb poems or stories or something." "I been working on some stuff but to be honest, my head been a little messed up lately. I ain't felt like writing too much." Janae empathizes with her, "Yeah, I know living here will definitely mess with your head. Well at least y'all going to get to go to Arizona for spring break, that should be fun." Ebony has no idea what Janae is referring to, "What you mean Arizona?" she says puzzledly.

Janae turns up her face in surprise, "Y'all going to Arizona with your Auntie Barbara for spring break. I heard your Mother and "him" talking about it earlier. Your Auntie got y'all a plane ticket and everything. Y'all pose to spend some time with y'all other cousins out there. Ben, RiRi, Corey, KeKe, Tiff, Jamie and they families. She ain't told y'all?" Ebony is excited, "No she ain't told us nothing about it. FeFe! FeFe!" Ebony calls after her sister who is in the room playing with the baby. "Unnhuh," Felicia says coming out the bedroom holding Lexi. "You know we pose to be going to Arizona with Auntie Barbara for spring break?" Ebony asks. "What? Who said that?" Felicia says as the excitement begins to drum up in her voice. "Janae said that Mamma was talking about it earlier. I know she ain't mentioned anything to us." "Ayyyeeee turn up! Won't he do it! I told you my God performs miracles, I been praying that I would go somewhere! And you coming with me! Ayyyeee it's finna be litty! Come on Lexi lets go back and finish playing!" Just like that Felicia is back in the room.

Janae turns to Ebony, "Well you know what's about to come for the next week. You might as well get ready for it. Yo Mama about to try and hold this over y'all head for the entire week. She finna be on one." Ebony exhales and says "Girl, I already know..."

Back to the Happy Place

The next six days flew by. As she suspected, her mother tried as hard as possible to hang the trip over their heads. However, the girls had kept the house clean and stayed clear of their Mother so she couldn't find any excuse to keep them from going on this trip. During this time Ebony had to go to the "Happy Place" about 4 times. The only difference was that she was a bit more creative because of the trip. Usually, the happy place has about 5 places that Ebony has created; the restaurant, the volleyball match, the beach in Hawaii, the reality TV show she stars in and her downtown New York business corporation that she runs.

Ebony is excited about the trip for obvious reasons but to top it all off, Auntie Barbara, is that Auntie! Technically, she is their Great Aunt, she is the sister of their Grandmother Juanita who passed away suddenly while Ebony and FeFe where very young. Auntie Barbara is a successful lawyer and business woman. She has a huge house and always sends them great Christmas gifts, not to mention that she buys them school clothes every year as well. Whenever Auntie Barbara is in town, she always picks the girls up and allows them to stay in the hotel with her. Being with her is non-stop fun, that's why the girls affectionately call her "Funtie Barbara".

Ebony and Felicia are leaving tomorrow after school. Ebony can't sleep because of the excitement that tomorrow is going to bring. So when she hears the dreadful sequence of sounds begin she just closes her eyes and takes her mind to what she thinks her Aunt Barbara's house is going to look like. Ebony imagines the pool that she is going to be swimming in tomorrow. Ohh it looked so fun on the pics that her Aunt posted on Instagram. Ahhh she can't wait to try on her Auntie's business suits and high heels. "I'm going to have sooo much fun!" Ebony is so anxious and filled with excitement that she fails to recognize that she is no longer being violated until that door sound snaps her out of the newest destination of the "Happy Place."

76

A hint that something is wrong

Ebony and Felicia just landed in Arizona about an hour ago. Auntie Barbara has taken them out to a restaurant. As they sit at the table and wait for their food Auntie Barbara strikes up a conversation.

"So ladies how is school going?" Simultaneously they give different responses, "Good." Says Felicia, "Okay." Says Ebony. "Oh, I see we got two different things going on here, Felicia you first, you are the youngest." "School is good for me but school is probably better for Ebony, she got offered to try for a ten thousand dollar scholarship. But it was out of town and you know my Mama ain't taking us nowhere... But Auntie her stuff is really good." Barbara is pleasantly surprised but not in total shock because she knows that Ebony is talented. "Wait, you were offered to try for a ten thousand dollar scholarship for what? I'm a bit confused?" Ebony gives Felicia the evil eye because she would have never brought this up. "Oh Auntie it's nothing, I wrote something and a teacher submitted it to some, I don't know. It's no big deal." Felicia immediately recognizes that this is a different version than what Ebony originally told her so she speaks up, "I thought you said something about you having to go out of town to some type of competition, you didn't say Dr. Dease submitted something." Ebony is making the "girl hush" face at Felicia, who isn't intimidated and makes the "What you going to do?" face back at her.

Aunt Barbara searches for clarity, "So did you have to submit something or did you have to go out of town for something? Dr. Dease, why does that name sound familiar?" Barbara looks over at Ebony who is growing uncomfortable with the conversation. Instead of pressing more Auntie Barbara decides to let it go. "You know what, let's talk about that some other time. Who wants to talk about school when you are on spring break right?" Ebony is relieved and says, "Exactly Auntie!" "Ebony storytelling is a gift, with the ability to write you can do so many things. You can write songs, poems, books, commercials… There are so many opportunities that you can take advantage of through writing. You gotta let me read some of your work before you leave." Felicia chimes in, "Auntie I be trying to tell her to let God use you… She don't be trying to hear me though." They all laugh at Felicia's perfect comedic timing. The rest of the dinner was fun-filled talk and catching up, however, the seed of curiosity into Ebony's work has been planted in Auntie Barbara. So has the name Dr. Dease, Auntie Barbara is sure that she knows a Dr. Dease back home.

Fun Times & Warning Signs

A couple of days have gone by and it's Easter Sunday. Ebony and Felicia are hanging out by the pool at Auntie Barbara's house. Ebony is writing and Felicia is taken what is likely ten thousand poolside selfies. Felicia ask "Did you call Ma and tell her Happy Easter?" Ebony says, "Girl, Mama is the last thing on my mind, she will be alright, I will text her later… If you about to text her tell "we" said Happy Easter so I don't have to make that call." Felicia has a little stunned look on her face and says "Well alright, tell me how you really feel." Ebony looks over and says to her "Look Fe Fe, we ain't never been anywhere like this, never! I know that a week from today we gone be headed back home and I just don't want to think about that at all until I have to. We on vacation and I am going to take my time trying to remember all of this so I can think about it when we get back home. This is helping me with my Happy Place."

Felicia rolls her eyes and says, "Here you go with that Happy Place stuff, that doggone Journal is the only thing that we don't talk about… I know you say it keeps us safe but I don't know what that means and when you say that I can only read it if something happens to you, that scares me. I don't want anything to happen to you…" Felicia's mood goes from worried to lit and she says, "But you right, I'm gone text Ma and get back to enjoying this pool and Funtie's house, OKURRR!" Felicia gets up without waiting for a response and jumps in the pool and the two scream and laugh in fun. A piece of mind has slowly crept in and they both enjoy the worry-free environment.

Ebony is still laughing when she decides to get up to go into the kitchen to get something to drink. Auntie Barbara is sitting at the counter reading, "The Mask" by Andreia Denise. Ebony reaches for the refrigerator when Auntie Barbara notices the cuts under her arm.

Alarmed by the cuts Auntie Barbara reacts, "Oh my God Ebony, what happened? Are you okay?" Ebony is taken off guard by the question and is clueless as to what she is talking about, "YES! I'm okay, what's the matter..." Auntie Barbara gets up, walks up to Ebony and gently raises her arm. "These cuts, what happened?" Not being prepared and completely losing sight of the fact that the cuts would be visible in a bathing suit, Ebony quickly snatches her arm back and steps back. "It's nothing, I'm okay, Auntie. Everything is fine." Ebony tries to go back to the pool. Auntie Barbara calls her back, "Ebony, turn yourself around and come back over here now." Ebony knows not to be disrespectful and comes back slowly after a deep sigh, "Yes Ma'am..." "Now look, I am no fool, something is up. Your little story about the scholarship didn't make any sense and now those cuts look like you did them. Now, I know that you are on vacation and you came out here to enjoy yourself. I get that. Trust me, I don't want to ruin your good time for nothing in the world, but Ebony, if something is going on, you can talk to me. I understand that your Mother doesn't have you all in the best of environments and that's why I made sure that you and Felicia came out here. It's important that y'all see that there is more to life than your neighborhood. I promised my sister, that I would do what I can for her grandbabies. She loved you all more than anything in the world. And I love you all too! So Ebony, whatever it is, you can talk to me about it."

As Auntie Barbara is finishing her sentence, Felicia comes into the kitchen and her usual happy go lucky personality bubbles out, "Auntie this house is bomb! Period! And the pool, it got my Instagram lit! I got about 200 likes already this morning! Aaayyee!" Ebony uses her sisters over the top entrance as the perfect escape. Ebony slips out towards the pool as Felicia keeps going on, "Auntie, so this is what the Bible is talking about when it says, Your gifts will make room for you! Auntie like you got one of them Real Housewives or Love and Hip Hop type houses! This is incredible! And you didn't marry no rich man or drop no mixtape either... Wow, Auntie, this is bomb, like period... This is bomb!" Auntie Barbara is careful not to be rude so she says, "Thank you, Felicia. You have been saying this for two days. Thank you, I have been blessed... Yes this is the result of a lot of dedication to my gift." Auntie Barbara is eyeing Ebony ease out the room as the two of them briefly lock eyes. Ebony knows she got away for the moment but she can feel that Auntie Barbara is going to eventually have the conversation to get to the bottom of what is going on.

An Aunts Intuition & God's Timing

Spring break is rolling along and their days are filled with shopping, binge-watching shows, fake runway modeling, hanging out with their cousins RiRi, Tiff, KeKe, Ben, Corey, and Jamie. The girls are teaching Auntie Barbara the newest slang because she still says "Off the chain." Felicia taught Auntie Barbara how to do things on her phone, they've had a dance competition at the house, they went sightseeing and even visited some colleges. Auntie Barbara notices that everywhere they go, Ebony is keeping the journal titled "The Happy Place" with her. Oddly, Ebony is never really writing in it but is being very careful not to let the book out of her sight. Auntie Barbara's suspicion is growing deeper and her gut is telling her that something is not right.

It's extremely late on Saturday night and the girls fly back tomorrow in the early afternoon. Auntie Barbara sits in her bed as she is trying to decide whether or not she wants to fly back with the girls. Auntie Barbara wants to see their house for herself and talk to their mother face to face. Ebony and Felicia were pretty good in general about not letting things out about what is going on in the home. Yet, Auntie Barbara can't shake the feeling that something wasn't right especially after seeing what appears to be evidence that Ebony is cutting herself. Making the trip she feels would at the very least clear her conscious. Not exactly sure why but something tells Barbara to check her emails. She grabs her phone and hits the icon to open the app. She scrolls down in her inbox when she sees an email with Ebony in the subject line:

Dear Attorney Stansil,

I hope this email finds you well. My name is Dr. Dease and I am emailing you in regards to your Great Niece Ebony Williams. You are listed as an emergency contact with the school. I'm Ebony's English teacher and I recently spoke with her about the $10,000 scholarship competition she won and I would like to discuss options with you on how we can work together to get Ebony eligible for college. Ebony is an amazing writer and I would hate to see her talent go to waste. I'm reaching out to you because Ebony was adamant that I not contact her mother. As I'm sure you know $10,000 is a lot of money and could be the spark she needs to help her reach her full potential. Please feel free to respond to this email at your earliest convenience. And by the way we met briefly a few years ago at a Sorority luncheon in which we were both honorees. Please have a blessed day and I hope to hear from you soon.

Needless to say, the email is the confirmation that Auntie Barbara needed to make her decision. She doesn't even respond to the email, she simply closes the app, opens Safari and books her flight. After booking her flight she gets up to go tell her neices the "good news". Ebony and Felicia are in the room having fun when Auntie Barbara comes into the room, "Hey ladies, I am going to be flying back with y'all in the morning. I got some business to take care of back home so I figured, I may as well fly back with y'all." Felicia is overly excited as usual, "Ayyyeee! Teetee it's gone be lit! Turn up Funtee!" Auntie Barbara gives an "Oh my gosh" roll of the eyes to Felicia's extra antics. She quickly switches the conversation to what has been on her mind, "So Ebony when am I going to get to read some of this amazing writing, I see you kept your journal with you everywhere you went. I mean if this writing is scholarship worthy, I can't wait to read it." Ebony was quick to play it off, "Yeah no problem, Auntie, can I give it to you on the plane tomorrow morning?" Auntie Barbara sees that as fair, "Okay sure thing, just make sure that you don't pack it in your suitcase." Auntie Barbara leaves out the room and Ebony and Felicia continue having a fun. They are fully aware that their time in this "fantasy world" was coming to an end and they were determined to live up every minute of it.

I know the plans I have for you...

As soon as they board the plane, Auntie Barbara turns to Ebony and says, "Alright Ebony, I am ready to read your writing." Ebony purposely packed the journal that she told her she would let her read into her suitcase, Ebony begins a dramatic lie, "Auntie, why didn't you remind me, I forgot all about it and put it in my suitcase." Prepared for the excuse Auntie Barbara counters quickly, "No big deal, I see you have your "Happy Place" journal, I can read that one instead." Felicia turns to look at Ebony to see how she plans to get out of this one, "Oh no this isn't really my writing this is just some stuff I write down to practice. The other notebook is the one that makes sense." Auntie Barbara smiles and nods "No worries, I will read your work in due time."

About 20 minutes into the flight back, Ebony and Felicia fell asleep as planned because they stayed up the whole night. Felicia had the aisle seat and Ebony sat in the middle and Auntie Barbara had the window seat. Auntie Barbara is reading The Mask: Recognizing and Resisting Spiritual Deception by Andriea Denise when she notices Ebony's Journal, "Happy Place" fall from her lap to the floor and opens up. Aunt Barbara reaches down to pick it up and see the words:

I wish I could die every time he climbs on top of me...

Tears immediately begin to stream down her face as she reads the eloquently written heart breaking accounts of how her precious neice's innocence has been taken away repeatedly for almost 9 years. The beautiful 17 year old girl whose smile lit up the room and whose laugh touched her soul, was hiding a secret that Auntie Barbara could have never imagined. Ebony, her sweet Ebony is a damaged, abused girl who has no protector.

Auntie Barbara can't stop crying, nor can she stop herself from reading it. She wants to do both but the problem with the truth is you can't unsee it, once it has been revealed. Naturally, her emotions go from sorrow to rage, to compassion, to wondering if the same thing has happened to Felicia. The emptiness in her stomach is unimaginable. Auntie Barbara feels powerless and overcome with regret because she knew something wasn't right but she never thought this to be what Ebony was hiding. Barbara knows what she has to do but unfortunately she has to sit the next three hours on a flight with a world of haunting thoughts running through her mind.

Felicia finally gets to read "The Happy Place"

As the flight lands and they are on their way to the baggage claim both Ebony and Felicia notice a change in Aunt Barbara. Shamelessly, Felicia asks "What's wrong?" Auntie Barbara takes a deep breath before saying, "This world is a lot, this book, The Mask by Andreia Denise reveals so much, just how spiritually we deal with so much and sometimes we have to stop hiding and reveal our truth." Ebony can see a different look in Auntie Barbara's eyes, "What are you talking about Auntie?" Looking Ebony squarely in the eye compassionately she responds, "Ebony everything that is happening in the dark will always come to the light." Ebony knows that something is about to happen, she can feel it. After a momentary silent stare into the eyes of each other, they turn and wait for their luggage to come around the carousel.

After getting their luggage, Auntie Barbara tells the girls, "Wait here, I am going to go pick up the rental car and I will call you all when I am done with the paperwork." As Auntie Barbara walks off, she grabs her phone and looks up the number to Child Protective Services, she hits send. "Yes, I would like to report a case of child molestation, the address is 8243 Willowdale Ave. I need you to meet me with the police at this address in approximately an hour and a half... My niece is the victim and I will be their with her at that time... Thank you." Auntie Barbara takes a deep breath as she knows that what is about to happen is going to take a lot of strength. Auntie Barbara knows that only God is going to get her through whatever she is driving into and as she walks towards the car she calls on him for strength,

"God grant me the serenity to change the things that I can, to accept the things that I can't and the wisdom to know the difference. Amen."

On the drive home, Auntie Barbara isn't saying much, she is focused on the road and getting there as quickly as possible. Felicia innocently breaks the silence, "Funtie, me and Ebbs was wondering... Can we come back and visit for the summer?" Barbara gives a laugh to herself and says under her breath, "It's going to be more than just the summer." Felicia couldn't make out what she said so she says, "Huh? I mean, I'm sorry I didn't hear what you said Auntie?" An obviously distracted Auntie Barbara says, "Yeah sure, Felicia." Ebony who is sitting in the front passenger seat notices Auntie's behavior and although she doesn't say anything, is trying to figure it out.

After nearly 45 minutes they pull onto their block and Ebony notices four cop cars sitting at the end of the street. As Auntie Barbara pulls into the driveway, the cop cars flash their lights and drive slowly towards their house. Ebony and Felicia are getting out and looking at the cars and cops while Barbara heads straight for the front door and begins to bang on it.

Tabitha comes to the door and can be heard yelling "Who in the hell is this banging on my got dang door..." Her voice trails off as she notices Barbara and six policemen approaching from the driveway. Tabitha is puzzled but continues her tirade, "Barbara, what the hell these cops doing at my house... What is this?! Heffa you done set me up or something?" An officer comes up and asks "Ma'am are you Tabitha Vallon?" To which she responds, "Yeah and what the hell you want? What is all this about?" "Ma'am you are under arrest for child abuse and neglect as well as aiding and abetting a criminal and known pedophille." The cop says as he places the handcuffs on Ebony's mother and begins to recite the Miranda rights. The other cops go into the house and bring her boyfriend out in handcuffs.

Felicia is stunned by what is happening and by now is holding on to Ebony's arm. Ebony knows what is going on and why this is happening. A sense of relief comes over Ebony as she sees "him" walk right past her in handcuffs, she looks back towards the door and sees Auntie Barbara standing in the doorway. Ebony gives a thankful nod towards Auntie, to which Auntie returns a sorrowful nod as she begins crying again. Ebony opens her journal to a particular page and hands it to Felicia, and says, "I guess I won't be needing this anymore, so it's time I let you read it." A confused Felicia says, "Wait Ebbs, is this what all this is about?" Ebony responds, "Yeah, just read it, it will explain everything."

Felicia walks into the house, sits on the couch and begins to read:

Diamonds

Dear Fe Fe,

I love you so much and I want you to know that no matter what, I will always love you. I am keeping this journal because I am scared. I am scared of what may happen to me. When I was about 9 years old, "Slick" started touching me in my private areas. It all started one night when he woke me up to use the bathroom at night so I wouldn't wet the bed. I thought that Mama gave him the job to wake me up because no one ever did. Before she got with him they would just change the sheets in the morning. Well, when Mama got with Slick about a year later he started waking me up and then soon after that he would touch me and make me touch him. I knew it was wrong but he told me that he would kill me and Mama if I told. He told me 'If you and your Mama are dead then I can have FeFe all to myself that's what's going to happen Ebony if you say anything'. Slick knew how much I loved you and how much I would protect you. He knew I would do whatever it took to protect you. I was so scared, I wouldn't talk to anybody. That's why I flunked the 3rd grade. I just sat there the whole year, afraid that he was going to kill me if I said 'anything' to anybody. I was too young to know that when he said that, he was talking about what he was doing to me. I thought he meant don't say a word to anybody so I didn't. Well, I did tell Mama one day but she didn't do anything. I told her one day when I was 13. That is when he went from just touching me to raping me. I'll never forget I got an A on my spelling test and he had to pick me up from school that day, it was the beginning of my 6th grade year. You were still in 5th at Banneker School so Ma picked you up. He took me to get some Ice Cream and then we went home and he told me to take off my school clothes and put on my play clothes and I could go outside. While I was changing he came into the room and climbed on top of me. It hurt so bad and I cried and I cried... That night when he left out I ran into her room and I told her what he did to me. She told me to stop making stuff up and that I am just having a nightmare. I told her I wasn't and she told me to go back to sleep. I came back with the bloody sheets and she yelled to get out her room and leave them sheets right there. So I knew then telling Mama wasn't going to help. I told Janae and she said that he comes to the basement and does the same thing to her. She didn't tell because they would have put her back in the system and split her and Lexi up. So that is why she went to move in with her boyfriend Reggie. Janae told me that if I want to learn how to deal with this, I should create a "Happy Place". She said a "Happy Place" is where you can take your mind and spirit when things are happening to your body that you don't want to think about... Fe Fe, I go to my happy place so I don't have to feel what happens to me. The rest of this Journal is all the places, details and emotions that I had when this was happening to me. I want to tell someone so bad! I just don't know what I would do if they take me from you... If something happens to me give this to the cops and its a sheet under my books in my trunk in my room with evidence of 'him' on it. I love you and I hope that whenever you read this I can be here to hug you afterwards....

Love Ebbs   12/25/16

83

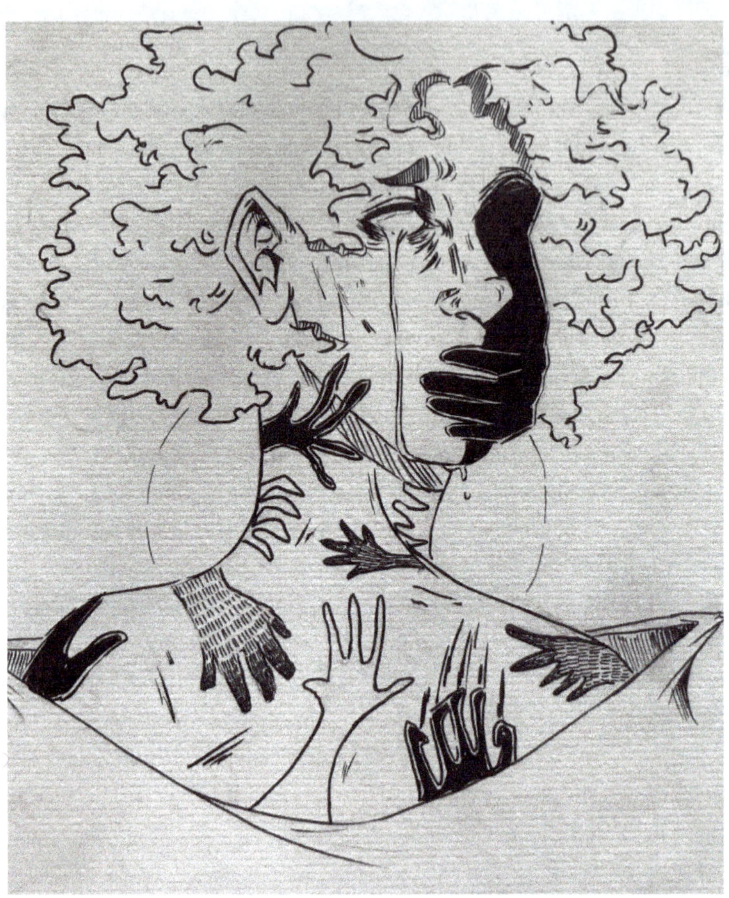

"Silence"

An Original Drawing by:
Charity Neal   Age: 16

This Beautiful drawing was inspired by the story:
Ebony and the Happy Place

@charliehates
@cnstudios

The Big Picture

It's a socially accepted norm in the Black community that "What goes on in your Mama's house, stays in your Mama's house." Too often the code of silence around this issue protects the perpetrators at the expense of the victims. I am not saying that each case of sexual violence on young girls falls within this category, however, the bottom line is that victims very often feel unprotected.

In some cases, it can be argued that it is human nature for individuals to overcompensate for things they feel left voids in their lives. In the story, I tried to highlight that Ebony was making a sacrifice to endure her abuse to protect her younger sister Felicia. Ebony was not protected by her mother and thus Ebony felt that she had to be the protector of her younger sister. The bottom line is Ebony should not be in a position to make that choice.

Simply put, Ebony's mother and father both failed to appropriately protect Ebony. Not only did they fail to protect her, Ebony was fed irrational narratives that promotes adults to act irresponsibly and not be held accountable... Why else would you not want your children discussing what goes on in their "Mama's House?"

It is our duty to protect children. If you are Ebony or know of one... SPEAK UP!!!

Where You Can Find Help

Rape, Abuse & Incest National Network (RAINN)
Call 1-800-656-4673
www.rainn.org

Chapter 4
It Wasn't Always Like This...

Any relationship in which a person is made to feel bad or guilty
for not appeasing to the wishes and desires of
the other person in the relationship is in an
abusive relationship.

In no circumstance imaginable should a person have to do things
that will not make them happy simply to avoid conflict or
confrontation from someone else. That is not sacrifice
that is abuse.

If you or someone else you know are in a relationship like this,
I am encouraging you to leave the relationship as well as to speak
to a professional to begin the healing process from the relationship.

With that being said, please allow me to introduce to you
Neveah.

Neveah is currently in an abusive relationship with her boyfriend
Khalil. Neveah just turned 17 a few months ago. She lives alone
with her mother who is a Correctional Officer at the juvenile facility
across town.

Nevaeh loves doing hair and has a job washing hair at the salon a
few miles from her house. We meet her after work on a Thursday
night. The shop was busier than normal for a weeknight. Nevaeh
was supposed to get off at 9 o'clock but is running over.

Her boyfriend Khalil is sitting outside of Nevaeh's job waiting for
her to get off. Khalil is already upset because he feels Nevaeh isn't
texting him back right away. So an argument awaits Nevaeh who is
tired from a busy day at work. Nevaeh opens the car door and gets
in the car.

86

<u>It Wasn't Always Like This...</u>

"Hey, I don't even know you but I hate you...
.... Tried and tried but she never could escape you"
                                    - Eve 'Love Is Blind'

<u>Thursday April 18, 2019</u>
<u>10:19pm</u>
    "Hey babe... whew... I am so glad to be -" Khalil cuts her off, "Don't hey babe me... Bro what took you so long to answer my text and why you got me out here waiting all day? I thought you said you got off at 10? It's 10:19?" (Nevaeh is so over the constant drama on top of the fact that she is tired. Nevaeh doesn't have the energy to argue so simply begins to explain "Khalil we were busy today. I am at..." Khalil cuts her off again, "Whatever. Shut up! You're ungrateful... I don't even know why I'm still with somebody so dumb..." Nevaeh has had enough, "You right, I don't know why I'm still with you either... It's over Khalil, I mean it this time... You can let me out now... I'll walk the rest of the way just don't ever talk to me no more. I hate you!" Nevaeh grabs the door with both hands as if she is ready to get out of the car the next time it stops.

    Khalil sees her and grabs for her shoulder to pull her off the door while still driving. "Girl, what the heck are you doing, get off that door! You ain't going nowhere, you belong to me! Let my door go!" Khalil is yelling as he continues to try to get a grip on Nevaeh. While reaching over he scratches her face. Nevaeh screams "Owww - you mutha ooooh - you scratched my face Khalil! You scratched my face Khalil! Let me out of this dang car now! I'm not playing with you! Let me out!" Khalil has no remorse, "So I don't care about your face! I told you before if you try to leave me I am going to kill myself!

*** OK I'm sorry to interject right here but I don't want what just happened to go unnoticed. Khalil just threatened to kill himself if Neveah left him. Khalil is attempting to do a few things when he makes that statement. Let's break it down real quick and then we will get back to the story.
1st he is trying to tell her that his life means nothing if she is not in it or that he doesn't want to live without her. Sounds sweet right? Not so much. 2nd he is trying to make her feel guilty. If he were to kill himself (which is highly unlikely) then it would be because Nevaeh left him and she would have to forever life with that on her heart. Lastly, this is an attempt at controlling her. She wants to leave as she stated but he uses what he can to keep her in the relationship. Control...*** Alright, let's pick the story back up where we left off...

Nevaeh could care less about Khalil's empty threats at this point. She can't believe Khalil has scratched her face, she says screams in disbelief, "I don't care what you do. Go kill yourself and make both of us happy... You scratched my face. Let me out of this stupid car now!"

Khalil is used to his threat of killing himself working, so when it doesn't he feels that he has lost all control. Khalil yells, "You don't care if I kill myself?! Okay then I'll kill both of us!" Neveah yells back, "Whatever Khalil just stop the car so I can get -" Without a warning, Khalil grabs her head and slams it against the dashboard while screaming "JUST SHUT UP!!! I SWEAR TO GOD IF YOU DON'T SHUT UP!!! I'M GOING TO... OHHH SHUT UP NEVAEH!!!"

Nevaeh is fearing for her life at this point. Hoping to protect herself she keeps her head down between her legs the rest of the ride while crying uncontrollably. Nevaeh is too scared to come up. Khalil is fuming and continues to rant, "You see... You see what you made me do! I didn't want to put my hands on you but you kept trying me! You know I don't play that! Just do what I tell you to do and we don't have to go through this! I text you, text back... Not when you want to, when you see it, text me back! You understand?!" Khalil finally notices that Nevaeh is still crouched over. "Bae... Bae... Bae sit up... Bae sit up! Come on Bae sit up! Bae you know I didn't mean to do that but you were making me mad Bae... Bae, I'm sorry. Come on Bae! Come on Bae..." Khalil is pulling on her jacket not too hard to get her to sit up.

Khalil pulls up to Nevaeh's house and continues pleading to Nevaeh who still is in the same position. "Bae we at your house... Come on sit up -" Nevaeh feels the car is in park and she doesn't hesitate to grab her bag and pops open the door as fast as possible and runs to her front door. She opens the door, runs upstairs and goes straight to her bed and cries.

Thursday April 18, 2019
11:36pm

A little more than an hour goes by and Nevaeh decides to take a shower. She finds the strength to make it to the bathroom. Nevaeh was hoping this was all a dream until she looks in the mirror at her partially swollen and slightly bruised face. This is real. The bruise is showing up greenish-brown on her caramel skin that has a precious mahogany undertone. Nevaeh is in disbelief that Khalil left a mark on her face. While this is not the first time he has hit her, this is however the first time that he has hit her and left a mark on her face. Khalil usually leaves marks that Nevaeh could hide rather easily. "But this..." She thinks to herself, "This is

"Nevaeh"

An Original Oil Painting By:
Karma Griggs   Age: 14

This Beautiful painting was inspired by the story: It Wasn't Always Like This

Instagram: @paintitkarma

foul... this is like... really some messed up stuff..." The tears are streaming down Neveah's face as she struggles to comprehend what just happened. While she is seeing her face in the mirror, she is definitely trying to look for her soul...

Neveah reaches down for the roll of tissue to wipe her tears as her phone goes off for the 43rd time in the last minute, indicating that she has a text message. She already knows who it is and what it is likely to say... Nevaeh doesn't want anything to do with Khalil at this moment and definitely doesn't have the energy for anything more than the shower that she is about to take and hopefully some peaceful sleep. Neveah cuts her phone off as she wipes her tears. She knows that Khalil hates to be ignored and her not responding probably has him boiling with anger but Neveah doesn't care... "I'm done with him. I'm for real this time..." she thinks to herself. Nevaeh is trying to figure out how things got to this point because Lord knows, "It wasn't always like this."

"Let's get in the shower Veah..." She says to herself attempting to make it through this horrific space she is in. Reaching for a towel she notices that her NDL bracelet is all twisted up. NDL - the initials of her and her besties, Devan and Lacy. She used to be much closer with them before things got serious with Khalil. Seeing her bracelet almost broken reminds her of the day when she began to hide the true Khalil from her friends. Nevaeh allows her mind to drift back to that pivotal day...

To help paint this picture, we gotta go back a little over a year ago. Nevaeh and Khalil's relationship was a little more than 3 months old. This day started out like any other but ended with Nevaeh's life never being quite the same. We find Nevaeh in the cafeteria with her girls and Khalil.

<u>Wednesday, March 8, 2018</u>
<u>11:33am</u>

<u>Stage 1: Isolation: The First Phase of Abuse</u>

"Bae, I'm gone eat lunch with Lacy and Devan today okay?" "Do whatever the hell you want to, you been getting on my nerves anyway so, go ahead and sit with your little stupid friends." Before Nevaeh could even respond, Khalil grabs his lunch tray, gets up and storms off. Khalil throws the rest of his lunch away and walks out of the cafeteria. Nevaeh doesn't want to make more of a scene, so she puts on a fake face and walks over to the table where Lacy and Devan are sitting. Lacy noticed Khalil's antics and ask Nevaeh, "Girl what was that all about?" Nevaeh was caught a bit off guard, "What was what all about?" Lacy whole face changes to that classic

"Really" look. Nevaeh recovers quickly though, "Oh Khalil... Girl he mad he got to go make up Mr. Fords, Algebra II test." Lacy isn't buying it but decides to leave it alone. However, she does make a mental note of it.

Nevaeh quickly changes the subject. "Girl spill the tea on what happened with Jazlyn and Sharod..." No sooner than Devan starts talking, Nevaeh begins to feel her pocket blowing up, she knows that it is Khalil, but ignores it because she is not in the mood to argue. Nevaeh doesn't know what he is upset about to be honest, so she ignores the "thousand" text messages. Moments later, she feels the vibration of an incoming call. Her mother was supposed to call at lunch to tell Nevaeh what shift she has to work today. Nevaeh slides up the phone in her pocket and sees it's Khalil... She hits the ignore button. Nevaeh is trying to keep up the image of Khalil that she has painted to Lacy and Devan.

Khalil is growing furious because he is being ignored. Nevaeh, on the other hand, has no idea why he flipped out. Being that it was early in their relationship, Nevaeh is still putting Khalil's feelings first. Above all else, she didn't want to lose what they have. Still trying to hide what's happening from her girls, Nevaeh continues the conversation at the table. Her phone is vibrating the entire time, Khalil is blowing her up. When Nevaeh and her friends get up to put their trays away Nevaeh decides to finally check her phone...

91

Bro answer dis phone b4 I kill
myself at dis skool

I knew u was like all dem other
thots who want me 4 my 💰

Ion even kno y I'm wit u

Keep playing w me u gone b
single af

I hope ya lil frndz gone take u
home

U so stupid

I h8 when u act dumb

Pick up da phone

While Nevaeh is reading, Devan notices the change in her face and instead of asking what is wrong, Devan looks over at the phone and begins reading the text also. Devan gets heated immediately, "Girl, Khalil sent all that! Unh unh girl, you need to drop him... Girl he crazy! Anybody who would send that will be going upside your head before you know it..." Lacy has been asking the same questions repeatedly the entire time, "What it say? What he say? What it say?" Nevaeh finally snaps back into reality and quickly tries to get control of the situation. "Girl shhhhhh, dang!" Not knowing what to do, she walks out of the cafeteria real fast and into the bathroom. Lacy and Devan are her day ones, so of course they follow her.

Keeping it 100 - It really doesn't matter what happened when they got to the bathroom. Why? Because in spite of all the perfect, sensible advice that Lacy and Devan gave her, Nevaeh still needed to talk to Khalil and see where all this was coming from. So of course, she texted him back.

Ion kno wat all da xtras 4 but we can talk afta skool when u take me home

Lacy and Devan were giving her advice to get out before it gets worse, while they all huddle up and waited for Khalil to respond. Khalil sees the text and the games begin. He doesn't text back. Nevaeh is appeasing her friends with all the "I know's" and "you rights" to everything they are saying but she is truly waiting on his response. After three minutes and he hadn't responded she texted him again.

Bae Y U trippin! Call me! Ion even kno where none of dis is coming from! Bae stop playin and text me back! 🧡 😘 😭

Delivered

Lacy sees what Nevaeh is typing and immediately goes in on Nevaeh, "Girl you stupid, I know you didn't let this fool talk crazy to you like that and you still calling him bae." Nevaeh defends her actions, "Yea because he is bae, y'all don't get it, Khalil be going through a lot and he needs me... I know he don't mean any of this stuff! He just frustrated..." Devan takes this one, "Vaeh, that doesn't mean he has to take his frustrations out on you! Tell him go play Fortnite or something! You ain't nobody punching bag."

While all this is going on, Khalil sees the text, but he is shifting the energy. Just a moment ago, Khalil was the one feeling frustrated about the situation. Now, Nevaeh is the one feeling some type of way.

Ok ladies, please pardon the sidebar, however, let me breakdown what is happening. Khalil has set his trap of isolation and Nevaeh has walked right into it. Khalil makes Nevaeh feel jealous for picking her friends over him. He also attacks her self-esteem in the process, by constantly calling her stupid and dumb. Khalil doesn't stop there, he makes her feel dependent on him by telling her that he won't give her a ride home and threatens to not come spend time with her when she wants him to.

I want to make sure y'all recognize all he is doing here. Khalil is telling Nevaeh, if you choose your friends over me, then you are stupid. (Mental abuse) Khalil's consistent threats of withdrawing his love and effection if she doesn't act according to his wishes is the emotional abuse. To make it plain, isolation is defined by words such as loneliness, seclusion, confinement, and insulation. All of which can be perfectly applied to Neveah both mentally and emotionally.

As you may have guessed, Khalil never responded to the text. They all left the bathroom eventually and went to class. Oh yeah, Nevaeh flunked Mrs. McIntosh test 6th period. Oh she studied all night for it, but she couldn't focus. Her mind was completely on what is wrong with Khalil. Yes, ladies, your grades are often a casualty of a mentally and emotionally abusive relationship.

Khalil is taking this mind game to the extreme. Nevaeh couldn't focus in 6th period because she was anxious about what was going to happen on her way to 7th-period class. The route that Nevaeh takes to 7th period allows her to cross paths with Khalil, because his class is in the opposite direction.. Nevaeh tries to play it cool when the bell rings. Yet, her stomach is full of nervous butterflies as she walks out of the class and down the hall. She is about to turn the corner into the hallway where she would normally see Khalil. Her heart is racing, she turns the corner and... No Khalil.

Khalil, a master manipulator, purposely took a different route just to mess with Nevaeh's head a bit more. Khalil is in total control of the situation. For Nevaeh the anxiety of the eventual confrontation has turned into a stomache ache. First, Khalil wasn't texting her back and now he wasn't in the hallway. Nevaeh doesn't know what to think.

Nevaeh is in her feelings as she sits in 7th period trying to figure out how a day that started out as any other typical day has become an emotional train wreck. At this point, Nevaeh just wants things to go back to normal between her and Khalil. Everything was great yesterday, yet today without warning she finds herself captive to Khalil's desires. Nevaeh feels she can't take another moment of this, and is willing to do anything to get things back to a good place with Khalil.

What Nevaeh doesn't realize is that an abusive relationship is much like a drug addiction, you are willing to do whatever it takes to get that feeling you had in the beginning back, but sorry, it's gone.

Nevaeh sat the entire 7th period distracted by what's going on and 15 minutes before class let out she makes up her mind that she is going to confront Khalil about the situation. She comes up with a quick plan, she asks to go to the restroom, but has no intentions to go back to class. She is going to wait in the restroom by Khalil's class so she can be right outside the door when the bell rings.

Things are playing out as Nevaeh hoped and when the bell rang Nevaeh is standing in the middle of the hall in front of the door. As Khalil comes out of the class and into the hallway he sees Nevaeh. Immediately, he gives her that irresistible look that says, "I'm sorry Bae, I love you..." You know, that look that only "Bae" can give. Nevaeh wasn't anticipating that, so she had no defense when that face was followed by him opening up his arms to give her a big hug. Nevaeh couldn't resist and walked right into his outstretched arms.

The ever conniving Khalil gives her an endearing kiss on the forehead as they hugged. As Nevaeh looks up into his eyes, he whispers, "I'm sorry Bae, lets get outta here, we'll talk in the car." Khalil puts his arm around her shoulders and Nevaeh put her arm around his waist. It was like nothing ever happened and as they held one another and walked out the school.

As they were walking down the hallway, Lacy and Devan are in complete shock to see them all hugged up. Lacy turns to Devan and says "I know this heffa aint..." Nevaeh is somewhat embarrassed when she sees the looks on her friends faces. However, she makes her choice without saying a word. As her girls looked on, she put her other arm around the front of Khalil's waist and dropped her head into his shoulder. This said it all, she is choosing her man.

Wednesday March 8, 2018
3:47pm

Stage 2: Reconciliation: The Second Phase of Abuse

It's the same day, a few moments after leaving the school holding each other like they are "soooo in love." The two get in the car and Nevaeh goes to break the ice. "Babe what -" Khalil calmly shushes her, "Shhhhh." He gives a subtle shake of his head and Khalil grabs his phone. Nevaeh sits back and tries to figure out what he is doing. He scrolls through and finds the song he is looking for. Khalil grabs the aux cord and puts it in his phone and turns up the volume just enough. No more than a moment passes when, Ella Mai's "Trip" starts to play through the speakers. Nevaeh turns and looks at Khalil with a face that says, 'like really.' Khalil gives her that same face he made coming out of the classroom before looking her deep into her eyes and mouthing the part of the song that goes, 'my bad for tripping on you!'

'Dang he is so cute' Nevaeh thought to herself. So when Khalil leans over for a kiss, of course everything in her is saying "this fool really think he about to get a kiss after all this drama he put me through?" But that little silly thing called her heart melted away her defense when he didn't break eye contact on his way to her lips. Khalil gives her a small peck at first and says, "Bae, it won't happen again... I promise." Nevaeh feels like that is some BS so without thinking she turns her face towards the window and away from him. Khalil remains calm and simply takes his left hand up and ever so gently grabs her chin and turns her face back to those puppy dawg eyes. Khalil whispers again, "Bae, I'm serious... You know I love you..." Nevaeh looks back and gives him a peck this time.

Khalil knows he has her! Khalil kisses her again, this time it's a passionate french kiss for about 7 seconds. Khalil pulls back, looks her in the eyes and says, "I love you Vaeh cakes." To which she responds, "I love you too, K Bae."

Khalil sits back knowing that she is trapped squarely in his web of deceit. Khalil puts the car in reverse and proceeds to exit the school parking lot. The song finishes playing and Khalil hits the off button on the car stereo. He turns to look at Nevaeh, knowing full well that she is about to buy whatever he is about to sell her. He begins to say exactly what he began plotting the moment she texted him back and he shifted the energy.

"Bae look, when you said you was going to eat with Lacy and Devan it just took me back to what happened with me and Ahronai. She let Takyra and Jalisa get all in her head about me. They got her all hyped up to not like me and eventually we broke up. I mean it's cool or whatever because I got something waaay better in you but still. Like if you gone keep running to your friends every two seconds, let me know." Nevaeh is a bit in shock as she begins to realize that she is being asked to choose between him and her friends. "Khalil, Lacy and Devan was my friends before you became Bae. You sound crazy asking me to choose right now."

Khalil, wasn't expecting resistance but he plays it cool, shifts his intentions and guilt trips her all at once. "Bae, I ain't asking you to choose, I would never do that. I see y'all lil bracelets or whatever. It's obvious them your girls and I am cool with that. What I'm saying is let our time be our time. We don't have that many classes together so I need to be with you on lunch hour. If not then they can give you a ride to school and back home everyday... Oh my bad they don't got no car... And instead of calling me to come over when your Mom working nights, have them come sleep with you so you don't be scared like you be claiming..." Nevaeh is processing it all, "Khalil you know that is different -" Khalil was quick to not let her finish. "Different how? When you need me I gotta be there for you but when I say I need you, it's "they been my friends before you was Bae." Is that fair?" Nevaeh quietly thinks to herself, how did we get back to arguing so quickly. While she pauses, Khalil says, "Exactly." Nevaeh then makes the big mistake, she goes along to get along instead of speaking how she truly feels. Nevaeh simply wants the argument to end so she says, "You right babe, I got you..." The moment she did that, the floodgates of abuse were wide open. Neveah remembers looking down at her NDL bracelet and adjusting it as she wondered if she should have listened to her friends who had told her just a few hours ago to get out while she could...

<u>Thursday April 18, 2019</u>
<u>11:53pm</u>

Nevaeh mentally has come back from reliving the painful memory. She musters up enough strength to get in the shower, yet she is still in a daze as the water runs over her body. She grabs her scrubber and soap and begins to wash his scent off of her. The thought of what just happened is surreal to her because she never thought that their fights would get this far. She finishes washing off and steps out of the shower. Nevaeh grabs her towel and wipes her face, she stops with the towel over her mouth when her eyes meet the mirror and she sees the marks on her face. Momentarily, she had forgotten that the marks were there.

Just seeing the bruises ramps up the emotions of her pain and simultane-ously lowers her self-esteem.

Nevaeh puts on her robe, grabs her phone and powers it on. Immediately her phone begins blowing up. In minutes she has 68 unread text messages, 47 new voicemails. All from you know who, Khalil. Nope not tonight, she doesn't have any energy left to give him. She knows that responding to him will only start another senseless argument. Typically, their arguments can last for hours and include a few hundred text messages back and forth. Nevaeh isn't in the mood for all this so she puts her phone in her robe pocket and heads to her room. After lotioning up, she heads to her dresser to get something to put on. As soon as she opens the drawer, right on top is the matching shirt her and Khalil had made for the city-wide drill team competition. Seeing the shirt triggers another memory she would like to forget. This was the shirt he was wearing the first time the abuse turned physical...

It was a little over 7 months ago, their Junior year had just started. This particular day was the City Wide Drill Team Competition. All the JROTC Programs from the cities 5 high schools compete in a gymnasium to see who had the best program. This was a huge citywide event in their hometown and everybody would be there. Nevaeh and Khalil were matching from head to toe. They wore matching airbrushed shirts, red jeans, and brand new Carmine 6s. Her gold chain had a pendant that read Khalil and his matching pendant read Nevaeh. All of which Khalil paid for. Khalil works at a clothing store in the mall but the most of his money comes from a settlement his parents got a few years back. They didn't blow it and even bought Khalil a car when he turned 16.

Khalil uses his money to control the girls he dates and Nevaeh is no exception. Neveah unfortunately, is oblivious to the underlining possessive web Khalil is weaving with the showering of material gifts. To her it is a statement of love, to him it is a mark of ownership.

<u>Saturday, September 22, 2018</u>
<u>6:43pm</u>

Nevaeh remembers that she had just posted a few pictures after getting dressed as she waited on Khalil. She thought nothing of it when her friend Deonte left the message 🔥🔥😍🥰 under her pic.

Nevaeh responded to his comment with the same response she did everyone else who commented on her pic

Thanks ❤️ 😘

Khalil saw it and was furious! Immediately his mind was set on ruining her night. So as Neveah was on the couch going back and forth between Instagram and Snapchat the text came through:

Bring ur dumb self outside

Having no clue as to what this text is about, Nevaeh angrily grabs her purse puts her charger inside of it and heads for the door. "Ma, Khalil is here, I'm gone..." "Waaaiiitttt" her mother yelled from the kitchen, as Nevaeh opens the door. Nevaeh is annoyed with the thought of the argument that awaits her in the car. Nevaeh turns and waits for her mother with a look of disgust written all over her body language. Her mother stops when she sees Neheah's energy. Mistakenly thinking Nevaeh is upset with her request, her mother goes on, "Uggh - I just wanted to give your gorgeous self a kiss before you left... Khalil little nappy head butt can wait... He kno' betta than to be sitting in the car without coming in to speak to me too... But I am going to let him get away with it today, next time he betta come speak, I don't play that... NT ways - I'll text you if they call me in to work tonight." Still annoyed Nevaeh, gives her a kiss and walks out the door while saying, "Love you too, Ma... See you later."

Her mother holds the door ajar as she watches Nevaeh walk to the car. Khalil hits the horn and acknowledges that he sees Ms. Winbush at the door. She signals for him to roll down his window. Khalil does so and leans his head out a bit and pleasantly says, "Hi, Ma..." To which Ms. Winbush answered "Boy I told you about that Ma stuff... And next time you better bring your butt in here and speak to me... You know I don't play that!" Khalil feeling a bit guilty replies, "I'm sorry... It won't happen again" he says with a sly smile on his face. While he is talking, Nevaeh gets into the car. Ms. Winbush yells "IT BET NOT... Y'ALL BE SAFE!!!"

Khalil rolls up the window, turns to Nevaeh and goes in, "What took you so long..." Nevaeh starts to answer "My Mama cal-" "Whatever, next time hurry up!... And why you blowing kisses to this thirsty nigga under your pic? Bro I bought you them shoes, that shirt and you wearing my necklace in the pic and cuz this weirdo put a flame under your pic you gone blow him a kiss... You got me out here lookin' like a goofy!" Nevaeh raises her voice "OH MY GOD!!! REALLY - I SENT THE SAME THING TO EVERYONE WHO COMMENTED - MY MAMA, YO MAMA!!! MY AUNTIE - REALLY!!! YOU CALLING ME NAMES OVER SOME STUPID STUFF LIKE THAT!!! YOU THE DUMMY - IF I WANTED TO GET AT HIM I WOULDA RESPONDED TO ALL THOSE TIMES HE TOOK HIS SHOT IN MY DM'S!!!

Typical Khalil, he can dish it, but he can't take it. Clenching the steering wheel in anger, "Who you calling a dummy!" he says taking his eyes off the road as he turns towards Nevaeh, who is texting on her phone. "Who the hell you texting?" he yells reaching for her phone. Nevaeh moves her hands back... "I'm texting Devan to come outside... You finna be on her street... DUH!!! YOU DUMMY!"

Khalil's frustration is boiling over as he pulls up to Devan's house. Looking straight ahead he says in a cold threatening voice, "Vaeh you better stop fu... Ooohhh you betta stop playing with me... Call me a dummy again and see what happens..." "Boy bye, you told me to Bring MY DUMB SELF OUTSIDE - Here, you wanna see the text that you sent me!!!" She says as she puts the phone up to his face. "You can call me dumb but I betta stop playing when I say the same thing to you... Boy Bye!" "You oohh... You lucky Dev-" Khalil stops abruptly as Devan reaches for the door handle and gets in the car.

An excited Devan gets in the car, "Wsup Sis! Ok I see y'all in y'all matching outfits... Yaasssss!!!" Nevaeh changes her mood to hide the tension between her and Khalil, "Thanks! You know how we do boo!" Devan puts on her seat belt and turns her attention to Khalil, "Wsup Big Head" she says as she shakes his shoulder. "Thanks for the ride..." "You good" Khalil says dryly. "Uhh, what's wrong best friend?" Devan says to Khalil, Nevaeh jumps in to respond as she gently rubs his face, "My baby just thinking about how much he love me that's all."

I know, it is crazy that Nevaeh is trying to cover up what's really going on. Sadly people are prideful and would rather mask the abuse than have the judgment and criticism of their friends and family.

Stage 3: Unpredictability: The Third Phase of Abuse

So about an hour or so goes past at the competition and everything was going great. Their matching outfits got a lot of attention as they walked in the building. This too was by Khalil's sinister design. Neveah naively thought this was a mutual expression of their love. From Khalil's perspective, their outfit was all about marking his territory, Nevaeh belonged to him.

At the intermission, everyone went out to the concession area. Nevaeh walked out with Devan and Lacy, while Khalil walked out with his boys Kadafi and Tavares. Nevaeh and Khalil were separated only briefly, however, Khalil is careful not to let Nevaeh out of his sight. Khalil made sure to position himself where he can see her every move.

As typically the case in a big event like this, some random thirsty dude takes his shot at Nevaeh. Khalil is watching the whole time as buddy is trying to spit his game at Nevaeh. Much to Khalil's surprise, he sees Nevaeh pull out her phone. One of her pet peeves is to be ignored so, she is mindful of making eye contact while the guy gives it his best shot. Neveah momentarily breaks eye contact to read and answer a text. Nevaeh lays him down nicely when she points to her necklace that says "Khalil." Innocently, Nevaeh keeps it pushing with her girls, not knowing that Khalil saw what appeared to him as her getting his snap.

Khalil is heated yet careful not to cause a scene. Khalil knows that the silent treatment and the cold shoulder when they get back to their seats will push her buttons. This continues for the rest of the competition. Nevaeh was blindsided by his attitude, but she has gotten used to the fact that any little thing can set him off. Careful not to make things worse nor obvious, Nevaeh shifts the majority of her interactions to her girls. Inside she is trying to figure out what is wrong with him now, while putting on the front that she is enjoying herself. Nevaeh hasn't learned the lesson that when you avoid conflict with someone else, you start a war within yourself. A million thoughts ran through her head, yet she can't point out what it could be. Truth is it could be anything. Despite how hard you try when you are in an abusive relationship, fault can be found in everything. Nevaeh like so many other victims of abuse lives in constant torment by the self placed pressure of being perfect just for someone else's pleasure.

When dealing with mentally and verbally abusive people like Khalil, it is important to remember that the truth and logic hold very little weight in their mind. The only thing that matters to an abuser is their perspective. What Khalil saw from his perspective is all that mattered. However, what looked like her getting her phone out to get the guys snap could not be farther from the truth. As the guy was talking to her, she felt her phone go off. It was a text message from her mother:

Veah, hope you are having a good time. Just got called into work. See you in the morning. Take that chicken I left in the sink and put it in the fridge

What Khalil saw was Nevaeh responding to her Mother's text. Nevaeh texted back:

Too bad, from Khalil's point of view, Nevaeh was falling for a thirst trap. Khalil was upset... And he was going to make sure she felt his anger.

K. Luv u. Competition is 🔥 Wirt just eliminated West Side. L Dubb & Velt up now. Text u when I get 🏠

Becoming emotionally drained from trying to figure out what changed his attitude, despite sitting directly next to him Nevaeh texted Khalil:

Wats wrong w u?

when Khaill feels
the phone vibrate in his pocket, he grabs it, reads the text, he turns to her gives her a very cold stare and texted her back:

OML I H8 U!!! U a dumb thot!!!   And with that, Khalil has succeeded in ruining Nevaeh's night. Through craftful manipulation by Khalil and unsuspecting choices of her own, Nevaeh finds herself in love with a ticking time bomb. Let's skip ahead to the ride home when the "bomb" known as Khalil detonates.

Stage 4: Physical Abuse - When mind and emotional control fail

Khalil pulls up to Devan's house and Nevaeh turns and says to her "Alright Devan, - I'll text you later and let you know what time I'll be ready to go tomorrow." Devan responds, "Ok girl and thanks again Khalil" Khalil nods and says "Yup." Devan closes the door and Khalil waits to make sure she gets in the house before pulling off. Khalil starts to pull off when, Nevaeh says, "Ok, now what gave you this stupid attitude?" Khalil who can finally begin to release this anger begins yelling, "Don't try to play me, I saw you talking to that lame nigga at intermission. Putting his Snap in your phone! You so stupid!" Nevaeh screams, "OH MY GOD!!! I told you to stop calling me stupid… But you bout to be the one who feelin' dumb!" Nevaeh begins scrolling through her phone to show him the text message that her Mom sent to her while the guy was trying to talk to her. Nevaeh has found the message and puts it in Khalil's face, "Look you Dumby it was my…" Khalil snatches the phone out of her hand, throws it back towards her while yelling, "Get that out my face." The phone hit the dashboard before falling to the floor. A stunned Nevaeh immediately starts looking for her phone. She spots it by her foot and picks it up. Nevaeh presses the home key and sees that her screen is cracked.

Khalil just cracked her "baby". "You cracked my screen you stupid…" Nevaeh is punching Khalil in the chest and shoulder while screaming and cursing him out. Khalil is trying not to lose control of the car but quickly pulls over and puts the car in park. Khalil turns to Nevaeh and punches her in the side of her face. He then grabs her arms and begins to shake her, yelling to her "Calm Down!!!" Nevaeh quickly realizes his strength and stops trying to fight him. Nevaeh yells, "Ok let me go!!!" "You going to calm down?!" he says. Nevaeh doesn't care what he is saying. She simply wants to be let go. So after about a couple hundred times of saying,

"Let me go Khalil... Let me go, let me go Khalil" and him saying "Are you going to calm down?" Khalil eventually does.

Khalil puts the car back in drive and continues on the route to take her home. Nevaeh is completely turned towards the window and is visibly shaking with anger and frustration. So when Khalil finally pulls up to her house and turns to apologize, Neveah has jumped out of the car and the door is closing before he can even get his apology out. Khalil rolls down the window and yells "Bae" in the direction of Nevaeh who is running to the door. Nevaeh gets inside, closes the door and collapses right on the couch. Nevaeh remembers the "puddle" that her uncontrollable tears created on her shirt. She knew that their relationship would never be the same after this point. Nevaeh was right, it only went downhill from there. Once a relationship turns physically violent there is no turning back.

Friday, April 19, 2019
12:14 am

If I just wouldn't make him upset: Self blame

Disgusted by the reminder, Nevaeh angrily grabs the shirt and throws it aside. The shirt is the first of many reminders yet to come of just how much Khalil is involved in her life. She grabs some sweats and a long shirt out of the drawer and sits back on the bed. Physically exhausted, she just wants to go to sleep. Neveah puts on her clothes knowing that with so many things running through her head, she won't be getting any sleep for a couple of hours.

Nevaeh is lonely by design. Khalil has isolated her. She is afraid of being judged by her friends and terrified of what her mother would do if she ever found out that Khalil was putting his hands on her. Nevaeh feels that this cross is hers alone to bear. Neveah lays on the bed trying to think of what she can do to stop what is happening to her and at the same time keep Khalil. Nevaeh would typically self medicate on the "good times" to get through rough patches and arguments. Now that the abuse has turned physical, she does an inventory of her behavior in hopes to find the prescription needed to make their relationship well. Unfortunately, she has began to blame herself because... It wasn't always like this.

In classic abuser fashion, Khalil has convinced Neveah that he needs her. Believing that she is the key to his happiness, Nevaeh doesn't even consider something other than herself being the root cause of Khalil's issues. She doesn't have the skill set to recognize that there is nothing that she can do or actions of hers that she can change that will allow him to heal. Neveah will continue a fruitless search for which of her actions are causing Khalil to erupt. Convinced that somehow all of this is her fault Naveah falls asleep as she searches for answers.

Friday, April 19, 2019
7:14 am

<u>What's Done In the Dark Will Eventually Come To Light</u>

After a few hours of restless sleep Nevaeh is getting ready for school. Nevaeh made sure she got up early to put on makeup to cover the bruises Khalil left on her face. Of course Khalil is still blowing up the phone and Nevaeh is still ignoring him. Neveah is in the mirror putting her hair in a style that covers her eye when she hears her Mom walk in from work.

Before her mother could put her bags down, she hears Nevaeh scream "Maaaa… Can you take me to school?" Her Mom disgustedly responds, "Why you ain't riding with Khalil?" which Nevaeh normally does. Nevaeh responds, "He has something to do… He said he was going to school later!" Nevaeh yells from up stairs. Nevaeh's Mom pays it no real mind but doesn't feel like taking her to school. After a long night at work she was really looking forward to lighting a candle and preparing a hot bath in order to relax. Upset by the abrupt change in her plans she yells, "Hurry your self up girl! Daaang! You could have texted me so I could have had my mind ready for this mess! Goodness! I wanna take a bath and lay down! Hurry Up!"

Nevaeh comes down after about two minutes and cautiously yet carefully rushes out the door. Her mother gets up from the couch and follows her out the door and into the car. "Oh you trying to be funny, huh?" Careful not to turn to her mother, she cleverly says, "What? I'm trying to hurry up so you can get back and relax." Liking the sound of that, her mother is momentarily quiet as she backs out and begins to drive towards Nevaeh's school. She notices that Nevaeh has her hair down over her face in a style she doesn't normally wear and says, "That is cute. Did you learn that at the shop?" Nevaeh plays along, "Yeah." Her Mom notices that the normally talkative Nevaeh is quiet, but she is ready to get back to the house and doesn't say much for the ride to school.

After what feels like a few moments they pull up to the school. Neveah reaches for the door while saying, "Thanks for the ride Ma, I love you." Trying not to be seen she doesn't wait for a response from her Mom. So her Mom picks up her phone and text Nevaeh:

I luv u 2

Nevaeh sees it and at the same time Khalil is sending her what seems like the millionth text message. At the same time that Nevaeh is responding to the text message. Nevaeh's mother is turning out of the school parking lot when she notices Khalil driving past her. She immediately gets the feeling that something isn't right. Call it a mother's intuition but she knows for a fact Nevaeh just told her that Khalil wasn't coming to school until later. Her mind gets to racing, Nevaeh rushed out the house after asking for a ride, she had a new hairstyle, she was quiet, now this confirms she lied about Khalil. Everything is not adding up. While she is doing the math, she gets a text message from Neveah.

God doesn't make any mistakes. Nevaeh sent her mother the text intended for Khalil. Now her Mother knows what is going on. All at once, tears rush towards her eyes, knots begin to form in her stomach and sweat begins to cover both her forehead and palms. A parents greatest fear has now become Mrs. Winbush's reality. "Khalil is putting his hands on my baby, how could I have missed that?" She thinks to herself as she makes a U Turn and heads back towards the school. "Siri Call Uncle Jay." She says as a plan of action begins to formulate in her head. Uncle Jay is a Police Officer. The phone rings twice before a deep voice says... "Wsup Baby Girl?" Her Mom responds, "Hey Unc, I need you to meet me at Vaeh's school right now, I think her little boyfriend is putting his hands on her..." Jay responds, "What!!! I'm on my way..." Her mother says "OK" and speeds back to the school.

The Truth is Revealed

When she gets to the school, Ms. Winbush hops out the car quick and walks swiftly towards the entrance. She goes through the metal detector and is greeted by the security guard, Ms. Theus. "Hey Ms. Winbush." Not in the mood for small talk Nevaeh's Mom responds "Good morning" not to be rude but keeps it pushing right into the office. "Good morning Mrs. Meyers, can you please call my daughter Nevaeh Winbush to the office so I can speak to her it's an emergency." The Principal, Mrs. West is coming from her office when she sees Ms. Winbush. Noticing the worried look on her face she asks, "Good morning Mrs. Winbush is everything okay?" Mrs. West says in a concerned tone of voice. "I'm not sure, I just need to talk to Nevaeh and I'll know. Right now, I don't think so." Ms. Winbush says while fidgeting with her keys. "Ok, well let me call her down." "Mrs. Meyers already called her but thank you."

"Okay, well I am going to make sure everything is okay in the halls. When Nevaeh comes down, y'all can have my office. Just let me know if I can help." Mrs. West says before leaving the office. "Thanks again Mrs. West." Ms. Winbush replies feeling supported.

A few anxious moments passed before Nevaeh gets to the Main Office. Nevaeh is puzzled as to why she has been called to the office first thing in the morning. When she walks in she looks over and sees her Mom and begins to wonders if she left something in the car. Nevaeh cautiously enters the room. "What's wrong Ma?" Her Mother says, "I thought you said Khalil wasn't coming to school until later today, I saw him when I dropped you off..." Nevaeh begins thinking of her lie... Her mother cuts her off and says "Ah ah Ah Don't even answer that, come here, lets go in Mrs. Wests' office." They both walk into the office.

After closing the door, Ms. Winbush walks over towards Nevaeh and slightly moves her hair back from her face. Nevaeh quickly jerks her head away. "Girl get yourself over here" she says before reaching at her hair again. Nevaeh exhales and slowly walks a few steps back in towards her mother. Ms. Winbush is beginning to cry as she notices the scratch and bruise that is somewhat covered by makeup.

A stunned silence overcomes the room. Both mother and daughter are in disbelief as they silently acknowledge the once hidden reality. Nevaeh's disbelief is rooted in embarrassment, while Ms. Winbush's stems from the thought of failing her child. With tears streaming down her face Ms. Winbush reaches to get her phone and shows Nevaeh the text that was meant for Khalil. Nevaeh just drops her head and begins to cry out... "Mama I'm Sorry..." Ms. Winbush wraps her arms around her hurting child. "Baby, shh... Don't be sorry. It's my fault. I should have been more involved. Vaeh, I'm the one who owes you an apology. I'm sorry Vaeh. It's going to be okay. We gone get through this. It's gone be alright. Let it out. Mama's here."

By this time Uncle Jay is knocking at the door of the office and comes over to embrace his family. Uncle Jay doesn't hesitate, "Where is he?" Nevaeh who is feeling all types of emotions, part relieved, part guilty, part ashamed, says to her Great Uncle, "He's in class." Mrs. West is now at the door trying to figure out what is going on. She knocks as she enters and asks "Is everything alright?" "No but it will be." Officer Jay replies. "We have a case of dating violence. I need to see Khalil Johnson. It seems that he has been assaulting Nevaeh as recently as last night." Shocked, Principal West looks over and notices the bruises on Nevaeh's face. "Wow. Well I will have to notify his parents also. But sure thing, I will call him down now." Mrs. West says before going over to her desk and calling the secretary and informing her of the necessary instructions.

About 3 minutes pass before Khalil walks into the main office. Noticing him enter Principal West leaves out of her office to speak with him. "Khalil, you need to go with Officer Jay." "Why wsup?" Khalil begins to get agitated. Hearing Khalil's voice from the main office, Nevaeh and

Ms. Winbush stand up. Khalil notices them through the window of Mrs. West's office. Nevaeh and Khalil lock eyes and in that moment they both know that the laughter, the lunches, the car rides, the jokes, the love is gone forever. The essence of what Nevaeh and Khalil shared was genuine at one point and has to be acknowledged. However, those days are gone and now it's time for Nevaeh to admit to herself that the majority of what they share at this point is fabricated. In that moment Nevaeh realizes that she is never going to catch that "high" of how things used to be. Their past is now nothing more than a delightful memory and Nevaeh must finally come to grips with her painful reality.

As Nevaeh looks into his eyes the memories of what was, slowly turns into, what now? Khalil drops his head in shame. It has finally dawned on Khalil that he will have to pay the consequences for his actions. As he does, Officer Jay says, "I think you know what this is about." Khalil's chin is in his chest as he gives a slight nod of acknowledgement to Officer Jay. They both slowly begin to walk out of the school.

Real Friends & Realizations

Nevaeh and her mother remained in the office for about fifteen minutes after Officer Jay escorted Khalil out of the building. Nevaeh told her mother what happened last night and was trying to get herself together to leave the school. The bell rings and after a few moments both Devan and Lacy enter the office. They all had 1st period together and since Nevaeh didn't come back to class they were coming to check on her. They brought Nevaeh's bookbag and as they are walking in, Nevaeh and her mom are walking out of Mrs. West's office. "Hey Ma" says Lacy who is happy to see Ms. Winbush. Devan waves to Ms. Winbush, but amongst Lacy's usual excitement, she notices that Neveah isn't really looking up. Immediately concerned she asks, "Vaeh... what's wrong?" Nevaeh had just pulled it together enough to get out of the school, however seeing her girls she begins to lose it slightly. Nevaeh knows that speaking it will break the dam of emotions she just built so instead she takes a deep breath and holds her head up. She looks Devan in the eye for a second before dropping her head and reaching down to straighten her "NDL" bracelet. Lacy and Devan look down at what she is doing and subconsciously grab theirs as well. Nevaeh is still silent as she raises her head back up yet this time she can't find the strength to look either of her friends in the eye. Instead of telling them what is happening, she moves the hair that is covering her eye and reveals the bruise. Without words, they both instantly hug her, which said exactly what Nevaeh needed to hear from her "sisters."

"Girl don't even trip, we here for you, sis!" Lacy says sorrowfully. "Yeah Vaeh, what's done is done, we got your back like for real for real."

Says Devan offering reassurance. Overwhelmed by guilt Nevaeh tries to apologize, "Y'all I'm so sorry, I shouldn't have let Khalil -" "Unh unh, don't do that girl, we gone get through this but don't apologize. We got you." says Lacy. The friends all hug again.

Principal West respectfully breaks up the supportive moment, "I'm sorry ladies, I know this is y'all friend but I know she has things she has to take care of and y'all got a class to get to. I don't want to be rude but I am sure y'all will get all caught up once everything is taken care of." Nevaeh pulls back from the hug and says, "I love y'all! I'll text y'all later alright." Lacy and Devan wiped their tears, said "OK" and head back to class. Nevaeh and her mother leave the school.

The Inconvenient Truth Is Revealed

When they get to the car, Ms. Winbush continues apologizing "I'm sorry Vaeh. I'm so sorry Vaeh. I know I should have been there. I been working so much. How did I miss this Vaeh? I'm sorry baby... I'm sorry." Nevaeh cuts her off in a moment of clarity, "Ma this ain't yo fault... This on me. Khalil made me feel like I wasn't enough, like I needed him. I lost myself in Khalil... This is my fault. Don't apologize Mama... I should have left him a long time ago."

Navaeh's phone rings as she is speaking, it reads... "K Bae Mama". Nevaeh swipes to answer it. "Hello""Vaeh, the school called and said Khalil is being arrested and I need to go to the police station. Do you know what this is all about?" Nevaeh says softly, "Yes Khalil hit me last night..." Khalil's Mom cuts her off and says, "Ok where are you at right now?" Nevaeh answers, "I am in the car with my mother we are heading to the police station so I can make a statement." Nevaeh's mom chimes in, "No we are going to the hospital right now." Nevaeh corrects herself. "Mrs. Johnson, my mother said we are heading to the hospital right now." Mrs. Johnson replies, "Nevaeh, I'm so sorry Khalil put his hands on you! I am going to get to the bottom of this okay!" "Yes Ma'am." "Ok Nevaeh, I'm sorry again, let me make some calls, tell your mother that I'm sorry and I will be reaching out to her as well. I'll talk to you soon Nevaeh and again, I'm sorry!" "Alright Mrs. Johnson, bye bye." "Ma Khalil mom told me to tell you she sorry. And -" "I heard her. Yeah she is sorry. A sorry parent, raising a woman beater ... Oooohhh. Ooooohhh. You know what let me calm down..."

Friday, April 19, 2019
9:46 am

Nevaeh and her mom are sitting in the ER when, to their surprise Khalil's mom walks in. "Mrs. Johnson... Khalil is at the police station."

Says a puzzled Nevaeh, Khalil's mom nods and says, "I know sweetheart. But I came to check on you. I'm so sorry Ms. Winbush... I am so sorry for what Khalil has done. I want you to know that I completely support whatever you all want to do in terms of Khalil. We are not going to fight your decision to press charges." Nevaeh's mom says aggressively, "We are not taking it easy... I'm telling you that now!"

Khalil's mom drops her head momentarily before looking up and saying, "I don't want you to take it easy... I want your help..." "Help with what?" Says a confused Ms. Winbush. Mrs. Johnson looks away and tears begin to stream from the corner of her eye. Ms. Winbush knows immediately what that look means. Lost for words, Ms. Winbush simply reaches out and hugs Khalil's Mom. Neveah is lost, "What? What do you need our help with?" Khalil's mom wipes the tears from her chin and says to Nevaeh. "I need you alls help because I am going to press charges on Khalil's father. He has been beating me since before Khalil was born..." Nevaeh begins to tear up. Trying to comprehend the situation Nevaeh naively asks, "Wait, Mrs. Johnson why did you stay with him all these years?" Mrs. Johnson takes a moment to find the absolute truth to give to Nevaeh. After giving it some thought she responds, "Well... I don't know... I just know that... it wasn't always like this..."

108

Resources for Victims of Dating Violence and Domestic Abuse

National Teen Dating Abuse Helpline
Call 1-866-331-9474
www.loveisrespect.org or text "loveis" to 22522

National Domestic Violence Hotline
Call 1-800-799-7233
www.ndvh.org

Rape, Abuse & Incest National Network (RAINN)
Call 1-800-656-4673
www.rainn.org

Online Resources

That's Not Cool
www.thatsnotcool.com

Break the Cycle
www.breakthecycle.org

National Center for Victims of Crime - Dating Violence Resource Center
www.ncvc.org

A Message From The Author

I wrote this chapter with the hope of triggering readers as well as taking them on the emotional roller coaster that goes along with being in an abusive relationship. I tried my best to make it obvious that Nevaeh should leave Khalil repeatedly throughout the story. I also tried to show you that leaving is also easier said than done...

A part of me feels that I would be remissed to not state the obvious that if anyone feels the need to put their hands on you, then it is impossible for them to truly see your worth. You can and you have to understand that you can do bad all by yourself...

Simply put, it will not get better, it will only get worse and there is nothing that will change in the future. A rule of thumb is that what you permit is what you promote.

This means that if you permit (allow) him to hit you... Then you are promoting (encouraging) him to hit you...

Whether you understand it or not, you are only receiving the treatment that you have indicated that you are willing to accept...

Nothing says you know your worth louder than leaving once you recognize that you are not being valued, that goes beyond just being physically abused, mental and verbal abuse is also grounds to leave...

Your Beauty is Your Worth...

- Alan Gaines

Section 3:

Dolphins

Dolphins are a universal symbol of Beauty, Intelligence and the Strength to Endure Tumultuous Surroundings.

Dolphins have a long standing history of being a positive omen to those who spot them in the ocean.

Dolphins are superior communicators whose presence is often seen as majestic and even representive of hope.

In This Section You Will Meet
Two Young "Dolphins" Whose Stories Will Shine
the Light on Global Issues That We Often Turn
A Blind Eye To. Please Allow These "Dolphins" to
Inspire Hope...

Chapter 5
Amukelani
(Accept / Recognize)

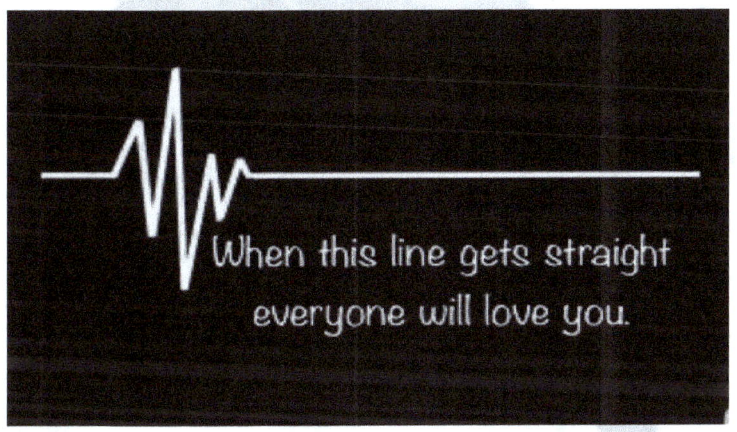

111

This was one of the final post made by Khensani Maseko before she took her life. A life gone far too soon. A Life that brought smiles, love and hope to so many people. Yet her death shined a light on a bigger global tragedy.

Rape is a global issue.

This issue is taking place at an unprecedented rate along the African Coast.

According to the World Population Review the four leading countries in the world with the highest rape rates are in Africa. Something has to be done about this crisis.

This story is told from a 3rd person view and attempts to give readers a look at this issue from a victims perspective.

Meet Fanisa...

"Queen"

This Beautiful Drawing is courteousy of: D. Marie

Amukelani - Accept / Recognize (Xitsonga African Language)

It's a Thursday afternoon and typically, Fanisa (pronounced Fa-NEE-Sa) would be just finishing her classes for the day. Thursday nights are ladies night at the clubs in Grahamstown and just two weeks ago this time Fanisa was in her dorm room with her suitemates being college kids looking forward to a night of dancing and fun. Now, she is at home trying to decide if life is worth living. School officials sent her home while they conduct a formal investigation. Neither Fanisa nor her parents believe anything is going to come of this "investigation," yet they agreed to it because that is the schools policy. Never in her worst nightmare would Fanisa have thought that her life would be in the center of anything of this magnitude. So as she sits looking at the wall feeling soulless, thoughts that were once unthinkable, begin to grow stronger inside her head by the moment...

Fanisa feels the "comfort" of home as she sits on her bed, yet this feeling of protection and security she has longed for since the moment she was violated may not be enough as she tries to figure out how to go forward. Honestly, she doesn't want to go forward. Fanisa doesn't know what "justice" is or would look like, so that isn't her desire either. Her desire is simple, for the act of rape to never have existed in the world...

Her emotions are turning darker by the second as Fanisa lays back on her bed and stares blankly at her ceiling. She begins to reminisce (think) about the first time she heard of the tragic culture. She couldn't have been no more than 5 or 6 years old. Fanisa remembers hearing that her Uncle was a part of a group that took matters into their own hands when it happened to an 8-year-old girl in town near the market. Fanisa didn't understand what was going on but she can vividly recall her parents pleading with her Uncle to ask God for forgiveness.

Fanisa's eyes drift from the ceiling over to her desk in the corner of her room. She spots her notebook from her 10th grade Civics class. Finding the strength to pull herself off of the bed she walks over and picks it up. Opening the book and looking through the pages, an ironic smirk runs across her face. Fanisa was 15 when she took the class. It was there in the 3rd seat on the first row, where Fanisa found her purpose. As the page turns over in her notebook, fumes reach her nose and take her back to better times. Moments that were filled with life, the complete opposite of what she is feeling now. The scent reminds her of the spirited debates and engaging lessons that "cut the light on" for Fanisa and fueled her passion to become a lawyer. Learning that so many girls of all ages were being victimized, she knew that she could not look in the mirror with a clear conscious if she didn't take a stand. Fighting the "Rape Culture" consumed Fanisa and at such a young age, she made up her mind that bringing an end to this was going to be her life's mission.

Now that she has become a victim of the thing she has devoted her life to eradicating, Fanisa has reached the ultimate paradox, "Do I take my life in hopes that my death will help change the law? Or do I continue to fight and have faith that I will be instrumental in getting the laws changed, to provide the necessary protection for girls?" Sadly, minute by minute, Fanisa is leaning more towards taking her life than she is living with the shame of rape. Fanisa knows that Mount Kilimanjaro is a meer molehill in comparison to the mountain she has to climb in order to be a victor and not just another victim.

Hlori - Wonder (Xitsonga African Language)

Fanisa is still thumbing through her notebook when she comes to the phrase that began her quest, "The Law Vs. Tradition". Fanisa remembers that she wasn't chosen to speak on this particular debate, she was a researcher. Her group had to argue the side of the Law. Fanisa always had a passion for history and learning about the past. Her father Akinwole is a history teacher and instilled in her the value of unbiased research. So when Fanisa got the task she was ready to make sure that the presenter was over prepared for debate. Fanisa's father had a saying that he picked up from one of his American college professors Dr. Candice Love Jackson, that goes, "You can't tear down Masters house without his tools." Simply put, you need to know everything about your enemy if you are going to defeat him... Armed with a strategy to prepare, Fanisa began to study the opposition's argument for the debate. That is when she first learned of Ukuthwala.

Reading her notes evokes emotions even stronger now than they were when she originally learned of the Ukuthwala tradition. Ukuthwala is a ritualistic tradition that involves a man and his friends or family, abducting (kidnapping) a girl and forcing her family to agree to allow him to marry her. When the tradition began hundreds of years ago the "ritual" only involved girls who were of marriageable age, typically between 16 and 21 years old. The kidnapper would have to give the family of the girls some type of compensation if the family agreed to the marriage.

While preparing for the debate, Fanisa found two key elements that creates the paradox which enables the rape culture to thrive. First, the tradition like many other customs that have been passed down through generations, is accepted as a "way of life" so very few people question the practice. This unchallenged acceptance has led to the ages of the "girls" being kidnapped now being primarily between the ages of 12 and 15 years old. The second factor and definitely the most alarming, is that many countries on the African continent don't have laws against sexual assault.

Furthermore, the countries that do have laws against sexual assault rarely prosecute or convict the men who commit the rape. Illogically, the burden of proof that the sex was nonconsensual is completely on the victim. Fanisa was even more devastated to find out that if a woman fails to prove that she is raped, she is likely to be convicted and sent to prison for falsely accusing someone of rape. While these realities would stop most people in their tracks, this only added fuel to Fanisa's fire and her mission to end the rape crisis in her beloved Mother Africa. Learning of this soul - crushing reality, Fanisa thought she would be ready for anything as she got more involved in the fight but things only got worse...

Tears are streaming down her face as she reads her notes. What was once sympathy has become empathy now that she can feel what those girls went through while being held captive as a part of the Ukuthwala ritual. Fanisa recalls being moved to tears then just like she is now as she learned that the kidnappers raped the precious little girls to "force" the parents to accept the "marriage". This forced the parents hands to accept the marriage. The perpetrators know the parents will accept the "marriage" because to refuse would mean that their daughter could face criminal charges for Zina, or unlawful sexual intercourse. A crime that would bring shame and stigma to the family.

The suicidal thought grow stronger with every word Fanisa reads. The notebook is bringing back a continuous stream of painful emotions that she can't help but relive. She is at the final bullet point on the page when she reads the note that was most heartbreaking of all from the research:

***There are no laws against marital rape in most countries that still allow the "ritual" to take place.**

Fanisa heart dropped in that moment because she knew that this fact essentially means that once a girl is taken as a part of Ukuthwala, she is realistically a sex slave. God's timing is perfect because amidst the darkness, Fanisa sees the note she made that day that brings her the comfort she needs right now:

Romans 8:28. "And we know that God causes everything to work together for the good of those who love God and are called according to his purpose for them."

For it was the only way she could mentally cope with what her mission in life would entail. Fanisa had faith that she would find the answer.

Kanelani - Engage (Xitsonga African Language)

In a daze, Fanisa looks up from her notebook and her eyes gravitate to the framed picture on her desk. The picture is of her with Seodi White, Fanisa's biggest inspiration. Seodi White, one of Africa's leading Women's Rights Activist, gave the keynote address at the conference hosted by the organization Fanisa started at her High School. The conference, Singila. Sisimuka. Ponani. (Nurture. Rise. Live To Tell the Tale.) focused on how legal pluralism, or the existence of two or more legal systems within one population, is largely responsible for the consistent oppression and victimization of girls and women. Fanisa was proud to have orchestrated such a well-attended conference. More importantly she was empowered by the fact that so many young girls and women were able to learn about how European Colonialism in Africa left the bloody trail of patriarchal dominance in government that drives such ridiculous and outrageous fallacies in the administration of laws designed to protect women, if such laws are even on the books at all.

Fanisa's research uncovered just how little is being done to prosecute men who rape women and girls. Being proactive Fanisa was determined to educate as many people as possible on just how vulnerable and unprotected women in general and girls like her, in particular, are in regard to the rape culture. Looking at the picture, she remembers that it was taken with White after Fanisa presented in one of the breakout sessions. Fanisa was happy to be the lead presenter in the session Systematic Silence.

Seodi White was amongst the overcrowded room that gave Fanisa a standing ovation after she masterfully globalized the sentiment of rape beyond the borders of Africa. Fanisa opened her session by playing a clip of famed American Basketball Coach Bob Knight's interview with Connie Chung. In the clip Knight infamously claimed that "If rape is inevitable, relax and enjoy it." With that, Fanisa immediately had her audiences attention. Fanisa craftfully exposed the mentality that drives the rape culture. Moving from Knight to the controversial comments made by Egyptian lawyer, Nabih al-Wahsh, who stated in late 2017 that "...when you see a girl walking down the street with her behind showing, it is a patriotic duty to sexually harass her and a national duty to rape her."

Fanisa's promising legal future was on full display when she followed those comments up by informing her audience of the ruling and subsequent explanation made by judge Aaron Persky of Santa Clara California in the case of Brock Turner. Turner was unanimously convicted of rape by a jury, yet Judge Persky sentenced Turner to 3 months in county jail. Fanisa wasted no time in pointing out how rulings such as this play an immense role in why women fear speaking out when they fall victim to sexual assault.

Fanisa remembers seeing the faces of the crowd overcome with sorrow as she read from the testimony of Brock Turner's accuser who stated that being raped in public by Turner robbed her of "my worth, my privacy, my energy, my time, my safety, my intimacy, my confidence, my own voice." Fanisa can still feel the anger from the audience as she read Turner's defense in which he points to "the party culture and risk taking behavior of college" as justification for his actions. Fanisa recalls the tears rolling down the faces of members of the audience when she read Judge Persky's rationale for the lenient sentence. Judge Persky reasoned, although the victim is likely to have "physical and devastating emotional injury" to sentence Turner to prison would have a "severe impact" on Turner and essentially "ruin his life."

Thinking back on such a high moment in her life is now bittersweet for Fanisa. She wants to feel the strength and courage that exhilarated from her as a presenter, however, it's the troubling nature of her presentation that she now faces as a victim. The tragic irony of Fanisa's life is that she actually knows just how unlikely it is that the man who victimized her is going to be brought to justice. Finding the strength to fight and be the voice for so many was much easier when she hadn't been violated. Fanisa looks at the picture one last time while thinking to herself "How did I go from being the next champion of the movement for Gender Equality, to another one of the ever-growing number of people who can use the hashtag MeToo?"

Rivoningo - Light (Xitsonga African Language)

Fanisa grabs a tissue from the desk only to hear the buzz from her phone that she placed on silent. It's a text message that she doesn't care to read so she swipes to dismiss it. Seeing her screensaver takes her mind back to the first event she sponsored as Ms. Varsity, an on-campus symposium to expose the detrimental effects of the "Virgin Cleansing Myth".

Fanisa thinks back to when she first read about the origins of the Virgin Cleansing Myth and how it dates back to 16th Century Europe only to gain prominence in 19th Century Victorian England. The myth is nothing more than a bogus cure, never proven by medical science, for syphilis and gonorrhea. The myth somehow reemerged in Africa amidst the ongoing AIDS epidemic. Fanisa relives the tears she shed as she learned that the Virgin Cleansing Myth has victims as young as 3 months old. The thought of the internal trauma that countless toddlers have endured always gets to Fanisa. So as she thinks back on it, the water works begin again. Fanisa knows the statistics all too well, 70 percent of rape survivors

"African Queen Made in Amerikkka"

This Beautiful Drawing is courteousy of: Lacist Wortham

in some African countries are 15 years old or younger.

As her spiral continues, Fanisa's thoughts go to the 5-year-old girl in Sierra Leone who was left paralyzed after being raped by her Uncle. This brings her emotions back full circle as her mind drifts to the "beginning" when Fanisa's parents confronted her Uncle. Fanisa thinks about him often, he died two years ago in a car accident. Maybe if he was still around she would have more strength to go forward. Her Uncle was always so proud of her, he would tell her that she fought this war the way it should be fought, through arming the people with knowledge and putting constant pressure on politicians. Although he chose "vigilante justice," he was proud of Fanisa and discouraged her from ever allowing her frustration to take her "over the edge" as he put it.

One conversation that they had in particular stayed with Fanisa. During her senior year in High School she asked him about that incident when she was 5 or 6 years old. He remembered it well. He told her, "I killed my best friend, I found out that he had raped his ex-girlfriend. I asked him why did he do it and he didn't give me a real reason. I asked him was this the only girl he had raped, he told me no, he had raped a young girl who was 13, several years ago. I asked him why did he do that? He asked me, if I remembered the time that I got arrested after the soccer match when we were 11? I told him I did. He told me while he was in custody, the officers raped him for 3 days, then they let him go. He told me years later when he was 18 he found out that he was HIV positive and shortly after that he raped the 13-year-old girl who was a virgin. Fanisa remembers asking her Uncle, so what did you say to him after he told you all this? Her Uncle responded, "Nothing, I blew his head off.

Felani - The One Worth Dying For (Xitsonga African Language)

Sometimes when you are searching for answers, the smallest most simple things come to you at the perfect times. Fanisa's mom comes in the room to check on her and although she has no idea that Fanisa is thinking about suicide, she gives her daughter a soft kiss on the forehead, looks her deep in the eyes and says simply, "To you the world may mean nothing, to someone else, you mean the world, Fanisa you mean the world to me." After a tearful hug she left the room. God's timing is perfect because that is what Fanisa needed to hear. Immediately she felt energized, she knew that she couldn't allow the person who assaulted her have the ultimate victory. Fanisa knows it is too many people she must fight for. Too many people who look up to her and too much left to accomplish to take her own life. Fanisa goes to her phone and posts a picture of Khensani Maseko, with the same caption Maseko left before the 23-year-old law student took her life after being raped on campus... "No One Deserves To Be Raped"

In Loving Memory
of
Khensani Maseko

May your fight & spirit live on...

24.07.1995
03.08.2018

120

This Chapter is
Dedicated to My Grandmother
Inez Davis

Granny I Love You So Much...

I am dedicating this chapter in particular to you because you always stressed to me that I must care about the world... You have always been a loving spirit that showed me that we must learn to laugh and protect our peace...

Thank you Granny for teaching me the most valuable lesson that nothing in the world is more precious than
A Peace of Mind...

Chapter 6
The 75,000

In America today over 64,000 Black Girls and Women are missing.
In addition to that approximately 11,000 Black females are
currently considered runaways.
This puts the total of Black Girls and Women unaccounted for in
America at an alarming 75,000.

While the number 75,000 is staggering in and of itself, this
number is magnified when one considers the mothers, fathers,
sisters, brothers, aunts, uncles and grandparents who are all being
affected by the absence of their loved one...

Beyond the Social Media post that appears on our timelines, very
little National media coverage is being given to this ungoing Crisis.
Many will argue and I would agree that this is due to these individuals being people of Color. However that is not the point because the
pain of losing a loved one in any fashion truly knows no boundaries.

Out of Respect to everyone who has a loved one who is missing regardless of their ethnicity and nationality I wrote this story from
the perspective of a Mother whose Daughter has gone missing.

I would like to introduce to you, Mrs. Loretta Stansil.
Her daughter Tanesha is missing and they are the subject of our
next story...

The 75,000

<u>The Ongoing Nightmare</u>

Mrs. Loretta is in her bed but she can't sleep... Mrs. Loretta wants to cry but she is out of tears... Mrs. Loretta wants to do a lot of things but her life has been on pause since October 13th of last year. Not able to sleep nor cry she does what she has done every day for the last 7 months 26 days and 11 hours for what seems like the "gazillionth" time. She re-plays "that day" over again in her head.

It started like every other Saturday and most of her days in general, with her morning "Success Schedule." The 42-year-old entrepreneur, got up at 3:30 am, did her 30-minute workout and 15 additional minutes of cardio to her "Retro and Ratchet Mix" on Tidal. You know, a little Aaliyah, Mary J, Total and SWV. Mixed with songs like Suge by DaBaby, Roddy Rich's The Box and Nipsey's Grinding All My Life. Followed by the weekly review of her stocks and other investments, a quick look ahead to her calendar to see what she has on her plate for the upcoming week and then her bath. She was uber excited because her daughter Tanesha was taking the SAT that morning. After her bath, she slipped into some jeans and her Bowie State hoodie and made Tanesha a big breakfast. Midway through cooking her breakfast Tanesha came to the kitchen and with the biggest smile on her face she gave her mom a hug from behind as Mrs. Loretta was scrambling the eggs. Mrs. Loretta turned over her left shoulder and kissed Tanesha near her ear. Tanesha gave a soft "Thank you Ma" acknowledging that her mother made her breakfast for the SAT. Mrs. Loretta turned around and said, "Hey, hey, hey - big day today, you gone knockout that SAT and then the homecoming is going to be litty!" Tanesha gave a smile and annoyed, "Maaaa!" Tanesha had been telling her mother to stop using that term because she thought her mother was doing too much, always saying that something was going to be "litty!"

"Smells good Ma", Tanesha said before Mrs. Loretta gave another playful retort, "Period!" "I can't with you today Ma, I'ma go and get ready. Thanks again for the breakfast I'll be back down in a few." Tanesha went back upstairs and Mrs. Dolphetta continued cooking as The Carters Everything Is Love Album played through the Amazon Echo Show in the kitchen. Shortly after Tanesha made her way up to her room, her father Ernest entered from the garage into the kitchen. Mrs. Loretta, turns at the sound of her husband opening the door. "How was your run babe?" "It was cool. Bae you in here doing the thang! I see you! Smells great as usual!" Ernest says as he walks over to give her a small kiss on the cheek. "Thanks Babe... I'm just trying to make sure that everything goes according to plan."

Mrs. Loretta says as she continues fixing plates. "I think Tanesha is going to do great... Babe, you sure we should let her drive by herself? She can catch an Uber over to the stadium and I can drive her car." Ernest grabs a few grapes from the plate and pops them in his mouth. "Babe, you are worrying too much. Tanesha will be fine, the drive is all of 15 minutes away. The girl has a 4.7 GPA, she does everything we ask of her, and she has done a great job of picking friends. Every one of her friends are going somewhere and doing something with their life. Tanesha isn't a baby anymore. We gotta start cutting that cord baby. I know it's hard but hey that's why we pray. And what do you always say, nothing happens to you, everything happens for you. Loretta, everything is going to be fine today. I know that our rule is that she has to drive with some-one else in the car but this one time is not going to hurt. At some point in life, she is going to drive somewhere alone babe."

Mrs. Loretta recalls being comforted by her husbands' words. "You right babe." Mrs. Loretta responds as Tanesha walks into the kitchen. "Good morning Padre" Tanesha says to her Dad as she walks over and grabs her plate. "Wsup Ms. 1560!" Referencing the score Tanesha plans to get on the SAT. "Ayyyyyeeee!!!" Tanesha says beaming with confidence at the score she has knows she is going to get. All three grab their plates and head into the dining room and have a seat. Ernest reaches out both hands as Mrs. Loretta and Tanesha each grab his hands and the family bowed their heads for prayer. Ernest begins the prayer "Lord heavenly Father we come to you humbly and thankful for allowing us to see another day. We not only want to pray over this food but also Tanesha's SAT test this morning. We ask that you allow her to relax and work at a good pace. Lord, we ask that you allow her to reach her goal of 1560 Lord. Lord, we ask for our safety as we leave the house today. We ask for safe travels and your grace over this family today and always. In your son Jesus name, we pray. Amen." "Amen" Both Tanesha and Mrs. Loretta said simultane-ously.

The rest of the breakfast that morning was pretty chill. After ev-eryone finished eating, Ernest headed out to the game. A few of his college buddies were going to start tailgating pretty early. Bowie State wasn't too far from their home in Kettering, Maryland. Shortly after he headed out, Mrs. Loretta and Tanesha hopped in the car and headed over to the local high school where Tanesha was taking the SAT.

"Alright Nesha, you need to DJ this thang! What you want to hear to get you pumped up for this test? Wait, you know we got to listen to this first." Mrs. Loretta starts scrolling in her phone. Tanesha calls it out, "You know it Ma - go head and put on... Your BOY E T!!! You know I gotta hear that Lion or the Gazelle!"

It's their "pregame" ritual to listen to ET The Hip Hop Preacher before any big test Tanesha has or any meeting involving a deal for Mrs. Loretta. After the Lion and Gazelle, they listened to the Dr. Thomas mixtape and Tanesha began to lock in as she rode pretty much silent yet with a confident swag for the rest of the trip.

Tanesha didn't need to take the SAT again because she had already scored 1495 on the test in March. Tanesha was taking it to meet her personal goal of 1560. Tanesha had a full ride to Bowie State University, her parent's alma mater, on a Bioinformatics scholarship. After a rather brief ride, they pull up to the school and Mrs. Loretta and Tanesha held hands as Mrs. Loretta started a small prayer. "Alright Lord, we ask one last time that you be with Tanesha. You promised to be with us always and we ask right now that you be with Tanesha as she takes her test, please give her patience, confidence and discernment, Amen." Tanesha gives her agreeance "Amen." "Alright Nesha, give me a kiss... Mmm mua... Good luck!!! Put on your thinking cap!" Mrs. Loretta says affectionately. "Thanks, Ma, I'll text you when I am done." "Ok love you!"

Mrs. Loretta went and got a quick mani-pedi and ran a few errands. Around noon, she was back in time to pick Tanesha up. Mrs. Loretta sat in the parking lot about 10 minutes before the students started coming out of the building from the test. Tanesha was in the 2nd wave of students and came to the car with a smile and a sassy swagger filled walk, which immediately got Mrs. Loretta excited.

Tanesha opened the door and before she could sit down her mother asked, "How was it?" Tanesha responded in her best Beyonce voice, "And I Slay... And I Slay..." Mrs. Loretta gave her a high five and uttered loudly, "That's my baby!" Now, of course, she didn't know her score but she was super confident. "You were right Ma, seeing it a second time allowed me to be much more comfortable with how things were going to go." "Hey, all glory to God. Okay, let's get you back so you can head on over to the game." The homecoming game started at 1:00 pm and since Mrs. Loretta had planned on staying for an alumni event afterward, they allowed Tanesha to drive her car alone to the game. Although they still had reservations about breaking their rule, Ernest's calming rhetoric put Mrs. Loretta mildly at ease.

After they made it home, Tanesha quickly went up to her room to get dressed. Tanesha put on her black and metallic gold LeBron 15s. Tanesha's Bron's matched perfectly her black BSU hoodie that had "Nesha" airbrushed on the back and "S.S.S." on the front pocket, both in yellow and white letters. S.S.S. was the name of her squad, the Super Savage Squad. After a few moments admiring herself in the mirror, she came downstairs.

Tanesha gave a slight knock on the door as she walked into her parents' room where Ms. Loretta was in her walk-in closet and said: "Alright Ma, I'm heading out..." Mrs. Loretta came out of the closet and walked over to Tanesha, gave her a slight hug and kiss on the cheek. "Love you Ma, I'll see you at the game or maybe after..." As they walked towards the door Mrs. Loretta kicked into mommy mode. "Nesha be safe please and don't forget to call me when you make it okay." "Ma, yes and yes. I'm going to be fine. I will see you later Ma." "Okay baby I love you... Don't forget to call me when you make it."

Mrs. Loretta watched Tanesha get in her car, a blue Nissan Versa, plug the aux cord into her phone and pull out the driveway to the faint sounds of H.E.R. coming from the car. She stayed there until Tanesha's car was no longer in her sights. Mrs. Loretta never once thought that this would be the last time she would see Tanesha.

Mrs. Loretta still doesn't allow the thought that her baby is gone forever to enter her mind. So as she sits up on the bed in the middle of the night replaying the nightmare she is living, she grabs a tissue to wipe the tear that doesn't come out of her eye. This scene has been on repeat so much that wiping her eye is now a habit. Mrs. Loretta continues going over the rest of that day thinking maybe she can find something she missed as she continues the mental replay.

A Mother's Intuition

After Tanesha drove off, Mrs. Loretta remembers going back into her room and getting dressed for the game. She packed her outfit for the alumni event in her garment bag and after exactly forty-three minutes from the time Tanesha left, Mrs. Loretta pulled out and headed to the game. She recalls that she looked down at her watch when Tanesha pulled off and checking her phone when she got in the car. It's the little details such as this that mark the events that change your life.

About halfway to the school, Mrs. Loretta hits a bit of traffic because of a car accident that appears to be pretty bad. Highway patrolmen have only one lane open and are directing the slow-moving traffic as onlookers try to get a sneak peek at the wreckage. Something tells Mrs. Loretta to look over to her left, away from the wreck and when she does, she notices a car that looks very similar to Tanesha's' Versa, parked at the BP gas station off of Annapolis Road. Being this area is popular with Semi-Trucks, Mrs. Loretta's "Mommy senses" went up and she immediately called Tanesha. No answer... Mrs. Loretta remembers thinking to herself, "Maybe the game is too loud and she can't hear her phone." Being that she wasn't 100% sure because she only saw the car in passing, she thinks to herself "Maybe I am tripping." Attempting to put her mind at ease, she called

Ernest to see if he had heard from Tanesha… No answer. Again, she thinks to herself maybe the noise of the game is why he didn't answer his phone also. But still, something didn't sit right with her because they have a rule that Tanesha never breaks, which is to call or text that she made it wherever she is going. Tanesha can text either parent and because Mrs. Loretta couldn't get a hold of Ernest, her mind begins racing even more. This was the very moment she began to worry and this feeling hasn't left her in nearly eight months.

After wading through the traffic, Mrs. Loretta makes it to the stadium. Filled with worry, she parks and rushes inside right before halftime. She speaks to a few familiar faces but only hurriedly because she is trying to make sure that Tanesha is ok. Mrs. Loretta was supposed to sit with her Sorror's but instead of going over to where her line sisters were seated, she headed directly for where Ernest was sitting with his frat brothers. When she gets to her husband he is holding a red cup and his back is turned to her. Mrs. Loretta pokes him in the back and says "Baby, did Tanesha text you or call and say she made it?" Ernest goes from laughing to a pleasantly surprised smile and a half "Oh hey bay-" when he turned to notice his wife. Recognizing the look on her face he bends over to his shorter wife and plugs his ear with the hand not holding his cup to hear clearly what is being said to him.

Leaning in, Ernest asks "Say what bae?" Mrs. Loretta repeats herself and ask "Have you heard from Tanesha? She was supposed to call or text when she got here and I haven't heard from her, did she call you?" Ernest responds, "Nawl" as he is going into his pocket to retrieve his phone, he continues speaking. "Let me check though, its loud in here and I ain't checked my phone in a minute." Ernest presses the home button and only sees the missed call from his wife. "Nawl baby, I only got a missed call from you…" Mrs. Loretta face went from worry to concern and Ernest saw it. "I'm going over to her seat." Trying to calm his wife down he said to her, "Baby, she probably forgot, there is a lot going on today, SAT, the game, you know how it can be… You know that Tanesha has never been one to not call or text when she gets where she is going. Babe, in a few months she is going to be on her own, so we can't trip too tough. Look it's finna be half time, we can call her then. You know what, check her Snapchat or Instagram, I am sure she has already posted some pictures or made a story whatever they call it. Going over there would be embarrassing."

Mrs. Loretta saw his logic and says "You right… Let me check her pages…" She grabs her phone and pulls up Snapchat… nothing… She pulls up Instagram… Nothing. Mrs. Loretta's stomache starts to knot up with fear.

Mrs. Loretta follows Tanesha's best friend, Marie on Instagram she knows Marie would definitely have pics up from the game by now. Mrs. Loretta checks Maries' page... Marie already posted three new albums. Mrs. Loretta begins scrolling through them and what she is looking for is missing. She doesn't see Tanesha in any of the pictures.... "Oh my God Ernest! She isn't in any of the pics! Where is my baby! I'm going to kill this girl when I find her!" Mrs. Loretta says as she gets more revved up with worry. "Baby she is fine I'm sure. I'm tracking her location on my iPhone now."

The locator on Tanesha's phone picks up, it is at the BP gas station on Annapolis Road. Ernest turns towards Mrs. Loretta showing her the phone, "It looks like she is at the BP on Annapolis." Mrs. Loretta's face turns white with fear, "LET'S GO!!!" she yells while grabbing Ernest by the arm as she starts up the stairs. Ernest's line brother David, yells to them noticing the worried parents rushing up the stadium steps, "Everything cool?" Ernest halfway turned around and yelled back, "Tanesha is missing!" David barely hearing anything but Tanesha, rushes after them. David catches up to the quickly moving couple and ask the same question, "Everything cool?" to which Ernest responds "Don't know yet. Tanesha is missing." Mrs. Loretta remembers Ernest blindly following her to the car, he could tell by the panic that something wasn't right.

The three of them hopped in her Lexus LC500 and as the doors slammed, Mrs. Loretta explains, "I saw what I thought was her car at that BP and that's why I called you on my way over here. Now I know it was her car. Something is not right and we don't have a lot of time, I can feel it!" While she was talking, Mrs. Loretta was cautiously speeding out of the parking lot.

When they got to the gas station, Tanesha's car was in the same spot she saw it on her way to the game. The car may not have been fully in park before Mrs. Loretta hopped out of the car and used her second key fob to pop the lock on Tanesha's car. Ernest and David opened the doors on the car and everyone looks inside. Mrs. Loretta sees her phone in the armrest between the two front seats and notices that her car keys are still in the ignition. Mrs. Loretta knew that something wasn't right, there is no way Tanesha would have left her phone. Mrs. Loretta vividly remembers this moment because it was the first of the countless tears that have fallen from her eyes since Tanesha has gone missing. In a panic Mrs. Loretta announces her discoveries "Her phone is right here and her key is still in the ignition. This isn't like Tanesha! Oh, Jesus where is my baby!" Ernest jumps in right away. "Let's go inside and see if anyone saw something." Mrs. Loretta followed behind her husband as he rushed inside. David stayed with the car.

128

Ernest asked the store clerk, "Have you seen this girl?" while holding up the picture in his phone. No luck, the cashier who was a white male in his early twenties, had just started his shift. Looking at the phone and trying to recollect he replies, "I'm sorry sir, I just clocked in about 10 minutes ago..." When he looked up from the phone and saw the concern and fear in Ernest's eyes, the clerk went from dismissive to trying to be helpful and responded, "Hold on a second, I'll ask the person that is just getting off, he is still in the back."

A few moments passed before the clerk returned with his coworker. A tall Black male that looked to be about the same age as the white male clerk. Ernest showed him the picture and the black clerk said, "Yeah, she was in here about an hour ago..." He said with a puzzled look. "She bought a portable cellphone charger, two bags of hot chips and some gum... She had on a BSU hoodie that had SSS on the front... She walked out right before the car accident." Mrs. Loretta frantically asked, "Did you see where she went?... Why is her car still here?... Can we see the security camera?..." The young man is trying to respond and process all the questions at the same time so his response is, "She left out the... I'm not sure... Uhh... I'm sorry M'am I can't let you see the security camera..." And with those words began another nightmare in and of itself.

129

The Darkside of The 75,000

Mrs. Loretta is still stoicly laying in the bed, only now she is no longer reminiscing about that dreaded day that Tanesha went missing. Mrs. Loretta has come back to her grim reality and looks over at the empty space in the bed next to her. Every morning for the last 22 years prior to Tanesha's disappearance, she has awakened to her husband's beautiful face. Now that space is void, Ernest hasn't slept in the bed next to her in what feels like an eternity. In reality, it's been five months since her husband has warmed the sheets next to her. Tanesha's disappearance has put a tremendous strain on their marriage. The truth is they are both depressed and facing the realities of self-imposed guilt. Since the time of her disappearance they have played the blame game with each other, confided in one another, argued, fussed, played strong for their church, self-medicated with alcohol, stopped being intimate, soothed themselves with home videos of family moments and the list can go on. Every imaginable emotion has been experienced by the Stansils' and that is just within the walls of their own home.

Mrs. Loretta is still staring at the empty spot in their bed. Although she so badly wants to be held by him right now, she knows that Ernest is in the one place he can't seem to leave. Which ironically, is the one place she can't bring herself to go into, Tanesha's room. Being that going in there is not an option, Mrs. Loretta moves her eyes from where her rock would normally be, to now staring at the ceiling. Not really focusing on the ceiling as much as she is looking to the heavens, Mrs. Lorretta is trying to find the strength to keep going through all this madness. Her strength has been found in prayer. Mrs. Loretta's faith has been tested tremendously but she knows that Tanesha is still out there somewhere. She can feel it. Knowing that giving up is not an option, Mrs. Loretta says the serenity prayer and climbs herself out of bed to start her day.

The New Normal

Gone is the "Morning Success Routine" that was synonymous with her building her businesses. Now, her life is a constant hunt for Tanesha and holding the authorities accountable. Hunting for Tanesha has actually been the easy part, getting the proper attention and holding police and authorities accountable has been the real nightmare. The Black Lives Matter Movement was started around Black Men who have been shot at the hands of Police, which brought a lot of attention to the issue, unfortunately, there is no hashtag associated with the Missing Black Girls and Women of America. Just the occasional "Missing Person" post on Facebook or Instagram that we repost and keep going on to the next thing on our timeline. Well, those "Missing Persons" and Black Girls and Women, in particular, have families that unfortunately can't just scroll to the next story on their timeline. The timeline of their life is currently stuck on this story and they must fight with every fiber of their life to keep the possibility of bringing their loved ones home, a reality. And that is the fight that Mrs. Loretta is taking head-on with the same vigor (strength) that she developed to be a great mother, excellent wife and revered businesswoman.

Mrs. Loretta sits at the counter in the kitchen with four slices of toast in the toaster. She made two glasses of orange juice and waits for Ernest to make his way to the kitchen. Mrs. Loretta opens her phone and begins to make the posts she makes every morning on all social media platforms associated to the disappearance of Tanesha. Mrs. Loretta has created a group dedicated solely to bringing awareness to the 75,000 Missing Black Girls and Women, which includes daily updates and a timer for how long it has been that Tanesha has been missing. Mrs. Loretta knows that she must remain vigilant in order to prevent Tanesha from becoming just another cold case.

After a moment, Ernest comes into the kitchen and walks over to her and gives her a subtle kiss to her forehead. "Good morning love," he says with a heartbroken tone. Mrs. Loretta closes her eyes as he gives her the kiss and attempts to reconnect to the not so distant memories of when life was normal. With the obvious pain in her heart and on her face she gives him a slow, introspective "Hey babe", as she puts down her phone. "Same script today?" Ernest asks his wife, which implies if anything needs to be changed to the routine they have created to effectively search for Tanesha.

"Yes... let's hope we hear something back from the lawyer or the private investigator today." Mrs. Loretta is referring to the hope that they get to finally see the security camera footage. "I already prayed about that this morning... God's got us babe." Ernest says clinging on to hope. Mrs. Loretta finishes her orange juice before replying, "I know babe... I know she is still alive, I can feel it... I don't know what it is yet but I just know 'Nesha still out there..." Ernest walks over to her while she is talking to grab her hand and slowly rubs his thumb across the top of hers. Ernest looks at his wife and lifts her hand to give it a kiss and a reassuring "I know Babe." Ernest slowly lets her hand go and says, "Let's go bring Tanesha home..." The same phrase they have said every day since she disappeared.

Ernest grabs the stack of flyers that he passes out every day from 8 to 9 am at the gas station and along the fifteen-mile stretch of Annapolis Rd where Tanesha went missing. After passing out flyers Ernest goes to city hall five days a week to make sure that his district committee person and councilman are devoting time to Tanesha's disappearance. While the Stansil's are ever vigilant in their devotion to bringing Tanesha home, it is a fight on many levels. Here is how...

Blockade of Beauracracy

The Stansil's had no idea that they would have to go through lawyers and private investigators to get access to the security camera footage. Well, it's been nearly eight months and they still are navigating "store policy" and are yet to see what was caught on video. A fact that the Stansil's hopes will soon change. However, that's not the only fight the couple has on their hands as they try to bring Tanesha home. The systems in place that should be willing to help have tons of protocol that they must navigate, starting with the police.

Mrs. Loretta goes to the local police and sheriff's department to ask for updates, EVERY DAY. The Stansil's understand that "The Squeaky Wheel, Get's the Oil". If they let up, they feel that the detectives and police will get the impression that the family has given up hope. The Stansil's are correct in their assumption because police and city officials don't like bad press and must keep up the appearance that they are doing everything they possibly can to solve the case. So Mrs. Loretta is at the station every morning between 8:30 and 9:00 am to get an update and give the police anything that she has come across. This relentless approach has recently begun to pay dividends and things have become more cordial between the Stansil's and the police. Initially, it was very contentious as the police were dismissive and would not press the issue with the gas station to see the footage. Without the video, Tanesha's case is considered a missing persons case and not an abduction. If her case is considered an abduction the level of police involvement increases. Mrs. Loretta knows this and keeps pressing for the footage. The inability to immediately see the footage prevented authorities from issuing an Amber Alert, which cost the family valuable time and support in trying to find Tanesha. A piece of "Red Tape" that has prolonged their nightmare. Sadly this story is too often the case with missing Black females.

As typically the case with Black girls who are missing, Tanesha hasn't gotten much media coverage. The local news station ran a brief segment on Tanesha's disappearance the day after her abduction. However, despite daily calls, emails and Mrs. Loretta going to the TV station every Thursday at 4 pm to petition that they run another story on Tanesha for the nightly news, Mrs. Loretta is consistently rejected. Mrs. Loretta doesn't just stop at local media, she has reached out to CNN, Fox, and HLN (Headline News) to get some media attention focused on Tanesha's disappearance, nothing.

Understandably, Mrs. Loretta has a resentment towards the media which still gives the occasional story to Elizabeth Smart, Natalie Holloway and Joan Benet Ramsey, all famous cases that had a white girl at the center. Yet, despite her most valiant efforts Mrs. Loretta can't get any attention for her baby nor the other 75,000 Black Girls and Women who are missing. Naturally, a part of Mrs. Loretta feels that maybe Tanesha would have been found by now if she had gotten half the attention that has been given to cases that involve white females. The Stansil's are careful to guard themselves against that type of negative thinking. They remain empathetic because regardless of race, they know what the families of any missing person are enduring, the same nightmare that the Stansil's are living every second of every day.

Mrs. Loretta is on her way into the Police station when she gets a call from the Private Investigator. Seeing the number come up on the display console of her car via the Bluetooth connection, she says a little prayer to herself... "Lord let this be good news..." She hits the button and says "Hello" with a slight hint of hopeful suspense in her voice. The P.I. responds with a cheerful, "Good morning Mrs. Loretta..." The optimism in his voice allowed her to exhale, she knew that her family's prayers has been answered because they will be able to see the tape today. "Alright, I can tell by the tone of your voice that you got good news for me." "I do, you and your husband can head on over to the precinct. The tape is available for viewing" the private investigator says. "Thank you, Jesus! I truly appreciate all that you have done. The fight is not over but this is a big step... Thank you, thank you, thank you! Okay, let me call my husband! Thanks again." "No worries, I will be in touch soon." Mrs. Loretta lets out a "Thank You Jesus!" as she hears the disconnecting beep come from her speaker.

The police have had the tape since two months after the disappearance and although they have reviewed it, red tape and company policy have delayed the family from seeing the tape. Mrs. Loretta was ecstatic, her mind immediately shifted to calling her husband so he could meet her at the police station to view the tape.

Wasting no time, she immediately hits the button on her steering wheel, "Call Color of Love" through the Bluetooth audio in her car. Ernest is at the gas station passing out flyers when he hears his phone ring in his pocket. He reaches for his phone and sees it is his wife and while answering his phone, he gives a passer-by a flyer. As he answers the phone Mrs. Loretta hears, "... Find our daughter, she was last seen at this gas station. So if you can, hang on to this and if you see her can think of anything that can help us bring her home we would appreciate it... Thank you." Turning his attention to the call, he answers "Wsup Babe?... You hear anything from..." Interrupting him but not to be rude, purely out of excitement, Mrs. Loretta responds, "Babe we can view the tape, get over here as fast as you can! I'll see you when you get here okay?..." A sense of relief and optimism comes over Ernest who simply says, "God's got us Babe. We are going to bring her home!"

The Tape

By the time Ernest gets to the police station, Mrs. Loretta is already in a backroom sitting at a table with a small TV on a pushcart. The detective left the room to tend to some other obligations as Mrs. Loretta chose to wait until her husband arrived to watch the video with him. Ernest comes in the room and an anxious Mrs. Loretta gets halfway out of her seat to embrace her husband, they exchange a quick kiss as Ernest anxiously pulls up a chair. "Where's the detective?" Ernest asks curiously. "He stepped out... He will be right bac-..." Mrs. Loretta is cut off mid sentence by the detective that entered the room. "Good morning Mr. Stansil" the detective says as he pulls up a chair. "Okay, now what you all are about to watch is going to be very disturbing. Although you are not about to see your baby get murdered, I want to caution you to brace yourself, it will be hard to watch."

Now the detective is just doing his job, but that is the last thing Mrs. Loretta needed to hear. She was already squeezing Ernests' hand, but upon this news Mrs. Loretta nearly loses her composure as a tear swells up in the corner of her eye. She says a small quick prayer to reassure herself. The detective turns and hits play. Simultaneously, Ernest and Mrs. Loretta hold their breath. The TV comes on and Tanesha's Blue Nissan Versa pulls up and she gets out of the car. Tanesha walks swiftly into the store, where another camera picks her up. Tanesha goes directly to the check out counter and says something to the tall Black cashier. He nods and points toward the phone chargers. Tanesha appears to smile and nod before grabbing hot chips and getting in line. Tanesha goes into her back pocket and pulls out her money. The customer in front of her has finished her order and she places the two bags of chips on the counter. Tanesha points at the chargers As the cashier gets her a charger, Tanesha looks down at the gum on the checkout counter, grabs it and places it next to the chips. The cashier rings up her total and you see Tanesha hand over a single bill as a payment. The cashier takes the payment and returns her change. Tanesha smiles and mouths what her parents believe are the words "Thank you" as she takes her items and leaves the towards the exit.

The parking lot cam picks her up walking out towards her car. While she is walking, Tanesha reaches in her pocket and appears to notice that she doesn't have her keys. She walks over to her car and looked in. Her reaction appears to show she sees that she left her keys in the car. Tanesha is then seen reaching in her right back pocket for her phone and notices that she doesn't have it either. She looks back into the car and then slams her fist in disgust across the top of her car as if she realized that she left her phone inside also. Obviously frustrated from her body language, Tanesha looks around and spots a man getting out of his semi-truck. Tanesha begins to walk toward the man and it appears that she asked to borrow his phone to make a call because she stops about 10 feet from him and points back towards her car. The man gets back in his semi-truck and appears to hand her a phone. Tanesha hands it back quickly as if she asked him to unlock the phone. The man cracks an embarrassed smile before handing her the phone back.

Tanesha begins dialing on the phone when everyone in the video raises their heads simultaneously and look in the direction of Annapolis Rd. A few people run in the direction of the highway. Mrs. Loretta knows that the commotion everyone is looking at is the car accident that caused the traffic she was caught in on the way to the Homecoming game.

The video shows Tanesha walking maybe four or five steps in the direction to get a bit of a better view of the accident. What happens next is the moment that the detective tried to prepare them for...

The man who gave Tanesha the cell phone can be seen going back to the trailer portion of his truck quickly opening it up and walks up behind an unsuspecting Tanesha and grabs her around by the mouth and violently snatching her towards the opened trailer. Mrs. Loretta lets out a small scream as she covers her mouth in shock of what she is watching. At the same time, Ernest balls up both of his fists and grits his teeth in frustration. Ernest feels emasculated by virtue of him being powerless as he watches his daughter whom he is supposed to protect being kidnapped. The two keep watching as, Tanesha drops the phone because she was completely taken by surprise and the force he grabs her with. Tanesha flails her arms and legs attempting to free herself from the abductor. The man drags Tanesha to the back of the truck and throws her inside the trailer and quickly slams the door shut. The man picks up the cell phone Tanesha dropped and quickly gets back into the cab of the semi-truck and pulls off. By Gods' grace, the license plate is captured on the surveillance camera.

The detective cuts off the tape, turns toward the Stansil's and notices both of them crying. He slides a box of tissue between them before saying, "I know this is hard to watch but let me tell you the good news... Those plates have been traced to a trucking company out of Sandusky, Ohio. We are working with authorities in Ohio to track that truck down and who would have been driving it on this particular day." The Stansil's were obviously devastated by what they saw and being that they were in a state of shock they really didn't hear too much else that was said by the detective. They got a copy of the camera footage to give to the private detective. Most importantly, the tape moves Tanesha's case from missing person to kidnapping. The victory that the Stansil's were hoping for the entire time.

Ernest and Mrs. Loretta walked out of the police station holding hands and trying their best to keep their composure as they left the station. As they entered the parking lot, Ernest tries to break the painful silence, "Babe I --" Mrs. Loretta cuts him off by simply raising her hand in a gesture Ernest understands as she doesn't want to talk about it right now. Mrs. Loretta shakes her head as she says "Babe just follow me home..."

After a 20 minute drive the two open the door to their house where Mrs. Loretta buckles in the doorway. She had been holding it in the best she could but seeing that video took her to a whole new level. Mrs. Loretta is crying uncontrollably. Ernest manages to get the door closed and just holds his wife. Of course, every possibility of what could have happened to

Tanesha had already ran through her mind. However, seeing her baby physically attacked is an image that will live with her forever. Mrs. Loretta needed to see the tape but now that she has, she wishes she had not seen it. Visually seeing Tanesha abducted has allowed the one thing she has blocked from her mind to enter it... Tanesha could be dead.

Mrs. Loretta is not ready to accept that fact but now she is entertaining the possibility because of what she saw on the videotape. This was the moment that the bottom had fallen out for her. When we feel we are at our lowest point is when God is closest to us. Amidst the pain Mrs. Loretta heard the words of her Pastor Royce Thompson as she sat on the floor crying asking herself, "How am I going to make it through?" Pastor Thompson had preached that you are "in between" and although you are no longer in your comfort zone, don't worry because "God will..." Pastor Thompson's words rang true and clear... In these moments of darkness and despair, God will... Get You Up, when you feel you can't stand... God will... Get you through when you feel you can't go any further... God will." Mrs. Loretta found strength in the only thing that can restore anyone who life seems to be getting the best of, her faith in the Lord. She reminds herself that nothing happens to us, for if you believe in the Lord, you know that everything happens for us.

136

Empathy and Advocacy

Mrs. Loretta sits with her legs crossed at the ankles and safely tucked under her seat. She is wearing blue jeans and a black blouse neatly peeking out from under her black leather coat. Mrs. Loretta is in a place she never imagined she would be, a grief counseling group session. Ernest sits closely to her right with his left hand supportively resting on her right thigh. It's been nearly three months since they have seen "The Tape" and Mrs. Loretta is in a daze as another group member is passionately sharing about her daughter who will have been missing a painful four years this coming January. Mrs. Loretta has been a vibrant addition to the group since they joined six weeks ago. Tonight, however she isn't her customary (usual) upbeat self.

Searching for a moment of clarity, Mrs. Loretta is trying to figure out how she got to this place in her life. Being a parent in general and of a girl in particular, Mrs. Loretta thought that the extent of what she was going to have to guard her child against during her high school years, was immature boys who only want one thing. Or mischievous friends who would try to encourage her to drink, smoke or break curfew. Oh, how she wishes that was the case. Instead, Tanesha is now a part of a group no parent wants their child to be a part of, one of the missing people in America.

Although the stories from the other members of the group are heart-wrenching, Mrs. Loretta finds peace among the group. In the eleven months since Tanesha has gone missing, the Stansil's have gone from respected members of the community to being viewed as a charity case. At times it feels as if they are a bit of a circus attraction. Wherever they go, either individually or as a couple, it seems that people tend to stare, point or whisper. Mrs. Loretta knows that people have good intentions and want Tanesha to return safely, which is why she never loses her cool. The misery of what has happened and the thoughts of what Tanesha could be enduring is more than enough of a mental struggle. However, when you couple that mental anguish with people either being unusually nice to them or awkward interactions because they don't know if they should bring Tanesha up, Mrs. Loretta feels like a fish out of water every time she goes into the community. For two hours every Wednesday night, Mrs. Loretta can feel understood by someone other than Ernest. So as her turn comes around to share, Mrs. Loretta's thoughts are a bit clouded as she begins to speak:

"Good evening everyone. Tanesha has been gone eleven months now and the pain doesn't go away as you all know. Being a member of this group for over a month now has really helped me and my husband deal with this reality. Initially, we thought that coming to a group like this was for people who had given up hope. Well, that very first meeting we came to, my husband and I quickly realized that this is so much more. I want to thank each and every one of you all for being so supportive and honest with your stories. Your honesty and openness have helped us so much on ways to deal with Tanesha being abducted. Please don't call me selfish but I am convinced that being a Black Missing Woman or Girl, is the worst thing in America. My heart goes out to all the parents who had their baby's lives taken at the hands of police or racist. My husband and I have attended rallies and marches going back over 20 years when James Byrd was murdered in Texas. We went down to support the Jena 6, in Louisiana, so we know first hand how crooked this system can be. However, those families had the chance at closure, they know what happened to their baby, I truly empathize with their pain. But I am sorry, it feels like no one cares about the steadily growing number of Black Girls and Women Missing in America. They don't get the media attention, they don't get the…"

Mrs. Loretta is overcome by emotion and stops as she becomes choked up, her husband wraps his arm around her and pulls her close as a tear begins to make its way down the right side of his face. Mrs. Loretta quickly regains her emotions and finishes with, "I just want to thank y'all… I truly do… I don't mean to be selfish with how I feel and I know some of you are missing a son. And you may feel the same way about how hard it is trying to get the attention for him, I want to acknowledge that. I do…

However, 75,000 black girls and women are missing in America... we HAVE TO DO SOMETHING ABOUT THIS... The Nation of Islam has a saying 'A Nation Can Rise No Higher Than Its Women' so what does that say about us as Black People if we don't even talk about or acknowledge our beautiful Women and Girls that are missing... I'm sorry but there isn't any hashtags like Black Lives Matter or MeToo for us... When a Black Female goes missing, they become invisible and I am tired of it because my Tanesha is not invisible. Every day, EVERY DAY. I show my face at that police station. Every day, my husband passes out flyers along the fifteen-mile radius where Tanesha was abducted. I have been to every TV station, every radio station, I have created a social media account on every platform devoted to bringing not just my baby home, but all these beautiful Black girls who have gone missing while the world seems to turn a blind eye. Something has gotta change, we can't keep scrolling, we can't keep swiping, we have to start speaking up, we have to start speaking out. We have to create some type of technology that tracks hot spots of where all our babies are being taken from. We have to be proactive if we are going to not only bring our babies home but also make sure no more babies get taken. Our girls are the future mothers of the next generation. We must protect them and treat them like the precious jewels that they are. Black girls and women are not invisible. They exist. Tanesha exists, she is out there, she is alive, I know it, I FEEL IT, I FEEL MY BABY IS OUT THERE, FIGHTING..." Mrs. Loretta again is overcome with emotions, she takes a deep breath and says, "Thank you all for letting me share." The room is silent but every eye in the room has shed tears during her passionate input. Mrs. Loretta takes her seat and Ernest leans in to give her a supportive kiss on the cheek. The group facilitator thanks her for her honesty as she hands her a box of tissue. The meeting continues and Mrs. Loretta quietly slips back into her daze searching for answers as to how she got to this point. Seated amongst what feels like the only people in the world aside from her husband that knows what she is going through, Mrs. Loretta knows what must happen next. She has to go into Tanesha's room, something is telling her the answer she has been searching for is inside.

Breakthroughs Part 1:

Mrs. Loretta stands at the door of what may as well had a force field around it for the last 11 ½ months, Tanesha's bedroom. Her husband has barely stayed out of it and has kept it up since Tanesha's disappearance. Being in the room for him has kept Tanesha close to his spirit. Mrs. Loretta, on the other hand, has felt in order to bring Tanesha home, she must remain focused on the details of the case.

In her mind, reminiscing is an acknowledgment of times that are gone forever, Tanesha is coming home so why go in her room to reminisce?

Upon walking in she sees a portrait of Dr. Anne - Marie Imafidon and under her picture the word Vision. Dr. Imafidon is one of Tanesha's SHEroe's and a world leader in Math and Computer Sciences. Dr. Imafidon is leading a global charge to get more women into the STEM (Science Technology Engineering and Mathematics). Dr. Imafidon is a big reason that Tanesha is interested in Bioinformatics. A smile comes over Mrs. Loretta's face as she thinks about how much Tanesha would talk about Dr. Imafidon. Mrs. Loretta can hear Tanesha go on about how she is going to meet her one day and even work on a project together. Mrs. Loretta knew that having goals and people to inspire you would be a huge part of raising Tanesha to be the young women she always imagined her daughter to be. That is why portraits of Michelle Obama with the word Class and Beyonce' with the word Swag adorn the other two walls.

While the pictures serve as a reminder of the determination and mindset that Tanesha brought to the world, Mrs. Loretta's eyes drift down to the dresser and right next to the 42-inch flat-screen is a diary. Mrs. Loretta slowly walks over to the diary and picks it up. She notices the diary is opened to the page dated October 12, 2018. The day before she was abducted, Mrs. Loretta begins to read the diary entry...

Dear Diary,

Today was a good day and I am sorry I am not going to give you a recap because I am super excited about tomorrow! My life is never going to be the same after tomorrow. I can't wait to slay this SAT in the morning! I am shooting for a perfect score but I told everyone 1560. Either way, I am ready for it and I am more excited about that then the rest of the day. I know Homecoming gone be lit! Especially after Bey slayed Coachella, I can't wait to see what the bands going to do at half-time! I should be there just in time coming up from the SAT.

When I get this perfect on the SAT I am going to be set... A perfect score on the SAT will help my resume when I apply for the Doctoral program at Oxford where I am going to meet Dr. Imafidon! My Grandma Barbara Jean would always tell us if you claim it, it's yours! Well, diary I am cutting our night short because I need some rest because I got to Rise and Grind like my father always says! Whatever happens tomorrow, I am going to always remember the words of my true hero... Mama, she always tells me that God requires us to do our best and prepare beyond what is expected. Since we pray for his will to be done, nothing happens to us everything happens for us... So whatever happens tomorrow, I know that it is going to happen for God's Glory!

Good Night

139

Mrs. Loretta wipes the obvious tears from her eyes. Although the prophecy of Tanesha's words were emotional, it was Mrs. Loretta's own words that resonated from what she just read. Nothing happens to us, it happens for us... Mrs. Loretta knows that this is a message from God to respond to a calling. She feels that God has chosen her to experience this horrifying ordeal because she is fortunate enough financially to forge the fight in this fashion. Her mission is to put these 75,000 missing women at the forefront of the minds of America in general and the Black Community in particular. Mrs. Loretta falls to her knees and praises God for this moment and this tragedy. She wails into tears but is releasing her will and submitting to God's will... Mrs. Loretta is thankful that she has a God-fearing child that He has used as the instrument to reveal to Mrs. Loretta her greater purpose in life. Mrs. Loretta is reminded of the words of Tanesha's Godmother, Mary Davis. Mary always tells her that obedience is the key to unlocking your blessings. Mrs. Loretta had avoided going into Tanesha's room because she feared the emotions that she would feel. However, when she let go of her pride, she was able to find what she was searching for throughout this whole ordeal. Mrs. Loretta has been called to advocacy for the 75,000 families who have been muted, simply because the are looking for a Missing Black Female. Mrs. Loretta had her breakthrough...

140

Breakthroughs Part 2

Tanesha is sitting on the floor tied to a beam in a dirty basement. She is bound by a chain that is around her left ankle. Tanesha has been secretly chipping away at one of the links every day for the last 4 months. At any moment she is going to break the link and be one step closer to the freedom she so strongly desires. Tanesha has been counting the days via the sunlight that has hit the basement. Tanesha has been in this basement for seven months. In the first four months of her abduction she was shipped around from place to place for three to four days at a time. Eventually, she wound up in this basement and hasn't moved since.

Tanesha knows that she has to have a sense of urgency because when she first got down in the basement it was eight other girls in the basement. One by one the girls have been taken out over the last two months. Of the nine females who have been in the basement, which includes her, only three girls remain. The others have yet to be replaced and Tanesha knows that at any moment one of the other two girls who were there when she arrived is going to be taken out. The girls and women have all formed a bond of sorts, sharing each other's names and where they are from, in hopes that if any of them get free they can spread the word that the others are missing and not dead. One of the young ladies, Vickie has been rather quiet the whole time. Unlike the other ladies who have been held captive, Vickie doesn't seem very enthusiastic about escaping. She rarely if ever talks about being free and has never mentioned any family that she is eager to see. Vickie appears to be older than Tanesha but not by much. However, when Tanesha looks into her eyes she knows that whatever Vickie has been through has "aged" her more than the brief 20 plus years she has lived on earth. Vickie doesn't express it but you Tanesha can feel the painfilled energy Vickie exudes.

It's night and Tanesha knows it from the light that creeps in from the cinderblock basement window. The light has been gone for about three hours when Tanesha feels it. The chain has broken and finally, her ankle is free. She knows that in a few hours her ordeal is coming to an end. As she has done every day and night since the moment she has been abducted, Tanesha says a prayer to God. Tanesha has asked repeatedly that God puts on the armor of God over her. Recounting the scripture found in Ephesians 6:10 -18 Tanesha ask God to put on; The shoes of peace, the belt of truth, the breastplate of righteousness, a shield of faith, the helmet of salvation and the sword of the spirit. Tanesha knows that this battle is for God's glory and he is going to give her the strength she needs to break free. Tanesha has been very careful to not tell any of the other women that she has been trying to cut herself free. She simply didn't trust anyone enough to jeopardize her chance to reunite with her parents and get back to living her life.

Keenly aware that she has to make her move while she has the chance, Tanesha waits a few hours after the other two girls were asleep and she begins to carry out her plot. Tanesha looks around the basement to go over in her mind one last time what she has been planning since the moment she woke up down here. The basement has nothing in it but an unfinished bathroom, a deep freezer, a microwave, a water cooler and a metal cabinet that blocks the door that leads outside of the house. The unfinished bathroom is a sink and shower head with a floor drain under it. The women shower twice a week at gunpoint unless they are menstruating and they get an extra shower that week. The water cooler and microwave are next to the metal cabinet that has the primary purpose of holding their hygiene products, which are only tampons, spray deodorant, soap, and shampoo.

The women are being held captive by a slender white male that appears to be a trucker. He has long stringy dirty brown hair and an overgrown mustache. He is a chain smoker that makes no conversation or interactions that would indicate he has a human side. Tanesha has a long-held feeling due to the methodical nature of the kidnapping, she is in a cog of a human trafficking ring. Tanesha has been paying very close attention

141

to his every move and has devised a plan that she will be putting in action in the next few hours. The freezer is next to the stairs and on top of it is where he keeps his lighter. The lighter is for the cigarette he lights up every morning while making their "breakfast." Breakfast every morning is always two packets of fruit-flavored oatmeal.

With the scene scoped out, Tanesha slowly gets up and grabs the lighter and slips it into her pocket. Next, she goes over to the cabinet and grabs a bottle of spray deodorant. Tanesha puts the spray bottle back behind the pole that she was tied to, then creeps back to the cabinet and grabs some shampoo and walks over to the stairs. While Tanesha is screwing off the top of the shampoo bottle she hears a whisper... "What are you doing?" Tanesha could have sworn the other two women were sleeping so she frighteningly turns around to see where the voice came from. Something tells her to look in the direction of Vickie who is sitting up. Tanesha is frozen and the same question is asked in an even lower whisper, "What are you doing?" Tanesha slowly walks in Vickie's direction and says... "I am getting out of here... when he comes down I am going to -" "Shhhh," Vickie says in a hushed whisper. "Come here!" she motions to Tanesha, who comes next to her and takes a seat.

142

Hidden Figures...

Vickie opens up to Tanesha; "You know, I wish I was you... I mean... I wish I had your life... I been listening to you talk. You going places, you gonna do big things... I know it... Honestly, when you first came down here, something told me you were going to be the one who got us out... That's why I don't really say much... When you came, I don't know why but I felt like hope came... But for me, that also meant that reality was coming along with it... I remember seeing on my timeline that it was 64 thousand Black women missing in America. Something told me to click on it, so I did. The article said that it's another 11 thousand Black girls who can be added to that number because they are considered runaways. That's 75 thousand of us Tanesha. I'm one of the 11 thousand... But Tanesha, ain't nobody looking for me... Ain't nobody looking for me because ain't nobody ever wanted me... If I get out of here, I don't have no place to go. I ain't got no family that will be waiting on me... I never knew my daddy, which sadly ain't no surprise. My mom been in and out of jail since I was 2 or 3... My granny died before I was born so I lived with my granddaddy and he is the devil..."

Tanesha turns and looks with a puzzled face. Vickie senses the change in Tanesha when she says this, yet Vickie keeps looking forward and reaffirms her statement. "Yes... he is the Devil... I was about 7 or 8 years old when he started pimping me out to some of his nasty old friends every time he lost one of the poker games he would have at our house, he would use me to pay off his debts." Tanesha drops her head after hearing Vickie's heartbreaking truth. Careful not to interrupt she keeps listening as Vickie continues.

"I was 10 years old when my 3rd-grade teacher began to get worried that my breath was smelling too bad. All the kids were picking on me for it... Well, that and the fact that this was the 2nd time I was in 3rd grade... Ms. Edmon, she really loved me... She asked my granddad if it was ok if she could pick me up for school one day and of course he was too drunk to even understand what was going on... So he agreed and she came by the house and saw the kind of dump I was living in... But that isn't why she reported him, nope... When we got to school that morning before all the other kids arrived, she took me in the bathroom and pulled out a brand new toothbrush and toothpaste. She pulled her toothbrush out and started brushing her teeth and showing me the correct way to brush mine. When it was my turn, I opened my mouth to start brushing like she just showed me. Ms. Edmon stopped me and asked me to open wide, she began to look in my mouth and I will never forget her eyes coming into focus on one of the sores inside my mouth and her eyes filling with tears... She grabbed her phone and I guess she googled something. The next thing I know was that I was in the nurse's office answering questions and she was looking in my mouth... From there was a nice lady that came in wearing some fancy clothes. I remember the nurse saying something about Oral Gonorrhea, then the nice lady taking me to get ice cream and then to my house to get my stuff... She told me that I wasn't going to be living there anymore. And I probably wasn't going to be seeing my granddad for a while. I figured whatever I said to the nurse when she was asking me questions had something to do with why I wasn't going to see my Granddad again but I didn't care. I hated what he was making me do to those men..." Vickie is still pouring out her heart.

"From there, it was the group homes and having to learn how to fight because the girls didn't like me or jumped on me over some boy that I didn't even like... This went on for about four years living in foster and group homes. Until I was around 15 when my mama finally got out of jail and said she wanted me to move in... She wanted me to move in alright... So she can use me... The first thing she did was make me get a job because she couldn't really get one because of her record. I was working at Popeyes Chicken as a 15-year-old who barely completed 8th grade and my mom was taking my money and shooting dope into her foot with her little 'dusty' boyfriend... I would have to hide my money in a water bottle when I was at home. She would go through my things and take my debit card, I hated

143

living there. I stayed with her for about three years. One night right before my 19th birthday my mom's little junkie boyfriend's brother was in my room when I got out of the shower. He was laying on my bed when I came back in the room. Now, I had ignored all the drugs and my mama and her boyfriend fighting... My Mama turning tricks in the room with random men so they could cop some drugs... I ignored it because I just wanted a place to lay my head at night and not have to worry about being back in a home or all the crazy mess I had lived through... But I was not finna go back to doing stuff to nobody. I refused to go back to doing that... So when I told my Mama that her boyfriends' brother needs to get out of my room, she had the nerve to say to me... 'Vickie, he just wanna talk'... I knew what that meant... She had me messed up... I went to the kitchen grabbed the 9mm out of the drawer and pointed it straight in his face... I told him to get out of my room... I got dressed, grabbed my things and left the house... I didn't look back... I lived with friends on their couches for a few nights at a time and when I got my last check. I got in my car and said I was going to LA... Well, I was until I caught a flat on the side of the road and a trucker came to help me out... So I thought... I ended up here... At first, I thought about leaving and trying to escape and all that but... but... where would I go? No one is going to be so happy to see me if I get out of here... When I think about all the stuff that happened to me, I feel like whatever happens next may be better than what has already happened... Tanesha... I just want to die to be honest with you... I just want God to take me out of this nightmare that I can't seem to wake up from..."

Tanesha has tears streaming down her cheek when she looks over to Vickie and says, "I know that this may not mean anything to you, but my Mother always tells me that everything that you go through is for God's glory... So nothing happens to us... It happens for us... We have to find the reason God allows us to experience what we endure. His word promises that we will never be given more than we can bear... Vickie, from what you just told me... God thinks really highly of you because you are still here... Every day we wake up we have two things, a chance, and a choice. Vickie I'm getting out of here and when I do, I'm coming back for you okay?" Vickie just nods her head. Tanesha, leans over and gives Vickie a hug. Tanesha does so without really thinking, it was an honest natural reaction she intuitively picked up from her mother. Mrs. Loretta would always give her a hug whenever she would express how she was feeling so she figured this is what Vickie needed. It was, Vickie is overcome with a sense of relief and exhales while shedding tears as Tanesha holds her... Vickie has finally had her Breakthrough...

The Escape

Tanesha switches back to the task at hand which is to get free, so she picks up the shampoo bottle and continues dousing the last three steps on the staircase with it. Every morning whoever this guy is that is holding them captive opens the door and never closes it behind him. He comes down to the very last step before hitting the light switch. He puts out the cigarette he was smoking, grabs another one from his pocket. Next, he goes to the freezer to grab his lighter. He lights the cigarette and makes their breakfast. One by one he unties them and allows them to go to use the bathroom at gunpoint, before tying them back up and giving them their morning oatmeal. The routine is clockwork, the same thing no matter what. Well, being that Tanesha is so good in Math, she has everything calculated. Another two hours past before she hears the door open. Tanesha says a quick prayer for strength because she knows it's go time!

Tanesha is sitting in the position she would normally be in when he comes down the steps. Tanesha knows that it is twelve steps on the staircase and she should hear a slip on the 10th step. She is counting the creaks in each stair like she has done each day for the last 2 months in her mind as she prepares for this one shot at freedom. Tanesha's heart is racing as she counts silently in her head as she hears each creak... domp 5... domp 6... domp 7... domp 8... domp 9... Everything stops... her ears go silent the world around her pauses, she looks out and her eyes come into focus as his foot slowly goes to the 10th step that is filled with shampoo... In an instant, she has a vision of her mother running toward her crying tears of joy to hug and hold her. She sees an image of her Dad fall to his knees overwhelmed by the fact that their prayers have been answered...

Tanesha quickly snaps out of her peaceful premonition. With the moment at hand Tanesha gets a rush of confidence because she knows this is it. His foot hits the 10th step and just as she anticipates, he loses his balance, but instead of falling back like she thought he would have, he slips forward unto the 11th step with the same foot, when he goes to put his other foot down, he falls back! Blooooowhhh! By this time, Tanesha is up and on him with the spray deodorant and the lighter! Tanesha's make-shift blowtorch has set him on fire! Tanesha is burning him in the face, neck and chest area. The cigarettes in his pocket have caught on fire and so does his shirt! Once Tanesha notices the package of cigarettes ignite she runs up the stairs and out the door that he never closes that leads to the basement. Tanesha looks to her left and sees what appears to be the front door, she runs as fast as she could to it and gets it open. She runs onto the porch and jumps from the top of it past the 3 small steps. Tanesha is barefoot, wearing the same jeans and undershirt she had on since she was abducted. She runs out of the front yard and into the street as fast as she can. Tanesha is screaming to the top of her lungs, "HELP! HELP! HELP! I'VE BEEN ABDUCTED PLEASE LET ME SEE THE PHONE!!! I NEED A PHONE!!!" Tanesha sees what appears to be a convenience store as she gets to the next block. Tanesha runs in the store still screaming.

The obviously startled female store clerk tries to calm her down. A black male who appears to be in his late 30's was pumping gas as Tanesha ran in screaming, followed her inside the store. He yells to Tanesha, "Miss are you okay, WHAT'S GOING ON?!!!" Tanesha turns to him and asks, "CAN, I SEE YOUR PHONE PLEASE!!!" The guy doesn't respond he just unlocks his phone and hands it to her, because he can tell something is not right... Tanesha grabs the phone and dials the number that she remembered being taught as a little girl, the number to her home... 555 - 938-3874

Answering God's Call

Mrs. Loretta is brushing her teeth when she hears the house phone ring. Ernest at the dresser getting an undershirt out when he looks up at the phone and sees an Ohio area code come across the caller ID. He pauses and looks back in the direction of the bathroom and Mrs. Loretta by this time has made it to the door because they both know that something isn't right. They don't even give out their house phone number anymore and it rarely rings, if ever. So when their eyes meet, they are simultaneously thinking the same thing, could this be? Ernest rushes over to the receiver, answers the phone and gives a puzzled, "Hello..." What he hears coming from the other end of the phone was the answer to so many prayers, "Daddy!" Ernest falls to his knees in disbelief. Mrs. Loretta is stunned and can only think of the Worship Notes that her childhood friend Mikaya had sent her which she had just read as a part of her morning Bible reading which was Romans 4:20 - 21 which reads "Abraham never wavered in believing God's promise. In fact, his faith grew stronger, and in this, he brought glory to God. (21) He was fully convinced that God is able to do whatever he promises."

Mrs. Loretta's nightmare was over. A settling peace came over her because she knew it would only be a matter of hours at the most before she saw her baby... But more importantly, Mrs. Loretta knew this moment would eventually come because she knows that obedience is the key to unlocking your blessings. Mrs. Loretta had accepted her calling to become the voice of the other 75,000 Missing Black Women and Girls In America. God selected the Stansils' and now that Mrs. Loretta had accepted her calling her life had taken an unsuspecting turn with a newfound purpose.

Tanesha's abduction was a part of a bigger plan at work which gave a new meaning to Mrs. Loretta's long held belief that nothing happens to you, everything happens for you...

147

If you have any information that could lead to the safe
return or help in any fashion for someone you know or
may have seen who is missing
please contact

The Black and Missing Foundation
by phhone
@
1-877-972-2634
or online
@
www.BAMFI.org

You can also report information to the
National Center for Missing & Exploited Children
@
800-843-5678
(800-THE-LOST)

148

If you have any information that could lead to the safe
return or help in any fashion for someone you know or
may have seen who is missing
please contact

Forgotten Children Inc.

(800) 445 - 1326

4401 Atlantic Ave. Suite 200

Long Beach, CA 90807

www.forgottenchildreninc.org

149

Section 4:

Butterflies

The life cycle of a Butterfly represents the
transformative powers that lies within all
humans.

When A Butterfly is born (caterpillar)
it immediately begins
to eat (take in) the leaf (the environment)
that it was born on (into).

After the Butterfly (caterpillar) has had
enough of the life that it has been given,
the Butterfly (caterpillar) creates a cocoon
(draws within to protect itself from the outside)
and finally reemerges.

While in the cocoon the Butterfly internalizes
the life it had roaming the earth in its lower self
(caterpilar) yet it reemerges fully equipped with wings
and fully capable of Flying to Heights
Unimagined prior to its Transformation...

In This Section You Will Meet
Three "Butterflies" Who Represent The Ability To
Transform Ourselves Into The Person We Are
Destined To Be...

I Am A Queen
An Original Poem & Drawing by
Janiyah Browning
Age: 11

Chapter 7
Baby Girl

"In Order to Be A Man, You Must See A Man." This saying was echoed repeatedly in my house when I was growing up. Being that this saying implicates that people learn by example, I would often wonder what happens when a girl doesn't see a man?

Allow me to pose the question to you, what are the effects of an absent or emotionally detached Father on his daughter? Much has been made and rightfully so about how males who grow up without a Fatherly figure manifest into emotionally damaged and detached men who have problems establishing and maintaining relationships.

However, what is lost in this is that we often make the assumption that since girls have their Mothers they will be alright. This chapter challenges that notion as well as highlights how some of the behaviors we see in young ladies today are simply the remnants of fractured relationships between Fathers and their Baby Girls...

Please allow me to introduce to you Kenyatta aka KeKe.

Kenyatta has a rocky relationship with her Dad. Don't get me wrong, she loves him to death, however he feels it is okay to hop in and out of her life when it is convenient for him.

A decision that left Kenyatta no other choice but to create KeKe, who protects Kenyatta whenever she is "In her Feelings."

152

Kenyatta lays in the bed staring at the ceiling with the sheet up to her chest. She feels dirty as she is trying to wrap her mind around her actions of just moments ago. No matter how hard she tries, Kenyatta can not explain why she keeps finding herself in this situation. Although the situation is one she is in total control of, Kenyatta tends to become extremely vulnerable when she begins to think about her Dad. Sorry for the letdown but there is no tragic event that I am going to tell you about that took him away from her. Her father simply made the all too familiar choice to not be involved in her life. For arguments sake, abandonment can be considered tragic in terms of the emotional wreck it created inside of Kenyatta and all the other boys and girls like her who live daily with the emptiness that it creates. To deal with the pain, Kenyatta created KeKe. A hardened version of herself who has one job, to protect Kenyatta whenever she is "in her feelings."

Kenyatta ignores the arm that has been placed over her waist area and continues staring emotionlessly at the ceiling for what seems like the millionth time that she has tried self-therapy. Whether it is the unconnected emotionless activities she just partook in or the sleepless yet tearful nights alone in her room, KeKe plays the role of doctor when Kenyatta is the patient looking for a prescription when her life lacks answers. Kenyatta is searching to fill that empty void that her Dad left when he distanced himself from her. Emotionally, allowing KeKe to act recklessly on her behalf is not working for Kenyatta either. She is yet to find the remedy because she is looking for things outside of herself to fill an empty void inside of her heart.

Kenyatta is still gazing at the ceiling trying to make sense of her life when the soul searching turns into a full-on emotional flashback to one of the more painful memories from her childhood. The moment Kenyatta began to realize that her Dad didn't mean it when he said, "I'll always be there for you Baby Girl…"

The ceiling fades away from her sight and the infamous day begins to replay itself vividly in her mind's eye. Kenyatta's flashback begins almost 6 years ago about 1 week after her 5th-grade graduation…

High Hopes Come Crashing Down

"Ma! Which shirt should I wear? I know I am going to wear my True Religion Jeans but which shirt should I wear? This green one? Or this blue one that I got for graduation? Ma?!! Wake up… which one should I wear? Ma wake up?" Kenyatta remembers being so excited that morning trying to wake her mother up.

"Little girl… If you don't stop screaming… It's too early for all this…

Hand me my phone off the charger so I can see what time it is..." "Here you go Ma..." an 11-year-old KeKe hands Katrina, her mother the phone. She looks at the phone. "Girl! Bye! Bye get out of my room... KeKe it is 7:42 in the morning you know I just got off work a few hours ago... I know you are excited to spend the day with your Daddy, but girl he won't be here until 4 o'clock to come get you... That's a whole 8 hours... Go watch Ant Farm or something... Let me get some more sleep... When I get up, I am going to do your hair and I am going to help you pick out an outfit... Right now, let Mama sleep okay... I know you can't wait to spend the day with your Daddy... But let me get some rest okay..."

"Okay, Ma... I love you, I'm gone make me some cereal, you want some?" "Nawl baby thank you, let me sleep okay... Your G Ma left yet?" "No, she finna leave though... She putting on her hair and makeup..." "Aight, well let me get a little more sleep baby then I will get up and get you together okay..." "Thanks, Ma..." "KeKe... if your Daddy don't come, then we going to do something special tomorrow because I'm off. Okay?" "Ma, he coming because he promised me he was coming at the Graduation" "Yeah baby... I know, I am just saying... nothing, nothing... I'm tired. Okay let me sleep and when I get up we going to get you ready okay?" "Okay... You want your door closed or can I leave it open?" "Leave it open because you said GMa bout to leave." "Okay"

"KeKe, grab my phone right there and call Safi for me... Put it on speaker" After two rings a voice comes from the phone, "Wsup Girl... What you doing?" "I'm ova here flat ironing KeKe hair.... Girl, this child been up since about 5 this morning all excited to go with her Daddy... Came in my room at bout a quarter to 8 trying to get me to help her pick out her outfit... I told this child, girl bye! You got all kinds of time before he gets here... Anyway, girl what you Amiyah and Steven got up for today? I see y'all 'Doing it big' on vacation!" "I know right! Girl, we are gone be back in back in this water today more than likely... It is soooo beautiful! We going to this nice restaurant for dinner... Other than that, nothing much... Just relaxing and enjoying this beautiful painting God made..." "Well okay, girl... y'all enjoy tell Miyah and Steven I love them and I'll call you later to tell you how KeKe's day went with her Daddy..." "Okay girl, love you!" As the phone beeped off, KeKe remembers the hopes began flying from her mouth.

"Ma, when my Daddy gets back from taking me out today he going to ask you to marry him and we going to be a family." (Katrina rolls her eyes as she continues to do KeKe's hair, she bites her tongue not trying to destroy the hope in her baby's spirit.) "We gone take vacations like Auntie Safi and nem.' I can't wait, it's gone be so much fun. And we gone move outta GMa house and get our own house and then..." "Girl calm yo self down... Now where you getting all this he going to ask me to marry him stuff from? Did he tell you that when you talked to him yesterday?"

"No... he said Baby Girl, you can have anything that you want... anything. All I have to do is ask him for it and he is going to give it to me. After we go get something to eat, he going to take me to get some summer clothes. But I don't want any clothes, I mean I do, but when he said he going to give me anything I want, I stopped thinking about the clothes... I got enough clothes, but I don't got my Daddy. I want my Daddy more than anything... So after we done eating I am going to tell him what I really want... You two, to get married, so you can be happy sometimes Ma... and I can be Daddy's Baby Girl every day, not just sometimes... So that's why I couldn't sleep and I been up because today I am going to get my Daddy forever and make you happy again Ma... Today is special..."

(What Kenyatta didn't see was that Katrina's tears had created a nice little wet spot on her shirt. Katrina wept as she tried to decide if she even have the courage to burst her baby's bubble. A major part of her feels that he isn't going to even show up today. The tears were from the cross that she bears as a single mom… It seems that Daddy is always viewed as the hero, who all he has to do is show up and save the day. Katrina knows that if she gives her daughter a dose of reality in this moment that Mommy will assume the role of the villain. The ongoing dilemma of the single mother, do I hurt my baby with the truth or do I comfort her with a lie…)

KeKe remembers hearing Katrina sniffle, "Mama are you crying? It's okay, true love makes me cry sometimes too..." Katrina rolls her eyes before saying,"Okay, you're done... ot ot ot... (KeKe hopped out the chair and was about to take off running) Don't even try to go running around, you'll mess up your hair. Go have a seat. Yo daddy supposed to be here in about an hour or so. Don't mess up your hair KeKe, I'm not playing!"

"Okay, but Mama can I sit in the living room and watch TV while I wait for him?" "Go head KeKe" "Yes!!!"

45 minutes had passed when Katrina comes from her bedroom and heads to the kitchen. As she passes the living room she sees Kenyatta turned around with her knees on the couch looking out the window. Katrina is preparing her mind to deal with the potential let down and the emotional wreck KeKe is going to be if her Dad doesn't show. She takes a deep breath and tries to divert KeKe's attention.

"KeKe, sit on that couch right. Don't wrinkle your shirt baby. It's 3:50, He not even off work yet. He coming as soon as he gets off I'm sure." "Okay but I just want to see him drive up... what kinda car he got Ma?" "I don't know... why?" "So I can know when I see it comin' up the street..." "He'll be here KeKe... and if he don't we going out tomorrow, okay?" KeKe doesn't even entertain the thought of him not showing up. Katrina leaves it alone and heads back in her room after grabbing some salad from the refrigerator.

Another thirty minutes go by, "Ma can you call him" KeKe remembers screaming from the same position her mother told her not to sit in. "Oh never mind, this is him right here... (A car slows down but keeps driving down the street) No, it's not... Maaaaaaa!!!! Where he aaatttt!!!! CAN YOU CALL HIM!!!! KeKe is frustrated. Katrina hears the anxiety in her voice.

As Katrina anticipated having to do, she put on her bomb squad hat and went in to diffuse the situation. Katrina calmly enters the room before speaking in a patient tone of voice.

"Kenyatta Shellerray! It's not even 4:30 yet, I know he running a little late. I'll text him baby but I can't keep calling him every two seconds. Your Daddy said 4 o'clock but obviously, it's going to be a little bit later so just chill out baby... I'm texting him now and I'll let you know what he says when he texts me back ok?" "Yessss.... Okay, but... ohhh... Okay, okay..."

Kenyatta thinks back on how she sat the next 7 hours getting her hopes up with every car that passed. She believed her Dad was coming because she wanted him to so bad. Kenyatta sat there looking out the window while the wounds of a diminishing self worth begin to open in her mind. He told her that he was coming so why shouldn't she believe him? What was she supposed to do? This is the day that she began to lose faith in her Daddy's word. With every passing car and moment she sat on the couch as the crippling idea that something was wrong with her began to formulate inside her. Was it something she said or did that made her father not want to come to see his baby girl? KeKe is still staring at the ceiling as she relives the agonizing pain of rejection. Kenyatta fell asleep on the couch fully clothed waiting on her Dad.

Her GMa came in from working a double shift and put her in the bed. Kenyatta remembers her mother coming in her room the next morning to telling her to take off the outfit she was so excited to wear just 24 hours ago. Kenyatta and her mom went to the movies, out to eat and for ice cream the next day. However, she doesn't remember that. Rejection is the only memory she can't seem to shake. The pain of this particular let down gave birth to the idea of KeKe. Although she was too young to formulate a persona, Kenyatta began to feel that something had to be done to protect herself from these emotions. Baby Girl was tired of being hurt and having her hopes crushed. While, KeKe would be "born" later this was the moment that led to her creation.

Kenyatta gives her control which isn't always a good thing. The problem is that KeKe was created from lack and not love and thus incapable of providing the healing Kenyatta needs. So KeKe, like many women and men alike, feels that intimacy is an expression of love. Her Dad's absence has resulted in self-constructed persona who lacks the key elements of time, integrity and sacrifice. Which are foundational components of all healthy relationships, however, KeKe doesn't know how that feels or looks. As a result KeKe consistently misconstrues physical affection for love and in turn, leaves Kenyatta draped in guilt and regret after every case of mistaken identity.

In Order to Fix it You Must Face It

Kenyatta deliberately goes back to those moments of pain from her childhood to justify her poor choices and decisions instead of simply taking accountability. By allowing KeKe to take control she can look at herself in the mirror and be okay with her reflection. Although KeKe takes the blame, Kenyatta still has to nurse the wounds. No matter what she tries, Kenyatta can't escape the reality that to fix it, you must face it. That's why ignoring her Dad's absence and acting like it doesn't bother her only makes the wounds deeper.

However, KeKe has convinced Kenyatta that by reliving the pain and feelings of rejection from her father she can validate making selfish choices like the one she just made. An emotionless withdrawal from KeKe's bank of self-worth that was spent irrationally on someone who she doesn't have a connection with. Continuing down this dangerous path will inevitably make Kenyatta compassionately bankrupt.

Kenyatta sits up and thinks to herself, "I gotta get it together... where are the rest of my clothes." Finally dressed and ready to go, KeKe looks at her phone that reads "1:11 am" She has two missed text messages so she opens them up. "Oh brother," she thinks to herself as she sees that they are both from Jeremiah. KeKe opens them to read them because she hates having alerts on her screen... the first one reads:

> Hey beautiful, lmk if u still want
> 2 C my AP English notes

The second text was sent twelve minutes later and read

> & the invitation still open if u
> want 2 go 2 church. If I don't
> hear from u then c l @ school n
> don't forget Ms Ledbetter
> calculus quiz is Monday. Good
> night.

KeKe rolls her eyes in annoyance after reading the text. Jeremiah is really into her but isn't the type of guy that she would typically date. KeKe is scared that if she gives him a chance that Kenyatta will really like him. If Kenyatta was to fall for Jeremiah and he were to break her heart she is not sure where she would end up emotionally. To prevent this, she allows KeKe to deal with him. So essentially, to this point in their friendship, Jeremiah is collateral damage that can be counted as a casualty belonging to Kenyatta's relationship to her father.

KeKe is ready to go as she sits on the side of the bed and continues scrolling through her phone. A voice says "I'm ready" which prompts KeKe to grab her things as she walks out the apartment and to his car. The seven minute ride home was mostly silent and as the car pulls up to her house she shoots him a quick lie... "I'll call you later..." KeKe is out the car and as she enters the house she sees the lights from his car fade out as he drives away.

Kenyatta, Katrina, and GMa still live in the same place. The only difference GMa stays most nights over Mr. Thadeus's house who she met at the church. GMa says it's because she wants to give Kenyatta and Katrina more space but Kenyatta thinks that GMa has finally opened up to a man for the first time since her PawPaw died and left them the house when Kenyatta was a baby. Kenyatta teases GMa with the line from Baby Boy from time to time... "Hey, Mama gotta live too..."

Pain can distort perception

It's now 1:48 am and because her mother still working those midnights Kenyatta, who is a Junior in High School, is coming and going as she pleases which is a gift and a curse. In terms of the gift, this has made Kenyatta super responsible. Kenyatta is on her stuff, she is an A student, the Student Government Association Secretary and is Vice President of the Yearbook at her school. Kenyatta is lined up academically to go to the college of her choice after graduation. As for the curse, Katrina's work schedule allows Kenyatta to self medicate with males whenever she gets the case of the "Absent Father Flu."

Kenyatta is feeling dirty both emotionally and literally. She takes a quick shower to both get clean and hopefully feel refreshed. she puts on some pajamas and gets in the bed simply putting the night behind her. For Kenyatta, forgetting nights like this is the easy part. She knows that by Monday morning she wouldn't have thought twice about it. That's because what she did meant nothing to her, but why she did it, Kenyatta can't shake that easy.

The rest of the weekend went by rather uneventfully, besides another Saturday evening text from Jeremiah asking her would she like to come to church to which she laid down softly...

Thanks but I'm busy tomorrow morning

Jeremiah doesn't flinch and simply responds:

Np - don't forget to study for the Calculus quiz. C u Monday beautiful

Jeremiah is used to it, to this point in their relationship he continuously does nice things for Kenyatta only to have the desired emotional connection rejected like a LeBron chase-down block. (Sorry ladies - search it on YouTube if you don't get the reference.)

Jeremiah is careful not to smother her and does things to let her know that she can count on him. While Kenyatta is genuinely appreciative of Jermiah, she feels that allowing KeKe to guard her heart from any and everything that could cause similiar damage to what her father has left behind is still the best way to proceed when it comes to getting involved in a serious relationship.

A few weeks have passed and everything is still status quo in their friendship. This particular day is a Friday and Jeremiah walks KeKe to her bus as he does on most days. On the walk, he asks "What you got planned for this weekend?" KeKe lights up, "Me, my Mama, My Auntie Safi and my cousin Amiyah are going to see Alvin Ailey this Sunday! It is awesome! We go see it every year, it turns into a full girls thing, we have a lot of fun!" KeKe goes on and on about it never stopping to ask him about his plans. She never does when they talk but Jeremiah doesn't let on to her being self-absorbed around him. He just grins and bears it.

Jeremiah cuts her off as he goes in his bag, "Well I see you gone be busy but I got you something..." He pulls out "Becoming Michelle Obama" and hands it to her. "I heard you talking about it in class last week and I figured you would like it... I also got you this book, "Free Heart" it's by Shacora Moore. It's about a girl who is going through some things because of her home life. I heard you mention a couple of times how you feel about your Pops and I figured you would like it. Mrs. Moore is actually coming to our church in a couple of weeks but I already know you ain't trying to go so... Anyway, here is your bus, enjoy your weekend and I'll see you on Monday... Oh yeah and Revelations is dope, Alvin Ailey was a beast... Be safe..."

Jeremiah walks off and Kenyatta is pleasantly surprised. She has

159

to admit that just how much he has paid attention to her is very attractive. As she gets on her bus she thinks to herself, she needs to speak up the next time KeKe puts up the wall when he is around.

It's Sunday, KeKe and Katrina are at Aunt Safi's house. KeKe is in Amiyah's room and they are catching up like long lost sisters. KeKe and Amiyah are a few months apart in age however, they live forty-five minutes away so they don't get to hang out as much. Steven, Amiyah's Dad calls her to his room. He tells her it is really important. Amiyah peeks her head into the door of her parents' bedroom...

"Yes Daddy?" "Miyah can you get me water out the fridge?" "Really Daddy?!" Amiyah says lovingly as she really thought that he wanted something important. "Ok, I wanted to see what you were wearing but I am thirsty." Amiyah jokingly rolls her eyes. "You want some ice?" "Aww baby girl I sure do and before you go make it, look in my pants pocket over there. I got something for you." "Oooohhh some money?" Amiyah says excitedly. "Yep get that fifty dollar bill and don't tell your mother," Steven says as if to indicate he wants to keep the peace between him and his wife. "Now, why would I do that?" Amiyah retorts jokingly. "Miyah, you know you are Team Mommy." Her father says with a frank look on his face. "Not when you give me money!" They both laugh. "That was a good one! Love you Baby Girl." "Love you too Daddy."

Yep, you guessed it… KeKe is feeling some type of way. Although she feels guilty for the jealous emotions she is experiencing, this conversation touched a nerve. A nerve that takes her back to the beginning of her 8th grade school year, KeKe begins the painful daydream...

KeKe remembers coming up the stairs of the church. KeKe's Dad had just lost his mother, Grandma Ethel. She was going into the church for the funeral. As she reached the top of the stairs she saw a beautiful little girl in a black dress just inside the open doors of the church. The little girl could not be any more than 3-years-old. As she skipped around and played off to the side, her innocence brought a smile to KeKe's face. The little girls' shoe came off while she danced around carefree. After a moment the man standing next to her recognizes what happened. He bent down to help her with her shoe and said the words KeKe will never forget.

"Aww Baby Girl, I got you. I'm always going to be here for you, let Daddy take care of that." KeKe froze immediately because she knew that voice. Her eyes traveled curiously up from the little girl and her shoe to the man who said it. At the moment all she could see was the top of his head because he was bending over to help the little girl. Kenyatta stepped out of the line of people making their way inside the church's sanctuary and towards the man helping the girl. When he finally lifted his head up after fixing her shoe and giving her a slight kiss on the forehead, the man and Kenyatta locked eyes.

Kenyatta's assumption was correct, that voice was her Daddy's. Immediately, she began to feel some type of way. Whatever her father said as he made his way over to her that day is still lost on Kenyatta, she was numb. The same jealous emotion she is feeling now, came over her then, only stronger. This precious 3-year-old girl was getting everything Kenyatta always wanted from her Daddy. Luckily for Kenyatta this happened at a funeral. While everyone else mourned the loss of Grandma Ethel, Kenyatta was able to let tears of yet another heartbreak flow unquestioned. As Kenyatta cried that day in the church she made up her mind that she wasn't going to let any man or boy have her heart ever again. This was the moment Keke was born. The decision was final, she was only going to look out for herself because she couldn't trust anyone to care about her feelings the way she does.

Ironically, Kenyatta created KeKe, who is an emotionally detached spitting image of her father. As the saying goes, "The man you despise is the man you become." Her Dad, an emotionally damaged individual himself, has gone through life manipulating women to get what he wants without any true emotional connection with them. Kenyatta's mere existence is the result of one of the many empty relationships her father has had with women. Sadly, his inability to create and sustain healthy relationships is becoming a generational curse that he is passing on to his daughter.

An outside perspective provides clarity

"KeKe. KeKe. Keke..." "Huh? Yeah, my bad... I was daydreaming." KeKe says as Amiyah calls to get her attention. "I'm tripping. Were you asking me something?" "I was telling you that your phone was going off. It said, Jeremiah." KeKe looks at her phone and rolls her eyes. Amiyah notices KeKe's disgust and asks the question. "Who is Jeremiah?" "This boy who likes me. He always calling or texting me about school or church. He cool but I ain't feeling him. I don't know... It's kinda hard to explain." KeKe says with a touch of irritability yet still trying to shake off the flashback. "Well, no shade but it sounds a bit like you like him but you have a reputation to uphold and don't want people judging you. What is wrong with a guy trying to keep you up on school and wants you to go to church? He seems to me like the kind of guy who at least wants what's best for you. I know my Mom and Dad would want me to be with someone like that." Amiyah says as she tries to comprehend KeKe's logic. KeKe goes to defend her position but Amiyah perspective is making Kenyatta want to speak up because she has seen Jeremiah in this light, yet she has trusted KeKe to protect her. "I guess you are right but... I don't know how to put it." KeKe says.

Amiyah still isn't sure what could be the problem with Jeremiah based on what KeKe has described so far. "What? Is he ugly? Is he too short? I mean something has to be a deal-breaker for you not to be into him. I'm missing something? You got a picture of him?" KeKe responds, "Nawl he not ugly. He cute." (KeKe grabs her phone and pulls up a picture. She shows Amiyah) Kenyatta continues, "I mean, I guess you right. He is thoughtful, he bought me "Becoming" by Michelle Obama and this book "Free Heart" by Shacorra Moore. It is really good. And he knew about Alvin Ailey. His Mom took him to see it before. He is smart he gets good grades... He a good dude. I guess I don't know. I don't know, maybe I'm tripping but I don't know. I just never thought about him like that until right now."

"Look KeKe, you know what both our moms would say. No need to rush into boys, they're going to be there. Which is true. At the same time, if he is a good guy and he really likes you, I wouldn't be treating him wrong because he is going to remember how you treated him when y'all was in school. If I were you, I wouldn't be pushing him away. I'm not saying you have to date him but I don't see the harm in him from what you saying. You told me about other dudes before and this seems to be the only one about something. But hey you do you... I'm just telling you how I see it." "Yeah, you right. It is a lot of dudes out here who only into their body count. I guess with Jeremiah, he likes me likes me. You know what I mean? I'm not trying to get my heart broke, I had enough of that with my Daddy. I'm not about to go through that with no dude." (KeKe says as she lets Amiyah in on the real reason she doesn't want Jeremiah or any guy to get too close to her.)

"KeKe I understand that. If that is the case just tell him. He sounds like he would really understand where you are coming from. To me, it doesn't sound like he is the type of guy who would try to hurt you. But at least tell him the truth instead of stringing him along. Me personally, I think you should give him a shot. But that's just me." Amiyah says. KeKe sees Amiyah's point about Jeremiah. She pauses for a second as the realization begins to simmer, then replies "Miyah you right, I don't have much to lose..."

162

It's Monday morning at school. As Kenyatta is getting off the bus she is feeling a little awkward because she is actually anticipating seeing Jeremiah today. This is weird because she would normally allow KeKe to put that wall up around her heart. Kenyatta has put KeKe away and is allowing herself to be vulnerable. Between the gift he gave her on Friday and the conversation she had with Amiyah she feels it is the right time to let down her guard and allow Jeremiah get to know her. As she walks into the school, Kenyatta begins to feel the unfamiliar sensation of butterflies are in her stomache as she walks down the hall. Kenyatta smiles when she finally sees him where she usually sees him, by the lockers talking to his bros Damon and DJ. Normally she would walk past him and go to her locker. Not this time, she walks right up to him.

Putting her guard down...

"Excuse me, Damon and DJ, can I borrow your boy for a minute, Thank You." (Kenyatta didn't wait for a reply she just grabbed his arm and pulled him away.) Pleasantly surprised Jeremiah says to Kenyatta, "What's all this about?" Kenyatta responded, "Nothing, I just missed you... I got a lot to tell you about my weekend, I want to hear about yours and I want you to walk me to class." A happily confused Jeremiah tries to play it cool, "Ohhhkay... Yeah, no that's cool... Uhh so you wanna talk first or you want me to tell you what I did?"

KeKe is a little annoyed by his innocence as she thinks to herself, "I got my work cut out for me if I am going to get him to be the kind of guy I like." Instead of saying what she is really feeling, she turns politely to him and says, "Jeremiah just walk with me to class... We going to have a lot of time to talk..." Switching into a semi seductive and somewhat manipulative mindset she grabs his hand and interlocks his fingers with hers and says, "So Alvin Ailey was dope, Revelations, oh it never gets old...." The two walked into class and continued the conversation during independent work time. KeKe begins slowly letting down her guard and allowing him into Kenyatta's emotional space...

They spent the whole week acting like a couple with no official title. Funny thing is they didn't even discuss it. Kenyatta was low key tripping because KeKe had her believing that guys like Jeremiah didn't exist. Jeremiah wasn't trying to get anything from her, nor was he some lame who always asked her to go to church. Jeremiah has three sisters so he knows a lot about what girls like. When you couple that with the fact that he is being raised in a stable, college-educated two-parent home, Jeremiah was bound to be different then most guys his age. Jeremiah consistently sees his Dad treating his mother with respect. Jeremiah was simply mimicking his Father whenever he is with Kenyatta. This strange relationship was off to a good start and KeKe was finally allowing Kenyatta to confide in someone other than her Mother, GMa and her best friend Tracyonna.

As soon as you think things are going good...

It is lunch hour on a Friday a few weeks later and Kenyatta is sitting in the gym with her squad Tori, Dacquanesha, Xaaria, Yalinda, Tyra, Alaysha, Kaylyn, Rene and Tracyonna. She is scolling through her phone when a text comes through:

Hey Baby Girl I need you to call me when you get a chance. It's important.

 Kenyatta's whole mood changed and Tracy noticed it, she gave her a look that said "What's wrong?" when the two made eye contact. KeKe rolled her eyes and shook her head to indicate "Nothing" but Tracy knew something was wrong. She thought to herself, "I'll check on my girl later."

 The text caught Kenyatta off guard, however, KeKe went right to work. She sent Jeremiah a text even though she is looking at him on the court playing basketball. The text read:

U wanna come ova 2ma nite? My moms gotta work 😘😘😘

KeKe gets up from the bleachers and walks to the edge of the court where Jeremiah was playing. Jeremiah notices her and she tells him, "Check your phone when you get a chance." "Yep," Jeremiah responded and kept playing. KeKe gave a nod and began calling her mother as she walks outside.

 Katrina answers the phone a bit frantically because KeKe never really calls while she is at school. If they need to communicate during school hours, it's usually through text. "KeKe... Wsup, everything okay???" "Yeah, I'm fine... but what is wrong with my Daddy, do you know? He come texting me about some he need me to call him it's important... Something didn't seem right about that, he know better than to say he need me for anything... So do you know what he wanna talk to me about?" Katrina takes a deep breath and says, "Yeah KeKe, I know exactly why he wants you to call him... He told me a few months ago what was going on but he made me promise not to tell you. He didn't want to get you all worked up about it... It is health-related and I know you going to worry until you find out so you might as well go ahead and call him so you can know what's going on..." KeKe responds, "Ma you starting to scare me now..." Katrina responds, "Well Ke it is a little scary but just gone head call him. I don't gotta go to work until later so if you need me call me back, okay?" "Alright Ma, let me call him and see wsup." KeKe says as the anxiety builds. "Love you KeKe... Bye" Katrina hangs up and is mentally preparing to pull out that old bomb squad hat and diffuse the situation once KeKe finds out what is going on with her Daddy.

 A puzzled KeKe is trying to gather her emotions of what possibly could be going on with her Daddy. While KeKe has built a protective shield around her emotions when it comes to him, the fact still remains, he is her Daddy. From KeKe's vantage point the relationship is frigid, she takes every chance she gets to throw darts and low blows reminding him of all the let downs and empty promises. Through it all he still buys her school clothes and even pulls up on occasion. For her sanity, KeKe hasn't allowed Kenyatta to love him in the way that she once did. Obviously torn KeKe and Kenyatta are contemplating what to do next.

164

While KeKe is scrolling back through her phone to the text. A sweaty Jeremiah comes up and hugs her trying to be funny and get his sweat on her. Instead of the "Ugghhh get off me!" reaction he was anticipating, KeKe falls back into his arms because she desperately needs to be held right now. "Oh! Okay, this what we on…" An unsuspecting Jeremiah says as he holds her up. "Did you get my text?" KeKe asks. Jeremiah responds, "Yeah I got it… I got a couple of questions though? Like what time you want me to come over because I wanna meet your Mom and I am sure my Mom would want to meet her too… Also, my curfew is 11:30 and I like to be in 30 minutes early, so my parents won't be worried. And… nothing, nothing…"

"What Bae, say it…" Kenyatta demands, "Okay, what is your Mom being gone have to do with anything? I mean, don't get me wrong I am attracted to you like that but… You my girl and all but I am not trying to get at you like that… I mean I am into 'you'… Your smart, you're strong, you're confident, your obviously gorgeous… But I am just not ready for all that… Not to say that was where it was going to go but I am just being upfront. We don't truly, truly know each other like that yet either… And I made a promise to God to save myself until marriage. I am in Young Men of Valor… I get clowned for taking an oath to save myself but hey I got faith that when it comes time for that it will be worth it. Like Tony Dungy speaks about in his book, Uncommon. I wanna be Uncommon." KeKe got lost about halfway through because she definitely wasn't expecting all this and she is still thinking about what could be wrong with her Dad. Irritated by his rant she responds. "Tony who? What are you talking about Jeremiah?" "Hey, you asked, so there it is… Oh and I am only going to come if you finally take me up on that offer to go to church with me…"

"Okay, Yeah I'll go with you to church… and ugh yeah well that was a lot… N E ways… Something is going on with my sperm donor and my Mom won't tell me wsup…" Jeremiah switches immediately to being concerned about the situation, "What's going on? What she say? What happened?" Jeremiah asks. "Ion't know what's going on, I just got this text from him saying, he NEED me to call him, which is weird because he never ever uses the word NEEDS when he talks to me… And he called me Baby Girl' which I told him never to call me again. So this got me in my feelings for real because I think something is wrong with him…"

Jeremiah is puzzled but asks, "Well did you call him? Why worry yourself sick trying to figure out what is going on when you can just call him and find out?" KeKe responds, "I know. But if I find out now then I know the rest of my day is likely to go bad and I don't want to have to go off on anybody." Jeremiah offers support, "Ok, well I'll just catch the bus home with you, so I can be there for you when you call and talk to him, I'll text my Dad to come pick me up from your house, if that's okay with you?"

"No, I'm cool, thanks, but I should be okay..." KeKe says instinctively, still unaware of how to accept support from a male. The fact that a guy could be there for her without wanting something in return is a concept she hasn't even conceived yet, so she misses the sincerity of Jeremiah's offer.

My Mind's Playing Tricks On Me...

The rest of the school day KeKe is truly in a daze and she can't focus on anything but what could be wrong with her Daddy. On the bus ride home from school KeKe sits staring out of the window. she is in a paradox in terms of her father. Feelings of guilt naturally invade her thoughts. Despite the insults and jabs she throws and all the painful letdowns and empty promises he has made over the years, Kenyatta still loves her daddy. The thought of him dying is becoming more overwhelming by the second. Luckily the bus makes it to her stop just as the lump in her throat was about to turn into uncontrollable tears.

KeKe gets off the bus, makes the short walk up the block to her house and goes inside. Normally her first stop is to the kitchen to grab a snack but she doesn't have the appetite today. KeKe looks down at her phone, scrolls over to her Dad's number and prepares to hit send... She can't do it... She puts the phone down and looks at the ceiling. Those mixed emotions of guilt start to creep back into her head. Usually, she arms herself with a 'funky attitude' when she calls him because she wants him to 'feel' the pain that she has inside that comes from his absence. KeKe can't bring herself to get that attitude because 'what if he is dying?'. 'KeKe just call him... You are driving yourself crazy...' Kenyatta finally takes over the dilemma, because truth be told, she is the one who has been affected the most by the actions of her Daddy. Kenyatta grabs the phone and tells KeKe to be quiet. She presses the number, sits back on the bed and waits for the ring. After about the 3rd ring his voice says.

"Baby Girl" he pauses out of habit because it's right about now that she would hit him with a stank, "N E WAYZ, Look I'ma need a ...." and KeKe would go on with her demands of what she wants. However, this isn't the case because he is talking to Kenyatta who regardless of what he has done and KeKe may feel about it, Kenyatta is and will always be his "Baby Girl". So, when he hears "Yes Daddy... you said you needed me to call you, whats up?" he is taken back and gives a startled, "Oh yeah, well, I wanted to tell you, hol' up... You sitting down Baby Girl?"

Kenyatta is annoyed by the unexpected delay, "Yeah Daddy, what's going on, Mama told me that whatever it is you told her she couldn't tell me so Wsup?!!!" Her Dad comes right out with it, "Look Baby Girl if I don't get a new liver then the doctors say I got 9 months at the most..."

Tears begin making their way towards Kenyatta's chin immediately. Kenyatta went silent, not knowing what to say because in that moment, Kenyatta realizes her mistake. She had allowed KeKe to spend so much time being angry and upset at all the pain and things that he didn't do, that she failed to take advantage of the moments they did share.

Even more, hearing that the sand in his life's hour glass was running out she begins to feel saddened as thoughts of the bigger picture formulate in her mind. It's beginning to dawn on her that it is a possibility he won't be there to walk her down the aisle when she gets married or maybe not at her graduation from High School next year. Ironically, happy memories began to come to the forefront. Kenyatta can only think of the things he did to put a smile on her face and how she gave him a hard time, wishing now that she would have done more to cherish those moments.

While trying to find the proper words to say to him, her Dad ends the awkward silence by getting to the real reason he said he needs her. "Kenyatta, Baby Girl, uh, I know this is crazy and your mother doesn't even know this... I went to the Dr. on Thursday and he told me about the live liver donation program. The Dr. told me that more than likely the closest match with this is usually one of your children. The Dr. said that finding a living donor is my only chance at living. Baby Girl, I don't wanna die and I hate to.... I hate to have to ask you but... Can you find it in your heart to come with me to see if you're a match?" Kenyatta was floored. Not knowing how to respond nor how to feel about his request, Kenyatta looks to escape, "Daddy, let me call you back... this is a lot right now... I gotta go..." Kenyatta hears "Baby Gir-" before she hangs up the phone and just sits with her tears. She cut the phone on silent before dropping it on the bed. She doesn't even have the strength to wipe her face so she just falls back on the bed and lets it all go.

Kenyatta takes control...

Numb from the news Kenyatta falls asleep but it is more like just being in a trance because she doesn't get any rest. When she finally comes to, she looks at her phone and is shocked that it's 10:39 p.m. Kenyatta had no idea that the conversation took so much out of her. Kenyatta gets up and makes her something to eat listlessly going through the motions for the rest of the night with her mind totally consumed by the bomb that was dropped on her by her father.

The next day was more of the same empty carrying on of her daily routine. Kenyatta and Katrina spoke about what her father asked buy only briefly because Katrina could tell that Kenyatta was still processing the situation. Something tells Kenyatta to check her phone which she had forgot that she put on silent. When she finally gets to her phone it is ringing.

"OMG, it's Jeremiah!" she thinks to herself. Kenyatta had completely forgot that she invited him over.

"Hello". Jeremiah was expecting a more upbeat response and quickly decides to gloss over his expectations and simply responds "Ok yeah, my mom and I just pulled up, we are outside if it's 3743 Oakdale Dr." KeKe responds, "Yep you are in the right spot, ok... here I come."

Kenyatta is too mentally drained to even check the mirror before going to the door. As Kenyatta opens the door, Jeremiah begins to smile at the sight of her. "Hello..." Ever confidently Jeremiah responds "Hey babe... This is my mother Inez... Mom this is Kenyatta..." They both reach out their hands and say "Hello" simultaneously. Kenyatta is trying to find the energy to be her usually upbeat self, somehow she assembles up enough strength to call her mother to the front so she can meet Jeremiah and his mom. "Maaaa.... Jeremiah and his mom are here." Turning to Jeremiah and his Mom as she closes the door behind them "Please, have a seat... can I get you anything to drink? My mom should be out shortly... And please Mrs. Turner... Excuse my appearance... I am having a rough day..." This jogs Jeremiahs' memory and in a concerned tone, he says, "Oh right! You did have to talk to your Pops... How did it... Oh well, I'm sorry it must not have gone too well... Aww babe I'm sorry... What happened?"

Jeremiah forgets his mother is in the room and being so excited with concern he didn't give Kenyatta the opportunity to respond to his rapid-fire line of questioning. Realizing that he is excited he stops himself and says, "My bad... Let me calm down..." Kenyatta is still spiritually processing the conversation with her Dad, so instead of reliving it she dismissively says, "No your, good, it's a lot but... yeah... Uh, well when I called him he sa-"

Katrina's voice comes from around the corner just prior to her actually, entering the room. "Hello... I'm Katrina, Kenya's mother..." She says extending her hand out to Inez. Kenyatta stands up and lets her mother finish before saying, "Mom, this is Jeremiah" The ever pleasant Katrina continues, "Oh nice to meet you, please have a seat... Don't stand for me, the pleasure is all mine... Oh, Kenya he "is" handsome..." Inez proudly looks at her son and grabs a microscopic piece of lint from his head and runs her hand over his waves, as Jeremiah blushes. Katrina still speaking, "So what you all got up for tonight? I haven't heard of any plans I just know that KeKe invited you over." Kenyatta and Jeremiah look at each other because they never actually discussed having any plans. Kenyatta looks and feels exhausted and says "I don't know to be honest... I was thinking just find something to binge-watch... Jeremiah hasn't seen the second season of Atlanta yet..." Everyone's mouths drop and eyebrows raise at the disbelieve of Kenyatta's claim.

"That's not totally true, I haven't seen all of the second season yet, I saw, of course, the Barbershop episode and I did an editorial piece on the Fubu episode for the school newspaper... I am a huge fan of this Black directorial emergence. I mean from Shonda Rhimes, Lena Waithe, Ava Duvernay, Ryan Coogler, Donald Glover, Mara and Salim Akil and my favorite, Jordan Peele. His imagery and creativity are off the charts..." A very impressed Katrina turns Jeremiah's mother and says... "Well, Mrs... Inez is it?..." Jeremiah's mother nods in agreement. "You and your husband have done an amazing job with Jeremiah and I have only been around him for a few minutes. Kenya told me that he knew about Alvin Ailey and I mean just hearing him now... Thank you for raising a fine young man... Well, whatever they get into I know that these two are going to behave. Well, at least Jeremiah is..." Katrina says laughing at the shot fired at her daughter. Kenya turns and makes a face of playful embarrassment.

Mrs. Inez stands up and says, "Well I have somethings to take care of. Jeremiah, you know your curfew. You have all the numbers if you need anything... Kenyatta, it was nice meeting you and I am looking forward to seeing you Sunday morning for church. You are still coming right?" Kenyatta says proudly, "Of course, I am looking forward to it..." Mrs. Inez spills some tea that Jeremiah wasn't expecting, "Looking forward to it? That sounds good... Jeremiah said you had been dodging his offer to go to church for quite some time..." "Ooohhh the shade Darling! The Shade!" Katrina says to poke fun at her daughters obvious unexpected embarrassment. The all laugh as an embarrassed Jeremiah nudges his mother before looking at Kenyatta with a regretful face of "I'm sorry." Kenyatta is too emotionally drained to even make herself mad at him for painting a slightly negative image of her to his mom. Katrina sees Mrs. Inez out of the house as Kenyatta and Jeremiah settle in on the couch.

Jeremiah understands that he was invited over to provide emotional support so he jumps right in, "So what happened with your Pops, everything good?" Mentally fatigued, Kenya knows that she has to relive the moment so she simply lays it out there, "He is dying and needs a liver transplant and if that wasn't enough, he asked me would I go with him to see if I am a match... Something the doctor said about trying your children or something. I started fading out of the conversation when he told me he was dying and barely heard him asking me about seeing if I am a match. I don't know, I mean that's my Dad and I love him but he has me screwed up inside. I feel like he has caused me so much pain and I have so many parts of me that is damaged because of him. I know this sounds selfish but for so long and so many times he has hurt me... I don't know if I should give a part of myself for someone who I feel has taken so many pieces of me... I know that sounds horrible but... I don't know...

169

Jeremiah isn't giving his opinion. He is giving an attentive and compassionate ear. Which is exactly what Kenyatta needs at the moment. After a contemplative pause by Kenyatta, Jeremiah speaks up "Oh wow, I'm so sorry to hear that, I know your relationship with your Pops is rocky but man, I'm sorry to hear that he is dying." Jeremiah grabbed her hand about midway through his sentence to give a little more reassurance to Kenyatta. Unlike most who would try to take advantage of this emotional vulnerability in Kenyatta, Jeremiah leans back and begins to ask more questions to help her process her emotions. "So, what are you thinking in terms of seeing if you are a match? I know you said you don't know but what is going through your head?" Kenya leans back and pulls both knees into her chest, ironically, she is sitting in the fetal position as she begins speaking.

"Honestly, I have a feeling that I am going to be a perfect match and if I am, I am not sure that I want to give him anything. Let alone a piece of my liver. It's like I said he has taken so much of me, I can't even count how many times he has hyped me up for something only to let me down. It's crazy..." A reflective Kenyatta opens up even more.

"I was making straight A's all through middle school and he never came to one parent-teacher conference... When we won the Spell Bowl in 8th grade you remember everyone was all happy and I was kinda down? I remember you asking me was everything cool? And I said yeah my stomach was hurting. That's because we won and I was the only person that didn't have any family in the stands. My grandma was out of town and my mother was scheduled to work a double and I begged him to come and he never showed up after he promised he would... I can keep going. It's really hard to love someone so much who keeps letting you down. You just don't know how much I wanted him to be there for me... But he is never there when I need it or really wanted him. For real for real, he can take all these Jordans he bought me for my birthday back. He can have all these school clothes, these Airpods, my iPhone... all these material things don't mean nothin' to me. He can take it all back if just one time he showed up when I wanted him to. It's like if I ask him to buy me something, oh he gonna break his neck to get it to me. But when it comes to his time and to be there for me when I need someone to talk to about things. Important things, real life stuff, like school or how to manage money, college, whatever... It's an excuse... Oh, I got to work, or I got this or I got that, I'll call you right back... He ain't never there, so I don't even ask anymore... I just can't believe now he needs a piece of me when all this time I couldn't find peace because I never really had what I needed from him."

Jeremiah leans up and grabs her hands and asks, "Have you prayed about it?" KeKe rolls her eyes, "Jeremiah you know why I never would say yes when you would ask me to go to church? It's because I used to pray so hard for my Daddy and my Mom to get back together.

I used to pray so hard that my parents would be like my Auntie Safi and Uncle Steven. I would ask God every night for my Daddy. Like EVERY NIGHT Jeremiah. I saw my mom struggle and be bitter towards men. I saw us be low on food and I would eat and my mom would say that she was okay because she ate at work when I knew she didn't. Times over here have been hard Jeremiah. And I would ask God to make them better by bringing my Daddy back to us. For so long I thought that my Daddy was the thing that would make my life complete. I prayed so hard, it felt like God was ignoring me. I would hear things like, 'You have not because you ask not' and other little references to the Bible. I became so disappointed that for a minute, I stopped believing in all that Bible stuff that they be saying. God never answered those prayers about my Daddy so I got turned off by the whole God has the answer stuff..."

Jeremiah smiles and says, "Oh you are going to love church Sunday... Just do me one favor. Please have an open mind and be willing to receive the word. Often times we are very defensive and we have our minds made up about things and because of that, we can't be nurtured the way we need to be by the word. So just do me a favor and come with an open mind for me please?" Kenyatta hears the sincerity in his voice and is a little surprised that Jeremiah didn't try to convince her that her stance on God's failure to answer her prayers is wrong. Swayed by his unexpected gesture Kenyatta responds, "You know what because you asked me I will honestly open myself up and listen to what the preacher has to say."

Jeremiah smiles again and says in a playful tone "Awww... Thank you, I feel special that you would do that for me..." as he flitters his eyelids and puts his right hand over his heart as if he is flattered. Kenyatta laughs as she gives him a slight kick with her left foot, "I can't stand you... I wasn't trying to laugh..." She says letting go more of the built-up tension that she has from the whole situation with her Dad. Jeremiah becomes assertive, "Ok look, whatever you decide, I am going to be right here to support your decision. I see this whole thing is taking a lot out of you and it hasn't even been a full day of you knowing what is going on. So let's park this whole thing right now so I can get caught up on Atlanta" Kenyatta likes this take-charge side of Jeremiah so she sits back and leans her head onto his shoulder as she resumes the fetal position. These feelings of being assured, comforted and supported are foreign to Kenyatta, KeKe and Baby Girl for that matter. She embraces them as she sits next to Jeremiah who is unaware that his compassion for her has begun to fill those empty voids she has inside.

As expected Jeremiah left at 10:30 to be home 30 minutes prior to his 11:30pm curfew. The night ended with a soft kiss on the lips and an

"I can't wait to see you in the morning bae..." from Jeremiah. Kenyatta closed the door and went back to her room. She climbed on her bed and thought to herself, "What a day! Thank you, God for a great day." Kenyatta was in the all too familiar position staring at the ceiling, only this time she didn't need any therapy. Kenyatta felt valued, Jeremiah's presence and support had reminded her that this feeling only comes from within. The idea that physical affection is how "love" is expressed began to fade. The continuous river of letdowns led KeKe to build a dam of deceit around Kenyatta's soul. Tonight, Jeremiah reminded her it's okay to play in the water.

A Heavenly Word Awaits

Sunday morning came and Kenya woke up with a funny feeling. The feeling wasn't that something bad was going to happen, more like something unexpected. Kenyatta couldn't quite put her hands on what the feeling was as she got dressed for church. Amid the whirlwind that has recently become her life, going to church was just the thing that Kenyatta felt she needed despite having evaded Jeremiah's offers for so long.

"Ma can you put the latch on my necklace for me?" she yells out as she finishes putting shea butter on her elbows. "Bring it here!" Katrina yells back from the other room. "Really! You coulda got up and came in here. I'm the one going somewhere." Kenyatta mumbles under her breath. "Say what, I ain't hear you!" "Nothing Ma, here I come," Kenyatta says as she grabs her necklace from her dresser and heads into her mother's room. "Ohhhh! Look at you! Periodt. Periodt! This boy has got you in a dress! You look good KeKe." An overjoyed Katrina says showering her daughter with compliments. "Thank you, Ma. I don't know how long I am going to make it in these tights though. They driving me crazy already." "Girl bye, you gone be alright. Did you get your GMa Bible? She got one in the armoire. Just make sure you don't mess it up. You know how your GMa is." Kenyatta's phone rings as her mother finished her sentence.

"OOh that's him! They probably outside." Kenyatta says imploring her mother to hurry up. "Ok gimme a sec. This thing doesn't wanna... Ok, there it is. Go ahead and grab your shoes, I'll get the Bible." They both went out of the room in opposite directions to grab what they needed before heading to the door. "Okay baby have fun," Katrina says as she gives her daughter a kiss while opening the door to let Kenyatta out of the house.

Seeing the door open, Jeremiah gets out of the car and walks to meet Kenyatta on her way to the car. "Babe you look good. I can't remember the last time I saw you in a dress. Wow!" Jeremiah says to which Kenyatta simply responds,

"Thank you." Jeremiah gets the door before holding her hand to help her in the car. "Good morning." She says speaking to everyone in the car. "Good morning." Everyone responds simultaneously. By this time Jeremiah has walked around to the other side and entered the car. "Dad, Kenyatta. Kenyatta this is my Dad. Ernest, well Mr. Turner." Jeremiah says making the customary introduction. "Hello," Kenyatta says nervously. "Good morning. well, it's nice to finally meet the young lady my son can't stop talking about. Alright, Jeremiah, she is real. I thought you were making her up for the longest time." His father says jokingly. "Oh my gosh, Ernest! Kenyatta please excuse my husband." Inez says mildly embarrassed. "Hey, Jeremiah been talking about the girl but we ain't never met her, I thought he was being catfished," Ernest says poking fun at his son, getting a laugh from Jeremiah's sisters sitting in the back. "How she going catfish the boy if they got class together? He sees her every day! Just drive please." "Oh yeah, you're right. My bad. No in all seriousness, we prayed for you and your father last night." Ernest says as he looks at Kenyatta through his rear-view mirror. "Thank you..." Kenyatta responds introspectively.

Kenyatta goes to make a face at Jeremiah as if she didn't want him spreading her business. "Before you go getting on Jeremiah, we are an open family. He brought it up in our nightly prayer. We prayed for your strength and discernment. You have a difficult decision and we pray that God gives you clarity. Either way, we are here to support you, so if you need anything don't hesitate." Ernest says encouragingly. "Thanks a lot, Mr. Turner," Kenyatta says as she turns to look out the window in hopes that she won't have to talk much more about the situation. "Jeremiah tells me that you want to be a journalist. Are we riding with the next Jemelle Hill?" Ernest says changing the subject. "I'm a big fan of Jemelle Hill but I don't see myself covering sports." Kenyatta proclaims. "Ernest would you let that child be. She just got in the car." Inez interjects in hopes of stopping the twenty-one questions. "Hey, I'm just trying to get to know the young lady. The way J talk about her, she's going to be around for a long time." Kenyatta turns and smiles at Jeremiah upon hearing his father's endorsement.

The rest of the car ride to church was filled with Jeremiah's parent's playful banter. When they got to the church, they sat near the front in the third pew. Not too long after they got seated the services begin. The choir got going and everyone was up and singing along before Pastor Shacora Moore came up to deliver the word. As she approached the pulpit, Kenyatta looked over at Jeremiah remembering that she is the author of the book he gave her. She sat very attentively as she begins to speak. Pastor Moore starts her sermon:

"God is Good all the time and _________ (The congregation responds All the time God is Good). Amen, Amen. God is in the blessing business and if you have been blessed, turn to your neighbor and say - 'I've been blessed'... (The congregation turns to the person next to them and says - I've been blessed. Kenya looks at Jeremiah and half-heartedly says, "I've been blessed" thinking to herself about the situation she is dealing with in regards to her Father.) Pastor Moore continues:

There is something even better than being blessed... I know some of you may be saying, "Pastor what could be better than being blessed?" And I say to you, the one thing that is better than being Blessed, is being a Blessing... We live in a world where everyone wants to be blessed and looking for something from God. But Jesus, I say Jesus, walked around being a Blessing. Jesus healed others, Jesus raised the dead, gave the blind sight... Jesus was the great teacher... Jesus was and is to this very day the physical and spiritual embodiment of being a Blessing... Don't look to be blessed, look to be a Blessing... Can I get an Amen... Amen...

Now, some of you in here are old enough to remember a time when people were wearing these fabric bracelets that had the initials W.W.J.D., now some of you, probably the young folk are asking yourself what does that stand for... Us "Old Folk" as they like to call us knows that it stands for What Would Jesus Do... Now some people may ask, "How do you know what Jesus would do... I tell you that I know because Jesus and God Almighty so loved us that they gave us a book filled with Prophecy and Evidence of what Jesus would and did do... that book is the Bible, or as I like to refer to it as the B.asic I.nstructions B.efore L.eaving E.arth. Today we are going to talk about being a blessing because when you are a blessing you are being like Christ... Can I get an Amen? Amen Amen. Ok so please turn with me to the New Testament and Matthew, Chapter 25 Verse 31 - 40. When you have it please give an Amen... (Pastor Moore takes a drink as the congregation finds the verse) Amen.

Alright, and it reads;

But when the Son of Man comes in his glory and all the angels with him, then he will sit upon his glorious throne. All the nations will be gathered in his presence and he will separate the people as a shepherd separates the sheep from the goats. He will place the sheep at his right hand and the goats at his left. Then the King will say to those on his right, Come, you who are blessed by my Father, inherit the Kingdom prepared for you from the creation of the world. For I was hungry and you fed me. I was thirsty, and you gave me a drink. I was a stranger and you invited me into your home. I was naked and you gave me clothing, I was sick and you cared for me. I was in prison and you visited me. Then these righteous ones will reply Lord, when did we ever see you hungry and feed you? Or a stranger and show you hospitality? Or naked and give you clothing?

When did we ever see you sick or in prison visit you? And the King will say, " I tell you the truth when you did it to one of the least of my brothers and sisters you were doing it to me!"

Amen - Now God makes it very clear to us that when we are doing for the least of those that we encounter in this world, we are doing it very clearly to him. Now let's get to what it is the Lord is saying here. He says that you are doing it TO me. Not for, not because of, but TO me. So it is clear that when you find it in your heart to Be A Blessing you are doing it TO Christ, not for Christ, Not for yourself not for some grace not for mercy but being a blessing is doing it TO Christ... Oh, you don't hear me I want you to think about all the things that have been done TO you... I say think about the things that have been done TO you... Tap back into that pain, that hurt, that emotion of darkness of betrayal and anguish of things that were done TO you... When something is done TO us we take it personally it usually stings and it usually hurts... For Christ has that same emotional connection but of Joy when we find the COMPASSION in our hearts to do for the least of the people we encounter. Can I get an Amen...

My son tells me sometimes that I tend to take things to a whole nother level... Or as some rapper said some time ago - It's levels to this... I say that to you today... It's levels to this... Matter of Fact turn to your neighbor and say "Neighbor... It's levels to this..." (Kenyatta is being moved by the sermon and which is often the case, the word seems to be tailored directly to her and so now with a smile and a little excitement, she turns to Jeremiah and looks him in the eye and says) "Neighbor... It's levels to this!"

Pastor Moore continues, "Jesus took being a Blessing to the ultimate level because he gave his life for us and washed away our sins... Now, it is only one Christ, so I am not going to ask you to make that commitment physically because he is the savior. But I will say that we must never forget what was the reason that God gave his only Son... So that we can be... FORGIVEN... Oh, Pastor said that word... FORGIVEN... The ultimate level of being a blessing starts with FORGIVENESS... I look around & I see people sitting up and folding their arms and give me a "Huh, I am willing to forgive but I ain't going to forget..." To that, I say if your memory is in the way of your letting go, then you ain't truly forgiving the person or people who are in need of your forgiveness... Now, here is where that levels thing comes in... Jesus gave up the one thing that we all are trying to hold on to... Life - so that you could be forgiven and accepted into God's Kingdom. Christ accepted his fate of suffering and pain and betrayal so that we can be accepted into the place of ultimate love, God's Kingdom."

175

"Now, let me stay here for a moment. Please turn with me to first Thessalonians Chapter 5 Verse 14 and when you are there please give an Amen… Amen alright and it reads: Brothers and sisters we urge you to warn those who are lazy. Encourage those who are timid. Take tender care of those who are weak. Be patient with everyone. See that no one pays back evil for evil but always try to do good to each other and to all people. Always be joyful. Never stop praying, Be thankful in all circumstances for this is God's will for you who belong to Christ Jesus."

Amen. Now let's unpack that just a little bit… Paul tells us here to "Take tender care of those who are weak…" Now that is saying a mouthful because often times those who are weak, were once Mighty… And I am willing to bet when those who are weak today, who was Mighty yesterday, acted yesterday, as if they were never ever going to be weak one day… That is why when you see them weak today, you often think to yourself, well that is what they deserve… I know it, I have seen and I must admit I have thought that way once or twice myself about people, but I must always remember what Paul said, to take Tender Care of those who are weak… He doesn't mention anything about who they were before they became weak. He is telling us to deal with people for who they are in their current state. That is why the next line says… Be patient with every-one…"

Patience is an association with time. Paul is telling us to give people time. The Bible says we don't know the moment nor the hour… We must give everyone time… Oh, I am speaking to someone in here because I can feel it… The spirit is telling me that someone needs to provide tender care to someone who is weak and that very person needs your patience… Oh yes… Remember when you take care of the least of my people Christ said you are doing it TO him! Amen, Amen…

Paul says to be thankful in all circumstances because this is God's will for those who belong to Jesus Christ… We must be thankful we are in the storms. We must be thankful that we are experiencing trials and trib-ulations. We must be thankful that we have dark days and cold nights. We must be thankful that we have experienced pain and hurt and agony. Why? Because that is the evidence that you belong to Christ! For it is when we experience what he endured are we being made to be more like our Savior.

He gives us the test so that we can have a testimony for others who will see God in us and become believers! Going to the next line Paul says that we must "See that no one pays back evil for evil…" Okay, now that is true Forgiveness… When you forgive you don't allow what was done to you stop you from doing what is right… For that is how you must do for the least of God's people… Forgive what has been done to you and give to those who are in need as Christ gave so freely to us… So we can be forgiv-en! Can I get an Amen…

Kenyatta has tears rolling down her cheek. Jeremiah is still wrapped up in the message and doesn't notice she is crying. Something tells him to look over at Kenyatta, allowing her to have her moment, he smoothly hands her his handkerchief and keeps listening to the word. Kenyatta wipes her face as the words have brought up emotions she tried so hard to bury. The word perfectly summed up her feelings about the situation with her father. For her the rest of the service is a blur. Jeremiah's family hung around the church for about 20 -30 minutes after the service. While they were walking to the car, Kenyatta notices she has four missed calls from her Dad and a text message from her Mom that reads:

KeKe your dad was rushed to the hospital late last night. Give him a call ASAP!

Jeremiah notices the change in Kenyatta's face and asks her "What's wrong? Is everything Ok?" Kenya responds, "No. It's my Dad he is in the hospital let me call him..." Kenya dials the number... "Hello, Daddy? What's wrong?" Her dad responds "Baby Girl, they say my liver is failing worse than they initially thought, do you think you can come to the hospital and see if you are a match?" Kenyatta can't help but think about the sermon. Less than an hour ago she got a heavenly message on how we must take tender care of the weak and that in the Final judgment God recognizes those who took care of the least of those we encounter.

However, KeKe is thinking about being left on the couch all those nights waiting for him and the million times he let her down... "Hello? Hello? Baby Girl you still there?" She hears her Dad's voice but both Kenyatta and KeKe are stuck, they know whatever they decide, it has to be in the best interest of Baby Girl...   THE END

Sorry, but you gotta make your own ending to this one. I can't finish it. But you can take this moment to think about the person or people who need Forgiveness from you. What would you do if you and that person switched roles with Kenya and her Dad? I wrote this story for many reasons but I want you to know that only you can fill the void and empty places that the people who are supposed to love you have left. And that starts with forgiveness. I know it's hard and I don't know if it is even fair to write an ending that would have Kenya to give her Dad a liver, because his track record is that he is likely to continue to let her down. On the other hand, this could give him a new lease on life and allow him to see his mistakes and shortcomings in regards to the parent that he has been towards Kenya. While these are all worldly ways of looking at things, when we find ourselves in situations like these it's important to remember what the Bible tells us we should do.

A Message From The Author

There is a belief that A Woman is Supposed to Learn what it means to be loved by a Man from their Father...

Unfortunately, not every Father has done what it takes to show their daughters the love that they deserve...

With that being said, I urge any young lady that is dealing with the issues that Kenya faced to understand that the love you must have for yourself is greater than any and all the love that you can receive from either of your parents...

Self Love is God's Love and Essentially All The Love You Will Ever Need...

– Alan Gaines

179

"What's Broken Underneath"

An Original Drawing by:
Charity Neal   Age: 16

This Beautiful Drawing was inspired by the story:
Baby Girl

@cnstudios
@charliehates

Chapter 8
Beauty Is A Beast

What you are about to read is the
story of two 17-year-old girls who are
dealing with the issue of Beauty.

The story is going to be told through
discussions they are having. Theresa with her Social
Worker, Mrs. Davis and LaShawn with her Therapist
Dr. Griffin.

These girls were born on the same day in the same city.
Ironically, each conversation takes place on the same
exact day at the same exact time. While their worlds are
completely different, they face the same
enemy...

The Idea of What Is Considered...

BEAUTY

181

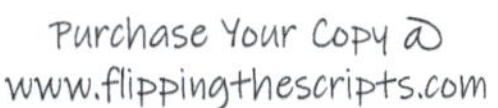

Theresa Rushing

Mrs. Mary Davis

Wednesday, September 22, 2018 8:37 am

Theresa comes in the office and sits down with an obvious scowl and negative body language. Its Theresa's first day at the Day School attached to the Juvenile Justice Center she just got shipped to on Saturday. The Center has a mandated 72-hour observation policy for all new students. This prohibits them from going to class or partaking in any of the routine activities until they have been in the facility for the allotted time.

This is her initial meeting with the social worker. Theresa has been in and out of foster care and residential living facilities since she was six years old. This upcoming drill of sorts is something that she is already over in her mind before Mrs. Davis even asks the first question. Little did Theresa know Mrs. Davis is a vet and she senses all the attitude Theresa is ready to give before she even sat down. Instead of reading from the notes in the file she is holding, Mrs. Davis takes an unconventional approach:

<u>Mrs. Davis:</u> Let me guess, you Team Cardi huh?
(Talk about a catchy icebreaker. Theresa is completely blindsided by the question and unintentionally relaxes all the muscles in her face and sits up and answers.)

<u>Theresa:</u> Yea! How'd ya kno?

<u>Mrs. Davis:</u> Uh-huh, my daughter is a little bit older than you, she is Team Cardi too. You kinda remind me of her a little bit.
(Theresa's whole mood has changed and she hasn't even recognized what Mrs. Davis is doing with the conversation. As Theresa thinks to herself "How I remind you of your daughter and I ain't been in here 5 minutes?" Mrs. Davis is going into her phone to show her a picture of her daughter. The picture has both her children and her husband on it, Mrs. Davis has a 19-year-old daughter and 14-year-old son. Mrs. Davis hands Theresa the phone.)

183

<u>Mrs. Davis:</u> See there... y'all kinda favor...
(Mrs. Davis knows that there is no true resemblance at all but Theresa has Pocahontas Braids and in one of Mrs. Davis's favorite pictures, her daughter happens to have the same hairstyle. Theresa doesn't see a resemblance but feels awkwardly obligated to be nice since Mrs. Davis is being nice to her.)

<u>Mrs. Davis:</u> Me personally, I can't get with all that gyrating, but I do like that Cardi is real. She has no filter but she is honest and I like that. I get the feeling that we actually see her for who she truly is.

<u>Theresa:</u> (Looking up from the phone she responds) You got a nice family... Misses???

<u>Mrs. Davis:</u> Misses Davis, Mary Davis. Everybody calls me Mrs. D though... You can too... Look at us talking bout Cardi and Nikki and forgot to introduce ourselves... Now I'm gonna keep it straight with you.

What's in this here file ain't going to have no impact on how I treat you or what I think about you. What I think and how I treat you, is going to be based on what and who you reveal yourself to be from our personal interactions. I give everybody a clean slate... I get to know people for who they are and more importantly who they want to be... Now, I got a question that I am going to need you to answer.

It may seem very simple but everything is going to make sense in your life when you can answer this question correctly. In order to answer this question, you must listen carefully...

Theresa: Lady, my life ain't gone make no sense with one simple answer. I'll play your little game though. What is this question that holds all the answers? (Theresa says while doing the extras)

Mrs. Davis: (Laughs to herself in her head at the bravado and defensive reaction she is getting from Theresa) The simple question is, **why are you here?**

Theresa: Lady... you got the report but if you want to hear my version of it then I'll tell you what I am in here for? (Theresa says in an annoyed tone.)
Mrs. Davis: Let's get something straight, I introduced myself as Mrs. Davis or even Mrs. D,

Mrs. Davis: Now you have called me "Lady" twice, the first time I let it slide... Now that you have done it again... I have to correct you. Theresa, I haven't disrespected you and I would appreciate it if you don't disrespect me again. You have two options of what you can call me but "Lady" is not one of them... Now that we have that squared away,

I never asked what are you in here for, I asked **why are you here?** However, now that you have offered to tell me, I am interested in what you feel you are in here for.

Theresa internally recognizes that she is wrong for calling her "Lady." However she doesn't currently have the tools to understand that she should apologize for her behavior. Theresa's actions are simply a reflection of Theresa's social immaturity and weren't intended to be disrespectful. Theresa begins to tell her version of what happened that led her to "Juvie".

Theresa: Ok **Mrs. Davis**, (Theresa says while rolling her eyes, Mrs. Davis gives a little "hmmh" but doesn't show too much emotion. Mrs. Davis knows that she must be the change she wants to see in Theresa)

my mom got locked up last Thursday. I wasn't there I was staying over my boyfriend Corky house. Somebody had called the cops on her and her boyfriend for fightin', they always be fightin, when Eddie heard the cops comin up the street, he ranned out da back door. Eddie, thats her boyfriend, when the cops got there my Mama had forgot that they were baggin up when they started arguing. So they got her on possession with intention to distribute.

<u>Mrs. Davis:</u> I'm sorry to hear that, have you spoken to your mom since this incident occurred?

<u>Theresa:</u> Nawl, I mean me and my mom don't really talk like that anyway, I mean she been in and out of jail my whole life, so she more like my older sister who look after me from time to time than she is my mama... I mean I been in and out of foster care and living with different family members in between her being out or being locked up. This has been going on since I was like 4 years old so, I mean its normal...

Mrs. Davis: No Theresa, that's not normal and I don't want you to accept that having a mother who goes in and out of jail is normal. It is not normal, living in Foster care or between family members houses and bouncing around is not normal. I don't want you to think this is normal because when we accept certain things as normal, we don't find the fault in it. When we don't find fault in things like this, we are likely to pass it on to our children. Do you want your children to have that kind of life?

(Theresa's face shows obvious signs that she had never looked at her situation from the perspective that Mrs. Davis has just given her so she simply replies...)

Theresa: No.

Mrs. Davis: Good... Baby, those things aren't normal... Now, let's back it up a bit, you said a lot. And I want to honor that I heard you and acknowledge what you are telling me. However, you didn't tell me how what happened with your Mom connects to why you are sitting in front of me.

Butterflies

<u>Theresa</u>: My bad, yea the next day after my Mom got locked up, I went back to the house to get the stash from the basement. Corky had told me he heard my Moms got locked up so I knew that the cops didn't get the work from the basement. So, I went back over there to get it and I guess the cops was still watching the house waiting on Eddie or something but when I came out, they let me get to the end of the block before they swooped on me. They got me on drug possession so that's why I am here.

<u>Mrs. Davis</u>: What were you going to do with the drugs?

<u>Theresa</u>: I was gone sell'em! What you mean? Man, I'm tryin' to get the bag out here...I mean they got me on possession because I had the work... they gave me possession with intent to distribute.

I just shut up when the police dect-uh, office-... Whatever, the man who arrested me. When he said intent to distribute I ain't no dummy so I just shut up and let them roll with that. I ain't got no lawyer so I ain't say nothin' else...

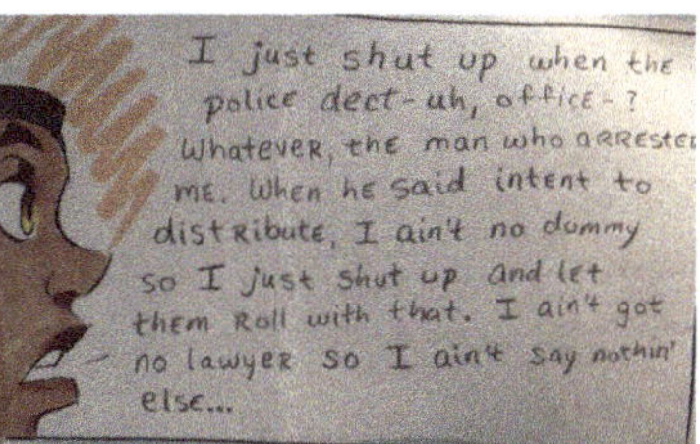

But to answer your question, I went back to get them so I could sell them. I was gone get that work off. I mean I can't only get the little money Corky be giving me... I need all mine...

Mrs. Davis: Alright... hey, I understand getting your money, I definitely know that we need to do it legally but... I understand. Okay, let's back this up a bit. You said that Corky gives you money. Tell me a little about how you got with Corky. I'm interested in hearing about this relationship.
Theresa: I got busted a few times for stealing clothes from the mall. It

wasn't a lot. It's like misdemeanor shoplifting or something. I stole some lingerie and a sexy little outfit. I told the cops it was for my Mom and they believed it so they kinda let me off.

Mrs. Davis: What did this have to do with Corky? I am a little confused...

Theresa: I stoled the stuff right after I got with Corky. Corky is a Baller, he a D - Boy, like a big D - Boy

Butterflies

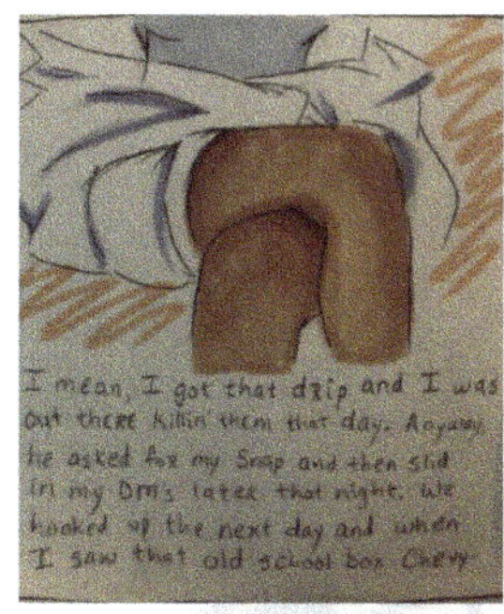

and I know how they be.
They always got a lot of girls, but they like to take
care of they girls too... When I first met him it was at a football game.
Him and all his boys was saying I was so fine and that they was gone get
me. I mean I got that drip and I was out there killin' them that day.
Anyway, he asked for my Snap and then slid into my DM's later that night.
We hooked up the next day and when I saw that old school box Chevy

sittin' on rims with the leather seats... I knew I had to put it on him. So,
I had Eddie drop me off at the mall because I knew I needed something to
blow his mind. I mean everyone else be using me because I am pretty...

so once I figured out I could
use my looks to my advantage, that's what I been doing...

Mrs. Davis: That is very interesting, let me make note of that... 'I figured
out I could use my looks to my advantage. That's what I been doing.'

Okay, as much as I hate to cut this short, but the initial meetings are only supposed to be 20 minutes and we pushing right up on 30 minutes. Plus, I have a meeting. I have to be in the conference room in about 10 minutes.

Also, I kinda wanna see how you do on the unit and just a touch of homework on you before we meet again ok?

<u>Theresa</u>: That's cool.

<u>Mrs. Davis</u>: Alright now... I don't want any bad reports on you when I follow up with your teachers ok? (Theresa nods in agreeance)

Also, I want you to think about why you are here, okay?

<u>Theresa</u>: Ok Mrs. Davis (Theresa agrees verbally but is still lost as to what Mrs. Davis means by the question.)

Theresa gets up to leave the room.

Butterflies

Mrs. Davis: It was so nice to meet you... Don't leave just yet...(Mrs. Davis

says while getting up.) Come give Mrs. Davis a hug...

(Theresa is shocked by the request and turns around in total surprise.)

Theresa walks over to her and shyly opens her arms. Mrs. Davis brings her
in tight, Theresa feels the comfort in the embrace and momentarily allows

life's worries to fade away.
Mrs. Davis goes to let go and Theresa holds on just a second longer. Mrs.
Davis senses Theresa's response to the hug and gives her words of reas-
surance.) Oh child don't you worry, I am gone love on you no matter what...

194

LaShawn Thorpe

Dr. Gloria Griffin

Wednesday, September 22, 2018. 8:37 am

LaShawn is nervously fidgeting with her jacket zipper as she sits alongside her mother, Mrs. Thorpe, in the office of Dr. Gloria Griffin, a board certified clinical therapist. Dr. Griffin makes small talk while Mrs. Thorpe completes the consent forms for LaShawn to receive therapy. This is the initial meeting and LaShawn is trying to overcome the anxiety that she feels inside as she is about to embark on uncharted waters.

Mrs. Thorpe requested that she begin therapy after a recent incident at school has triggered a change in LaShawn's behavior. Surprisingly, LaShawn didn't give much resistance to the idea when her mother suggested it. LaShawn is a great student in school and very kind hearted. However, due to the fact that she is a plus sized individual LaShawn has been the target of bullying since she was a kid. In the past, LaShawn hasn't shown how much the ridicule has bothered her, however this recent incident appears to have been the last straw. LaShawn has become withdrawn, which prompted her mother to seek professional help.

Dr. Griffin: Thank you so much Mrs. Thorpe. (She says as she receives the form from Mrs. Thorpe.) Ok, now I want to hear a little more about why you guys are here. From your perspective what do you feel is going on with LaShawn? I understand you are worried about a recent event that happened which prompted you to reach out to me. Can you tell me about it?

195

Mrs. Thorpe: Yes. Okay, it was about three weeks ago. LaShawn was in the bathroom at school washing her hands and another girl who is popular (Mrs. Thorpe rolls her eyes at the overblown idea of high school popularity) at the school took a selfie and LaShawn was in the background. The girl posted the picture to Instagram and everyone started making mean comments about LaShawn. Calling her names, zooming in on her and even making memes of her. It was cruel and hurtful. LaShawn isn't that type of person to be mean to other people and although she knows its a cold world, she didn't do anything to bring this on herself. Since then, I saw a change in my baby, she is depressed... She doesn't really want to go to school, she isn't coming out her room much, she's just not herself anymore and I am concerned.

So I reached out because, although people have said mean things in the past, this feels different. I have always told her to embrace herself and for the most part she has, but I just know this has been hard on her and I think she needs more than just my help on this.

(Dr. Griffin takes a few notes as Mrs. Thorpe was speaking and now that Mrs. Thorpe has finished she addresses the situation.)

Dr. Griffin: First, I really want to express my sympathy to you LaShawn. I can't fathom your pain and I want you to know that I hate that you

are experiencing such a painful moment. And mom, as a parent, I know that we are protective by nature, so I can only imagine the range of emotions that you must have been feeling over these past few weeks. I just want you to know that you did the right thing by reaching out and finding help for LaShawn.

Butterflies

There is a stigma that goes with seeking therapy and I want to commend you for understanding the value of mental health. I want to assure you that, I will do all that I can to help you and your family get through this.

I want you all to know that I am here to help you both deal with this situation so we can get Ms. LaShawn back to loving herself and being happy again. (LaShawn has begun to tear up) Mrs. Thorpe, I am going to ask you to step out and let me talk with LaShawn alone. We are going to push up around 35 or 40 minutes or so feel free to step out and even make a quick run if you need to, LaShawn will be fine here.

(Mrs. Thorpe gets up to leave but is sure to give LaShawn a hug. She whispers a soft, "I love you" into her daughter's ear and gives her a kiss on the cheek before exiting the room.)

<u>Dr. Griffin</u>: (Looking at LaShawn with a caring smile says to her) You are such a beautiful girl.

(LaShawn isn't used to hearing compliments, but more importantly, she doesn't have enough self-esteem to believe what Dr. Griffin sees, which is that LaShawn is beautiful. Although she thinks that Dr. Griffin is being nice because it's her job to help, LaShawn drops her head in a symbol of shy disbelief at the compliment and replies gingerly "Thank you" as she wipes another tear with the kleenex in her left hand.)

198

<u>Dr. Griffin</u>: LaShawn, I just heard your mother give her concerns but I wanna know from you, **Why are you here?**

<u>LaShawn</u>: (LaShawn takes a deep breath and starts to speak.) Because I... (LaShawn stops again. She is fidgeting with the strap of her purse as she tries to find the words to express how she feels.) Because I am ugly and I hate the way I look...

(Saying the words breaks the dam of emotions she has been holding in for far longer than just the 3 weeks since the incident her mother described. With the tears beginning to flow heavily, Dr. Griffin gets up and hands LaShawn more kleenex.)

199

Dr. Griffin: Oh LaShawn, I understand that may be how you feel but that doesn't make it true! I hate that you are hurting but I am glad you are being honest with how you feel. Your feelings have to be faced in order to move forward. This is good, I know it hurts but allow all of it to come up... It is okay, let it out, LaShawn.

(Dr. Griffin patiently allows LaShawn to let go of what she has been holding in. After a few moments of weeping LaShawn brings herself back together to continue the conversation.)

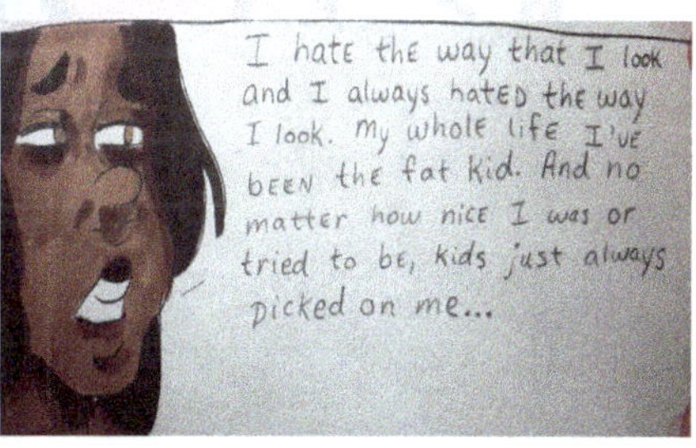

Lashawn: I hate the way that I look and I always have hated the way that I look. My whole life I've been the fat kid and no matter how nice I was or tried to be, kids just always picked on me...

Dr. Griffin: LaShawn, when you say picked on, let me know what you mean by that. I do know what it means to be picked on, but I want you to explain, so I can get a clearer picture of what types of things you have experienced...

LaShawn:
Going back to when I was in like second or third grade, the boys in my class and in my grade would remix songs on the radio to make fun of me... Like the Lil' Wayne

song, 'A Milli' - they would switch the lyrics and say stuff like 'A MEAL' E' one of the lines was, "LaShawn eats the cafeteria/ compared to our plate, this just isn't fair' or 'If you can't eat them then you pop'em / LaShawn ate all the Orville Reddenbaucher'... Just mean stuff... The T.I. Song, 'You Can Have Whatever You Like' - they would say 'Snacks on deck, Kool Aid on Ice, And Shawn eat chips all nite... She be eatin' whatever she like...

200

(Dr. Griffin can hear the pain in her voice. LaShawn is recounting the painful memories with tears streaming down her face. Strangely as it may seem, finally speaking these horrid memories is liberating. So amid the tears LaShawn's voice doesn't crack)

Dr. Griffin: Wow, I am so sorry that you had to go through that... Unfortunately, kids tend to be very cruel and often disregard other people's feelings to be funny...

LaShawn: Cruel is too easy of a word... I call it evil. One day when I was going to my seat on the bus, they threw a McChicken at me... It didn't hit me... So I acted like I didn't see it, but when we got to school, I went straight to the bathroom to cry...

Being... (LaShawn takes another deep breath) being, "Big" is not easy.

Dr. Griffin: That is horrible. I can't imagine what you have had to endure. While I do want to honor your emotional space right now, it seems to me that your mother may not be fully aware of all the baggage you are carrying.

My perception from what she stated was that she feels like the incident with the selfie is an isolated situation. Am I correct?

LaShawn: Yes, to a certain extent she knows. However, I am not sure that she gets the full picture. My Mom has enough to worry about and I don't want to be another part of what she is going through.

202

<u>Dr. Griffin</u>: While I understand your position. First, it is very important to know that we must never view ourselves as a burden to those who are responsible for us. Your parents have the right to know all that you are experiencing because it is their responsibility to protect and provide for you the best they can. If they are unaware of what you are dealing with than they can't do their job to the best of their ability.

Lastly and more importantly, I want to back it up for one second. You expressed that it is not easy being "Big" as you put it. I want to discuss that a bit further. I sincerely acknowledge the trauma and ridicule that you have experienced in regards to your size. However, I want you to consider embracing the way God made you. You must understand that everything about who you are is exactly the way in which God intended you to be.

203

Unfortunately, the world has created a perception and ideal of beauty. I could ask a question that I already know the answer to, which is were the "skinny" or "pretty" girls treated the same way? I know the answer is very likely to be no, but the question I really want you to consider is why weren't they treated in the same cruel and evil way that you were treated?

LaShawn: I never thought about that, I guess because there ain't nothing wrong with those girls... I don't know?

LaShawn, there isn't anything wrong with you either... Society has just made it acceptable to make fun of people who are larger in size than others. I think the term they are using now is "Fat Shaming". LaShawn, there is only one true way in which you can overcome the feelings of worthlessness. That is through self-love which means you must embrace LaShawn. Every thought, every emotion, every curve, everything that is you, must be internalized with love. Then and only then can you present your true self to the world with love and appreciation...

LaShawn, it is going to take a lot to get to this point. However a failure to do so will leave you spiritually insufficient and the feelings that something is wrong with you, will haunt you forever... LaShawn, I want you to understand something... True healing can never come from accepting a faulty ideal...

Dr. Griffin: LaShawn, there isn't anything wrong with you either... Society has just made it acceptable to make fun of people who are larger in size than others. I think the term they are using now is called "Fat Shaming". LaShawn, there is only one true way in which you can overcome the feelings of worthlessness. That is through self-love which means you must embrace LaShawn. Every curve, every emotion, every thought, everything that is you, must be internalized with love. Then and only then can you present your true self to the world with love and appreciation. It is going to take a lot to get to this point. However a failure to do so, will leave you spiritually insufficient and the feelings that something is wrong with you, will haunt you forever... LaShawn, I want you to understand something... True healing can never come from accepting a faulty ideal.

Here is what I mean, you will never be truly happy with yourself if you go out of your way to embrace an ideal that is given to you by the outside world. LaShawn, let's say you lost weight and got to a size that the world tells us is acceptable. If you lost the weight only because you wanted people to stop talking about you, then let me be the first to tell you that you are likely to still be unhappy because the reason you did it will not have come from within. Now, if you felt that a size… "whatever?!" would make you feel better about who you are and would allow you to be the best LaShawn you could possibly be, then by all means, you should make the decision to do so. The difference is simple, you must accept yourself and make every decision from the standpoint that you have LaShawns' best interest in mind. Not from a position that you no longer want to be talked about or made fun of because of how you look. Alright let's pause for a second right here, I know that is a lot, so tell me how you are feeling about this idea that I just proposed to you?

<u>LaShawn</u>: (LaShawn takes a moment to think about it before responding.) I mean, I never looked at it like that, but it makes a lot of sense. My whole life I just remember thinking, 'What people are going to say if I do this… Or if go there… I have been so wrapped up in what I thought people were going to say or do, that I haven't given myself the chance to think about myself and how I feel about me…" (LaShawn takes a deep breath and looks over towards the door staring at nothing in particular. She briefly goes to say something else but stops herself. She holds it in and slowly drops her head before wiping more tears.)

<u>Dr. Griffin</u>: LaShawn, this is a long journey to self acceptance and I want you to know that it has nothing to do with your size, I have clients in all shapes and sizes. The common thread amongst everyone I work with is that, they all are dealing with someone else's perception instead of embracing their own reflection… Now we are going to wrap it up here for today. However, before we do, I want to give you a little homework… I want you to take this book, it's titled, I Have Something to Say by Japonica Brown. Also, I am going to give you a few affirmations that I want you to say in the morning when you wake up and at night before you go to sleep. It will feel a little funny at first talking to yourself but stick with it. You don't have to only say it in the morning and night. You can say them at any time. Also, I want you to look up Chardline Faiteau, Erica Moise and Izzy Lopes. Find out what you can about them and we will talk more about them at our next meeting. One last thing, when we have our next session, I want you to tell me **"why are you here?"**

205

Thursday, November 18, 2018. 1:37pm

Theresa has just got into a fight at the day school. Theresa has been at the facility a little more than 7 weeks. This however, is her first incident. By now Theresa and Ms. Davis has developed a very strong relationship because Ms. Davis comes to check on her in class and sometimes brings her in the office just so Theresa can get a break. Theresa has that "Alpha Female" effect on the day school and facility. Theresa is the one person whose mood usually dictates how everything and everyone else goes. If she is feeling good, everything is good. If she is feeling in a funk, everyone seems to have an attitude. Today, completely out of character for her, Theresa started the fight. This has taken Ms. Davis by surprise and she now has Theresa in her office trying to get to the bottom of what is the real reason for this uncharacteristic behavior.

<u>Mrs. Davis</u>: Talk to me Theresa, this ain't you... Tell me what's going on... I mean you got a smart mouth but you ain't no fighter. Wsup? This doesn't add up... Talk to me...

<u>Theresa</u>: MAN SHE-

<u>Mrs. Davis</u>: Hold up... Bring it down Theresa... (Ms. Davis says in a calm voice, to get Theresa to regulate her emotions and recognize that she doesn't have to yell, even though Theresa is still excited by what just happened.) Now. We have been working on accountability, so I don't want to hear about her. I want you to tell me your role in what took place and the decisions that you made that have you in my office right now and not in class getting your education. Theresa, we already talked about how you gotta catch up because you behind in both reading and math. So, I am not understanding how you feel like you have time to be fighting. Mrs. Vaughn says that you spend most of your time in class, drawing... Theresa it's obvious that you have a gift, your drawings are beautiful. I got your pictures up all over my office but we talked about balancing your time with your gift and your education. Nowhere in that conversation did we mention that you would have time to be fighting? So please tell me what happened?

<u>Theresa</u>: Ok, so she...

<u>Mrs. Davis</u>: Nope, start again, if you need to take your time then please do... But you must start approaching everything from the standpoint of analyzing your role and the choices you made because when we fail to analyze ourselves first, we approach things from a thermometer mentality and not a thermostat mentality. We working on this, thermometers do what?

Theresa: Tell the temperature of the room...
(Theresa says rolling her eyes in disgust. Theresa and Mrs. Davis have done this drill what feels to Theresa like the one millionth time. She knows exactly where this is going.)

Mrs. Davis: Ok. Good, tell me what a thermostat does?

Theresa: Control the temperature of the room.

Mrs. Davis: Exactly... Now take a deep breath. Think about yourself for a moment as the thermostat that you are, that we all are. We control the temperature in our room of life. Take accountability for your actions and when you are ready, please tell me what happened?
(Theresa's leg begins to shake as she looks out the window. About a minute goes by before she looks back at Mrs. Davis and then abruptly drops her head and begins to cry. The tears are coming down in a painful, soul moving uncontrollable fashion. This long overdue build up of pain is finally coming out. However, Mrs. Davis has no idea what these tears are about. She comes around from the desk and places her hand on Theresa's back. Theresa feels the hand on her back and turns and grabs Mrs. Davis around the waist, buries her head onto Mrs. Davis hip and releases the pain via her tears.)

Mrs. Davis: Come on, let it out... Theresa this is good, let it out... Come on, come on... I know this has nothing to do with the fight... Let it out, let it out Theresa. Ok, Use your words to express how you feel! I'm here for you.
(Theresa takes her arm from around Mrs. Davis waist, takes her sleeve and wipes her nose. She opens her eyes to see the tissue that Mrs. Davis has out for her. Theresa grabs one and wipes both eyes before, ironically pulling her knees up to her chest so she is know seated in the fetal position. Theresa takes a deep breath and begins to speak. Mrs. Davis takes her seat.)

Theresa: Mrs. D, I fought that girl because I 'pose to go out on pass for the weekend with my mother. Remember she got out of jail, last month when they reduced her bond. (Ms. Davis is careful not to interrupt and simply nods her head in agreement.) Well, she 'pose to come get me tomorrow but I know she ain't coming... And before you say... 'How you know she ain't comin? Give her a chance...' I know she ain't coming because it's been the same story my whole life... My momma been leaving me and not coming to get me since I was born. I remember being like 4 years old and she left me over my cousin's house for like a month. It was a cookout or something and she left with 'a friend' and didn't come back and get me. I remember my Auntie having to track her down to see if when she was gonna pick me up. It turned into this big thing and my Mama finally coming to pick me up almost a month later. It's been like that my whole life. Livin' over here with this cousin or Great Aunt or Uncle for two or three months. Or over there with her Best friend or someone else she grew up with... My whole life I can't even count how many people I stayed with. But I know from the age of eleven to fifteen, I stayed in twenty seven different places with sixteen different people. That's before I went into foster care when I was fifteen. I was in eighth grade and fifteen years old because I had to repeat the sixth grade. I've felt abandoned my whole life Mrs. D. It would have been too embarrassing when she didn't show up tomorrow and I gotta sit on the unit looking stupid the whole weekend when everybody know I was 'pose to go out on pass. So now I don't gotta worry about how it look, I ain't going on pass because I got into a fight, not that my Mama don't love me enough to come get me...

<u>Mrs. Davis</u>: Okay, I hear all of that and we are going to address it, but I need you to explain how what you are dealing with gives you the right to jump on LaDeja? Sound like she had nothing to do with what you got going on inside of you. How does that give you the right to hurt someone else?

<u>Theresa</u>: Ms. D, you don't understand, when I be feeling like this, I just want someone else to hurt... And I don't really like her like that, she got too much mouth on her anyway, so I fought her...

<u>Mrs. Davis</u>: Theresa but you know that this behavior is not right?

<u>Theresa</u>: (Filled with anger and frustration she begins to cry before she yells) **It ain't right being left by my Mama! It ain't right what they did to me, when I was over there! Nobody cared about what they did to me at all those places she left me! That wasn't right! Why should I care that this ain't right? Nobody cared about my pain!**

<u>Mrs. Davis</u>: Theresa, Theresa, Theresa... What who did to you? When you was over where? Yes, oh God is so good and merciful, its time to free yourself from this pain... Let it out...

<u>Theresa</u>: Everywhere! It seem like everywhere my Mama left me that someone would touch me or make me touch them or do something to me or make me do something to them! That's what's not right! I don't care if it

ain't right! My life ain't right!

(Mrs. Davis gets up again and walks over next to Theresa in a show of emotional and physical support. Using what she knows about the importance of proximity support for people who have experienced trauma, Mrs. Davis shifts the energy in Theresa by simply walking over to her. Theresa trusts Mrs. Davis, who knows that when a person is opening up about trauma it's important to give them comfort as they process difficult moments. This helps them feel secure. Mrs. Davis simply grabs Theresa's hand and gently rubs her upper back which causes Theresa to pause momentarily. Theresa takes a deep breath, collects her thoughts and begins reliving her trauma.)

Theresa: When I was bout 6 or 7 I spent the summer with one of my Great Uncles. While I was there, one of my female cousins, she a lesbian now. She probably was then now that I think about it. She was like fifteen or something, she would always say, 'You so pretty, you gone be so fine when you grow up'. She would... She would, oh my gosh... I've never told anyone this. To be honest, no one has ever asked...
(Theresa looks back at the window but continues talking. She is emotionally too embarrassed to look at Mrs. Davis as she speaks about what happened.)

Theresa: She would make me do "stuff" to her and she would do "stuff" to me... (Theresa looks over at Mrs. Davis after releasing the painful memory. When their eyes meet, Mrs. Davis understands what Theresa is referring to. Theresa feels weird saying this yet it feels good to finally let this out. She is not too familiar with the feeling of liberation that comes from speaking your truth. However, with this sudden rush of courage she keeps going without missing a beat.)
        I was so scared, I cried the whole time... I begged my Mama to come get me when she finally called to check on me. I was crying an crying and she didn't say nothing but she will be there to get me on August 8th. It was like the middle of June when it happened. I didn't figure it out until I got a little older that she was in jail and couldn't come pick me up. When I tried to tell my Aunt, well my Great Aunt Ethel about it and all she said was 'Girls like boys and boys like girls. Quit making stuff up. Saying stuff like that when it ain't true can make people go to jail. She say "Don't nobody deserve to go to jail, 'specially not family, we protect family, you understand me...' That's what she said, of course I told her I understand but I didn't get why no one thought to protect me. Ain't I family?

when my Aunt Ethel didn't believe me, I knew nobody was gone believe me. So when people would touch me or make me do stuff when I was staying in other places, I wouldn't tell nobody. Most of the time it was family or someone who was one of my mama friends. When I was about 13 we had moved out of town and my Mama had us staying with one of her friends she grew up with. She offered to help my Mama get on her feet or whatever. well, she had a 17 year old son who would sneak on youtube or whatever other websites and be watching nasty stuff."

"Well, one night, he came in the room me and my Mama was staying in. My Mama and his Mama had went out to the club or something and he asked me did I wanna see something. So he showing me this nasty video and he said "You beautiful like my girlfriend... She want me to do this stuff with her but, I don't really know how. Can I practice on you so I can be good at it when I have to do it to her? It would really help me out." I always wanted an older brother and up until that point he was really cool. He would look out for me. We would laugh and joke, he made me feel like I was his real little sister. So when he asked me, I didn't mind helping him out. He would always tell me thanks for my help and be gentle. It wasn't until we got in trouble that I found out that what he was doing was wrong. (Theresa sees the puzzled look on Ms. Davis's face and explains further what happened.) We got in trouble because my teacher Mrs. McIntosh had us write an essay about a time or something that we did that was really nice or helpful. My life had been so crazy to that point, the only thing I could think about was what I was doing to help him out. So I wrote about it. Mrs. McIntosh told me to stay after class and asked me about my essay. At first she was asking me about like, the structure of the essay and stuff like that. Then she asked me was the stuff I wrote true. I was like "yeah". I saw her drop her head and tears started up in her eyes. She told me to go to class and I did. Before the next period was over, they called me in the office and I saw the cops and some social worker lady. That's how I got in foster care."

Mrs. Davis: Oh my God, I am so sorry to hear that baby! But I'm still a bit lost. Theresa, you said "We" got in trouble, did you mean "he" got in trouble?

Theresa: Well, it felt like we were in trouble because Foster Care was no better. Everywhere, I would go, "Oh you so Pretty or You too Pretty to be like this... to be like that." That's why I stayed running away. (Mrs. Davis notices that Theresa didn't answer her but let's it go.) I hated being told how I should act or having people always touching on me or doing stuff to me, so I would run away. But it was the last foster home that changed my mind... My Foster brother Eric, we called him Ric. He put me on game one day. It was the last time someone took advantage of me. Our foster Mom was working 3 to 11's and he would have his friends over to play Fortnite. They would smoke a little weed and what not, they would say little sly stuff about how I was So Fine this and that, but I wouldn't pay it no 'tention and Ric would always tell them to chill out. Well, I had came out my room to go to the kitchen and his boy Rell said something and I blew it off. Ric told him to chill out and before I knew it Rell yelling, she ain't gone keep teasin' me walking around here knowing that I wanna hit that... So I was scared and said 'Stop screamin, you know ain't nobody teasin' you!' He pulled a gun out, pointed it at Ric and told him 'Either she gone gimme some or I am going to shoot you and then rape her, either way I'm getting me some! This chick ain't your real sista no way! So why you care?' When his other boy Smoke didn't stop him or say chill out, that's when I figured they had set Ric up. So they both took turns on me. After it was done and they left, Ric came into the room to apologize and gave me the game. He said 'Look Rees... everybody wanna piece of you because you so pretty. Everybody gone always want the pretty girl or something from her. You better learn to use your Beauty to your advantage. They gonna take from you anyway so you would be smart to get something for yourself out of it." Since then, I been out here using what God gave me to get what I want. When I thought about it, he was right, everybody else was taking advantage of me, but me.

Mrs. Davis: Wow! Wow! Theresa, that is no way to live. Baby you must see your worth. No one had the right to manipulate or take advantage of you. I am sorry that all this has happened to you. But Theresa, you must realize that you are priceless. I understand your childhood has made it nearly impossible to see life in something other than a give and take fashion. But when you are the one taking from yourself, it is only a matter of time before there is nothing left to take. Theresa, what has using your looks to get what you want truly gotten you? More importantly, where are you going? All that will make sense Theresa, when you understand, "Why are you here?"

Theresa: Here we go with that again...

Mrs. Davis: You are right here we go again. Theresa, you know I love you and want what is best for you. But here is the truth, your way has led you to become self manipulative, which destroys your worth. Your way has you behind academically, with a 24 year-old drug dealer boyfriend.

while you are 17, sitting up in a juvenile alternative school picking fights because you don't want no one making fun of you or talking behind your back if your Mama don't show up to take you out on pass. Now Theresa, this isn't all your fault but you have to take some responsibility. Your decisions are based on a lack of knowledge and some very unfortunate circumstances, however they are still your choices... (Mrs. Davis continues.)

Again, why you are here and why you are in here are two totally different things and I know that we talked about that before. Right now, we are dealing with why you are in here. If you are going to find out why you are here, I'm sorry but Theresa, you are going to have to face your mother at some point because you are carrying her baggage. (Theresa gives Mrs. Davis a look of confusion) Yes. You are carrying your mother's baggage around. The choices you have made and continue to make are all to protect that little girl inside who was abandoned. Theresa, I get it. You know I do. You have to realize that you have created a wall of protection around yourself that is made of deceit, manipulation and now violence. To solve a problem Theresa, you must get to what is causing that problem. Your problem is abandonment. Whenever you feel abandoned you act out. Theresa think about what you told me about Corky... You said that he is a big drug dealer. Essentially, you are with him because of the protection that he provides. You know that you will not be in danger and you will get some sort of money. Now, I'm not going to pass any judgment, but I want you to think about at some point do you love him or do you love what he provides. Either way, from how I see it Theresa, it all boils down to your mother. You are doing whatever it takes to never be back in the situation of abandonment. Theresa you are right for protecting yourself the best way that you know how. I don't want you to think that I am blaming you. I simply want to help you get a different set of tools to protect yourself with. You need tools that are going to build you up, not the ones that you have been using that have torn you down. Do you understand what I am saying to you Theresa?

<u>Theresa</u>: Yea I do Mrs. D, but how am I going to do that in here? I'm 17. I'm not good in school. I ain't got no family that care for me like that. My mama done messed up every relationship by either stealing something or doing... whatever?! Don't nobody want to have nothing to do with me because of her. I mean, it is what it is now. My mama is who she is and I am who I am. I see what you saying about how I try to protect myself or whatever but, talking to my Mama ain't going to change her. So what is the point?

<u>Mrs. Davis</u>: Theresa, this has nothing to do with your mother. This is

about you. Forgiveness is more beneficial to the person doing the forgiving than it is for the person being forgiven.

<u>Theresa</u>: Mrs. D, you tripping! I ain't forgivin' my Mama! You got me messed up. Nah, you can miss me with that. I been through too much to forgive her, I been through things she don't even know about. I mean, no. No. I'm not forgivin' her. Mrs. D! Can I go? You done threw me off with that one! Like for real. I mean we cool but you tripping! I am ready to go back to the unit. I don't care. They can give me more time for fighting her. Whatever, I -

<u>Mrs. Davis</u>: Theresa. Theresa. Look at you, the moment I mentioned forgiving your mother, you are blowing up. This, (Mrs. Davis gestures in a circular motion) all this. Is telling me that you got some issues that you need to resolve with your mother. I'm not saying that you have to talk to her tonight. I understand that it is going to take you some time to get to that place where you can forgive and have the conversation you need to have with your mother. Theresa, here is the bottom line. We can talk. You can draw. We can do a lot of things that make you feel better in the moment. However, all that is putting a bandaid on the bullet wound. I can give you strategies. Drawing can give you a release, but your mother, she can give you answers. Answers, Theresa that is what you need. Answers, why did she leave you? Who is your father? What happened in her childhood that made her this type of mother? What was her childhood like? These questions will help you paint the best picture of all, the picture of Theresa.

Right now, you have the pencil, Theresa you have the paint brush, but you don't have the canvas. Your mother can provide the canvas. The answers are going to give you something to draw on and what is missing inside to draw from, Theresa. Without those answers, you are going to continue to manipulate or act out whenever you feel those emotions of abandonment.

Unless you address what causes these emotions, you will never overcome your struggles. Your mother holds that key Theresa. You have the power to make your past either chapters or the summary of your life. When someone looks back at your life when it is all said and done, what are they going to talk about? Theresa was pretty? Or Theresa momma left her over here and left her over there and people did bad things to her? Or that Theresa never got over all the things that happened to her and that's why she is like that. Theresa, you have to make a decision that you are going to be a victor and not a victim. Things in our life don't just get better we have to make things better... So Theresa what are we going to do? Make the past the summary of your life or a chapter in your life?

Theresa: Mrs. D, I don't know how to make my past a chapter, but I know I don't want it to be a summary... I am going to make my past a chapter... Can you help me?

Ms. Davis: Yes, I can. But you are going to have to trust me. Theresa there is no way around it but you are going to have to have that talk with your mother. If not, there is nothing that I nor anyone will be able to do for you.

Theresa: I'm sorry Mrs. D. I'm just not ready for that. I feel what you are saying but like my Mama not going even sit down and listen to me. I know she going to try to blame me and that's going to start an argument. Ain't no point in even talking to that lady. That is why I treat her like my big sister more than my Mama. When it comes to real stuff she be gettin defensive. I ain't even trying to deal with that, Mrs. D.

Mrs. Davis: Theresa, I understand that. Again, I am not saying that you have to talk to her tonight. Theresa, I am simply telling you that in order for you to deal with the type of feelings that made you jump on LaDeja. You are going to have to face it head-on. That is all I am saying. You don't have to do that until you are ready. Not a moment sooner. I am not trying to rush you, Theresa, I am trying to help you.

Theresa: You know what Mrs. D, whatever. If you want me to talk to her then I will but I ain't talking to her no time soon. I'll tell you that. Can I go back to the unit now?

Mrs. Davis: No, you are going to sit here and chill out. Look up there on my shelf and get your sketch pad. Go on over there and sit on the couch. But you ain't going nowhere until you calm down. I'll tell you what though, I am about to call LaDeja down here so you can apologize.

Theresa: Mrs. D I ain't bout to - (Mrs. Davis cuts her off, raising her voice.)

Mrs. Davis: Theresa you are going to apologize to LaDeja and that is final! (Theresa folds her arms sits back in obvious disgust. Knowing that she isn't going to win this battle of wills with Mrs. Davis, Theresa abandons the fight and picks up her notebook and begins to draw. About thirty minutes pass before Theresa looks up from her sketch pad and expresses her emotions to Mrs. Davis.)

Theresa: This felt so good, letting all that out... I think, no, I know I am ready to change. I think I am going to be able to do this Mrs. Davis.

Ms. Davis: (Comes around the table and gives her a hug.) Baby you are going to be able to do this and more. The big thing is that you are ready to make the change. We will get to work on what triggers you and why. Knowing what sets off our reactions helps us become aware of situations we need to avoid if we can. It's always better to be Proactive than it is to be Reactive. Proactive is the Thermostat, Reactive is the Thermometer. Now that you have calmed down, I am going to call LaDeja down so you can apologize...

"Theresa"

An Original Oil Painting By:
Karma Griggs   Age: 14

This Beautiful painting was inspired by the story:
Beauty Is A Beast

Instagram: @paintitkarma

Thursday, November 18, 2018. 1:37 pm

This session we find a more comfortable and confident LaShawn. LaShawn is excited because she enjoyed doing the homework she was given and is looking forward to the conversation with Dr. Griffin. LaShawn enters the office and has a seat after being told by the secretary that Dr. Griffin is ready to see her.

Dr. Griffin: Good afternoon LaShawn how are you today?

LaShawn: I'm blessed... I wanted to thank you for having me look up those phenomenal women! I had no idea of who they were but I was happy to learn that women who look like me could be so confident.

Dr. Griffin: Well I am happy to see that you did your homework! And yes, Black Girl Magic comes in all shapes and sizes. (Dr. Griffin is speaking with self-pride as well as love for her people.)

LaShawn: I have been on Chardline Chanel's website like every day. Seeing the women in such beautiful clothes and looking so happy and free. I have read all the articles on there like at least 5 times. Reading the stuff on there just gives me so much confidence in myself.

216

Dr. Griffin: I see! I'm glad you mentioned confidence because in one of our previous session we discussed taking this journey on the road to self-acceptance. And like I mentioned, it is impossible to accept yourself if you apply the agreed-upon definitions of society to dictate and control the image you hold for yourself. To say it more plainly, if you were to lose weight or alter your appearance in any way to simply fit in. Then you would have placed a higher value on the opinions of others than the ones that you should hold for yourself. I know that we covered this before, but I want to make sure that this sticks so lets stay here for a second. Tell me what that means to you?

Lashawn: It means that, anything that I do should be because I want to do it, not because I don't want people saying things about me?

(LaShawn is about 85% sure that she knows what Dr. Griffin is talking about, so her voice comes across with an initial hesitation, but grows stronger as she speaks before diving into a quizzical tone at the end.)

Dr. Griffin: Exactly! Yes, that is exactly it! (A smile comes across LaShawn's face. Her gut was right! Proudly she listens intently to what Dr. Griffin says next.) Ok, we are on the same page. Alright, let's transition. LaShawn can you talk about why you feel that you aren't really confident. Tell me where that comes from?

LaShawn: Well, I mean... My whole life, I never really got a compliment. Aside from people in my family, like my parents or Grandparents or Aunties. If someone said something nice to me it is usually like... "Oh that purse is cute" Or "Your hair is nice" or "I like those shoes". Never does anyone say "You look nice." So my whole life, I have known that things I might wear will look nice but never do I look nice.

Dr. Griffin: That is interesting... I don't want to interject too soon, tell me more about this, dig deeper.

LaShawn: It's like when I saw those pictures on the Chardline Chanel website, those women looked nice. They looked happy. Ok, like the Izzy Lopes site, The Thicky Chicky, I ordered a shirt from there and it fit me, I looked really good in it. That was honestly the 1st time in I don't know how long that I was able to put something on and really feel like it was made for me. Honestly, I stopped going to the mall to get clothes a long time ago. I stopped at first because things don't ever really fit me the way that I want them to. Then, when I would go in there and see all the little cute stuff for the smaller people, it doesn't look the same when it is in my size. That is not to mention the looks you get when you ask for this shirt in a 4x or 5x. It's embarrassing honestly. You can't get a lot of confidence from hearing, "I'm so sorry, the largest it comes in is a 2x." So instead of walking around the mall to hear that they don't carry my size or barely find something other than shoes, I just don't go anymore. I know that there are other stores like Lane Bryant, but those clothes make me feel old. Their stuff be alright but I get tired of flowers, stripes, and polka dots being all I have to choose from...

Dr. Griffin: This is good, let it out... Is it only a lack of variety in fashion that affects your confidence? I don't want you to stop there if you have more, lets get it out because we don't want to carry any more than we need to on our road to self-acceptance.

217

LaShawn: Ok... well, now that I am thinking about it, there is a lot of things that have affected my confidence. To be honest, I don't really go out too many places besides school or somewhere that I have to go, because I don't like the way the stares and whispers make me feel. Like, if we go to the movies it's the last showing of the night because it's not too many people there at that time. The last time I went to a matinee show, people were snickering and pointing when I was walking to the theatre with a bucket of popcorn and some Twizzlers. My mother saw it and told me to ignore it but of course, I couldn't enjoy the movie after that. That and the fact that the seat was digging in my hip the whole time." (LaShawn is allowing her emotions to flow freely, she continues uninterrupted.) "Going out to eat is the worse, people would give me those "She know she doesn't need to be eating that" look. Every time I would go out, it felt like I was an exhibit. Simple things people enjoy just aren't fun for me. So, I just stay in the house. (LaShawn pauses in thought, then looks at Dr. Griffin indicating that she is finished talking.)

Dr. Griffin: I feel there is more water in that well. Let's get it all out.

LaShawn: Not really, other than the things I missed out on at school. Last year, for the Sophomore trip they went to the Legacy Museum in Montgomery, Alabama. I didn't go because the airline the school booked through required that I buy a second seat. My parents could afford it but, I honestly didn't want to deal with the embarrassment of having two seats and an extension seat belt. I don't know Dr. Griffin, its just not a lot to be confident about. Like I said, being big isn't fun... There is a lot that I can't do...

Dr. Griffin: Ahh... There it is... Stay there... Is it a lot that you can't do? Or is it a lot that you will not allow yourself to do?

(Emotionally disgusted but recognizes that Dr. Griffin is right, she says half-heartedly)
LaShawn: I am not allowing myself to do... But who wants to go through all that?

Dr. Griffin: I am sorry LaShawn, we can't deal with buts... We have to recognize that our emotions are eternally tied to our decisions. Pain is inevitable, but suffering is optional. You have allowed the mean, cruel words and actions of others to become invisible chains that have confined you to your school and house.

Everywhere else in the world seems to be a place that can cause anxiety and feelings of embarrassment. While, I completely understand how and why you feel that way. However, that does not change the fact that you are making the decision not to go to those places. LaShawn, when you get to where we are going, you will make choices in spite of what people will say about you, not because of what you think they will say about you. Currently, you don't go to the movies or to a restaurant because of what people are going to say or do. When you accept yourself, you are going to go to the movies or out to eat in spite of, what looks and jokes you are going to get. You mentioned earlier, that those women on Chardline Chanel looked so beautiful and so happy. Why do you think that is? They looked beautiful and happy, because they are beautiful and happy. Beauty and happiness are qualities that resonate from within us, these are not qualities that can be given to us from the opinions of other people. Those women are confident in themselves and that is what you are seeing... You are seeing a choice... A choice that they made to love themselves just the way God created them... How do you feel about this? Do you see yourself being able to make this choice?

LaShawn: I get what you are saying. It's just hard to do when your whole life has been the same thing constantly on repeat.

Dr. Griffin: I understand that and I receive your pain. However LaShawn that cycle must be broken and is the very reason that you must do this for yourself. It has been 17 years of the same thing, so you have your answer, no one is coming to make you feel better about yourself. You are going to have to do this for yourself. You are going to have to make the choice to realize your beauty and show it to the world. You won't stop people from being mean but if you show them the light from within that exudes confidence and beauty they will have no choice to see you for who and what you are... LaShawn you are beautiful. But are you willing to embrace yourself?

LaShawn: (Half-heartedly) Yeah, I am...

Dr. Griffin: That's not going to do it... I don't need you to tell me what you think I want to hear. I want to know what you are willing to commit to... You may not be ready right now and that is okay as well... I just need you to know when you are ready, you must address your self confidence from every angle, not just the things you feel you can deal with.

LaShawn: What do you mean by that?

Dr. Griffin: What I mean is, up until this point you have shared with me what has been said or done to you. Which is what I have asked for thus far and I appreciate your honesty. However, we are about to go to the next level. To get there we are going to have to get into how you have dealt with what has been said or done to you... (LaShawn drops her head because she gets the feeling that Dr. Griffin is going to begin discussing her relationship with food.)

LaShawn: Do we have to go there?

Dr. Griffin: Do you want to continue feeling the way that you feel about yourself?

LaShawn: I mean I don't want to keep feeling like this about myself but...

Dr. Griffin: We can save it for next session, however we have to address everything in order to make the growth that we both want you to make. And yes that includes food... We will discuss that next session, but before we wrap up today, I have a question for you... You mentioned earlier that no one has ever given you a compliment on how you look. They only compliment your accessories or your hair, now let me ask you, have you ever felt beautiful? (LaShawn sits up as a puzzled look comes over her face, you can tell she is searching for a time in her memory bank that she felt beautiful.)

LaShawn: Uh, I mean, it was... No, I have never felt beautiful. (Her voice tails off in embarrassment. Embarrassment that stems from the realization that she was in control of her emotions yet has never given herself that confidence.)

(Dr. Griffin is saddened by the response and pulls up her bottom lip while slowly rocking her head at the sadness that has overcome the conversation. After a few seconds she finds the words and says)

Dr. Griffin: LaShawn it is impossible for people to see something in you that you have never shown them...

220

Poetry Inspired
by the theme of
Beauty is A Beast

Beauty is a Beast

Especially in a World were Likes often defines who is the most and who is the least...

There once was a time where the essence of an individual was a determinate of who was and just how pretty one could truly be...

But now the world is full of filters, A.I. and magic air brushes that distort what we see...

Therefore it is important that we fall in love with the mirror because nothing is more important than under-standing that beauty is no longer found in the eye of the beholder...

Beauty is Now and Will Forever Be...

Me

221

An Original Poem
by

Alan Gaines

January 12, 2019. 3:27 pm

This meeting comes the day before Theresa is set to go before a judge on her case. The facility took her out to get suitable attire for court and to the beauty salon. Theresa has cut her hair very short. Upon returning she has a scheduled meeting with Ms. Davis and is worried about what may happen tomorrow at court. The meeting begins and Theresa's nerves are obvious. The conversation starts with Theresa being brought into the room by the staff member. Ms. Davis is sitting at her desk, she hears the knock on her door.

Mrs. Davis: Come in...

Staff Member: Good afternoon Mrs. Davis. I have Theresa Rushing here for your meeting, can she come in?

Mrs. Davis: Sure send her in... Thanks and have a blessed day...

Staff Member: I will. You too Mrs. Davis, I'll be back to get her when it's time for her to go back to the unit.

Mrs. Davis: Sure, no worries...

(Theresa enters the room with a rare blank stare on her face. Usually going to see Mrs. Davis is the highlight of her day. Today not so much. Mrs. Davis knows the uncertainty of the court hearing has Theresa worried.)

Theresa: Wsup Mrs. Davis? (Theresa says dryly)

Mrs. Davis: (Mrs. Davis notices that Theresa has cut her hair off but what is more obvious to Mrs. Davis is Theresa's mood as she enters the room.) Nothing much but I can see you in a funk. I already know you worried about what the judge is gonna do. Well guess what? The Lord's will is going to be done. Remember we talked about Cyntoia Brown and what she went through?

Theresa: Yea I remember, but Mrs. D, to be honest. I don't think I am strong enough to go through all of that, like she did... I just want them to like, gimme probation or let me stay up in here til I get my GED or my diploma or whatever...

Mrs. Davis: What I tell you all the time Theresa?

Theresa: Wise actions result in blessings and wrong actions result in consequences. If you think before you do you can predict what is next. But Mrs. D, that makes me feel like, the judge going to say something I ain't trying to hear, like for real for real.

Mrs. Davis: Theresa I tell you that because it gives you the power to choose what you have to be accountable for. I always tell you that you have to take accountability right?

Theresa: Yeah.

Mrs. Davis: Theresa we can't outrun our past. We can't hide from it either. Tomorrow you are going to have to face something that you have done in your past. In life we have to hope for the best and prepare for the worst. I am not going to sit here and tell you that the judge is going to get up there tomorrow and be lenient on you. -

Theresa: What's leny ain't?

Mrs. Davis: Lenient, basically it means to take it easy. Or show mercy. I been in this business for too long and most of the time these judges don't care nothing about people that look like you and me. They been locking black and brown people up left and right for a long time. Theresa I couldn't look myself in the mirror if I sat here and told you that everything was going to be alright tomorrow. I'm not trying to scare you. I'm trying to let you know that whatever happens you must be willing to accept it and I am going to be there with you through it all.

Theresa: Wait, you going?

Mrs. Davis: Ofcourse, we're in this together, I wouldn't let you go by yourself, I'll always be here for you.

Theresa: Mrs. D, like for real, you like the Mama I always wanted... Like, you be the only one telling me the truth and stuff like that... It's like, a lot of times I don't be doing a lot of bad stuff that I could because I don't want to disappoint you... That's also why I am so scared about tomorrow. If they send me away Mrs. D, then that mean that I won't get to see you and talk to you...

223

<u>Mrs. Davis</u>: Don't you worry about that. I want you to know that you mean just as much to me as I do to you… You were sent into my life by God for more than just a season. You have brought me back to focusing on God and you reminded me why I am here… (A smile comes across her face and she gives a wink. It finally clicks for Theresa)

<u>Theresa</u>: OOOOHHHHH!!!! YOU MEAN LIKE MY PURPOSE! WHY AM I HERE! I get it, I get it… I feel so dumb now! All this time you been talking about why God has put me here? Oh My God! It all makes sense… You were right! Oh my Gosh… WOW Mrs. D, I am like so freaking out… It makes so much sense… OMG… I am tripping, I been tripping this whole time… Give me a minute…

<u>Mrs. Davis</u>: It's okay… Take your time… (Mrs. Davis says with a smile and a laugh in her voice.)

<u>Theresa</u>: You know what's crazy, is I actually been thinking about that a lot, of course with my hearing being tomorrow or whatever… I been thinking like why would God put me through so much stuff and then send me to jail? Like no, it gotta be more to it, this can't be my life… That's why I cut my hair…

<u>Mrs. Davis</u>: I was gonna ask you about that. I like it. But I am a little confused by what you mean when you say that is why you cut your hair?

<u>Theresa</u>: See like, you the only one that really care. Like everybody else that's gone be the first thing out they mouth. "Why you cut your hair?" Anyway though, I cut my hair because, I was just thinking like God created me to be more than just pretty… I mean it's more to me than just being cute and having a nice body… But like my whole life, that is all people been doing. Just telling me I am so cute or so pretty. It's like people have never got to know me… To be honest, up until I met you, I really didn't know me… Like I told you, I was just gone be an Instagram model… Everybody else had been using my looks to get what they want from me… I told you dudes would buy me stuff or trick a little money on me to say that they was with Reesa. So I had made up my mind to get paid off my looks… But you been the only one to challenge me to do something with the gifts that God gave me. Like you always be telling me that being able to draw real good is a Gift and I gotta use it… I mean I haven't figured out just yet what I am going to do but I know I didn't want people to just think I was pretty… So I cut my hair because I don't want to be pretty no more…

224

<u>Mrs. Davis</u>: I get what you are saying but tell me how you feel that cutting your hair would solve this?

<u>Theresa</u>: I figured, if I wasn't pretty then people who really about something would have to take the time to get to know me. It wouldn't just be all about how I look. If I wasn't pretty then none of this would have happened to me. I was thinking like, since I can draw real good that if I was to draw my self portrait, it would be called Beauty is A Beast, not Beauty and the Beast... Like people get so wrapped up in how a person look that they never see the person. Like what I been thinking, it don't matter how people think you look, you gotta love yourself... Being up in here is teaching me that... I mean, you know Mrs. D, you be talking about the thermometer thingy, or the thermostat... Thermostat, yeah, thermostat that's it. I was thinking about all the stuff that happened to me and a lot of it wasn't my fault and people took advantage of me... But when I think about it, a lot of it could have been avoided if I didn't skip school. Or if I had said something when I had an opportunity to speak up for myself... I did feel invisible a lot of the time but when I think about the things you be saying and the Bible verses you be telling me, I do be seeing how they connect... I be wanting to blame God for things because it be hard to do your favorite saying, "To Take Accountability" (Theresa does air quotes to mock Mrs. Davis's repeated phrase. Mrs. Davis smiles from deep within because she knows that her words have had their intended impact) but I know I got to do it. I feel like I didn't take accountability before because I didn't love myself, so I blamed my Mama for everything. Now that I love myself, I gotta take accountability then I won't truly be able to live with what the judge says tomorrow in court. I guess I just need a mustard thingy...

<u>Mrs. Davis</u>: You mean a mustard seed of faith.

<u>Theresa</u>: Yeah that... I'm just scared Mrs. D....

<u>Mrs. Davis</u>: Let me tell you what I learned about FEAR. It is an acronym for False Evidence Appearing Real.

<u>Theresa</u>: Watsa acronym?

Mrs. Davis: An acronym, is when you take the first letters from other words and pronounce it as one word. So FEAR stands for F - false. E -evidence. A - appearing. R - real. So what we fear in life is not really there. We make it up in our minds and believe it. Theresa - you don't have anything to fear tomorrow.

Theresa: Mrs. D, how you know? You don't know what that judge is gonna to do?

Mrs. Davis: You right, but I know my God. Whatever happens is his will. And I am prepared for it. You gotta be too.

Theresa: Mrs. D. you really coming tomorrow? (Theresa says both surprised and anxiously)

Mrs. Davis: Of course, I told you I am going to be there, why would you ask me that?

(As soon as the words leave her mouth, it dawns on Mrs. Davis why Theresa asked the question. Theresa drops her head and begins reliving the let downs of her past. Mrs. Davis knows she has to lighten the mood.)

Mrs. Davis: Oh Theresa... don't you worry. I'm going to be there bright in early. Okurrrrrr!!!

(Theresa burst into laughter as she nods her head "Okay." She gets up and turns towards the door. Theresa looks back at Mrs. Davis, Theresa runs around the desk and gives Mrs. Davis a big hug. A shocked Mrs. Davis takes the hug and sheds a small tear because she is usually the one giving the hug to Theresa. The two silently embrace but the love between them is being spoken very loudly.)

226

"Theresa after hair cut."

An Original Oil Painting By:
Karma Griggs   Age: 14

This Beautiful painting was inspired by the story:
Beauty Is A Beast

Instagram: @paintitkarma

January 12, 2019. 3:27 pm

Dr. Griffin knows that this is the meeting in which she is going to have to address the issue of food with LaShawn. They have hinted at the topic at prior sessions but now Dr. Griffin knows that this issue has to be faced head-on.

<u>Dr. Griffin</u>: Good afternoon LaShawn, how are things going?

<u>LaShawn</u>: Everything is going good... I have been feeling better about myself lately... I'm good, I really am, I'm in a good space right now.

<u>Dr. Griffin</u>: That's fantastic! Are you still saying your affirmations every morning?

<u>LaShawn</u>: Yes! (Her voice raises excitedly.) I have and thank you... At first, it felt a little weird. But I kept saying them and then I began to notice little things like, I was feeling better about myself. Slowly but surely, saying them became believing them. Now, I say them more than just in the morning, I say them to myself throughout the day. I am really seeing a difference in how I feel about myself.

<u>Dr. Griffin</u>: Great, that is great... Everything starts with visualizing it first. I once heard that everything around us is at least the second rendering of it. The first rendering took place in the mind of it's creator. You must see it first! Alright, let's move on... So, is there anything that you would like to talk about, anything that happened that you want to discuss?

<u>LaShawn</u>: No... Nothing has happened, things, like I said, are going pretty well for me. I'm fine, we can talk about whatever you feel we need to discuss...

<u>Dr. Griffin</u>: Great, well again... I am glad to hear that things are going well for you and that the affirmations are working. Today I want to talk about how you have coped with your emotions in the past. Now that you have strategies to deal with emotional highs and lows, along with your affirmations, let's discuss how you would normally deal with situations in the past.

<u>LaShawn</u>: Well, huh, honestly I would eat. (LaShawn drops her head in embarrassment as she says the word. This is done more so out of habit than it is what she is actually feeling right now.) Food was my comfort... It's been times if I am down or sad emotionally, I would eat the whole thing of ice cream and when I was done, I would hate myself for doing it... I would call myself a fat pig or a stupid chunky monkey...

228

Dr. Griffin: Mmmm... I see, so you would beat yourself up after you ate... Interesting, why would you call yourself those names?

LaShawn: Because that's what I felt like... I mean who eats a whole quart of ice cream in one sitting? Fat people do and that is what I was when I did it, I was a fat person...

Dr. Griffin: Ahh - I hate to interject but I am listening and what you are saying now is more powerful than you realize. You are referencing yourself as fat in the past tense... You just said I "was" a fat person... This is a fundamental disconnection between what you were and who you are right now in your mental processing. You are not recognizing yourself as "fat". By not recognizing yourself as fat you are now mentally disconnecting and thus shedding the negativity that is associated with being fat from how you identify yourself. That is a great milestone in self-acceptance. Breaking any and all connections with things that we see as negative from being associated with our self-identity. LaShawn I am proud of you...

LaShawn: Thanks, Dr. Griffin. That makes me feel good... I know I am still a big girl but I get what you are saying... Thank you! (LaShawn is very happy with the confirmation from Dr. Griffin about her growth and her mood transitions to a happy confidence. LaShawn sits up and is more upbeat at this point of the conversation.)

Dr. Griffin: You are welcome... However, I want to be very clear, there isn't anything wrong with being "Big" - heck we all love big things, big cars, big houses, big bank accounts... Honestly, there is nothing wrong with being fat... The fact of the matter is that for you, the word "fat" has a lifetime of negativity associated with it. That is why it is important that you are disconnecting with it. If you play back what you said, you were downing yourself. From the way that you were describing it, it sounds like this "beating yourself up" was common practice. I want to make sure that you process this... You would eat food when you felt down and after you finished you would make yourself feel worse. Transitioning to now, you are starting your day with positive affirmations and you are feeling great about yourself. LaShawn, I want you to take note of the power of words. The Bible says in Matthews 15:11 "A man is not defiled by what enters his mouth, but by what comes out of it." Jesus goes on to say that "... the things that come out of the mouth come from the heart and these things defile a man." LaShawn, it is so important that we choose what we say in general, but more specifically, what we say about ourselves with the utmost respect and integrity. I know we have gotten a little off track but this is a point that will be very beneficial to your progress. Please continue with how you dealt with your emotions in the past.

LaShawn: Truthfully, food was and still is a comfort for me. If I did well on a test, I would reward myself with a slice of cake or some cookies when I got home from school. I don't really go anywhere so it wasn't like I was going to celebrate at the mall and buy myself something. So for me, it is food. A cake, cookies, chips... Thinking about it now, through good times or sad moments food has always been there for me...

Dr. Griffin: Let me make sure I am processing this correctly. In your mind you view food as a friend to celebrate happy moments with and a friend you pour your heart out to when you are down, would that be fair to say?

LaShawn: I never looked at it that way before but... Yeah, you can say that... Yes... I would agree with that... (LaShawn is processing while she is responding. Dr. Griffin's assessment makes more sense the more she thinks about it.)

Dr. Griffin: That is understandable, people generally celebrate things with food. Birthdays, report cards, good test scores, getting admitted into something, graduations, the list could go on... Food is usually connected with us emotionally. I know that there have been times when I was having a bad day, where I have driven across town to the mall to get a Cinnabun. I'll be the first to tell you I felt so much better after eating it. So don't get me wrong the act of turning to food is very understandable and I don't want you to beat yourself up for that. To celebrate or sulk with food is more common than you think. Alright, we have that established lets dig deeper. You mentioned in previous sessions about overeating, we dabbled around it but never fully addressed it. When do you feel like the overeating takes place?

LaShawn: Well mostly it happens when I am on the computer. I usually have a big bag of chips & a big thing of soda.

Dr. Griffin: So do you think if you cut down on how much time you spent on the computer you would decrease the amount of food you eat...

LaShawn: Yea, maybe... But I don't think its a good idea for me to really cut down on the amount of time I spend on the computer... I spend the majority of my time on my computer coding.

Dr. Griffin: Wow! That is amazing! I know this is about to get us off topic a bit but this is potentially something that we can build on, so expound on that more please.

LaShawn: Well, my Mom was, well she "is" a huge Prince fan. Before he died, she heard him discussing the need for Black children to get into coding. So my Mom did a little research and came across #YESWECODE. After that she began exposing me to coding. A few months later my mom learned that Black Girls Code was having a Hackathon event like two hours from where we live and we went. You can say the rest is history. I have full ride scholarships to all the Top HBCU STEM programs. North Carolina A & T, FAMU, Alabama A & M, Norfolk State, Howard, Jackson State, umm, Fort Valley State, Morgan State, Prairie View uh, I forget... It's a lot though... Kimberly Bryant is one of my SHEro's. She founded Black Girls Code and it has been amazing, like really has helped me. I do a lot of freelance coding on Fiverr. I make good money building websites and creating apps. People don't really know that I do it outside of my family but, yeah that's what I do...

Dr. Griffin: Wow. That's awesome, it looks like you are very close to finding out why you are here...

231

LaShawn: You keep mentioning, why I am here, what do you mean by that?

Dr. Griffin: Just what it says... Why are you here? It's actually not for me to explain as much it is for you to figure out... Experience is the best teacher. Trust me, there are going to be somethings that you experience that will give you a full understanding of why you are here... The Bible says in Proverbs 18:16 "Your Gifts Will Make Room For You and Bring You Before Great People". You seem to have a gift at working with the computer and you are working with some amazing organizations. The late great Chokwe Lumumba always preached that true achievement was attained when we were able to use our success to make the lives of people like us better. You should start thinking about how you can use your gifts to improve the lives of people who are experiencing what you are going through. Never forget that most people don't seek help for things such as depression. Therapy has a bad stigma, so most people never get the tools to improve their life. Give it some thought, we will pick this back up at a later date.

LaShawn: We always do... You don't forget anything Dr. Griffin...

Dr. Griffin: That's because I really take my craft serious... Missing a detail or forgetting something could be a matter of life or death... I work with people who are typically in a place where life has little to no value to them when they walk into my office. So, I approach what I do as a calling, not a career. I revere my work, for it is God's work, it is why I am here... (Dr. Griffin notices the light starting to come on for LaShawn as she finishes her sentence. With a budding sense of purpose LaShawn responds.)

LaShawn: I think I am starting to get what you mean by that now...

Dr. Griffin: Trust me, you will fully understand when the time is right... In the meantime, let's talk about some alternatives to eating while you are on the computer or snacking on something a bit healthier than a bag of chips... Again, let me remind you that eating isn't the problem... Your emotions and feelings you connect to them are the problem that we must address. Remember it's not what goes in our mouths but what comes out of it... Make sure that you keep saying your affirmations because as the Bible says the words we say are connected to our hearts...

LaShawn: I will, I'm going to do them even more because now it makes even more sense to me. All this time, I have been helping to build this negative image of myself because of the names I would call myself. I feel more confident knowing that I really have control over what I see and what I show people about who I am... This has been really helpful... Thank you...

Dr. Griffin: Your welcome LaShawn. Ok, I know that we are wrapping up this session however, something you said is bothering me just a little bit. You said that food has been your friend or companion through your good and bad moments. LaShawn, why food and not your parents?
(LaShawn begins to cry and puts her head in both of her hands. Dr. Griffin knows that she has touched a spot that LaShawn wanted to hide.)
LaShawn I know this is the end of our session. We will pick this up at a later session. Here is some tissue. Take your time. You can use my restroom if you need to gather yourself.

LaShawn: Ok, thank you Dr. Griffin. (LaShawn gets up and goes directly to the restroom. After gathering herself, she comes out.) Thank you, Dr. Griffin, I will see you next session.

"LaShawn"

An Original Oil Painting By:
Karma Griggs   Age: 14

This Beautiful painting was inspired by the story:
Beauty Is A Beast

Instagram: @paintitkarma

January 13, 2019. 9:07 am

Theresa gets out the van at the courthouse with a look of worry and concern on her face. The blank stare is a reflection of the uncertainty she feels inside. Theresa knows that in a little more than an hour a decision is going to be made that will determine the trajectory of her life. Theresa is in court today to see if her case will go to trial on charges of felony drug possession with intent to distribute. Theresa is looking at between 5 - 10 years in prison. However, she is holding out hope that the judge will reduce or even throw out the case because she is a minor with no serious crimes on her record. Theresa walks up the stairs with her head hung low, as she gets to the top of the steps she sees Mrs. Davis. The fact that someone in her life finally kept their word brings a huge smile to Theresa's face.

Theresa: Mrs. D!!! You really came! Oh my God! Thank you!

Mrs. Davis: Oh you are welcome! I told you I was going to be here. (Mrs. Davis reaches out and grabs both of Theresa's hands as she reassures her.) You ready?

(Theresa takes a deep breath. Convincing herself to be strong she says.)
Theresa: Yeah, I guess. I really don't have no choice, it's here now.

Mrs. Davis: Well, I been praying all night and all morning. So let's head on in. Remember no matter what, I am here for you...
(Theresa is still in shock because this is the first time someone she loves actually kept a promise to her as well as been there for her in a time of need. Theresa says what she feels.)
Theresa: "I love you Mrs. D."

Mrs. Davis: I love you too Theresa. Now c'mon, lets go on in.

After a few minutes of being in the hallway the bailiff opens the door to the courtroom. He looks around before spotting Theresa's public defender. He makes eye contact with him and motions them into the courtroom. Theresa and her public defender take a seat at the defendant's table. Mrs. Davis sits behind her in the first row. Theresa looks back and the worry that had subsided when she saw Mrs. Davis is back and written all over her face. Mrs. Davis sees the concern and gives Theresa a nod of reassurance. Theresa looks at Mrs. Davis and gets a feeling of support. Theresa nods back as if to say you thanks. Knowing that no matter what is about to take place, Mrs. Davis is here for Theresa is the victory she needs to face the moment. Theresa turns back around and although she is still nervous she gets a calming sensation that everything is going to be alright.

234

Baliff: All rise. The court of Lake County is now in session. The Honorable Amiyah Banks presiding."
(The entire courtroom stands until the Judge enters and takes her seat.)

Judge Banks: All may be seated. Alright, this is the preliminary hearing of Theresa Rushing. I see here that today I will be making a determination for trial. Ok, first I would like to hear the statement from the prosecution.

Prosecutor: Good morning your honor. The defendant, Ms. Rushing was arrested outside of the residence 4725 Miller Lane. At the time of her arrest Ms. Rushing had in her possession one-half pound of marijuana, a quarter kilogram of cocaine, four grams of heroin and a bottle containing 12 pills of oxycontin. Although the defendant has no drug-related priors, due to the amount and variety of drugs that Ms. Rushing had on her at the time of the arrest, we are motioning the court that Ms. Rushing is charged with felony drug possession with intent to distribute. That is all that I have at this moment, your honor.
(Theresa does her best to show no emotion as the prosecutor makes his statement. Mrs. Davis, however, drops her head in disbelief.)

Judge Banks: Thank you. Your motion will be taken into consideration. Next, we will hear from the defense.

Public Defender: Thank you, your honor. On behalf of my client, Ms. Rushing, we motion the court to have the case dismissed in its entirety due to the fact that Ms. Rushing has no prior drug-related convictions. She also does not have any known connections to drug dealers that would enable her to move such a high quantity and variety of drugs. For us to believe that a 17-year-old girl whose criminal history is highlighted by stealing lingerie in a mall could turn into a queen pin overnight is far fetched. Now, the amount of drugs in her possession was substantial, however, to charge a minor with no prior felonies as an adult and possibly up to ten years in prison, your honor, we feel would be cruel and unusual punishment.

Judge Banks: Ok let's not get too far ahead of ourselves. I understand your position and I will make a ruling that is fair once all of the evidence is presented. Counselor, can you speak to the progress that Ms. Rushing has made since the time of her arrest. I see that you have here listed a character witness for Ms. Rushing. A one Mrs. Mary Davis is she with us today? (Mrs. Davis stands up as the judge is speaking.)

235

(Theresa looks back in a bit of unexpected confusion. She sees Mrs. Davis get up from her seat carrying a folder and approaches the podium.)

<u>Public Defender</u>: Yes she is here today and willing to speak to the character of Ms. Rushing. (Judge Banks nods to Mrs. Davis permitting her to speak.)

<u>Mrs. Davis</u>: Good morning your honor. My name is Mary Davis and I am the director of counseling at the Lake County Juvenile Correction facility. I am here to serve as a character witness for Theresa. Your honor, Theresa is a very unique individual. Honestly, I have never met anyone quite like her in all my years in the profession. Theresa came to us in September of last year and during her initial testing, her scores indicated that she read on a fifth-grade level. As you know, that is severely behind for a 17-year-old. Theresa initially was very adverse to school but after a brief adjustment period, Theresa has increased her Lexile score over 400 points. This has allowed Theresa to qualify for her GED program which she started last month. I've never seen anyone in our system make that kind of growth so quickly. Your honor, the biggest thing I have seen from Theresa has been how she has helped the other girls in the facility. Theresa has encouraged the girls to take school more seriously as well as to make better life choices. The overall number of infractions on our female unit has decreased and Theresa is a big part of the progress we have seen. Lastly your honor. Above all else, Theresa is an amazing artist. I have some of her work here with me. (Mrs. Davis opens the folder and begins to show the judge the artwork. Judge Banks motions to the bailiff to get the folder from Mrs. Davis so she could take a closer look at the artwork.) Your honor, Theresa has a truly amazing gift. When I think about all the things that have happened to her thus far in her life. My fear is that if Theresa is eventually convicted of these charges, she will lose her will to continue using her gift. I have spoken at length with Theresa about how she can use her gift to help others. Theresa wants to use her talents and even her story to help others. Judge Banks I am asking that you consider not only Theresa's life but also all of the lives of the individuals Theresa could help if you give her a second chance. Thank you.

<u>Judge Banks</u>: Thank you, you may be seated. Ms. Rushing, is this your work?

<u>Theresa:</u> Yes it is your honor.

<u>Judge Banks</u>: I'm impressed. Ok, I had the chance to review the file while I was in my chambers and I was interested in what I would hear

today. Looking over the file I see a long history of being in and out of the foster care system. I see on various occasions your mother lost and re-gained custody of you. However, that is no excuse for you or anyone else to get involved in the world of drugs. I will be honest, I am finding it very hard to overlook the amount and variety of drugs that were in your possession at the time of the arrest. I have to be very careful with this ruling because it could very well set precedent.

On the other hand, you have no drug-related priors. So more than likely, you were going to have some type of encounter where someone was going to either physically do harm to you or take the drugs from you at gunpoint. Sitting in this seat I have seen this scenario played out that too many times to count. The way I see it Ms. Rushing, you were very lucky to be arrested. The underworld has very little sympathy for anyone when it comes to drugs and the chance to make money. That is why Ms. Rushing, I am also finding it very hard to have you stand trial for intent to distribute when I truly don't feel you were going to get the opportunity to traffic these drugs. Okay, so let me ask a few questions. Counsel if I were to dismiss this case and release your client where would she return to?

<u>Public Defender</u>: Your honor can I have a moment to speak with my client?

<u>Judge Banks</u>: Sure.
(The public defender leans over and asks the question to Theresa. After a brief conversation the public defender turns back to the judge.)

<u>Public Defender</u>: Your honor my client would like to speak on her own behalf.

<u>Judge Banks</u>: Ms. Rushing go ahead.

<u>Theresa</u>: Your honor, my whole life I ain't neva had no say in where I am going to live. My mama would just take me here or take me there and leave me. Or we would just pack up and move. I have lost count of how many people and places I done stayed in my life. When I was in foster care I didn't have no say. So if I didn't like it or when somebody would do some-thing to me I would run away. That was my way of saying that I didn't want to be there. But still nobody asked me. I really didn't have no say.

Even right now, I am speaking up for myself but in the end, this gonna be your decision. But since I got the chance to speak on where I wanna go, I'm taking it. If you was to let me go right now, like my Mama boyfriend's house is probably where I would have to go. But I don't want to go over there. My Mama not even here for this hearing. Honestly, I'm doing

237

good at the facility. Mrs. Davis been really helping me out and like I just got into the GED course. Your honor, I wanna stay there at least until I get my GED, so I can finally say I accomplished something in my life. If I get my GED, it will be the first thing I ever got in my life. I ain't neva made the honor roll. I ain't neva had no job. I ain't neva been in one place long enough to accomplish anything. This may sound crazy your honor, but it feel good to know where I am going to sleep and what to expect my day to be like. I know that sounds bad that I would rather stay in juvie or whatever but, if you let me go today, I will be back in the same world where I don't know what to expect from day to day. If I can stay up in here and get my GED at least when I get out I can like try to get a job or something. I can at least get a job with a GED and figure it out from there. That's what I want your honor.

(Theresa looks back at Mrs. Davis after speaking. Mrs. Davis stopped wiping the tears somewhere around the time Theresa stated that she was never in one place long enough to accomplish anything. When Theresa locks eyes with Mrs. Davis she knows that the tears are prideful. The realization that she has made Mrs. Davis proud moves Theresa's emotions and she begins to cry. Theresa turns back to judge confident that she can face whatever decision that is going to be made simply because she knows for sure that she will not be facing it alone. For the first time in her life she no longer feels abandoned)

<u>Judge Banks</u>: Ms. Rushing, that was very well stated and very heartfelt. I feel that your counsel, as well as Mrs. Davis, have done a tremendous job of showing your growth. However, it was your heartfelt words that have pushed me to the decision I am going to render in this matter. Theresa Rushing. I am dismissing the felony charge of drug possession with intent to distribute. However, I am placing you on a thirty-month probation. Eighteen of which are to be served at the facility you are currently residing in, contingent on the completion of your GED program. If you have not completed your GED program in eighteen months, the remaining twelve months of your probation must be spent in a halfway house. In the event that you complete your GED program in or before the mandated eighteen-month time frame, the remaining probation will be waived as time served. Ms. Rushing if you complete your GED program within eighteen months, the state will pay for you to receive transition to living services. Ms. Rushing do you understand my decision.

Theresa: Your honor, to be honest, I don't know what all that mean. But what it sound like is that it ain't goin' to be no trial and I can stay where I'm at until I get my GED. But I only got eighteen months to get my GED.

(Judge Banks smiles at her innocence. Theresa's response is justification for her ruling.)

Judge Banks: Something like that. I will let your counsel explain it to you more. One last thing Ms. Rushing, in regards to this artwork. The University has a young innovators conference in early March. Participants present projects in a variety of categories. The winners in each category are teamed up with professionals to help them develop their projects into fully operational charitable organizations. I am requiring you to enter your artwork. I will see to it that Mrs. Davis gets the paper work for the conference. You have a real talent and I want to make sure you find a way to use it to help others. And with that, this court is adjourned.

(Judge Banks hits the gavel. Mrs. Davis and Theresa share a very relieved and emotional hug. Both are crying throughout the embrace.)

239

Theresa: Thank you soo much Mrs. D! Thank you so much!

Mrs. Davis: Ahhh... you are so welcome! Ohhh God is good! God is so good! Okay make sure you thank the lawyer. (Theresa releases the hug and turns to the public defender.)

Theresa: Thank you so much sir. Thank you. Really thank you.

Public Defender: I'm just doing my job. Really you did all the work by making improvements in the facility. Judges always look at that stuff. I will be getting your paperwork to Mrs. Davis. And I will see you soon. You guys have a wonderful day.

Mrs. Davis: (Speaking to the public defender) Oh thank you so much we will, now that this is over. C'mon Theresa let's get outside so we can talk. (The two walk out the courtroom along with the assistant from the facility who is providing transportation for Theresa. They all continue out of the building, Mrs. Davis turns to Theresa upon exiting the courthouse.)

<u>Mrs. Davis</u>: Oh my God Theresa I am so proud of you! I know I been preaching take accountability but my God! You took control! Wow! I am so proud of you Theresa. I really am. I am really at a lost for words right now! I could not be any prouder of you than I am right now! That was amazing!

<u>Theresa</u>: Mrs. D, to be honest. I was only able to do it because of you. When I saw that you actually kept your promise to be here. I just got this feeling like everything gonna be good. Like, I just got this confidence in me that I ain't never felt before. Then when you was saying all that nice stuff about me to the judge. I knew that I was gone have to try my best to stay with you if they gave me a chance to speak. So really... thank you Mrs. D.

<u>Mrs. Davis</u>: Ahh gimme another hug! (The two embrace once again. After letting go Mrs. Davis continues.) Well, I'll see you back on the unit. And don't be waiting for me either because I am about to... what y'all call it... turn up? I'm bout to Turn Up!

<u>Theresa</u>: Ayyyyeee! Okay Mrs. D. I see you! Thanks again... (The two walk away in opposite directions. About ten seconds go by when Theresa remembers she had something to tell Mrs. Davis. Theresa abruptly turns around and calls to Mrs. Davis) Oh, oh Mrs. D.! Mrs. D.!
(Mrs. Davis hears Theresa and turns around.)

<u>Mrs. Davis</u>: Yes, wsup?

<u>Theresa</u>: Well, uhm... I think uhm... (Theresa drops her head and begins fidgeting with the button on her coat as she is searching for how to say what she is feeling. Theresa quickly realizes it's best to just come out and say it. Theresa lifts her head up and looks Mrs. Davis right in the eyes.) I think I'm ready to have that talk with my mother...

"The Me I See"

An original drawing by:
Daisjah Ball   Age: 14

This Beautiful painting was inspired by the story:
Beauty Is A Beast

January 13, 2019. 9:07 am

LaShawn didn't get much sleep after yesterday's session. She asked her mom if she could schedule an emergency session. Dr. Griffin's last question from the previous session didn't sit well with LaShawn and she feels that she must speak with Dr. Griffin immediately. Dr. Griffin makes the necessary adjustments to her schedule and fits LaShawn in on short notice.

Dr. Griffin: Good morning LaShawn how are you today? I honestly didn't expect an emergency session after yesterday's session. Is everything okay?

LaShawn: I'm okay, it's just that I know from yesterday that I am going to have to talk about my parents in our next session. Honestly, I didn't get much sleep last night and I know myself. I think this would be better if it came out now. I tried my affirmations last night and this morning and it didn't really make me feel better.

Dr. Griffin: Affirmations help us feel a certain way about ourselves, but I don't want you to think that affirmations are the cure to depression.

LaShawn: Depression? What do you mean by depression?

Dr. Griffin: Yes LaShawn, you are having a long-standing battle with depression. Please don't get too wrapped up in the word depression. Millions of people are battling depression. A large number of which do not even know that they are because depression manifests in many different ways. Depression is not only sitting in a room not wanting to get out of the bed or contemplating suicide. Depression can be going to the mall and spending all of your money on a consistent basis. Rage is a form of depression, alcohol abuse, the list can go on. In your case overeating was the case. However, that is not what you requested an emergency session to talk about, so lets get to what brings you here today.

LaShawn: I am ok. I guess, ok but wait, I didn't look at it like I was depressed. I know that I was getting bullied and it made me feel bad about myself but I didn't look at it like I was depressed.

Dr. Griffin: Most people fail to link depression to bullying because the focus shifts toward getting the person who is being mean and cruel to stop. The thought process is usually if you get the bully to stop then everything will be fine. However, little attention is given to the damage that has been done to the victim. I'm sure you can relate to that?

242

LaShawn: I do. It makes sense because in these sessions you only been talking to me about how I feel and my reactions.

Dr. Griffin: LaShawn the reality is you are not going to be in control of the mean things people say or the looks that they are going to give. So we must focus on your reactions to the things being said. You have to take control of your response to these things and build yourself up to a point where you have the confidence to be yourself no matter the circumstance. This requires that you are in an environment that promotes healthy responses and having difficult conversations when necessary. Which leads me to where we were going in the next session. Your relationship with your parents. Obviously, me bringing it up has struck a nerve with you so let's talk about it. If I remember correctly yesterday you mentioned that food has always been there for you. Tell me LaShawn, why is it that food was there and not your mom or dad?

LaShawn: Well my Dad, he works a lot. In his eyes, I can't do no wrong. I'm a Daddy's girl or whatever but he don't really talk to me. I guess you can say he is there but he is not there. My Dad works all the time but like he never comes to anything that I am having so, I don't know. He gives me whatever I ask for but I feel like I would much rather have his time. My Mom says he doesn't really know how to open up about his feelings but I guess. It's usually my Dad that buys the junk food. Sometimes my parents argue about it but for the most part, he just gives me whatever I ask for. I don't know if that's a good thing but he just want me to smile but we not close like I would want to be, you know...

Dr. Griffin: There are a lot of fathers like that. It sounds like there may be some issues that he may have with expressing his emotions that may stem from his childhood. I don't want to assume much about that. So please tell me about your mother. What is your relationship like with her?

LaShawn: In some ways, she is just like my Dad. My mom gives me whatever I ask for, but it's not like we are really close either. Most of the time, she just tells me what she wants me to do. Or since I get good grades she rewards me but I don't really talk to her. We talk but it is not like about things that are going on. I stay in my room a lot. From what she tells me, she was popular in school and even today she has a lot of friends. I think she has a problem dealing with the fact that I am the opposite of what she is or was in school. Or maybe I'm not what she expected her child would be in terms of my appearance and popularity. I don't know if she knows how to handle the fact that I am not

243

like she wanted me to be.

Dr. Griffin: What does that mean? Explain how you think your Mom wanted you to be?

LaShawn: When I was like five or six years old, she put me into cheerleading and ballet. She was really good at both when she was young and she can still dance really well. I hated both of them and I only did them because she made me. I was the biggest girl on the cheerleading team and I didn't really try hard. I remember my Mom getting really frustrated and her arguing with my Dad because he told her to pull me out of it. She went off about not letting me quit because I would become a quitter and it was a big argument. The next year she didn't sign me up anymore and I never went back. I just remember feeling like I was an embarrassment to her. After that my mom never tried to force me into anything. She would never try to get me out of the house if I didn't want to go. She became cool with me staying in and staying to myself. My Dad is a homebody and although we are there together it's always in separate rooms. My Mom would go out and do her thing and bring back food or clothes or whatever I needed. I don't know if it is because I am not outgoing and athletic like she was but she definitely became ok with me just being in the house on my phone or computer. I know that she loves me, I just feel that sometimes she doesn't know how to deal with me not being the daughter she thought she would have.

Dr. Griffin: This is very interesting. So the isolation is not only at school it is at home as well.

LaShawn: Yeah. I know my parents love me but we aren't just the type of family that talks and expresses it like that. My mom is on top of like my school work and me being set up and preparing for college, I guess you can say the important stuff. Just not the personal stuff I would say.

Dr. Griffin: LaShawn, nothing is more important than you. What college you get into means nothing if you are not prepared to mentally and emotionally handle the transition and freedom that comes along with leaving home. You are the most important thing and your parents are going to have to work to provide more interaction with you so you can get the emotional support you need. This is very important, as you progress through therapy it is important that your parents provide the support system necessary to reinforce the progress that you are making.

LaShawn: I agree it's just that... nothing. I agree.

Dr. Griffin: It's just that what? It's okay to express what you are thinking?

LaShawn: I just feel like my Mom really wouldn't be receptive. We don't really talk or say I love you like that so I am not sure that she is going to just open up.

Dr. Griffin: LaShawn, your Mom brought you to therapy. She cares for you more than you can imagine. A lot of times, parents don't know how to express their love so they show it in ways that they feel say I love you. You may want to hear the words or feel the embrace of a hug. Your Mom may not be the type of person that shows her affection in that way. That doesn't mean that she doesn't love you. What I think needs to take place is a conversation between you and your mother so you can express how you feel. More importantly, you can hear from her, how she feels about you. I'll arrange that for an upcoming session. How does that sound?

LaShawn: I'm okay with it.

Dr. Griffin: Great well, if there isn't anything further than that just about wraps up our time for today. Emergency sessions are generally shorter and rarely taken on an hours notice. I hate to cut it short but before I do are you sure that you are okay with me setting up the conversation with your mom?

LaShawn: Yes, that's fine. I feel a little better now that I spoke to you. Oh, I did have one thing, it's not about therapy or anything. I wanted to invite you to this competition I entered. It is at the University. I don't want to tell you too much about it. I kinda want it to be a surprise. The things I have learned in therapy with you is a big part of it so I would really like for you to come if you can make it.

Dr. Griffin: Sure thing. Just give all the information to my secretary and I'll be there. I like surprises so I can't wait. This is also a major sign of growth. To go from staying in because of what people may say about you to wanting to present in front of a room of people is amazing I'm proud of you.

LaShawn: Well, I am a bit nervous about it. But without giving it away too much, I will say that you encouraging me to find my purpose has a lot to do with why I have to do this.

Dr. Griffin: Alright! Well I am excited to see what comes of it. I will definitely be there. Thanks again for inviting me and have a great day. My secretary will be contacting your mother about our next session.

LaShawn: Thank you Dr. Griffin and I will see you at the conference.

246

The Conference
March 7, 2019. 9:53 am

Theresa enters the room with Mrs. Davis. Theresa is carrying a large art portfolio case. Mrs. Davis points in the direction of the sign-in sheet and the two go over to sign in before taking a seat in the third row of chairs. As Theresa and Mrs. Davis are taking their seats, LaShawn and her parents enter the room. Dr. Griffin was already in the room prior to Theresa and Mrs. Davis and is seated in the row in front of where Theresa and Mrs. Davis took their seats. Dr. Griffin turns around and notices LaShawn and her family and waves them over to the seats that she has saved for them. LaShawn and her parents have a short embrace with Dr. Griffin before going to sign in and returning to their seats. The room fills up with both spectators and participants and at 10:00 am sharp. The session begins as a man stands up and brings the session to order.

Good morning. My name is Rodney Williams Sr. and a few years ago I lost my wife, LaTanya or Nay as I called her. Nay is short for Renee. Anyway, my wife was a phenomenal woman and during her life, she devoted herself to the cause of helping young women. She wore many hats and got involved in lots of youth organizations to help young people reach adulthood with the proper tools for success. Today, in honor of her legacy we are going to choose five young ladies whose ideas we feel would go a long way to helping improve the quality of life for their fellow youth. The five individuals we choose will be an official LaTanya Williams Agent of Change Award Winner. This comes with a one thousand dollar stipend as well as being paired with a team of professionals to help develop and launch their ideas on a national scale.

The rules and rubric for scoring were given to each participant upon entering the competition online. Just remember when you come up to make your presentation, to state your full name, your cause, why you chose this cause and how your idea can help the youth affected by this problem. Thank you. Now, I will turn this over to the moderator, who will introduce our judges and get the presentations started.

<u>Theresa</u>: Mrs. Davis, you think I got a shot at winning this thing?

<u>Mrs. Davis</u>: It's not about having a shot. It's about you sharing your truth. Everyone in here is talented. Some more than others, I'm sure. But I don't want you worrying or doubting yourself. When they call your name, you go up there, tell your truth and show them your work. With or without winning today you have discovered why you are here. No matter what happens, your life has the direction it needs to be lived to the fullest. You'll be

247

fine. I'm here for you Theresa. Don't forget your cards, okay.

<u>Theresa</u>: Aight Mrs. D, thank you.

(The program begins and after about five presentations, the moderator calls up LaShawn. After a brief set up that includes getting her Prezi presentation to be displayed on the screen, LaShawn begins her presentation.)

<u>LaShawn</u>: Good morning. My name is LaShawn Thorpe. My presentation today addresses the issue of bullying. I chose this cause because since the time I started school, I became an immediate target for bullies. I have always weighed more than my classmates. In my mind, this was the only difference between my classmates and I. However, to some of them, this meant that I should be talked about, called names and made fun of. Because of the things that were said to me, I allowed myself to believe and feel like I was less than others. Being bullied went on for years and I dealt with it. To be honest, people still say mean and hurtful things.

Well about six months ago, I had another incident with being bullied. This time it was cyberbullying and I didn't handle it very well. Honestly, it was so bad that I didn't want to go back to school. My mom eventually got me the help I needed. I begin seeing a therapist, Dr. Griffin. She started me out by giving me affirmations. Dr. Griffin helped me to realize it is not what goes into our mouth but what comes out of our mouth that defiles us. Before I started seeing Dr. Griffin, I saw myself the way that the people that were bullying me did. Dr. Griffin gave me strategies that allowed me to not only see myself positively but helped me speak life into my existence as well. Therapy has allowed me to see that my worth was not something that could be determined by my outward appearance. My worth is determined by the love I have for myself. Therapy helped me understand that I could increase my worth by using my gifts to help others. That leads me to what I am going to share with you today. An app that I created called the B.U.L.L.Y. app. Bully is an acronym, (Theresa turns to Mrs. Davis and smiles at the memory) for Beauty, Understanding, Lonely, Learning, You. (LaShawn uses the clicker to the next slide which is displaying a prototype of the app she has developed.)

From my personal experience, I know that most people who are bullied usually deal with one or a combination of these five issues. They don't think that they are attractive. They feel like no one understands them. They often feel isolated and think that they are going at the world by themselves. Often times people who have learning disabilities or who struggle academically are prime targets for bullies. And finally, which I think all victims of bullying become subject to at some point is self-bullying. We begin tearing ourselves down, using the same hurtful language others have used towards us on ourselves and we essentially become our biggest bully. (LaShawn clicks to the next slide.)

The B.U.L.L.Y. app will allow users to get powerful affirmations throughout the day. Users of the app can preset text and video messages to be sent from the app to their phones at certain times of the day. Users can choose to have videos of prominent people giving inspirational messages or text alerts of positive quotes. However, the feature that I am most excited about is the "Beautiful You Selfie." Using this feature, when a person takes a selfie, not only can you change the filter, but they can also use the "Beautiful You" feature. This feature allows users to pre-record or use random affirmations that speak positivity with every pic. I created this feature because no one would ever tell me that I was beautiful or pretty. The compliments I would receive were always about either my clothes, my hair or an accessory that I was wearing. Dr. Griffin allowed me to see that beauty is something that emanates from within and if I wanted people to give me the compliment I desired, I simply had to show them. The Beautiful You Selfie feature will allow users to say to themselves the positive things that will help them build their confidence and ultimately see themselves as Beautiful, Just the Way They Are... (The crowd applauds.)

Furthermore, in therapy Dr. Griffin also exposed me to plus size women and blogs that allowed me to see myself for the beauty I have both inside and out. Knowing that other people my size embraced themselves and looked happy enabled me to see myself from a new perspective.

I was fortunate that my parents could afford to pay for a therapist and that they didn't have a negative view of mental health. All of this positivity was the perfect recipe for an issue that I was not aware that I was facing, depression. The majority of victims of bullying are silently battling depression. Unfortunately, bullying is seen as commonplace particularly in schools. And although most schools have an anti-bullying policy, very little is ever done to provide emotional support to the victims. In most cases, the person who does the bullying receives some form of discipline while the victim remains in the same environment where he or she was just embarrassed. (LaShawn clicks to the next slide.)

A look at the statistics of the relationship of bullying and suicide amongst young people made me realize just how many kids are going through the same things I've endured in schools. I'm not going to read all this data but I want to highlight that 4,400 bullying-related suicides occur every year according to the CDC. At the heart of the inspiration for my app were 3 suicides in particular; Nigel Shelby, the 15-year-old boy from

249

Alabama who committed suicide after he became so depressed from the constant torment of his sexuality. McKenzie Adams who committed suicide after the kids in her class bullied her for riding home with a white classmate. McKenzie took her life at 9 years old. And Seven Bridges from Kentucky. Seven was born with a rare condition that required him to wear a colostomy bag. He became so depressed from the bullying that he hung himself. Seven was only 10 years old. Their stories moved me to create this app and I hope my presentation moves your organization to fund it. Together we can help put an end to all this madness. Thank you.

(The audience gives a very loud round of applause.)

Moderator: Wow! That! Wow, that Ms. Thorpe I must say was very impressive. Judges these young people are making your decision extremely tough. Ms. Thorpe you may take your seat. Let's give her another round of applause... The next presenter will be...

(LaShawn makes her way back to her seat.)

Dr. Griffin: (To LaShawn) Oh my gosh, you were amazing. Talk about surprises! That was phenomenal. You have come so far from the shy young lady who walked into my office! I am so proud of you.

LaShawn: Thank you. Thank you. I couldn't have done it without your help. I truly appreciate you Dr. Griffin.

Dr. Griffin: You are so very welcome.

(The program continues and after three more presenters, the moderator calls up Theresa. Theresa nervously gets up and goes to the front. She begins to set up her art work. After setting up, she walks over to the podium and begins her presentation.)

Theresa: Good morning or whatever. Ok like um, I don't really know what to say but like here is my drawings and I know that I want to sell them or whatnot. Like the money can go to help people that are in foster care, like I was. I mean, I don't have all that fancy stuff like some of these other people that came up here but like I know that I can sell my work and give money to like helping them out. I mean, I don't know what else to really say.
(Mrs. Davis is trying to get her attention and tell Theresa to read off the

cards that she had prepared for her presentation. Theresa doesn't get what she is talking about and as she is trying to figure out what Mrs. Davis wants, one of the judges asks Theresa a question.)

<u>Judge</u>: Ms. Rushing, I see that you are nervous, which is very under-standable. However, your artwork is amazing and I want to help you out. The format is for presenters to introduce themselves. Explain your cause. Explain why you are passionate about this cause and how your idea helps people facing this issue.

Hearing the judge explain the format made Theresa remember the cards that her and Mrs. Davis worked on. As she reaches in her pocket to get them she makes eye contact with Mrs. Davis who is shaking her head in both relief and disbelief.

<u>Theresa</u>: Oh my bad, I didn't even introduce myself. Ok. My name is Theresa Rushing and me and Mrs. Davis, that's my counselor. We worked on these cards but I'm gone just tell y'all like some of my story if that's cool or whatever. (The judges nod in agreement almost as if to say go ahead at this point.)

Ok, so my project is called Pictures for Promise. The money from the pictures is going to like help kids in foster care. Um so like, well, why this really is something I'm passionate about or whatever is like because I was in foster care.

Ok, well let me just tell y'all about me. So when I was a little baby like 2 or 3 years old my mom used to leave me with family members or her friends. She would be drinking a lot and doing drugs or whatever. Cause of how she was living, she would be in and out of jail and I ended up in foster care. So like when I was in foster care or whatever, I had got molested and later on, I even got raped. But not only in foster care, like when I was left with family members or my mama's friends. People would touch me or whatnot. Wow, this is crazy, I'm just telling a room full of strangers my business.

But anyway like, I started running away and I ended up in juvie. That's where I met Mrs. Davis. And she would ask me, 'Why are you here?' At first, I didn't get what she was talking bout. Then like some other stuff happened and then when I got what she meant. Like what is your purpose in life? I began to see I could use my ability to draw to help other people that been through stuff or whatever. Ok so, I been in juvie so I couldn't really come up with no fancy presentation. But anyway, what I want to do is like sell my drawings and then get other people to sell their

251

drawings too and some of the money go to like building a dorm or something to help teens that are in the foster care system learn to live on they own. I'm in an independent living program and it is helping me a lot. I think if we could get more people out of foster care homes where they may be getting abused or whatever and into like a dorm, or a place where they can get skills to learn how to live on their own it would be really good. Cause like when I was doing some research with Mrs. Davis we found out that, hold up let me look at my card to find it. (Theresa looks through her cards.) Ok here it go, like kids in foster care are 27 times more like to be a victim of abuse or whatever. Like not all foster care homes are bad but like something needs to be done and that is what I want to do. I wanna sale my pictures to help kids in foster care. Ok, I know I am rambling a lot but like that is my presentation or whatever so if y'all got any questions, then y'all can ask them.

Judge: Theresa first let me say that I am so sorry that this has happened to you. Like I said previously, your art work is amazing. I do want to know what made you enter this competition and I have a couple of follow up questions after you answer that.

252

Theresa: Well, to be honest, the judge in my case made me enter this competition. Her name was Judge Banks. At my hearing, she told me that I had to enter this as a part of the ruling. I'm glad she did because it was some nice projects or whatever. But yeah that's why I entered the competition.

Judge: Alright. If you were to be chosen for funding, how would you use the money to further your project?

Theresa: I mean I'm not all the way sure but Mrs. Davis was telling me like that I need to get a website and some social media thingies to like help people know what I am trying to do. But like on the website, people could buy my art or other people's art who want to sell their stuff.

Judge: I think what you are attempting to say is that the money would be used for marketing purposes. Alright, that makes sense. Last question. You said that your project is called, Pictures for Promise. Can you explain why you chose that title?

Theresa: Yeah, like so when I was a kid, my Mama would always tell me that she was gone be right back and then she would say, 'I promise.'

She would always break her promise. So I lost hope. I figured that the kids in foster care probably used to people breaking their promise, I want to be the one who keeps a promise to them.

Judge: Thank you, Ms. Rushing, if none of the other judges have any questions you may be seated. (Theresa gathers her things and takes a seat.)

Mrs. Davis: Good job Reesa! You had me scared there for a second, I could tell you wer nervous to start. I was trying to say get your cards. But you did good! You were just like your girl Cardi - You were real! Good Job!

Theresa: Thank you Mrs. D! I was super nervous! Thank you!
(Mrs. Davis hugs her and nods to be quiet for the next presenter. After two more presenters the competition came to a close and the participants were informed that the winners were going to be announced at the closing ceremony later that afternoon. As everyone is leaving out of the conference room, Theresa made her way over to LaShawn and begins a conversation.)

Theresa: Hey, uh excuse me. I wanted to tell you that I think you are really pretty and that I hope you win because like your app I think it would really help a lot of people.

LaShawn: Oh thank you so much! I really appreciate that. Your art is beautiful. I'm sorry I didn't catch your name?

Theresa: My bad. My name is Theresa but everybody calls me Reesa.

LaShawn: Ok Reesa. Again your drawings were beautiful. If you want, I can help you build your website. I am pretty good at it. If you don't mind I can do it for free. I would love to help you out.

Theresa: That would be dope! Like how can I get in contact with you? I mean I am in juvie so I ain't got no phone. But if you give me your information I can have my counselor, Mrs. D keep it for me or whatever.

LaShawn: Yeah sure. Do you have a pen or something?

Theresa: Yeah let me just let Mrs. D know. That's who brought me here. She can just put it in her phone. Hold on, I will be right back.

LaShawn: Ok cool!
(Theresa walks over to Mrs. Davis and explains to her the situation. After the short conversation she goes back to LaShawn with the phone.)

Theresa: Aight, I'm ready, but like for real for real your app would be really dope. Like I wasn't bullied or whatever but I have tried to kill myself before and I used to think about dying all the time, so I know people really need it. Sometimes I still be feeling down.

LaShawn: I'm really sorry that all that stuff happened to you. That's really sad. It's crazy so many people are going through things and you can never really tell by looking at them... I'm just trying to help people out. You know to use my gifts to make people's lives better. what's crazy is if someone just look at you they would never think you would have wanted to kill yourself.

Theresa: I know right, the crazy thing is that most of the stuff happened to me because people think I am so pretty. Trust me, being "pretty" ain't always what it's cracked up to be. No matter how you look, everybody dealing with something. It's like, problems don't care who you are, they come for everybody...

Theresa's GED Party
May 18, 2019   2:34 pm

Theresa received her GED earlier today and will be discharged tomorrow morning. Mrs. Davis put together a graduation / going away party for her on the unit. Theresa will be moving into her own apartment as a part of the independent living services. Theresa looks a little sad during the celebration and Mrs. Davis notices and comes over to talk to her.

Mrs. Davis: Theresa, what's wrong? I thought you would be a little more excited about getting out of here. I know that eventually, we won't see each other as much. But I am going to be picking you up and taking you to school and work from time to time so everything is going to be fine.

Theresa: It ain't that Mrs. D. I know you got my back or whatever. I don't know... I guess I just got a lot on my mind. Like, this the only place that I ever had some sustili- what's that word?

Mrs. Davis: Stability?

Theresa: Yeah that. So like getting out of here is gone be crazy. I mean, just the whole thing got me tripping. LaShawn helping me put together the website and it raising all that money. The newspaper doing a story on me. Like, I owe this place a lot and I guess I am just sad to be leaving to be honest.

Mrs. Davis: Theresa, this place is not going anywhere and you already said you going to come back and work with the girls so you will be just fine, I promise you. But on another note, remember I said I had a surprise for you? It's in my office let's go get it. C'mon...

Theresa: Ok, because I was gonna bring it up that I didn't get your little surprise or whatever if you didn't give it to me before the party ended. (The two get up and walk to Mrs. Davis' office. When they get to the office Mrs. Davis opens the door and lets Theresa walk in first. Theresa sees the back of a woman who turns around at the sound of the door opening. It is Theresa's mother. The two lock eyes briefly. Theresa turns around and looks at Mrs. Davis, who gives a nod of reassurance. Theresa turns back and looks at her mother who makes a guilty smile at her estranged daughter.)

Mrs. Davis: I will leave you two alone. Theresa if you need me I will be right outside by the reception desk, ok?

(Theresa nervously nods at Mrs. Davis, who closes the door slowly and walks away.)

<u>Mom</u>: Theresa let me start by saying I'm sorry.

<u>Theresa</u>: I'm so glad you started with that because if you didn't I was gone... oooh ok, let me calm down. You can keep going because I know you got more to say.

<u>Mom</u>: I'm sorry and I know that my sorry will never take away the pain and all the things that you have been through. I know you have a lot of questions and I know that I have been the worst mother in the world. But let me tell you my truth and how I got off track and eventually ruined your life.

　　　Ok, when I was six your grandpa, my daddy died and that left just me and your Grandma. Well, when I was fourteen, your Grandma had a really bad stroke and I had to go live with my Aunt Ethel. That would be your Great Aunt. My mother, your grandmother never recovered from the stroke. She died six weeks later. Anyway I was living with my Aunt Ethel and you probably remember her husband Uncle Timmy.

<u>Theresa</u>: Is that the man that used to always give me $100 at all the barbeques and no one else?

<u>Mom</u>: Yes. That's him.
Theresa: Whatever happened to him?

<u>Mom</u>: Theresa, he would give you and only you $100 dollars because, Theresa, Timmy is your father.

<u>Theresa</u>: Wait, what? I'm not getting what you saying?

<u>Mom</u>: I know it's crazy Theresa just listen. One night, Uncle Timmy came home drunk. This was like a month after my mother died in the hospital, so I was staying with them permanently. Anyway, he came home drunk one night and came in my bedroom and he pulled my nightgown up and raped me. I kept telling him to stop but he wouldn't. When your Great Aunt Ethel came home she saw him passed out in my bed with his pants down and I told her what happened. She blamed me and put me out! She called me fast and everything else but a child of God. At the time I wasn't into boys, I was in 8th grade and on the honor roll. Up until that point I just knew I

was going to be a lawyer like Claire Huxtable.

Anyway, after she put me out, I went to stay with a friend Monica for about a month and then when my period didn't come I realized I was pregnant. I told Monica and she told her mom. Her mother was really nice about it but she couldn't afford a baby in her house. So they got me hooked up with a battered woman shelter and I was staying there for a minute but I didn't like it. They were trying to get me into the foster care system but I wasn't having that. So one day I skipped school with this guy who I met one day when I was walking to the store. He was always telling me he would take care of me and he had his own place so I just never went back to the shelter. Wasn't too long before I was laying up over there with him, I stopped going to school.

I started getting drunk like when I was four months pregnant with you. I remember sitting up one night trying to figure out why God chose to take my parents and then have my Aunt's husband rape me. I felt God really hated me because I got pregnant from the rape. My head was really messed up from everything that was going on. I thought if I got drunk enough we both would die. That's all I wanted, for us both to die. I didn't want to live. You wouldn't die and neither would I. So when I had you, I had just turned 15. I remember asking the doctor did you have alcohol fetal syndrome. I just knew he was going to say yes. So when he said no, I knew that something was special about you. I wanted to say God was looking out for you, but at that time I didn't believe in no God, because the God they be talking about wouldn't allow all this bad stuff to happen to me and he definitely hadn't answered any of my prayers.

Well, there I was, 15 years old living with a 22-year-old who had promised me that he was gone take care of me and my baby. Of course, I wasn't the only girl in his life like he told me I was. They would be calling the house and I got tired of it. I was trying to hold on to him, to hold on to something because it felt like everything was just slipping out of my grip. I couldn't keep them away from him nor him away from them. Eventually, all the arguing and fighting led to him putting me out. You was like 5 months or something. Again, I had no place to go and you were a reminder of what had happened to me. So I went back to getting drunk and then I started using drugs. I didn't know how to take care of no baby and I wanted to die. So I would go over people's houses that I thought were good parents and I would leave you. I thought that somebody would eventually take care of you. It didn't happen like I planned. Nothing seemed to happen like I planned, I guess...

I just know that I wasn't in the right state of mind to take care of you. I'm sorry. I know that this doesn't make it any better. But you deserve the truth Theresa so there it is. Theresa, I need help.

I'm stuck, I've been stuck in the same place your whole life. Theresa, in a matter of two months, I went from losing my mother, to being raped by my Uncle and being pregnant with you. To this very day, I still haven't had a chance to fully grieve losing my mother. I'm sorry, Reesa but this is my truth. You can't understand who you are until you know from whom you came. That's why I was never there for you. I didn't know how to be there for myself. That is not an excuse, that is the truth... (Tears are streaming down Theresa's face. She never knew the pain her mother endured and tears are the only emotion that she can give in the moment. Not expecting a response, her mother switches the subject.)

      If you don't want to ever see me again, I understand. Mrs. Davis reached out to me about five months ago and told me that you were on pace to get your GED. She told me that she wanted me to be there for you but I had to get cleaned up first. She helped me get in a treatment program. Theresa I've been sober for 117 days. Mrs. Davis been working with me a lot and she offered to help me pick out something for your graduation. I told her that I only wanted to give you one thing, the truth. Theresa you needed the truth so you didn't continue going through life with questions. This may not be all the answers you are looking for but this is the truth of why I failed you as a mother.

(Her mother wipes a tear and a momentary silence falls over the room. She looks up at Theresa who appears to be in deep thought about what she just heard. Theresa takes a deep breath and begins speaking)

<u>Theresa</u>: For so long, I hated you. Like really, really hated you. You don't know how many times I wanted you to just keep one of your promises that you made to me. All those places you left me. All the things that happened to me. All the nights I cried because I felt like no one ever loved me. I had a hatred in me that no one saw but was burning inside of me. I begin to not care about people because nobody cared about me. So seeing you like this, telling me your pain it all makes sense to me now. I mean my hatred for you didn't get me nowhere like Mrs. Davis would say. And I thank you for giving me your truth, you're right, I did deserve it and I hope it frees you. To be honest, like I don't know about us having a mother daughter relationship just yet, but you are right, I know that I can't keep carrying your pain. Mrs. Davis always tell me like that we can't carry other people's weight or whatever because it stops us from going at the speed God wants us to go at. She say the heavy load breaks us down. And when I think about it, I was broken. I honestly felt like I could never be made right.

<u>Mom</u>: Theresa I'm sorry. I'm so sorry. I never meant for any of this... I never planned on having you so- (Her mother pauses just as she allows the words to come from her mouth.)

<u>Theresa</u>: That's it right there... Mrs. Davis say, God don't make no mistakes, she right. First time she told me that, I thought to myself, 'He made me.' I felt like a mistake. For the longest time I thought that I must've been a mistake if nobody wanted me. It took me a long time to see that I ain't no mistake. God put me here for a reason. A lot has happened to me to make me see that but I see that clearly now. Mrs. D would always tell me the Bible say something like, what we go through now is nothing compared to what God going to give us later, or something like that.

     Well, my later starts now. I get out of here tomorrow and I don't know what it's gonna be like to live on my own. To be honest, I am a little afraid to be out in the world again by myself. But you know what, I ain't gonna worry because my life finally makes sense now. I'm finally feel free. I feel free because I know why I am here. God allowed me to go through those things so I can connect to the people I am here to help. Like, I never thought I would be getting interviews for TV shows and newspapers. To be honest, I never thought nothing good was going to come of my life. But God's plan was greater than my thoughts. I done been through so much that I know what's next has to be amazing. (A confident smile comes across Theresa's face as she continues speaking.)

     You know what, I never thought I would say this to you but... I forgive you. I forgive you, Ma. I don't know what's next but I don't want you holding on to the things that you didn't do for me because I'm letting it go. Holding on to what did or didn't happen hasn't done me no good so I am letting go. Forgiving you right now feels so good because I ain't letting my past control my future. (It finally clicks for her as she speaks it.) Wow, I am the thermostat. Hmm... (Theresa pauses at the self-actualization.)

<u>Mom</u>: Huh?

<u>Theresa</u>: Nothing don't worry about it.

<u>Mom</u>: Theresa, I have made a lot of mistakes and I want to have a relationship with you. When I had you, I didn't know how to do that. Honestly, I still don't, I am not sure what you would even need from me...

259

(A confident smile comes across Theresa's face as her mother speaks to her. Theresa realizes why God chose Mrs. Davis to be in her life. Theresa can finally live the lesson of the thermostat and the thermometer. Recognizing her power to control her situation she answers her mother.)

Theresa: Ma, I only need what I always needed... For you to be there. Only this time, being there is going to be on my terms. I'm not going back to depending on you. I'm not going back to hanging on to your every word. I've been through too much to put myself in that situation again. I'm sorry but them days are over. I am happy you getting yourself cleaned up and I know you gonna need support or whatever. But this time things are going to have to be on my terms. So once I get myself set up, I'll get your number from Mrs. D and I will call you.

Mom: You really gonna call?

(Theresa is in total control of the temperature. Feeling completely liberated she responds...)

Theresa: I promise...

LaShawn's Family Session
May 18, 2019   2:34 pm

Dr. Griffin has arranged the final session for LaShawn. In this session, LaShawn's mother has been asked to join the session. Dr. Griffin sets the tone and expectations of the conversation between Mrs. Thorpe and LaShawn.

Dr. Griffin: Good afternoon Mrs. Thorpe. LaShawn, good to see you as usual. Alright, this is the time in treatment where families begin to come into the sessions. These sessions are designed to begin the healing process in the relationships that impact the client most. Mrs. Thorpe I don't want you to be caught off guard by anything here today. I don't want you to feel as if you are being attacked in any way either. As I stated before on our call, LaShawn has a few concerns that she would like to express and you will have the opportunity to respond. I do want to caution both you and LaShawn to be careful not to make this a finger-pointing session. It's not about who is to blame, it is about feelings, emotions and the consequences of a lack of communication. With that, LaShawn I will let you begin.

LaShawn: Ok. Ma I love you. I know that you love me. I know that you do. However, I do feel like you are embarrassed of me. (Mrs. Thorpe sits up and tries to interject.)

Mrs. Thorpe: LaShawn why would -

Dr. Griffin: Please Mrs. Thorpe allow her to finish.
(LaShawn takes a deep breath and begins to finish her thoughts.)

LaShawn: Well Ma, I have always felt like this. I can go all the way back to when you tried putting me in cheerleading and ballet. I remember you having the biggest attitude when I didn't want to do it and even more of one when I wasn't really good at either one of them. I know you were very good at both ballet and cheer when you were a kid and in high school but Ma, it's like you have been distant with me since then. Honestly, I remember it wasn't too long after that I begin picking up weight.

But Ma that's not the only thing. You always hounding me Ma. You always coming in my room, going through my things. When I was in like fourth grade and I had some friends, you would always tell me. Don't trust none of the people you hanging around with. Girls like to keep up mess so watch who you be around. Ma it's like I never get a chance to figure things out on my own. Every little detail is picked at or analyzed. Ma I love you but you cause me to eat. I am always nervous when you come around.

It was worse when I was younger but, I would just eat to calm my nerves. I don't want it to sound like I am blaming you but this is how I feel... (LaShawn pauses and Dr. Griffin interjects.)

Dr. Griffin: Mrs. Thorpe do you care to respond?

Mrs. Thorpe: You know, it's whatever... I know this isn't supposed to feel like it's an attack but it sure feels like I am being blamed for all this. I mean, your Daddy is the one who buys all the mess you eat... And as for being embarrassed, who would be embarrassed of their own child?

Dr. Griffin: Mrs. Thorpe, I know this is hard to hear. However, this is LaShawn's point of view. I don't want you to dismiss her feelings. Let's keep the discussion going. LaShawn, is it more that you want to add?

LaShawn: Ok Ma, like since I won the competition for my app, you been on me to go to the gym and try to lose weight. Or you have been asking me about being a vegetarian or vegan. You have been saying stuff like, "You're not going to want to look back at those pictures and interviews ten years from now and see yourself like that..." Ma do you know how that makes me feel on the inside? But even before that Ma, you stopped taking me to the shop to get my hair done. You don't take me with you to get manicures and pedicures. You go all those places to make sure you look good. But you do my hair at home or you say let's do our nails and feet together when you feel it is time for me to have mine done. Ma you don't think I notice stuff like that? I feel like I am an embarrassment to you.

Mrs. Thorpe: Look, I was raised to care about my appearance and I am not going to apologize for that. It's nothing wrong with wanting to look good and being presentable. Me and your Daddy work hard to make sure that you have nice things and good clothes. It might look that way but LaShawn that is not the case. And yes I did say that about your pictures and interview but I am not apologizing. You should care about how you are going to look, now and years later when you are looking back at yourself. I don't see what is wrong with that LaShawn?

LaShawn: Since the moment Dr. Griffin started working with me, she has told me that I have to accept myself for who I am. At first, I didn't get why that was so hard for me. I would try, like really hard. The affirmations helped me. Yet deep down inside, it was some doubt if I ever would feel the way I needed to feel about who I am. Now I understand why it was so hard for me to accept me for me. It was so hard Ma because, I never felt like you accepted me for me.

(The room goes silent for a moment. Mrs. Thorpe drops her head as there is some undeniable truth in LaShawn's words. LaShawn turns to Dr. Griffin and speaks.)

<u>LaShawn</u>: Dr. Griffin, you once told me that I was going to have to do things I wanted to do, in spite of the reactions I would get. I am realizing now that includes my mother. (Looking back at her Mother now.) Ma, I love who I am. I want you to know that I could never be who I am and do the things that I will do without all the things that you have taught me. I would have never started coding if it weren't for you. I thank you for it all. But, Ma, I need you to know that not only do I love who I am, I love the way I look even more. If I make the decision one day to lose weight or change my diet, it will not be because you suggested it. If I make that decision it will come from me wanting to change something with the way I look.

    I used to think that I hated the way that I looked and how big I was. Now, that I think about it, the truth is my anger really belonged to the fact that I didn't feel loved despite how I look and how big I am. Ma, I know you love me. When Dr. Griffin told me about this session with you, I wanted you to accept my feelings, but truthfully, it doesn't matter if you accept my feelings or not. I accept how I feel. I accept me. I don't want you to feel bad Mama, I just realize that how I feel about me is the most important thing in the world. I can't worry about what you say or how you feel about me. I can't worry about what other people say. I can't worry about what other people think when I go out to the restaurant or to the mall or to the movies. I've lived that life and it wasn't a good one. Now, I am going to go and do the things that I want to do. You know as I am letting this out Ma, I can't help but to think about how Lizzo responded when Jillian Michaels made thos comments about her... she said:

"I have done nothing wrong. I forgive myself for thinking I was wrong in the first place. I deserve to be happy."

Dr. Griffin. Ma. I am happy. I feel happy. I feel free. I am free because I know that I am Beautiful... Just The Way That I Am...

The End

In Loving Memory
of
My Grandmother

Barbara Jean Bean

Grandma, you transitioned on my 4th birthday. For 30 plus years you have provided me heavenly guidance. Your last words to me were to always have Wisdom & Knowledge.
Grandma this book is filled with both wisdom and knowledge.
I am glad to know that I have made you proud. I Love You...

In Loving Memory
of
My Other Mother

LaTanya Williams

Ma, I am so glad I gave you your roses while you were here on earth. You were so instrumental in developing the husband that I am today. You would talk to me about what it means to truly build a marriage that will last. I am so grateful that since the age of 9 years old you were a major part of my life. You always told me to be thankful for the storm because it means that sunshine is soon to come. I love and miss you!

Ernest & Vickie Stansil

It's true you can't understand the value of your parents until you become a parent yourself, so as a parent let me be the 1st to say that your worth to me is incalculable...

Your continued support and lessons have and will forever be something that I treasure!

Thank you for the discipline, the consistency and unconditional love that has made me what I am thus far and what I am yet to become...

Most importantly, thank you for giving me the tools that allow me to learn the lessons you did not teach and obtain the things that you did not give. You have empowered me to get it for myself which makes it more worthwhile. I Love You Mom & Dad!!!

266

Carl & Delores Rushing

A lot of people are not fortunate enough to have a set of good parents. God has blessed me with 2 sets!

I am eternally grateful for the spiritual presence that you all have been in my life. When your daughter introduced me as her boyfriend nearly 20 years ago, I was just that, a boy...

With your influence I am proud to say that I am a God fearing man.

I am eternally grateful for everything you all do for us and our children absolutely have 2 of the world's greatest Grandparents!

I want to thank you all for accepting me into your family and allowing me to grow with you! I Love You Mom & Pops!

For My Sisters

Shellerray Barnes
The Definition of Strength
The Elegance of A Black Rose
Find Your Way Back On Stage
And Show the World Your Gift
Dance Baby Girl Dance...

Barbara Stansil
You Embody Peserverance
Your Path is Filled With
Abundance... Embrace Your
Gift and You Will Recieve
All God Has InStore...

Jeanene Rushing
Trust In Your Talent
Your Dreams And Gifts
Were Given to You Because God
Knows You Can Handle Them... Embrace Your Destiny

My Nieces

Tatyana Green
Lady Bug words can't express my love for you. I have watched you grow into a strong woman. Your story is not finished so please enjoy the journey.

Jalen Williams
I love you Jalen. Your future holds amazing things and endless possibilities. Keep your focus on the prize you want and put in the work to get it.

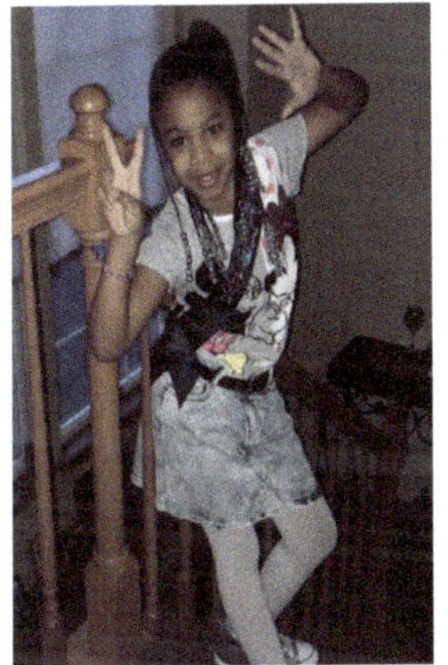

Jalayia Williams

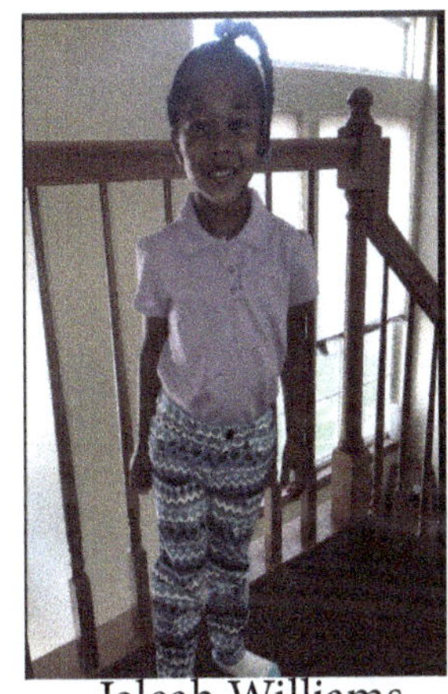

Jaleah Williams

Although your life is still just beginning, the time will come when you are reading this and you will fully understand that Beauty is our ability to showcase the God that lives within us. I love you both.

Bria Rushing
Success is not measured by our accomplishments. It is measured by the circumstances we over come as we go throughout our journey. Bria hone in to your abilities and write the story you deserve.

269

To My Son Hannibal
May you have an Uncommon reverence for Women.

I pray that you understand that your actions will always have a great impact on the people around you.

Your Mother and I are raising you to be a leader. That will often require that you take the road less traveled and make the unpopular decision. Let God lead your actions and find solace in prayer.

I am working to be the best example of a Man everyday in order to leave you a sound Blueprint.

You Are Your Own Man. Think For Yourself.
You Can Do Anything...

270

The Banks Family
(Steve, Amiyah & Safiyah)

271

I want to acknowledge the incalculable help and grace of Safi Banks. Without your reading and editing and pushing me to do better, to change this and suggesting that, this book would not be anywhere near the magnitude it is today. However, the one thing that I am most grateful for from you is the suggestion you made that I take my time. That is truly the best advice that I have been given and it had a tremendous impact on me doing the best that I could to get this right. I am better because of you and so many of your students can attest to the light and radiant presence you provide us all. Thank you for being the loving friend to my wife and the amazing person that you are to everyone you encounter... Thank you!

272

David & Dakisha Lewis

I want to give an extra special thanks to David and Dakisha Lewis. Brother there is so much I could say but I will respect your modesty and not go too much into it, however I will share that I am eternally grateful for the prayer sessions we hold prior to the many moments when we need to be lifted up. David Thank You from the bottom of my heart you are not my friend, you are truly my Brother... I Love You!

Charity Neal

@cnstudios
@charliehates

If you would like to purchase work
by Charity Neal

Visit her Etsy
@cnstudios

If you are interested in hiring Charity Neal
contact her at:

cnstudios@gmail.com

Special Thank You From the Author

To Hope and Charity Neal. In this millennial time that we live in and the overall importance of aesthetics, I owe you both so much. Ms. Neal thank you for allowing me to work with your fantastic daughter. To Charity, the rest from this point I truly feel is history. Your amazing gift of art has now been shared with the world and I encourage you to shine as bright as possible. I personally want to thank you for blessing my book with your phenomenal talent. This is hopefully the first of many projects we work on!

Beautiful... Just The Way You Are

Karma Griggs

@paintitkarma

Facebook
Karma Griggs

If you would like to purchase work by Karma Griggs
contact her at:

@paintitkarma
on Instagram

Special Thanks From the Author

To Samantha Myles and Karma Griggs. Thank you Ms. Myles for allowing me to work with your daughter on this project. Karma your talents are magnificent and I am super excited to see where you take them as you continue to hone in on your craft.

Books Highlighted In
Beautiful... Just The Way You Are

The Mask:
Recognizing and
Resisting Spiritual
Deception

Andriea Denise

Black // White:
A Poetic Concept
by Carol's Son

JD Phelps

Deserving Grace

C.L. Jackson

I Have Something To
Say

Japonica Brown

I Was Bitter, Now I'm
Better

Jerra Latrice

Free Heart

Shacora J. Moore

<u>Special Thanks</u>

To "My" Pastor Royce Thompson. Man your spiritual guidance and pointing me to the specific parts of the Bible has allowed me to not only grow but understand how to manifest my purpose. God told me to reach out to you in the darkest time of my life and you have definitely been the light I needed. Brother Thank You and I Thank God for YOU!!!

To My Closest Friend and Biggest Supporter, my big brother Sherray Williams. You have been on this journey with me as I wrote this book. Thank you for the support and encouragement along the way. It means the world to have someone like you pushing and encouraging me to see it through. Thank you Bro!

To Daisjah Ball & Janiyah Browning, I hope that seeing your work inspires you to work relentlessly at your craft and realize your God given potential.

To D. Marie & Lacist Wortham, thank you for sharing your gift! I appreciate it immensely.

I must thank my cousin Candace Randolph. Cuzzo your consistent positivity and spiritual presence is so inspiring! I am always uplifted by our conversations and you leave me inspired to do and be more. Thank you & our time is coming soon!

I want to thank all the people who read portions of the book and took their time to give me feedback along the way:

Kayana Dilosa, Tiffany Browning, Keishanie Taylor, Jerra Mitchell, Shacora Moore, Venitria McKinley, Comora McKee, Mia Evans, Patricia Smith, Amora Coles, Imogene Bibbs, Nalini Eldridge, Mikaya Clark, Mary Davis, Celistine, Aurelia Weaver, Gloria Griffin, Five Brown Girls, Nicole Cullors, Krishana Robinson, Marcus Ford, Rodney Williams, Aaryn Bernard, Christina Wherry, Kashley Brown, Lacist Wortham, Takeia Brooks, Ashanti McKenney, Tiffany Long, Tyronda Bandy, Tyra Cooley, Raven Osborne, Deajeh Munya, Devan Thomas, Amber Harris, Shellerray Barnes, Barbara Stansil, Jalen Williams, Otis Rushing Jr Ernest Stansil Jr. and last but not least, my mother Vickie Barnes Stansil.

Finally during the last stages of this book, one person pushed me to finish. Everyday she came in with the biggest smile and would ask me... "Mr. Gaines, when is your book coming out? Because I can't wait to read it." Thank You Maritza!

To you and everyone who reads this, remember that you are...
Beautiful... Just The Way You Are!!!

277